ABOUT *A BETTER WORLD*

The brilliants changed everything.

Since 1980, 1% of the world has been born with gifts we'd only dreamed of. The ability to sense a person's most intimate secrets, or predict the stock market, or move virtually unseen. For thirty years the world has struggled with a growing divide between the exceptional . . . and the rest of us.

Now a terrorist network led by brilliants has crippled three cities. Supermarket shelves stand empty. 911 calls go unanswered. Fanatics are burning people alive.

Nick Cooper has always fought to make the world better for his children. As both a brilliant and an advisor to the President of the United States, he's against everything the terrorists represent. But as America slides toward a devastating civil war, Cooper is forced to play a game he dares not lose—because his opponents have their own vision of a better world.

And to reach it, they're willing to burn this one down.

From Marcus Sakey, "the master of the mindful page turner" (Gillian Flynn) and "one of our best storytellers" (Michael Connelly), Book Two of the Brilliance Saga is a relentless thrill ride that will change the way you look at your world—and the people around you.

A BETTER WORLD

Also by Marcus Sakey

Brilliance

The Two Deaths of Daniel Hayes

The Blade Itself

Accelerant

Good People

The Amateurs

Scar Tissue

MARCUS SAKEY

A BETTER WORLD

THOMAS & MERCER

Published by Thomas & Mercer, Seattle

www.apub.com

Amazon, the Amazon logo, and Thomas & Mercer are trademarks of Amazon.com, Inc., or its affiliates.

ISBN-13: 9781477823941
ISBN-10: 1477823948

Cover design by Jeroen ten Berge

Library of Congress Control Number: 2014903386

Printed in the United States of America

For my father, who showed me what it means to be a man.

Cold liquid splashing across his face brought Kevin Temple back to himself.

He'd been on the road all night, a dedicated run from Indiana hauling a load of fresh vegetables. Fifteen minutes out of the depot in Cleveland, and he had that stale feel, too much coffee washing down too much beef jerky. What he'd really been craving was a double cheeseburger, but while it would surprise no one to see a trucker gone flabby around the middle, it was a point of pride that at thirty-nine he weighed only ten pounds more than he had in high school.

When sirens lit up the darkness behind him, he jumped, then cursed. Must've zoned out, gotten heavy on the pedal—only no, the speedometer read sixty-seven. He'd been tired, but not so whacked that he'd drifted out of his lane. A broken taillight? It was after four in the morning; maybe the cops were just bored.

Kevin eased over to the shoulder. He yawned and stretched, then turned on the interior lights and rolled down the window. A week until Thanksgiving, and the cold air felt good.

The state trooper was middle-aged, with a lean, wolfish look. His uniform was starched, and his hat hid his eyes. "You know why I stopped you?"

"No, sir."

"Get out of the cab, please."

It must be a broken taillight. Some cops liked to rub your face in it. Kevin slid the license from his wallet, grabbed the manifest and registration, then opened the door and climbed down. A second trooper had joined the first.

"Keep your hands where I can see them, please."

"Sure," Kevin said. He held up the paperwork. "What's this about, Officer?"

The trooper held the license up, clicked on a flashlight. "Mr. . . . Temple."

"Yes, sir."

"Cleveland your destination tonight?"

"Yes, sir."

"You do this route regularly?"

"Two, three times a week."

"And are you a twist?"

"Huh?"

The trooper said, "Are you an abnorm?"

"What are you—why do you care?"

"Just answer the question. Are you an abnorm?"

It was one of those moments, the kind when he knew what he *should* do, in that idealized sense of the word. He should refuse to answer. He should make a speech about how that question was a violation of his civil rights. He should tell this bigoted cop to shut his idiot mouth, throwing around a word like "twist."

But it was four in the morning, and the road was empty, and he was tired, and sometimes the *should*s get overwhelmed by the *willing to*s. So he settled for putting a little attitude into his voice as he said, "No, I'm not a brilliant."

The trooper stared at him for a moment, then flicked the flashlight up. Kevin winced and squinted, said, "Hey, whoa, I can't see."

"I know."

There was motion in his peripheral vision, the other cop raising a device that crackled electric blue, and then lightning struck Kevin Temple square in the chest. Every muscle locked up at once and he heard something like a scream coming out of his mouth and stars blew out his vision as claws sank into his ribs.

When the pain was finally done, he collapsed. His thoughts were slippery, and he struggled to process what had just happened. The ground was cold. And moving. No, he was moving, being dragged. His hands were behind him, and something held them together.

Then liquid splashed his face. The cold made him gasp, and he sucked some of the fluid into his mouth. It was foul. A pungent chemical presence he'd never tasted but had smelled a thousand times, and that was when panic swept out the last vestiges of pain, because he was handcuffed on the side of the road and someone was pouring gasoline on him.

"Oh God, please, please, don't, please don't—"

"Shh." The wolfish trooper squatted down beside him. His partner tipped up the gas can and stepped backward, pouring a trail. "Quiet now."

"Please, Officer, please—"

"I'm not a cop, Mr. Temple. I'm"—he hesitated—"I guess you could say I'm a soldier. In Darwin's army."

"I'll do whatever you want, I have some money, you can have anything—"

"Be quiet, okay? Just listen." The man's voice was firm but not harsh. "Are you listening?"

Kevin nodded frantically. The gas fumes were everywhere, ringing in his nose, burning his eyes, chilling his hands and face.

"I want you to know that it's not because you're a normal. And I'm honestly sorry that we have to do it this way. But in a war, there's no such thing as an innocent bystander." For a moment it seemed like he was going to add something else, but then he just stood up.

The purest fear Kevin Temple had ever known filled him, pressed him out of himself, wore him like a suit. He wanted to cry, to beg, to scream, to run, but he couldn't find any words, his teeth chattering, his arms bound, his legs rubber.

"If it's any comfort, you're part of something bigger now. An essential part of the plan." The soldier struck a match against the side of a pack, once, twice. The flame caught and flared. The bright yellow flicker reflected in his eyes. "This is how we build a better world."

Then he dropped the match.

THREE WEEKS EARLIER

CHAPTER 1

Arms wide and palms empty, hyperconscious of how many weapons were trained on him, Cooper was thinking about all the ways things hadn't gone as planned.

It had been a busy month. A busy year. He'd spent half of it undercover, away from his children, hunting the most wanted man in America. But when he'd found John Smith, Cooper had discovered that everything he believed was built on lies. That his agency wasn't just covert—it was corrupt, led by a man who was fostering a war for his own gain.

The aftermath of that discovery had been bloody and dramatic, especially for his boss. And the weeks since had been split between cleaning up the mess and reconnecting with his children.

But today was supposed to have been quiet. His ex-wife Natalie was taking the kids to visit her mom. Cooper had no meetings, no details to attend to, and at the moment, no job. He planned to hit the gym, then go out for lunch. Afterward maybe a coffee shop, spend the afternoon lost in a book. Whip up dinner, open a bottle of bourbon, read and drink his way to an early bedtime. Sleep ten straight hours for the sheer luxury of it.

He made it as far as lunch.

It was a hole-in-the-wall Arabic place he liked, lentil soup and a falafel sandwich. He was sitting at a two-top by the front window, hollow November sun glaring off the silverware, dumping hot sauce into his soup, when he realized he wasn't alone.

It happened just like that. One moment, the opposite chair was empty, the next, there she sat. Like she'd formed from sunlight.

Shannon looked good. Not *fit and healthy* good, but *make a man think wicked thoughts* good: a fitted black top that bared her shoulders, hair slipping past her ears, her lips quirked in that half smile. "Hi," she said. "Miss me?"

He leaned back, regarded her. "You know, when I asked you on a date, I meant soon. Not a month later."

"I had some things to take care of."

Cooper read her, not just the words, but the subtle tensing of her trapezius muscles, the sideways dart her eyes wanted to make but didn't, the alert readiness with which she took in the room. *Still a soldier, and not sure if you're on the same side.* Which was fair. He wasn't sure himself. "Okay."

"It's not that I don't trust—"

"I get it."

"Thanks."

"But you're here now."

"I'm here now." She leaned across to help herself to half of his sandwich. "So, Nick. What are we going to do today?"

The answer, it turned out, was perfectly obvious to both of them, and they spent the afternoon knocking pictures off the walls of his apartment. Funny, it was only the second time they'd made love—and the third and semi-fourth—but they had an unselfconscious comfort that normally required long intimacy. Maybe it was because he'd been thinking about her all month, waiting for her to appear, and the anticipation had been akin to actually being together.

Or maybe it was just that their relationship already had enough complications. He was an abnorm who had spent his career hunting other abnorms for the government. She was a revolutionary whose methods verged on terrorism. Hell, the day they'd met, she'd held a gun on him, and that hadn't been the last time.

On the other hand, she also saved your children's lives and helped you bring down a president.

As the top agent at the Department of Analysis and Response, Cooper had built a career on intercepting terrorists, usually before they struck. But the one who had eluded him—had eluded the whole country—was also the most dangerous. John Smith was a charismatic leader and a strategic mastermind. He had also been blamed for the slaughter of countless innocents.

After a particularly horrifying attack in Manhattan that cost more than a thousand lives, Cooper had gone undercover to find Smith. It was during that time that he and Shannon had first connected, first as mortal enemies, then reluctant companions, and finally lovers. But when Cooper had finally tracked Smith down, the man opened his eyes to a horrifying truth—the real monster was Cooper's mentor Drew Peters. The proof was a video in which Peters and the president of the United States planned a massacre in a popular Capitol Hill restaurant. It was a political maneuver, a way to polarize the country and place more power in the hands of the government. By blaming the attack on abnorm terrorists, Peters and those like him gained enormous power to control and even assassinate brilliants.

And all it cost was the lives of seventy-three innocent people, six of them children.

After Cooper discovered the truth, Drew Peters kidnapped his children and ex-wife as leverage. Shannon had helped Cooper rescue them. He had no doubt, none, that without her his kids would be dead.

So, yeah, complicated. He and Shannon were like those diagrams of overlapping circles. Parts of them might always be held back, but that middle intersection, oh man.

Regardless, the sex had been great, the shower had been great, the shower sex had been great. The conversation had been easy. She'd filled him in on her last month: time in New Canaan Holdfast, the enclave in Wyoming where abnorms were trying to build a new world. The mindset there, how people were getting worried. They talked about the tagging that was slated to begin next summer, the government's plan to implant a tracking device against the carotid artery of every abnorm in America. Starting with tier ones like Shannon. Like himself.

Near as anyone could figure, the abnorm phenomenon started in early 1980, though it wasn't detected until 1986, when scientific study revealed that for unknown reasons, one percent of all children were born "brilliant," possessed of savant abilities. These gifts manifested in different ways; most were impressive but unthreatening, like the ability to multiply large numbers or perfectly play a song heard only once.

Others were world-shifting. Like John Smith, whose strategic gift had let him defeat three chess Grandmasters simultaneously—at age fourteen.

Like Erik Epstein, whose talent for data analysis had earned him a personal fortune of $300 billion and prompted the shuttering of the global financial markets.

Like Shannon, who could sense the vectors of the world around her so completely that she could move unseen, just by being where no one was looking.

Cooper's own gift was for recognizing patterns in people. A kind of souped-up intuition. He could read body language, know by the motions of subcutaneous muscles what someone might be about to do. He could look at a target's apartment, and based on the books they'd read and the way they organized their closet and what they kept on their nightstand, he could develop a good notion of where they might try to run. It had made him an exceptional hunter, but it came at some cost. The things he had seen haunted him. There was an irony to being an elite soldier desperate to prevent war.

You're not a soldier anymore. And it's not your war.

A mantra he'd been repeating for a month. But repetition hadn't made it seem like fact.

"Did they interrogate you?" They were on the couch at that point, naked and sore, a blanket draped over them. Shannon had her head on his shoulder and one hand toying with his chest hair. "Your old agency?"

"Yeah."

"What did you tell them about Peters?"

"They didn't ask."

"Seriously? The director of a DAR division goes off a twelve-story building, and they're willing to let bygones be bygones?"

"I'm sure they knew it was me. But Quinn took care of that." Cooper's old partner had been the third member of the team that night. His friend had commandeered the building's security center and erased all trace of their presence. "If there'd been explicit proof, they wouldn't have had a choice. But without it, they'd rather avoid the scandal right now. They even offered me my old job back." He felt her tense. "Relax. I declined."

"So you're unemployed?"

"We're calling it a personal leave. Technically I'm still a government agent, but I've done enough for God and country. I need time to sort things out."

Shannon nodded. His gift, never idle, never under his control, put a thought into his head. *She has something to ask you. There's an agenda here, besides this.*

But when she spoke, all she asked was, "How are your kids?"

"Amazing. They both had nightmares for a while, but they're so resilient, it seems like it's behind us. Kate is in a nudist phase, keeps stripping off her clothes and running around the house giggling. And Todd has decided he wants to be president when he grows up. Says that if the last one did these things, we need a better one."

"He's got my vote."

"Mine too."

"And Natalie?" she asked, too casually.

"Good." Cooper knew enough to leave it at that.

Later, they went for a walk. Magic hour, the sun almost down and the light coming from everywhere at once. It had been a mild autumn, the trees a riot of color that had only started to fall in the last week. Blue jeans weather, leaves crunching beneath their shoes, red cheeks and her hand warm in his. DC in the fall, was there anything better. They strolled the Mall, past the Reflecting Pool.

"So how long are you here?"

"I'm not sure," she said. "Maybe awhile."

"Doing what?"

"Things."

"Ah. More things."

"It's getting worse, Cooper. That war you're always worrying about is closer than ever. Most people, norm or abnorm, just want to get along, but the extremists are forcing everyone to take sides. You know that in Liberia they've started abandoning babies with birthmarks? They believe it's a sign of the gifted, so they just dump them. In Mexico, brilliants have taken over the cartels and are using them against the government. Private armies headed by abnorm warlords and funded by drug money."

"I watch the news, Shannon."

"Not to mention that there are right-wing paramilitary groups popping up across America. The KKK all over again. Last week in Oklahoma, a gang of straights kidnapped an abnorm, tied him to their pickup, and dragged him around a field. You know how old they were?"

"Sixteen."

"Sixteen. School bombings in Georgia. Microchips implanted in people's throats. Senators on CNN, talking about expanding the academies to include tier-two or even tier-three children."

He turned away, walked to a park bench, and took a seat. The pillars of the Lincoln Memorial glowed white in the flood-lights, the steps still crowded with tourists. From this distance he couldn't see the statue, but he could picture it, Honest Abe lost in thought, weighing the issues that threatened to tear apart his union.

"Cooper, I'm serious—"

"It's too bad."

"What is?"

"I was kind of hoping you came to see me."

Shannon opened her mouth, closed it.

Cooper said, "So what does John want?"

"How did you—"

"Your pupils dilated, that's focus, and you glanced left, that's memory. Your pulse picked up ten beats. You laid out a bullet list of horrors, easy enough, but you did it in geographical order, far to near, which isn't likely to happen randomly. And you called me Cooper, instead of Nick."

"I . . ."

"That whole argument was memorized. Which means that you're trying to convince me of something. Which means that *he* is trying to convince me of something. So let's have it."

Shannon stared at him, the corner of her lip tucked between her teeth. Then she sat down beside him on the bench. "I'm sorry. I really did come here for you. This was separate."

"I know. That's what John Smith does. He dresses his agendas in plans and wraps his plans in schemes. I get it. What does he want?"

She spoke without looking at him. "Things have changed since he's been exonerated. You know he wrote a book."

"*I Am John Smith*. Really put his heart into the title."

"He's public now, lecturing and talking to the media."

"Yeah." Cooper pinched at the bridge of his nose. "And this has what to do with me?"

"He wants you to join him. Think how compelling that would be—Smith and the man who once hunted him, working together to change the world."

Cooper stared out at the fading light, the people climbing the stairs of the memorial. It was open twenty-four hours a day, which he'd always found moving.

"I know you don't trust him," she said softly. "But you also know he's innocent. You proved it."

It wasn't just Lincoln, either. Martin Luther King Jr. had stood on those steps and told the world about a dream he had. And now anyone could come here, any hour of the day, from the aristocracy to the guy emptying the trash—

The garbageman's posture is rigid, his hair is agency short, and he's been emptying that can for a long time.

While he does, he's looking everywhere except to his right . . . where a businessman is talking on a cell phone. A cell with a dark display. A businessman with a bulge under one arm.

And that sound you hear is the rev of a high-cylinder engine. Super-charged.

—and everyone was welcome.

Cooper turned to Shannon. "First, John is as innocent as Genghis Khan. He may not have done the things he was blamed for, but he's bloody to the elbows. Second, get out of here."

She was a pro and didn't make any sudden moves, just took in the space like she was enjoying the view. He caught the subtle tightening in her posture as she spotted the trashman. "We're better together."

"No," he said. "I'm still a government agent. I'll be okay. You're a wanted criminal. Do your thing. Walk through walls."

The sound was growing louder, engines coming from multiple directions. SUVs, most likely. He glanced over his shoulder, turned back. "Listen, I mean it—"

Shannon was gone.

Cooper smiled, shook his head. That trick never got old.

He stood and removed his jacket, took his wallet from his pocket, and set both on the ground. Then he stepped back and put his arms out, his palms empty.

They were good. Four black Escalades with tinted glass swept in at the same time from four different directions, a Busby Berkeley raid. The doors winged open, and men spilled out with choreographed precision, leaning across the hood with automatic rifles. Easily twenty of them, nicely arrayed, with clean firing lines.

The good news was that this team was so clearly professional, and operating with such impunity, that they were almost certainly governmental. The bad news was that there were plenty of people in the government who wanted him dead.

Ah well. Keeping his hands wide, he shouted, "My name is Nick Cooper. I'm an agent with the Department of Analysis and Response. I'm unarmed. My identification is in my wallet on the ground."

A man in a nondescript suit climbed out of the rear of one of the SUVs. He walked across the circle, and as he did, Cooper noticed that the guns were now swiveling to cover other directions.

"We know who you are, sir." The agent reached down, picked up Cooper's wallet and coat, and handed them back. Then he spoke in the clipped tone used to broadcast into a microphone. "Area secure."

A limousine pulled around the circular drive. It bumped up over the curb, glided between two SUVs, and stopped in front of them. The agent opened the door.

With a mental shrug, Cooper climbed in. The car smelled of leather. There were two occupants. One was a trim woman in her midfifties with steely eyes and an aura of intense competence. The other was a black man with the look of a Harvard don . . . which he had in fact once been.

Huh. And you thought the day was headed in a strange direction before.

"Hello, Mr. Cooper. May I call you Nick?"

"Of course, Mr. President."

■

"I apologize for the rather dramatic way this meeting came about. We're all a little bit on edge these days." Lionel Clay had a lecturer's voice, rich and deep and dripping erudition, rounded just slightly with South Carolina twang.

That's a polite way to put it. As the gifted continued to dominate every field from athletics to zoology, normal people were growing nervous. It wasn't hard to imagine a world divided into two classes like something out of H. G. Wells, and no one wanted to be a Morlock. On the other hand, the more extreme elements of the gifted weren't fighting for simple equality—they believed they were superior, and were willing to kill to prove it. America had grown accustomed to terrorism, to suicide bombers in shopping malls and poison mailed to senators. Worst of all had been the March 12th attacks; 1,143 people died when terrorists blew up the stock exchange in Manhattan. Cooper had been there, had wandered the shattered gray streets in a daze. Sometimes he still dreamed about a pink stuffed animal abandoned in a Broadway intersection. *We're more than on edge—we're batshit scared.* But what he said was, "I understand, sir."

"This is my chief of staff, Marla Keevers."

"Ms. Keevers." Though Cooper had been a government agent for eleven years, politics had never been his thing; still, even he knew of Marla Keevers. A hardcore political fixer, a backroom dealer with a reputation for ferocity.

"Mr. Cooper."

The president rapped his knuckles on the partition, and the limo slid into motion. "Marla?"

The chief of staff said, "Mr. Cooper, did you release the Monocle video?"

Well, so much for preliminaries.

He thought back to that evening. After Shannon freed his children, Cooper had chased his old boss up to the roof. He'd retrieved the video of Drew Peters conspiring with President Walker, and then he'd tossed his mentor off the twelve-story building.

That had felt good.

Afterward, Cooper sat on a bench not far from here deciding what to do with the video. The massacre at the Monocle restaurant had been the first and most incendiary step in dividing the country: not North versus South, not liberal versus conservative, but normal versus abnorm. Revealing the truth about that attack felt like the right thing to do, even though he knew it would have consequences beyond his control.

What was it Drew had said just before the end? *"If you do this, the world will burn."*

President Clay was watching him. It was a test, Cooper realized. "Yes, I did."

"That was a very reckless decision. My predecessor may not have been a good man, but he was the president. You undermined the nation's faith in the office. In the government as a whole."

"Sir, if you'll forgive me saying, President Walker undermined that when he ordered the murder of American citizens. All I did was tell the truth."

"Truth is a slippery concept."

"No, the great thing about the truth is that it's true." A hint of that old antiauthority tone was coming out, and he caught himself. "Sir."

Keevers shook her head, turned to look out the window. Clay said, "What are you doing these days, Nick?"

"I'm on leave from the DAR."

"Are you planning to return?"

"I'm not sure."

"Come work for me instead. Special advisor to the president. How does that sound?"

If Cooper had listed a hundred things the president of the United States might have said to him, that wouldn't have made the cut. He realized his mouth was open, and closed it. "I think maybe you have bad information. I don't know anything about governing."

"Let's cut through it, shall we?" Clay fixed him with a steady gaze. "Walker made a mess of things. He and Director Peters turned the DAR, which might have been our best hope for a peaceful future, into a private spy shop for personal gain. Would you agree?"

"I—yes. Sir."

"You yourself have killed more than a dozen people and leaked highly classified information."

Cooper nodded.

"And yet out of the entire catastrophe, you were the only person who acted righteously."

Keevers wrinkled her lips at that, but said nothing. The president leaned forward. "Nick, things are getting worse. We're on the edge of a precipice. There are normals who want to imprison or even enslave all brilliants. There are abnorms who favor genocide of everyone normal. A new civil war that could make the last one look like a minor skirmish. I need help averting it."

"Sir, I'm flattered, but I really don't know the first thing about politics."

"I have political advisors. What I don't have is the firsthand opinion of an abnorm who dedicated his life to hunting abnorm revolutionaries. Plus, you've proven that you will do what you believe is right, no matter the cost. That's the kind of advisor I need."

Cooper stared across the limousine. Scrambled to remember what he knew of the president. A history professor at Harvard, then a senator. He had a vague memory of an article he'd read, a piece suggesting that the real reason Clay had been chosen as VP was for electoral math. As a black man from South Carolina, he'd mobilized both the South and the African-American vote.

Jesus, Cooper. A vague memory of an article? That right there tells you whether you belong in this car.

"I'm sorry, sir. I truly appreciate the offer, but I don't think I'm the man for the job."

"You misunderstand," Clay said mildly. "Your country needs you. I'm not asking."

Cooper looked at—

Clay's posture, his body language, they've been perfectly in line with his words.

This isn't a PR move or a way to quiet you.

And everything he said about the state of the world is accurate.

—his new boss.

"In that case, sir, I serve at the pleasure of the president."

"Good. What do you know about a group called the Children of Darwin?"

ONE WEEK BEFORE THANKSGIVING

CHAPTER 2

Ethan Park stared.

The supermarket shelf was empty. Not thinly stocked. Not lacking variety. Empty. Cleaned out.

He closed his eyes, felt the world wobble. Long hours he was used to; the research team had been on the edge of a breakthrough for a year, and as they'd moved into proof-of-concept trials, the days had started blurring, meals eaten standing up, naps snatched in break room chairs. He'd been tired for a year.

But it wasn't until Amy gave birth to Violet that he discovered true exhaustion. The blackness behind his closed eyes felt dangerously good, a bed on a cold night that he could just wrap himself in, drift away—

He snapped to, opened his eyes, and checked the shelf again. Still empty. The sign above the aisle read SEVEN: VITAMINS – CANNED ORGANICS – PAPER TOWELS – DIAPERS – BABY FORMULA. Paper towels there were still plenty of, but on the shelf that until today had held Enfamil and Similac and Earth's Best, there was only dust and an abandoned shopping list.

Ethan felt oddly betrayed. When you ran out of something, you went to the grocery store. It was practically the basis for modern life. What happened when you couldn't take that for granted?

You return to your exhausted wife and hungry baby with a dumb look on your face.

Before they'd had a child, he'd scoffed at the idea that breast-feeding was difficult. He was a geneticist. Feeding the young was what breasts were for. How hard could it be?

Pretty hard, it turned out, for dainty modern-day breasts, breasts draped in cotton and lace, breasts that never felt wind or sunlight, never chafed and roughened. After a month of agonizingly slow feedings, of being patronized by a "lactation consultant" peddling specialized pillows and homeopathic creams, of Amy's nipples cracking and bleeding and finally growing infected, they'd called a halt. She'd tied down her breasts with an Ace bandage to stop milk production, and they'd switched to powdered formula. Their entire generation had been raised on it, and they'd done okay. Plus, it was so easy.

Easy, that was, until there was no formula on the shelf.

So. Options.

Well, at Violet's age, bovine milk was not ideal. Casein protein micelles were too taxing for a baby's developing kidneys. *On the other hand, cow's milk is better than no milk—*

The dairy case was empty. There was a piece of paper taped to it.

WE APOLOGIZE FOR THE INCONVENIENCE. RECENT ATTACKS HAVE DISRUPTED SHIPPING. WE HOPE TO BE RESTOCKED SOON. THANK YOU FOR YOUR PATIENCE IN THIS DIFFICULT TIME.

Ethan stared at the paper. Yesterday everything had been normal. Now there was no formula on the shelves. No milk in the fridge. What was happening here?

Baking.

He spun on his heel and jogged down the aisle, conscious of shoppers piling goods indiscriminately, clearing whole shelves into their carts, arguing and shoving. Ethan had a vision of the store an hour from now, cleared down to greeting cards and magazines and school supplies. Maybe no one had thought of . . .

Where the evaporated milk should be was just a glaring hole.

Ethan squatted down in front of it, stared at the back of the shelf, hoping a can or two had been missed. Knowing they hadn't.

Another store.

The front of the Sav-A-Lot was jammed, the checkout lines overflowing. The checkers looked stunned. Ethan pushed his way outside.

It was mid-November, cloudy and cold. He jumped at the honk of a horn, an Audi that barely slowed. The parking lot was overflowing, a line of cars backing out to Detroit Avenue. He climbed in the truck and tuned in WCPN as he spun out of the parking place.

"—reports of massive shortages across the entire Cleveland metro area. Police are asking everyone to remain calm. We're joined now by Dr. James Garner of the Department of Transportation and Rob Cornell of the Department of Analysis and Response. Dr. Garner, can you break this down for us?"

"I'll try. Early this morning there was a series of devastating attacks on the shipping industry in Tulsa, Fresno, and of course Cleveland. Terrorists hijacked more than twenty trucks and murdered the drivers."

"Not just murdered them."

"No." The man coughed. "The drivers were burned alive."

Jesus Christ. There had been a lot of attacks in the last years. Terrorism had become a fact of life in America. They'd all almost gotten used to it. Then March 12th had happened, the explosion in the new stock exchange in Manhattan. More than 1,100 people dead, thousands more injured, and suddenly there was no ignoring the unpleasant schism developing in America. But as hideous as that attack had been, there was something worse about this, something more brutal and intimate about pulling a living soul from his truck, pouring gasoline on him, and striking a match.

"—in addition, supply depots in all three cities were bombed. Fire crews stopped the blazes in Tulsa and Fresno, but Cleveland's depot was destroyed."

The announcer cut in. "All credited to the abnorm group calling itself the Children of Darwin. But these are major cities, with thousands of deliveries."

"Yes. But because of the attacks on drivers, insurance carriers had no choice but to withdraw coverage across the board. Without insurance, trucks are prohibited from even leaving the yard."

Ethan had made two stoplights but caught the third. His fingers tapped at the wheel as he waited.

"You're saying that after one day without deliveries, stores go empty?"

"The modern world is intricately connected. Businesses like grocery stores operate under what is known as just-in-time inventory. If you buy a can of beans, the scanner tells the computer to order more, and they arrive in the next shipment. It's an incredibly complex arrangement of systems. The Children of Darwin seem to understand that. Their attacks target the weak points in our own systems."

"Mr. Cornell, you're with the Department of Analysis and Response. Isn't preventing this sort of attack what the DAR is for?"

"First of all, thank you for having me. Second, I would like to remind everyone, including you, ma'am, to keep calm. This is a temporary problem caused by a violent but small terrorist organization—"

Ethan sped east, past a restaurant, a car lot, a high school. A new luxury market had opened near the river not long ago. It was pricey enough that people might not have thought of it. *Even if you're right, you won't be for long, so plan your moves. First goal is baby formula, whatever vegan moonbeam variety they have. Then milk. As much meat as you can pile in the cart. Skip the perishables, go for canned and frozen vegetables—*

The road to the store was jammed, cars honking and flashing, double-stacked in a single-wide lane. Forty yards ahead, he could see a mob surrounding the entrance. As he watched, a woman tried to force her cart through the crowd. Cries went up, and the ring of people tightened. A man in a business suit yanked at her shopping bags. The woman yelled, but he filled his arms and spun away, knocking the cart over in the process. Cans and bottles spilled across the pavement, and everyone dove for them. A thin guy tucked a chicken under his arm like a football and sprinted away. Two ladies with expensive hair fought over a gallon of milk.

"—again, we expect to have this problem under control soon. If everyone can just stay calm and work together, we'll get through this."

There was a crash, and the front window of the grocery store collapsed. The crowd surged in, yelling.

Ethan turned the car around.

.

When they'd moved to Cleveland, the real estate agent had assured them that Detroit Shoreway was the neighborhood they were looking for: a mile from the lakefront, two from downtown, solid schools, tree-lined streets, and a friendly community of people "like them"—basically all the advantages of the suburbs without being one. A great place to raise kids, the agent had said with a knowing look, as though visualizing sperm and egg meeting.

It had taken some getting used to. Ethan was a native New Yorker and mistrusted any place where you needed a car. Hell, a couple of years ago if anyone had suggested he'd end up in Cleveland, he'd have scoffed. But Cleveland was where Abe had set up his lab, and despite the fact that the guy was the most colossally arrogant prick Ethan had ever met, he was also a genius, and the second-place spot at the Advanced Genomics Institute was too good to pass up.

In the end, he'd been surprised. Much as he loved Manhattan, you could live in the same apartment for a decade and never meet your neighbors. It was a pleasant contrast to dwell amidst the simple Midwestern kindness, the backyard barbecues, and the I'll-get-your-mail-you-can-borrow-my-lawnmower-we're-all-in-this-together vibe.

Plus, he loved having a house. Not an apartment, not a condo, an actual house, with a basement and a yard. *Their* house, where they could turn the music up as loud as they wanted, where Violet's midnight cries weren't waking a downstairs neighbor. He was a reasonably handy guy, could wire a light fixture and drywall a nursery, and it had been such pleasure to make the place theirs one sweaty afternoon at a time, and then to sit on his front porch with a beer and watch the sun set through his maple trees.

Now he wondered if he'd been fooling himself. Manhattan might be congested and expensive, DC might be sprawling and hectic, but there was no way the markets wouldn't have milk.

Yesterday you would have said the same about Cleveland.

He killed the engine and sat in the dark. Tomorrow he could drive out of town, hit the highway, find formula somewhere.

Yeah, but she's hungry tonight. Man up, Daddy.

Ethan climbed out of the CRV and headed for his neighbor's house, a solid gingerbread thing with ivy devouring the southern half. They had three boys spread out at metronomic two-year intervals, and the rough sounds of play thumped through the walls.

"Hey, buddy," Jack Ford said when he opened the door. "What's up?"

"Listen, I'm sorry to ask, but we're out of formula, and the stores are cleaned out. You have any?"

"Sorry. Tommy's been off it for like six months."

"Right." Sirens started, a cop or an ambulance not too far away. "How about regular milk?"

"Sure thing." Jack paused. "You know what? I've got some evaporated milk in the basement. You want it?"

Ethan smiled. "You're a lifesaver."

"What neighbors are for, right? Come on in, have a beer."

Jack's house was crayon art and blaring cartoons and the smell of casserole. Ethan followed him down creaky basement steps into a half-finished space. On a carpet remainder in the corner, two recliners faced a huge tri-d screen, a new model with the enhanced projection field. The rest of the basement was given over to deep shelves packed with canned goods and cased food.

Ethan whistled. "You've got your own a grocery store down here."

"Yeah, you know. Once a Boy Scout." His neighbor bobbed his head, a not-quite embarrassed motion, then opened a minifridge and pulled out a couple of Buds. He dropped in a recliner, gestured to the other one. "So the supermarkets are empty?"

"The one I was just at, people started looting."

"It's the abnorms," Jack said. "The situation with them is getting worse every day."

Ethan gave a noncommittal nod. He knew a lot of brilliants; while abnorms raised the bar in every field, science and technology were where their advantages were clearest. Sure, there were days when it drove him nuts, when he knew that despite degrees from Columbia and Yale, there were people out there he would simply never be able to match. It was like playing pickup basketball with the Lakers; no matter how hot your skills were otherwise, on that court someone could always stuff the ball in your face.

Still, what were you going to do? Stop playing? No thanks.

"Every generation believes the world is going to hell, right?" Ethan sipped his beer. "The Cold War, Vietnam, nuclear proliferation, whatever. Impending doom is our natural state."

"Yeah, but no milk in the grocery store? That's not America."

"It'll be okay. Radio said the National Guard is going to start distributing food."

"To half a million people?" Jack shook his head. "Let me ask you something. You study evolution, right?"

"Sort of. I'm an epigeneticist. I study the way the world and our DNA interact."

"That sounds like a wild simplification," Jack said with a smile. "But I'll take it. What I want to know, have there been times like this? When a brand-new group just, you know, appeared?"

"Sure. Invasive species, when organisms are moved to a new ecosystem. Asian carp, zebra mussels, Dutch elm disease."

"That's what I thought. Those were all pretty disastrous, right? I mean, I'm not a bigot; I don't have anything against the gifted. It's the *change* that scares me. The world is so fragile. How are we supposed to live with a shift like this?"

It was a question often heard these days, bandied about at dinner parties, debated on news programs and in feedcasts. When the gifted had first been discovered, people had been more intrigued than anything else. After all, one percent of the population was a curiosity. It was only as the one percent grew to adulthood that the world had finally come to realize they represented a fundamental shift.

The problem was, from there it was a tiny step to hating them. "I hear you, man. But people aren't carp. We gotta find a way."

"Of course. You're right." Jack heaved himself out of his chair. "Anyway, I'm sure it'll work out. Let's see about that milk."

Ethan followed him through the basement. The shelves were stacked four high with cases of canned food, batteries, blankets. Jack pulled a twenty-four-pack of evaporated milk from the shelf. "Here we go."

"A couple of cans would be fine."

"Take it, it's no big deal."

"Can I at least pay you for it?"

"Don't be silly."

Part of him wanted to protest further, but he thought of Violet, and the empty supermarket, and he just said, "Thanks, Jack. I'll replace it."

"That's fine." His neighbor gave him a long look. "Ethan, this may sound weird, but do you have protection?"

"A pack of condoms on the nightstand."

Jack smiled, but only out of courtesy.

Ethan said, "I'm not sure I know what you mean."

"Come here." He walked to a metal cabinet and started fiddling with the combination lock. "Until the National Guard gets this all sorted, I'd feel better if you had one of these."

The gun cabinet was neat, rifles and shotguns locked into stands, half a dozen pistols on pegs. Ethan said, "I'm not really a gun guy."

Jack ignored him, took down a pistol. "This is a .38 revolver. Simplest gun in the world. All you need to do is pull the trigger." Fluorescent lights gleamed off oily metal.

"That's okay, man." Ethan forced a smile, held up the milk. "Really, this is plenty."

"Take it. Just in case. Put it on a closet shelf and forget about it."

Ethan wanted to make a joke, but the expression on his neighbor's face was serious. *The guy's helping you out. Don't offend him.* "Thanks."

"Hey, like I said. What neighbors are for."

∎

After the last two hours, walking in the front door of his house was like stepping into a hug. Ethan snapped the lock and stepped out of his shoes. Gregor Mendel sauntered over and rubbed his head against Ethan's ankles, purring softly. Ethan rubbed the cat's neck, then picked up the case of milk and followed the warm light flowing down the hall, looking for his girls. He found them in the kitchen, Amy holding Violet to her chest.

"Oh thank God." His wife's face lit up to see him. "I was getting scared. Have you heard the news? They're saying that people are looting stores."

"Yeah." He held out his arms, and Amy passed Violet to him. His daughter was awake and impossibly beautiful, neckless and pudgy with a shock of auburn hair. "I was there. Everything is cleaned out. The milk is a gift from Jack."

"Lucky he had some." She opened a can and poured it into a baby bottle. "You want to feed her?"

Ethan leaned back against the counter and switched his daughter to his left arm, bracing her weight on his hip. She saw the bottle and started to cry, a desperate sound like he might be teasing her. He popped the nipple in her greedy mouth. "Is this a whole can?"

"Five ounces." She read the label. "It's pretty caloric. We can probably water them down to stretch it longer."

"Why? There are twenty-three more cans."

"She eats four times a day. That's not even a week."

"The stores will be figured out by then."

"Still," she said.

He nodded. "You're right. Good idea."

They stood for a moment, both dead on their feet, but with a sweetness to it too. Everything had a sweetness these days, a golden glow like he was watching his own life in some sun-faded movie print. Becoming a father made everything fraught with meaning.

"Hey," he said, "want to hear something funny?"

"Always."

"Jack's a survival nut. His basement is stocked like a bomb shelter. He even gave me a gun."

"What?"

"I know." He chuckled. "He wouldn't let me leave without it."

"You have it with you? Now?"

Ethan balanced Violet in one arm, pinned the bottle under his chin, and pulled the gun from his jacket pocket. "Crazy, huh?"

Amy's eyes widened. "Why does he think we need a gun?"

"Said we should have it for protection."

"You tell him we had condoms?"

"He didn't seem to think that was enough."

Amy said, "Can I see it?"

"Careful, it's loaded."

She weighed it gingerly on an open palm. "It's heavier than I would've thought."

"I know." Ethan popped the baby against his shoulder and started rubbing her back. Violet promptly belched like a trucker. "You're not freaked out about it?"

"A little." She set it on the counter. "But it's probably not a terrible idea. Just in case."

"Just in case of what?"

She didn't answer.

Indestructible's Jake Flynn out of the closet!

Heartthrob Jake Flynn is well known for his abs. But it's the fact that he's an abnorm that's startling people. Last week the singer-turned-box-office-sensation announced he was a tier-five brilliant, a fact never before revealed.

Now, in an exclusive interview with *People* magazine, the hunky star comes clean about life, love, and being brilliant.

PEOPLE: Let's start with your gift. You're hyperthymesitic. What does that mean?

FLYNN: I remember certain trivial details with exceptional clarity. If you give me a date, I can tell you what I wore, what the weather was like, that kind of thing.

PEOPLE: May 3, 1989.

FLYNN: One of those days when you know spring has arrived. Blue skies, puffy clouds, the smell of things growing. I wore Spiderman pajamas. [Laughs.] I was five.

PEOPLE: You've always been private about being gifted. Why?

FLYNN: If I talked about it, that would have been the way I was framed. "Abnorm actor to star in blah, blah, blah." It's not that important to me, and I didn't want it to be that important to anyone else.

PEOPLE: Then why come out now?

FLYNN: People are getting so worked up about norms and abnorms. It felt like by not mentioning it, I was part of the problem. I just wanted to say hey, you all thought I was one thing, and now you know I'm something else. And yet nothing's really changed. So chill.

PEOPLE: Your gift must make learning lines easier.

FLYNN: I wish. It's not a matter of memory. I lose my car keys all the time.

PEOPLE: Abnorms are hot right now. What do you say to people who suggest you came out as a publicity stunt?

FLYNN: That's ridiculous.

PEOPLE: Why?

FLYNN: For one thing, it's about the twentieth thing I think of myself as. I'm a husband, I'm a father, I'm an American, I'm an actor, I'm a singer, I'm a Cubs fan, I'm a dog lover. On and on. After all of that stuff, it's like, oh yeah, I'm also an abnorm.

PEOPLE: What do you think of the growing conflict between norms and abnorms?

FLYNN: I hate it. For me being an abnorm is no different than having blue eyes. I get that there are tier ones out there, exceptional people who are changing the paradigm. But there are a lot more folks like me. I mean seriously—I know that it was raining in Denver on June 9th of last year. Because of that, my government wants to implant a microchip in my neck?

PEOPLE: When you put it that way, the Monitoring Oversight Initiative does seem a little silly.

FLYNN: The problem is that the media portrays this like there are two factions, norms and abnorms, and we're all supposed to choose sides. But really, it's a spectrum. At one end you have President Walker murdering his own people because he's afraid of what brilliants represent, and he wants the power to contain them. On the other, you have abnorm terrorists saying it shouldn't be about equal rights, that brilliants should rule the world. The extremists are the problem. Most people just want to live their lives.

PEOPLE: Speaking of lives, you and your wife, Victoria's Secret model Amy Schiller, recently had a baby girl—

FLYNN: Oh God. Not the name question.

PEOPLE: It's an unusual name.

FLYNN: I don't know what to tell you, man. We want her to be her own person, to not feel like she has to fit the world's constraints, and we both really like Thai food, so . . .

PEOPLE: Noodle Flynn.

FLYNN: Won't be any others in her kindergarten class.

CHAPTER 3

He was being the spider when the SUV finally stopped.

The truck was black. There were two men inside. It had been coasting to a halt for almost three minutes. It would be three more before the doors opened. Then five minutes to cross the half dozen paces to where he sat. He had plenty of time to be the spider. An ocean of time, massive, deep, crushing, and cold. Time like the Mariana Trench, thirty-six thousand feet deep. Time that weighed and warped.

The spider. Tan and black, an inch long. A wolf spider, he believed, although he was no great spider expert. He had been watching it for eleven hours. First had come revulsion, the primal skin-crawl. Eventually, the tracing of hair on her legs and abdomen—he had decided it was a female—came to look soft, almost inviting, like a stuffed animal. Eight eyes, shiny and complete. The fangs fascinated him. To bear your weaponry so blatantly before you, to move through the world as a nightmare. The spider regarded him, and he regarded the spider.

She was perfect. Stillness itself, until motion was called for. And then motion so fast and precise it could hardly be seen by the prey. Brutal and without remorse. For her the world was only food and threat. Were there vegetarian spiders? He didn't think so.

No, she was a killer.

From his position he could see both the spider and the SUV; he shifted focus to the vehicle. His eyes didn't move, of course; they were locked in the glacial pace of muscles, of flesh and blood.

But he had long ago learned to move his attention even while his body lagged behind. It was a simple thing to focus on the SUV and the two men inside it. The driver was speaking. It took twenty seconds for him to frame six words, and his lips were easily read.

Inside the SUV, the driver asked, "So who is this guy, anyway?"

"His name is Soren Johansen. He's the most dangerous person I've ever met." John Smith smiled through the windshield. "And my oldest friend."

Hello, John. I've missed you.

■

It was hardest with people.

There was a reason he was alone. In retreat, like a Buddhist monk on a mountaintop. And like the monk, he had been striving not for knowledge or wisdom but for nothingness. Not the idea of nothingness, not the exercise of it, thoughts sent drifting down the river as they intruded on his meditation. No, his comfort had come, when it did, in true moments of nothingness. Moments when he did not exist. Only in them did the relentless dragging of time not overwhelm.

When he couldn't be nothing, which was often, he became something else. Something simple and pure. Like the spider.

People, though, were neither simple nor pure. It was agony watching them move through life like they were fighting through wet cement. Every motion endless, every word taking an eternity, and for what? Motions without purpose or grace, words that wandered and drifted.

Therefore it surprised him to realize that he had missed John. But of all the gifted—and no one else was worth considering— John was most similar to himself. John lived in a multilayered view of the future, plans within plans, eventualities a year away set in motion by a conversation today. It was different than Soren's own perspective, but it provided a frame of reference, a means of understanding.

Like now, the way John jogged the fifteen feet to him, rather than making him suffer through the walk. The way he spoke in their old way, "Howareyou?"

Not a pleasantry, Soren knew. A question on multiple levels. John asking if he was holding together.

A flash of memory, vivid as tri-d: John Smith at eleven, talking to him on the playground of Hawkesdown Academy. Passing him a Kleenex for his bleeding nose, broken by one of the older boys. Saying, "It's better if I talk fast, isn't it?"

Saying, "You'resmartbutyou'renotthinking."

Saying, "Makeityourstrength."

Saying, "Andnoonewilleverhityouagain."

Teaching him about meditation, how to put aside the dizzying maelstrom of the future and exist only in the now. Teaching him that if he could control himself, he could use his terrible curse to do anything, use it against all the petty little ones who tried to hurt him. John understanding that the boy everyone thought broken was merely overwhelmed, knocked flat by every second.

People thought that time was a constant, because that was what their mind told them. But time was water. The stillest water vibrated and buzzed with energy.

John had taught him, and the next time the older boys came for Soren, he remembered. He became nothing but the moment. He did not plan. Did not anticipate. He merely watched them move in slow motion, and lazily, with a stolen scalpel, he cut the throat of the biggest one.

No one had ever come for him again. "I have more nothingness than ever."

Smith understood. "That'sgood."

"You need me."

"Yes."

"Out in the world."

"I'msorry. Yes."

"It's important?"

"Crucial." A pause. "Soren. It'stime."

He stopped being the spider then and became the man again. For a moment, the future threatened to swamp him, the terrifying infinity of it, like being alone in the Pacific in the middle of a starless night, all that water and time around and below him, the deepest hole in the planet sucking him down into darkness.

Be nothing. Be not the spider nor the man nor the future nor the past. Be the moment. Be nothing. Just like John had taught him.

Soren would rise and go with his friend into the world. He would do . . .

"Anything."

Treat Me Like the Filthy Twist I Am

18 yr old T4 male, slender, shaved. My father kicked me out—be my new daddy?

Norm Couple Seeking Abnorm Housegirl

We are: mid-40s, professional, fit, successful. You are: Tier 2 or 3 Reader. If you're who we want, you already know what we want.

Married Abnorm Looking for NSA Fun

There's a reason they call us gifted. Let's get twist-ed.

Lonely at the Top

T1 physicist seeking other Tier Ones for conversation, friendship, more if we're both feeling it. Age, race, gender unimportant.

Groupie Seeks Hot Abnorm Action

I know it's wrong, and I don't care. Must bring Treffert-Down test results and/or Academy diploma. I can host.

Knock Me Up

Attractive norm woman, 37, seeking T1 for night of passionate procreation. No condoms, no strings. Just drop your jeans and gimme those genes.

CHAPTER 4

Cooper wasn't used to it. Not one little bit.

It'd been three weeks since he'd taken that unscheduled limousine ride. Twenty-one days as a special advisor to the president of the United States, all of them work days—he had a feeling that weekends would soon be a distant memory—spent in meetings and conferences, poring over reports and sitting in the Situation Room.

The Situation Room, for Christ's sake. Twenty-one days wasn't near long enough to get used to it. Cooper waved his pass at the guard hut on Pennsylvania, waited for the buzz of the door.

"Morning, Mr. Cooper."

"Morning, Chet. I told you, it's just Cooper." He slipped off his jacket, set it atop his briefcase on the X-ray belt, then swiped his pass and typed his ID code into the machine. "How was your night?"

"Lost twenty dollars on the 'Skins to my son-in-law. Arms up, please."

Cooper raised his arms as Chet ran a wand up and down his body, searching for traces of explosives and weaponized biologicals. The wand was newtech, developed in response to the public outcry over delays at airport security. Best Cooper could tell, it hadn't sped anything up. "Bad enough he marries your little girl, he takes your money too?"

"Tell me." The guard smiled, gestured to the opposite end of the X-ray machine. "You have a good day, Mr. Cooper."

And just like that, he was through the fence and on the White House grounds. A long, curving driveway wound past the tri-d cameras at Pebble Beach, where the newsies waited day in and day out. Cooper put his jacket back on and walked, drinking in the building, the reality of it. The people's house, the symbol of the best the nation could stand for, the epicenter of global power—his office.

Well, sort of. In actuality, his office was in the OEOB, the office building across the street. But he'd barely seen it; his working hours had been spent almost entirely in the West Wing.

A marine in dress uniform executed a precise right-face and held the door for Cooper. In the lobby, he checked his phone and saw he was on time, a few minutes shy of seven. He passed the Roosevelt Room, stepping aside for a general and two aides. The carpet was thick and soft, and everything glistened, the furniture freshly polished. He'd never put a lot of thought into pondering what the air in the White House might smell like, but even so he'd been surprised by the answer: flowers. It smelled like flowers, from the fresh arrangements brought in every day.

A right turn took him past the Cabinet Room—*the Cabinet Room!*—and a handful of paces later, he was stepping into the president's outer office. Two assistants typed at keyboards projected onto antique desks, and their screens were polarized monoglass so thin that from the side, they vanished entirely. A funny juxtaposition of the old and the new.

Press Secretary Holden Archer was locked in conversation with Marla Keevers, the chief of staff looking smart and vicious in a gray suit. Both were seasoned politicians and gave little away, but to Cooper's eyes, the subtle stiffening at his arrival spoke volumes.

Relax, guys. I'm not after your job.

Cooper put his hands in his pocket and turned his attention to a gilt-framed painting, the Statue of Liberty draped in impressionistic fog. Nice enough, he supposed, though if he'd seen it at a street fair, he wouldn't have paid any attention.

"Mr. Cooper."

He turned. "Mr. Secretary. Good morning."

Though now the secretary of defense, Owen Leahy had come up through intelligence, and it showed. His posture suggested that not only would he not comment on the quality of the morning, he would neither confirm nor deny that it was in fact the a.m. There weren't many people who gave off so little to Cooper's eyes.

"Anything new on the Children of Darwin?" Cooper asked.

Leahy made a noncommittal face. "Have they found you an office yet?"

"Across the street."

"Ah." A tiny smile at that; Cooper had noticed people here put a lot of stock in the location of their office. Leahy continued, "And how are you enjoying working here? All these meetings must seem dull after the DAR."

"Oh, it's not that different," Cooper said. "Less gunplay, but still plenty of fatalities."

Leahy gave an *aren't-you-droll* chuckle. Cooper could see the SecDef preparing another veiled insult, but before he could fire it, a curved door in the southwest wall opened. President Lionel Clay stuck his head out, said to his assistant, "Push everything nonessential," then turned and walked back inside, gesturing over his shoulder for them to follow.

In the flood of morning sun, the Oval Office glowed, light bouncing off every polished surface. Keevers, Leahy, and Archer walked in comfortably, like it was any other room. Cooper squared his shoulders and tried to do the same, still hearing the same gentle roar in his ears he experienced every time.

"Owen, what's our status on the Children of Darwin?"

"We're getting a more complete picture, sir, but slowly." The secretary of defense began to brief the president, but it was clear that there had been no significant progress made.

Cooper had become something of an expert on the terrorist organization since joining Clay's administration. He'd devoured every memo on the Children, met with the DAR and the FBI and the NSA, spent hours staring at photographs of truckers burned alive. Yet for all the time he'd spent, he still didn't know very much. The terrorist organization seemed to have sprung to life full-formed. No one knew how large it was, where it was based, how it was funded, if it had centralized leadership or was just a loose network of terror cells.

"What it comes down to, sir," Leahy continued, "is that we've learned a lot in the last days—the bombs at the food depots illustrate their technical knowledge and chemical access, surveillance video shows that they used stolen police cruisers when attacking the trucks, our analysts are gaining insight through data-mining patterns—but none of it is giving us actionable answers."

"Maybe that's because they're fanatics. Lunatics," Keevers said. "They burned people alive. Why are we talking about the COD like a foreign regime instead of a cult?"

The president rubbed at his chin. "Nick? What do you think?"

Only his ex-wife Natalie and Shannon used his first name, but somehow he didn't feel comfortable asking the president of the United States to call him Cooper. He cleared his throat, took a moment to weigh his words. "Think how furious the whole nation was at what they saw on the Monocle video. Their own president planning to kill them."

Clay maintained a mild expression, but the three staffers exchanged glances, shuffled papers. He could feel them edging away. *Let 'em. As long as you're here, you may as well tell the truth.* "Well, now consider the brilliants' point of view. Tier-one children are forcibly taken from their parents and sent to academies. Without due process or a jury, the DAR terminates abnorms it deems a threat to society. Thanks to the Monitoring Oversight Initiative, every American gifted will be forced to get a microchip implanted in their neck—"

"We'll see about that one," Clay said. "I'm not a fan."

"That's great to hear, Mr. President. But even if you are able to get the law repealed—and you should—it won't change the fact that gifted are treated like second-class citizens."

"I'm not sure," Leahy said, "that I'm seeing the tactical value to this analysis."

"It's this," Cooper said. "Fanatics they may be, but they're not lunatics, and they have cause to be pissed off. I've spent my life hunting terrorists. I hate everything they stand for. But let's not pretend that they haven't been provoked."

"And let's not forget," Leahy said, "that they've killed thousands, burned innocent men and women alive, and are trying to starve three American cities. What do you propose, we sit around a table and chat about our differences?"

"No," Cooper said. "We can't negotiate with terrorists."

"So then—"

"But we could get someone to negotiate on our behalf."

President Clay looked thoughtful. "Who are you thinking, Nick?"

"Erik Epstein." The world's richest man had earned more than $300 billion using his gift to find patterns in the stock market. When the global markets were finally shuttered to protect against people like him, he'd turned his attention to a new project: building a home for brilliants. He'd leveraged his fortune to create an abnorm Israel in the heart of the Wyoming desert. "As the leader of the New Canaan Holdfast, he's got connections to the gifted community at all levels. And he doesn't condone terrorism, so . . ." Cooper trailed off. A look was passing between the other staffers. "What?"

"Of course, you don't know," Marla Keevers said. "You're new to this world, how could you? But you see, there is no Erik Epstein."

He stared at her, bemused. Remembering standing in a subterranean wonderland of computers beneath the New Canaan Holdfast, talking to Epstein. A strange and intelligent man with a gift of enormous power, the ability to correlate seemingly unrelated sources of data and draw patterns from them.

Of course, the same gift had made him a recluse, barely able to communicate with other people. Which was why his brother had served as the public "Erik Epstein," the one who did talk shows and met presidents. It was a secret known to only a handful of people.

"You see," Keevers continued, "it's clear that the man pretending to be Epstein is not the same man responsible for bringing down the stock market."

"Which makes diplomacy with him impossible," the president said. "We could never be sure who we were dealing with."

"But—" Cooper caught himself. He knew a truth these people did not, a truth that might matter. And yet, these were some of the most powerful people on the planet. If Epstein had chosen to keep them in the dark, there was a reason.

Last time you met Epstein, you promised him you'd kill John Smith. Instead, you spared Smith's life. Do you really want to screw the world's richest man twice? "I see."

"For now," Leahy said, picking up as if uninterrupted, "we're focusing on the situation on the ground. We're hoping to begin distributing food and critical supplies tomorrow."

"Tomorrow?" The president frowned. "The supermarkets were empty two days ago. What's the delay?"

Keevers said, "We'd actually consider that a win, sir. The National Guard doesn't maintain food reserves. In Tulsa and Fresno, we're negotiating with the grocery distributors, but the largest food depot in the Cleveland area was destroyed. We're having to coordinate with others across northeast Ohio."

"What about FEMA?"

"FEMA can't act until Governor Timmons declares a state of emergency and formally requests help."

"Why hasn't he?"

"He's a Democrat," she said. "If he comes to a Republican president for help, it'll make him look weak come reelection."

"Fix that. People are hungry."

"Yes, sir." Marla Keevers uncrumpled her d-pad and made a note. "In the meantime, the National Guard is trying to set up food distribution centers, but they're having trouble. There have been incidents at most of the grocery stores. Broken glass, fistfights, looting. The National Guard is trying to keep the peace, but while they're doing crowd control and defending stores, they can't build aid stations. And the longer the delays in delivering food, the more people are taking to the streets."

President Clay turned his back on them and paced to the window. He stared out at the Rose Garden, the morning sun neatly bisecting him. "Any fatalities?"

"Not yet. A few people hospitalized."

"We need everyone to calm down," Clay said. "The panic is worse than the problem."

"Yes, sir," Keevers said. "We think you should address the nation."

"This afternoon?"

Press Secretary Archer said, "We'll get better coverage this evening."

"Just a brief statement," Keevers said. "Prepared remarks. You are personally overseeing all attempts—"

"Efforts," Archer said, "not attempts. Personally overseeing all efforts during this difficult time."

"A season of adversity when Americans must come together—"

"—to demonstrate the spirit of resolve that defines the national character, et cetera."

"The National Guard has your highest confidence, and so do the people of Cleveland, Tulsa, and Fresno."

"Meanwhile, no stone is being left unturned in the hunt for those who vilely attacked our nation."

"Excuse me," Cooper said.

The rhythm of the room was broken, everyone turning to look at him like they had forgotten he was there. He smiled affably. "You said 'statement.' Shouldn't he take questions?"

"No," Keevers and Leahy said at the same time. Archer said, "Absolutely not."

"Three cities are in chaos," Cooper said. "There are food shortages and looting and the fear of riots. Why wouldn't the president answer questions?"

Keevers's face was tight. "Mr. Cooper, I don't think—"

"Actually," President Clay said, "he has a point. Why not take questions?"

The other three looked at one another. After a moment, Archer said, "Because, sir, the questions will be, who are the Children of Darwin? Where are they? What do they want? How close are we to stopping them?"

"Why not come out strong?" Clay asked. "Say that the situation is under control, that the COD will soon be neutralized by actions covert, swift, and final."

"Because intelligence suggests more attacks may be coming," the secretary of defense said. "If you say we've got it handled and an hour later something blows up, it looks like we're asleep at the switch."

"So tell the truth," Cooper said. "Tell people that you don't have all the answers yet. Tell them that the full force of the US government is being brought to bear. That terrorism won't be tolerated, and that the Children of Darwin will be caught or killed. And that meanwhile, you need your citizens to put on their big-boy pants and calm down."

A silence fell. It had a weight and a texture. It was a silence that spoke volumes; a silence filled with at least three people wondering just how dumb he was.

So much for "the truth shall set you free."

After a long moment, the president spoke. "All right. No questions."

Cooper leaned back in his chair. Fought the urge to shrug.

"But Nick raises a good point," Clay continued. "It's important to preserve people's confidence that the buck stops with the president, and if I make a statement and don't answer questions, it suggests we're hiding something. Holden, on the other hand, can defer and deflect. He'll do the briefing."

"Yes, sir."

"And, Owen, I want answers about the Children of Darwin. Not next week, not tomorrow, now."

"Yes, sir."

"Good." Lionel Clay circled behind his desk, put on his reading glasses, and began to flip through a file folder. His attention was absorbed immediately. A side effect of Cooper's gift was that he tended to categorize people as shades of color; hotheads felt red to him, introverts landed in shades of gray. Lionel Clay was the smoke-stained gold of café walls, comforting and sophisticated.

Which is great. But I wonder if right now we don't need a man who patterns like polished steel.

He stood up, buttoned his suit jacket, and followed the others out of the Oval Office. Marla Keevers waited until the door closed to jump him. "Big-boy pants?"

"Big-girl pants too," he said.

Her smile was thin and cold and died far from her eyes. "You realize all you accomplished was to get him excited about something he can't do."

"My understanding, he can do pretty much anything he likes."

"You're wrong. And now instead of the president telling the nation not to worry, we'll have the press secretary bobbing and weaving. Holden is good, but what we need is the leader of the free world telling his people that everything is okay."

"Even if it's not."

"Especially then."

"See, that's where we disagree. I think that the president's job is to protect the country. And telling them the truth is the best way to do that."

"Oh, Christ." She rolled her eyes. "I'd say that I hope you know what you're doing, but you clearly don't."

"We'll see," Cooper said.

"Yes," Marla Keevers replied. "We will."

Con$piracy around murder of DAR director
El Chupacabra
"Why is it called 'common sense' when it's so rare?"
User ID: 493324

You guys gotta hear this.

You know how three months ago, DAR's Drew Peters takes a header off a DC high-rise? The cover story is that he's overwhelmed with guilt about his role in the Monocle, so he uploads the video of him and Walker planning it, and then swan dives.

Crazy to begin with, because the dude was the head of Equitable Services, and that division killed God knows how many people, so why is he worried about the 73 in the restaurant?

But here's the wacko part. I've got a buddy in the DC police, and he told me that that same night, in that same building, there was a firefight in a graphic design studio. Apparently it was shot to shit, monitors blown up, glass broken. He says there was a lot of blood but no body.

My guy got to the scene and was turned away by the men in black. He thinks maybe DAR agents. And later that night, he gets a call from the police commissioner telling him that he's mistaken, there was no blood, no firefight.

Obviously something else went down. My take, Peters didn't release the video, it was actually whoever shot up the graphic design studio.

Which means that Peters was murdered. And no one is talking about it.

So the order had to come down from on high. Someone with juice was moving pieces behind the scenes.

Stay locked and loaded, guys. Dark days are coming.

Re: Con$piracy around murder of DAR director
Benito the Mighty
"Be still and know that I am God"
User ID: 784321

You just putting this together?

There had to be more people involved. Walker was the president, and Peters a director at the DAR. It's not like either of them did the wetwork at the Monocle. And no one has been able to find the shooters, which means they were whacked too.

And you're surprised that others are involved?

There's a whole shadow government at work here. They go on TV and do the magic show for us. Get us worked up because a mayor sends some girl a picture of his dick, or a senator says something racist, or an aide smokes crack. And we ooh and ahh and judge, and meanwhile, we never look at what they're really doing.

The decisions that drive the nation are made in dark rooms. Records are not kept, and press releases are not issued.

It goes a lot deeper than the Monocle. There's a cabal of people who are pulling all the strings, and they aren't afraid to drop bodies. Your cop buddy better be careful.

Re: Con$piracy around murder of DAR director
LadyKiller87
"You are all sheeple"
User ID: 123021

Smells like BS. Covering up the murder of a DAR director would take crazy clout.

Re: Con$piracy around murder of DAR director
Benito the Mighty
"Be still and know that I am God"
User ID: 784321

You're right, that would take, like, the president of the United States.

Oh wait—he was in on it. Dipshit.

Re: Con$piracy around murder of DAR director
El Chupacabra
"Why is it called 'common sense' when it's so rare?"
User ID: 493324

So how far does this rabbit hole go? Walker was president; who else is in his cabal? President Clay? SecDef Leahy?

Re: Con$piracy around murder of DAR director
Benito the Mighty
"Be still and know that I am God"
User ID: 784321

Could be. All I know is that my go-bag is packed and my cabin is prepped. Two pallets of canned goods, 200 gallons of water, and the hardware to defend it.

When the shit goes down, I'm going to ride it out in style. And woe betide any numb nuts who crosses my fence line.

Re: Con$piracy around murder of DAR director
BananaGirl
"Worry is a misuse of the imagination"
User ID: 897236

Dude, you don't need all that water. Just build a catch basin and a purification system. Here, check out the schematics.

CHAPTER 5

"Big-girl pants? He really said that?"

"And smiled like he was being cute." Marla Keevers sipped her coffee.

"It's quick, at least." Owen Leahy shook his head. As the secretary of defense, there weren't many people around whom he dared show his hand. But Marla was a friend, or as close to one as politics at this level allowed. They'd worked together under President Walker, and he'd quickly learned that she was one of those rare people who got the job done, whatever it took. He liked those people. He was one of them. "The president seems smitten."

"Cooper won him over right away. You know how? When Clay offered him the job, he refused."

"You're kidding."

"Nope. You believe that? Sitting in the limo, after a show-of-force pickup with twenty Secret Service agents, and the guy says no."

They were in her office, the doors closed, and Leahy had his foot up on his knee, the chair rocked back on two legs. These informal conferences had started as a way to keep the train on the rails during the transition from Walker to Clay, but they'd become chatty. "Was it a performance?"

"No. That's the weird thing. He honestly didn't want the job."

That was unnerving. This was Washington, DC. Everyone wanted the job. "So Cooper is the new fair-haired boy."

Marla nodded. They stared at each other, then broke into laughter. It felt good, absurd as the situation was.

"What a world, huh? Throw your boss off a roof, end up serving the president," Leahy said. "I guess we could always use that as leverage to control him."

"Cooper won't be a puppet. Plus, do we really want to open that particular can of worms?" Marla shook her head. "If the truth about that night came out, people would start asking who else was involved."

"I didn't have anything to do with the Monocle."

"Neither did I. But there are plenty of other things we have been . . . aware of." She left it at that, a gesture he appreciated. Deft.

"I don't know, Marla. Is it just me, or is the world going crazy? We're facing maybe the greatest crisis in American history, and the president is getting his advice from a Boy Scout."

"You know how many people Nick Cooper has killed?"

"Okay," Leahy said, "a dangerous Boy Scout."

She shrugged. A message pinged in on her system, and she glanced at it, typed a quick response. Leahy laced his fingers behind his head, stared at the ceiling.

"In 1986, when Bryce published his study on the gifted, I was just starting at the CIA. Done my four years in army intel, transferred over. I was the FNG on the Middle East desk, a junior analyst getting all the junk assignments. But when I read that study, I got up from my cubicle, walked straight to the deputy's office, and asked for five minutes."

"You didn't."

"I was young."

"Did he see you?"

"Yeah." Leahy smiled, remembering that day. January, and cold; his shoes had salt stains on them, and while he'd waited outside Mitchum's office, he'd licked his fingers to wipe the leather clean. He could still taste the tang of salt and dirt. "The deputy looked at me like I might be mentally challenged." He shrugged.

"No way out at that point, so I figured, screw it, today you either make your name or lose your job."

"What did you say?"

"I dropped the study on his desk, and I said, 'Sir, you can forget about the sheiks, and Berlin, and the Soviets. This is the going to be the conflict that defines the next fifty years of American intelligence.'"

"No." Marla was smiling broadly. "No."

"Yes."

"And?"

"He laughed me out of his office, and I spent an extra year as a junior analyst. But I was right. I knew it then, and I know it now." *And Mitchum does too.* It had taken five years before the deputy saw the truth, but when he had, he'd remembered who told him first. Deputy Mitchum had taken a personal interest from then on, and Leahy's climb up the ladder had accelerated dramatically. "Nothing in our history presents the same threat that the gifted do."

"Easy. The *New York Times* would pay a fortune to quote you saying that."

"The *Times* can bite me. I've got three children and five grandchildren, and none of them are gifted. How do you like their odds? Think in twenty years they're going to be running the world? Or serving fries?"

Marla didn't respond, just typed another message on her system. Leahy said, "What do you think of him?"

"Cooper?"

"Clay. He's been president for two months. The grace period is over. What do you think?"

She took her hands from the keyboard. Picked up her coffee and took a thoughtful sip. Finally, she said, "I think he would make an exceptional history professor."

Their eyes locked.

There really wasn't any point in saying more.

CHAPTER 6

It was the kind of crisp blue day that made a man proud to own his house, to be out in scrub clothes working in his yard. A beer on the edge of the porch, radio voices talking in the background. Ethan was partaking in that greatest of white-collar lies, "working from home," and not feeling at all bad about it. He put in plenty of hours at the lab. Besides, what the news had termed the "Crisis in Cleveland" had been going on for three days now. People would be running out of supplies, starting to get hungry. Hungry people did stupid things, and he wasn't leaving his wife and child alone.

"—expected to address the nation this evening. In advance of that press conference, the White House has reiterated that the National Guard is in the process of setting up aid stations to distribute food and supplies in each of the affected cities—"

One thing he'd discovered about owning a house, the damn leaves just kept falling. But he found a kind of Zen to stuffing the bags, soaking up the small details, the smell, the way each armful sent splinters to float in the air, lit by golden autumn sun.

"—have indicated that this will be mostly an inconvenience, with no lasting repercussions. They are asking that everyone remain calm—"

"Dr. Park?"

Ethan looked up. A man and a woman stood on the curb. They wore dark suits and sunglasses, and the man held out a wallet with a badge. "I'm Special Agent Bobby Quinn, and this is Special

Agent Valerie West. We're with the Department of Analysis and Response. Do you have a moment?"

Ethan straightened, his back singing. "Um. Sure."

"You are Dr. Ethan Park, of the Advanced Genomics Institute?"

"Yes."

Quinn nodded, taking in the yard, Ethan's torn clothes and dirty hands. "Would you mind if we came in?"

"What's this about?"

"Dr. Abraham Couzen. Could we talk inside?"

Abe? He shrugged, said, "Sure." Feeling a bit surreal—where but in the movies did government agents show up on your front lawn?—he led them up the steps and inside. "Have a seat. You want some coffee or anything?"

"No, thank you." The two agents sat side by side on the couch. Quinn said, "Nice place."

"Thank you."

"You've got a little one?" Gesturing to the infant swing.

"A girl. Ten weeks. Look, I'm sorry, I don't mean to be rude, but what is this about?"

"When was the last time you saw Dr. Couzen?"

"A couple of days ago."

"Can you be precise?"

Ethan thought about it. Abe came and went according to his own whims. *Actually, he does pretty much everything that way.* "The day before yesterday. At the lab."

"And you haven't heard from him since?"

"No. Has something happened?"

Quinn looked pained. "I'm sorry to tell you this, but yesterday a neighbor reported gunfire coming from Dr. Couzen's house. Police responded and found his back door kicked in. His home office had been ransacked, and Couzen was gone."

"*What?* Is Abe okay?"

"That's what we're trying to find out."

"Dr. Park," West said, "do you know of anyone who had made threats against Dr. Couzen?"

"No."

"Anyone let go from the institute recently, or who might bear a grudge?"

Ethan almost laughed at that. "Let go, no. Bear a grudge? Sure. Abe's not an easy guy to work with."

"How do you mean?"

"He's . . ." Ethan shrugged. "In the old days, they would have said he was brilliant, but that means something different now. He's not an abnorm, but he's an off-the-charts genius, and not the most patient person."

"What does that mean, exactly?"

"He's abrasive. Difficult. Dismissive of anyone not as smart as he is, which means he's dismissive of pretty much everyone."

"Including you?"

"Sometimes. But I didn't break into his house, if that's what you're asking."

"It's not," Quinn said, holding up his hands. "We're just trying to figure out why someone might have targeted Couzen."

"Targeted?" He looked back and forth between the two agents. "I'm sorry, I'm still catching up here."

"This wasn't a simple robbery," Quinn said. "They came in while he was home. There was a struggle, and Dr. Couzen is gone. At this point, we're assuming it's a kidnapping."

Ethan leaned back against the chair, trying to process what he was being told. Kidnapping? Who would kidnap Abe?

"Dr. Park—"

"Ethan."

"Ethan, can you tell us what Dr. Couzen was working on?"

"Epigenetic roots for variable gene expression."

The agents exchanged a glance. Quinn parted his hands, raised his eyebrows.

Right. Ethan said, "Have you ever heard of the Dutch famine cohort?" No change in the blank looks. "Toward the end of World War II, Germany starved the Netherlands. It was called the Hunger Winter; something like twenty thousand people died. As you'd expect, the women who were pregnant at the time gave birth to weaker babies. That part makes sense. But the surprise is that those children eventually gave birth to kids with the same problems. And so did *their* kids. In a nutshell, that's epigenetics."

"Whoa," Agent West said. "Seriously?"

"Cool, huh?"

"Yeah. So what, the starvation changed their DNA?"

Ethan found himself liking her. The other agent had a slick G-man feel, but this one was nerdy in a way he could relate to. "No, that's the tricky bit. Not the DNA itself, but the way the genes express themselves, the way they're regulated. Epigenetics is nature's way of addressing environmental changes without altering the DNA itself."

"But how?"

"Well, that's kind of the question."

Quinn said, "In the last few months, you've had some break-throughs."

You have no idea. "We've made progress."

"Can you tell us what you've learned?"

Ethan shook his head. "We all sign a nondisclosure agreement when we join the lab. The work we're doing could be worth a lot of money."

"I understand that, sir, but we're not geneticists—"

"I'm sorry, I really can't. I'm not allowed to tell my *wife* what we're working on. Abe is very serious about his NDAs." Ethan paused. "Wait a second. Are you suggesting that someone kidnapped him because of our work?"

"Whoever came in was after more than Dr. Couzen," said Agent West. "They took everything of value from his office, right down to his server hard drive."

Bobby Quinn said, "Your lab is privately funded, right?"

"Yes."

"By whom?"

"I don't know."

Quinn cocked his head. "You don't know?"

"Like I said, Abe is eccentric. He's been burned before. He didn't want to risk someone stealing our research and making an end run." Ethan had a guess on the identity of their benefactor, but now didn't seem the time to share it.

"Wait a second." Quinn scratched at his chin, a move that looked practiced. "You're saying that you do research you can't talk about, for an employer you can't identify?"

"We aren't refining plutonium. And funding is funding." *Although if our results are accurate, funding will never be a problem again. A whole lot of things will never be a problem again.* He pushed the thoughts aside, said, "I'm not really sure what this has to do with Abe being kidnapped."

"Ethan," West said, "I know this is all very sudden. But I analyze data for a living, and the data here is ugly. Couzen is in danger, and anything you can tell us about what he was working on might save his life."

What's the harm? Knowing the goal doesn't mean they'll be able to replicate the results. Shit, even you can't do that. Abe is the only person with all the pieces of the puzzle—

Wait a second.

"Why DAR?"

"Excuse me?"

"If he was kidnapped, why would the DAR be involved? Isn't that handled by the FBI?"

"We're working with them. He's a prominent guy, and we're doing everything we can to find out what's happened."

"But why would his research help? Epigenetic theory won't tell you who broke in his house. Shouldn't you be, I don't know, looking for fingerprints, sweeping for DNA?"

"We are," Quinn said. "We're doing all of the stuff you've seen on tri-d. But if you want to see your friend again, we need to know what you know."

Ethan stared, his nagging suspicion blooming into certainty. "You're not after Abe at all, are you?"

The two agents didn't flinch, didn't gasp. But the temperature in the room seemed to drop.

"DAR agents. Huh." He smiled. "You're after our work."

"Ethan—"

"It's Dr. Park," he said. "And it's time for you to go."

The agents exchanged a glance. Quinn said, "You know that we can subpoena you, right? That you'll be legally bound to share any information you have?"

"And if you do, then I will. With my lawyer. But I'm done talking." He stood up, his pulse racing. Part of him couldn't believe what he was doing, but the other part was absolutely certain he was right. These agents didn't give two collective shits about Abe. *They know what you're working on. They must. They may even know that you've succeeded.*

And that scares them.

He walked to the door, held it open. After a long moment, the two agents stood up. "All right, Dr. Park."

On the porch, Quinn turned, and his amiable pose dropped away. "Here's something you might want to think about, though, *Ethan.* Everyone we've spoken to says that you were his protégé. That he may have been the genius, but that he couldn't have done it without you."

"So?"

"So, Abe's blood was spattered all over the walls of his office." Quinn traced a hand down the doorframe and looked at him meaningfully. "You might want to consider whether you really want the same people to come looking for you." He smiled without warmth as he made a business card appear. "Call me when you get it through your head that you're in danger."

THE BEST DEFENSE AGAINST TERRORISM ISN'T THE GOVERNMENT.

It's you.

Spot a suspicious passenger on the train? Tell security.
Neighbor acting strange?
Make a phone call.
Child's playmate knows things
they shouldn't? Let us know.
Together, we can protect America.*

If you SEE something, SAY something.

THE DEPARTMENT OF ANALYSIS AND RESPONSE

* The DAR is an equal opportunity organization. Please remember to respect the rights and feelings of all. Abnorms are people too.

CHAPTER 7

It had been a lousy day, filled with frustration and burned coffee. But it got better once Cooper landed on the fourteenth moon of Saturn.

"Enceladus," his son said, "is the most likely place for life in the solar system. It's got lots of water and carbon and nitrogen."

"Sounds like just the place to search for little green men."

"Yes," Todd said. "But we have to secure the station walls first. It's negative three hundred degrees outside."

"Yikes." Cooper took one side of the blanket and draped it over the back of a chair, knotting the fringe to hold it in place. "We better not dawdle then. Special K?" He held out the other end to his daughter, who stretched it across the living room. He and Todd dragged the couch over to form one wall, then draped another blanket over the top.

His son surveyed the fort, his lips crinkled in a scowl. "We need a better ceiling."

"On it," Cooper said. He crawled from under the sagging blanket, went to the kitchen, and dug in the everything drawer for a roll of duct tape. On tiptoes, he wrapped a loop around the light fixture on the ceiling fan. Then he pinched the center of the blanket, tugged it up, and wrapped tape around it. "How's that, Captain?"

"Awesome!"

He smiled and crawled back inside. The overhead light glowed through the blanket in pinhole stars. The tent was just tall enough now for him to sit cross-legged in the center, watching his children continue to build. Todd worked in broad strokes, jamming cushions upright as walls, tugging the couch to narrow the entrance. Kate focused on the details, closing seams and carefully smoothing folds. Making order. It was her way.

Of course it is. She's gifted. Her world is all about patterns.

With the thought came an involuntary shiver. She wasn't just an abnorm; she was tier one. Of the four million children born each year in America, only a couple of thousand had that sort of power. According to the law, they were taken from their parents and sent to specialized governmental schools. The academies were an open secret, known about but not discussed. After all, the number of tier ones was small enough that the academies didn't impact most people. Like concentration camps in Germany, or internment camps after Pearl Harbor, or CIA prisons in Africa, the academies were a national atrocity it was easy enough to ignore.

But Cooper had been to one. He'd seen the way children were isolated and abused, how the teachers turned them on each other. How the faculty charted their secrets and constructed their greatest fears. The academies were brainwashing centers, pure and simple. Cooper had listened while Director Norridge calmly explained the process: *"Essentially, we take the negative formative experiences that all children experience and manufacture them according to psychological profiles and at a dramatically higher rate. From their youth we teach them that they cannot trust one another. That other abnorms are weak, cruel, and small."*

The powerlessness he'd felt in that moment had been equaled only by his desire to bounce the director's head off the desk until one or the other cracked. He'd managed to hold his temper, but he'd made a pledge at that moment: his daughter would never end up in an academy. Ever.

He ruffled her hair. She looked up over her shoulder at him. "Daddy?"

"Yeah, baby?"

"Will the Martians be nice?"

"Well, we're not on Mars, honey, so they won't be Martians."

"What will they be?"

"Toddster?"

"Enceladians."

"Will the Enceladians be nice?"

"Sure. It's too cold to be mean." He heard a sound, peeked out a slit in the blankets. "Actually, I see one now. It looks like a girl Enceladian to me."

Natalie's feet appeared in the door of the tent, then her knees as she squatted, and finally her head. "Can I come in?"

"What do you think, guys? A little cross-species cooperation? Thanksgiving on Enceladus?" The children looked back and forth at one another, then Kate nodded somberly.

His ex-wife grinned at that, said, "Phew. I've always wanted to be in a spaceship." She wriggled in beside him.

"It's a space *station*, Mom."

"Sorry. Does it have a tub? Because it's time for a little space girl to take her bath."

"No!"

"Yup. Come on."

"Can we leave the space station up?"

"Of course," Natalie said. "What else would we do with the living room?"

Together they got the kids moving, went through the nightly dance of snacks and baths and toothbrushing. The whole ritual was infused with a painful sweetness that Cooper lapped up.

Bright bathroom light reflecting off white tile. Silly songs. Superhero pajamas. Kate with toothpaste dripping down her chin. An impromptu dance party in the bedroom, Kate spazzing out, Todd a little self-conscious until Cooper chased him around and tickled him. Books read. Bargains struck. Books reread.

Then he was turning off the light on his daughter's side of the room and tucking the blankets around her tightly. Todd, almost ten and allowed to stay up to read, was already lost in a sci-fi novel and grunted a goodnight as Cooper kissed his forehead. He walked out of the room and closed the door behind him, feeling that mingled lightness and loss that attended the kids going down.

He descended the stairs and wandered into the kitchen. No Natalie. Nor in the playroom. The living room was dominated by the fort they'd made, the couch pulled out of position, coffee table pressed against the wall, duct tape dangling from the light fixture to the blanket. "Nat?"

"In the space station."

He laughed, crawled inside. His ex-wife sat cross-legged in the center of the tent. Cooper didn't know a lot about women's fashion, but he was pretty sure yoga pants were one of the great inventions of the last twenty years. Natalie had a bottle of wine open and two glasses. "They down?"

"Todd's reading."

"Where are we?"

"Enceladus," he said. "The fourteenth moon of Saturn. Or so our eldest tells me."

"That kid is crazy."

"Absolutely nutty," Cooper agreed. He took the glass she offered, took a long swallow.

"And how are you?"

Something he'd always loved about Natalie, her words and her meaning were more aligned than most anyone he'd ever met. It was a cousin to bluntness, but without the swagger; she wasn't in anyone's face, had nothing to prove. She just said what she meant. For someone with his gift, that was a wonderful relief.

He took her question the way she meant it, sincerely. "What do you call it when you're either swimming or drowning, but not sure which yet?"

"Treading water?"

"I guess."

"What's bothering you?"

He hesitated. It had been three and a half years since the divorce. They were friends, and co-parented well, but it wasn't fair to unload about his day. That was for married couples. "I'll figure it out."

"Nick," she said, gesturing at the tent walls, the blankets breathing softly in a draft. "You're safe. We're on Enceladus. Talk to me."

He laughed at that. Then he started and found it hard to stop. He wanted to share the good stuff, the walk down the drive to the West Wing, the feeling of stepping into the Oval Office, the thrill of seeing his words, his thoughts, translated into something that showed up on the evening news. But those parts were inseparable from the conference table battles that fed his growing frustration.

"Keevers and the rest, even Clay, they're stuck in old-world thinking. So focused on the day-to-day that they're missing the big picture." He laughed without humor. "They're honestly worried about how things will look come election time. And I'm sitting there saying, 'Guys, shouldn't we be worrying that there won't *be* an election?'"

"It's that bad?"

Cooper paused. Took a swallow of wine. Nodded.

"Then fix it."

"Huh?"

"Fix it." She shrugged. "You've got the ear of the president of the United States. Use it."

"It's not that simple."

"Was it simpler when you were hunting your own kind for Equitable Services?"

"No."

"All your life you've been fighting for a world where our children won't need to be afraid. I know the last year has been tough on you. But if things are as bad as that, then you need to gear up, soldier."

He looked at her, this exceptional woman he had loved for more than a decade, through their own ups and downs. Loved passionately once; then, when his gift and his job came between them, loved with respect even as they decided to live separate lives. "Gear up?"

"Yes. And one other thing." She set her wine glass down. It was a calculated move, carefully considered; he could see it in the play of her muscles, and the way her lips were slightly parted, and the way she leaned forward as she crawled over to—*whoa.*

Kiss him.

Full and firm, lips soft against his, her red-wine tongue dancing into his mouth. The feeling of it was at once familiar and novel, the electric brush of her upper arm against his as she leaned in, and the smell of her in his nostrils.

She held the kiss long enough to make it clear that it wasn't a friendly gesture, a peck between old lovers. When she broke it, she looked into his eyes and said, "I'm proud of you." Then she picked up her wine glass and crawled for the exit. Over her shoulder, she said, "Fix it."

Huh.

Huh.

Huh.

PRESS BRIEFING
BY PRESS SECRETARY HOLDEN ARCHER
11/24/13, James S. Brady Press Briefing Room

Mr. Archer: Good evening, everyone. As you all know, the situation continues in Cleveland, Fresno, and Tulsa. However, President Clay is personally overseeing recovery efforts.

The president asks that during this season of adversity, we come together as Americans, with the resolve that defines our national character. He has the highest confidence in the National Guard, as well as in the people of Cleveland, Fresno, and Tulsa.

With that, I'll take a few questions. Jon?

New York Times: *It's been four days since the hijackings. Do you have further information on the Children of Darwin? And is the president considering military action against them?*

Mr. Archer: Our intelligence community is the finest in the world. I can assure you that this government knows a great deal about them, and that no stone will be left unturned in the hunt for those who so vilely attacked our nation.

Like all terror attacks, the goal was to cause chaos and suffering for ordinary Americans. In that light, these can only be judged a failure; while they have led to temporary shortages, our nation is stronger than ever.

New York Times: *And military action?*

Mr. Archer: Internal security is handled by police, the FBI, and the DAR. I can't comment on their individual plans. I refer you to them. Yes, Sally?

Washington Post: *What about allegations that—*

New York Times: *I'm sorry, a follow-up. Defense department sources confirm that Secretary Owen Leahy has urged military, I repeat, nonpolice, response. Has Secretary Leahy called for the deployment of US troops on American soil, and would the president consider that?*

Mr. Archer: I'm not going to respond to a blind quote. Sally, your question.

Washington Post: *What about allegations that the Children of Darwin are planning further attacks?*

Mr. Archer: I can't comment on the intentions of a terrorist organization. But I can say that all efforts are being taken to keep American citizens safe.

CBS: *Are the Children of Darwin connected to the*

New Canaan Holdfast in Wyoming? Are they affiliated with Erik Epstein?

Mr. Archer: We've seen no evidence of that. And let's remember that the people who live in New Canaan, Mr. Epstein included, are United States citizens. This government respects the rights of all law-abiding citizens, normal or gifted.

NBC: *People in Cleveland are saying that the National Guard has no food to distribute.*

Mr. Archer: The National Guard is setting up camps in parks, churches, and gymnasiums. We ask that everyone exercise good sense when they visit, and understand that their neighbors also need help right now.

NBC: *I'm sorry, you didn't answer my question. Is there food available in Cleveland?*

Mr. Archer: I, ah, it's difficult to—I would refer you to the National Guard for operational details.

Associated Press: *There are also reports that guardsmen have threatened crowds.*

Mr. Archer: The National Guard is there to help. If a crowd is a danger to itself or others, it's possible that they employ nonlethal crowd control measures.

Associated Press: *I have reports of guardsmen pointing rifles* *at citizens, even firing warning shots. If the situation grows worse, will the president authorize the National Guard to attack civilians?*

Mr. Archer: I don't see it getting there. The president has the highest confidence in both the guard and the citizens of Cleveland, Fresno, and Tulsa.

Associated Press: *So the guardsmen will not be authorized to fire?*

Mr. Archer: I won't speculate on that.

CNN: *I'm quoting a senior White House source here who says, "We have no operational knowledge of the Children of Darwin, literally none. They're ghosts with guns."*

Mr. Archer: I can't comment on top secret intelligence. But I want to reiterate that every effort . . .

CHAPTER 8

It had been two days since government agents had dropped by to tell him that his boss had been kidnapped and his family was in danger, and Ethan had thought of little else since. Every stranger seemed filled with menace. Every parked car might be scoping out their house. He'd spent the time in an edgy fugue, peeking out the curtains and fingering the business card Special Agent Quinn had given him.

What had made it worse was not being able to share the whole load with Amy. Ethan had told her about Abe's kidnapping, of course, but he'd downplayed the notion it was connected to their work. For one thing, there was no proof. For another, there was no way to tell her that without telling her what he was working on. Which he couldn't do, not if he wanted to keep his job. Abe didn't mess around with that kind of thing; Ethan had no doubt his boss would fire him without a second thought.

And that can't happen. Not with a ten-week-old baby. Not when you're about to succeed.

He'd taken to keeping the gun in the nightstand, though. Just in case.

So when his neighbor Jack had called and invited him to the meeting, Ethan had jumped at the distraction. The idea was silly—a neighborhood watch to protect their homes? The cadre of lawyers and marketing execs was about as threatening as a middle school choir—but here he was, along with most of the guys on the block, crammed into Jack's living room, eating pretzels and drinking Diet Coke from red Solo cups.

"So what," Ethan said, "are we talking pitchforks and torches?"

"No, of course not." Jack looked disappointed. "This is about neighbors helping each other, that's all."

Ethan thought of the case of milk his neighbor had given him and felt a flush of shame. "I don't mean to be a smart-ass. I just don't understand."

"It's simple. Right now we can't count on the government to keep things working. It's been five days since the stores were cleared out, and still no food. There are robberies and arsons and shootings, and not enough cops and firemen to go around. The system has broken down, so let's work together to get through this."

"You mean like patrol the neighborhood?"

A man Ethan didn't know said, "Why not? I know it's not politically correct to say, but if you're a crackhead from the east side, who you going to rob? The crackhead next door who's got nothing? Or one of us?"

"We're not forming a posse," Jack said. "But if the government doesn't work, then it takes a village."

"I'm happy to help any of you," Ethan said. He looked around the room, mentally categorizing: *guys you stop to chat with, men you wave at whose names you think you know, men you wave at whose names you are certain you don't, total strangers.* Three or four of them were decent friends, guys like Jack. Or Ranjeet Singh, who, as Ethan's eyes met his, mimed King Kong chest beating. Ethan started to laugh, covered it with a cough. "I'm just not sure why we should make it formal."

"Because we need to organize. Let's say, God forbid, Violet gets sick. You think if you call an ambulance, it'll be here two minutes later?" Jack shook his head. "But Barry is a doctor. Or say that Lou is right"—nodding to Political Correctness—"and some bad characters come up here to rob your house. If we're organized, everybody on the block will show up to help."

"Bad characters?" Ethan cocked an eyebrow.

"You know what I mean."

"I'm not sure I do. How do I tell if someone is a bad character? If I don't recognize them? If they look poor? If they're hungry?"

"What's your problem, guy?" Lou was short but barrel-chested, with a coiled-spring tension.

"It's okay, Lou." Jack smiled, held his hands out, palms. "He's right to ask. And we should be able to answer. We're not a street gang."

That was smooth, Ethan thought. Jack had disarmed the tension without insulting anyone, and his use of "we" drew them all together on a subconscious level. The term *alpha male* had taken on a knuckle-dragging context, but in truth, it described a subtler and more powerful attribute than physical superiority. The desire to organize was ingrained in DNA; groups fared better than individuals, and so, *a priori*, the individuals around whom groups naturally formed tended to be very attractive. A survival advantage reinforced evolutionarily.

Gee, thanks, Professor. Ethan mentally slapped himself, then tuned back in to what Jack was saying.

"—is having a tough time. I think we all understand that. But if someone is trying to rob one of you, then to my mind that makes him a bad guy, and you should be able to protect yourself. And I'll have your back." Jack turned to look at Ethan. "Is that a definition you can live with?"

A glance around the room told Ethan that the twenty or so men looking back were already united into a tribe. *Let it go. No harm indulging the fantasy.* "Sure."

"One idea," an engineer named Kurt said, "we should set up a group on our cell phones, so we can send one text and it goes to all of us. Our own local 911."

"Great thinking."

"I've got an idea," Lou said. "We got a lot to organize, right? Let's put Ranjeet in charge of that. He's an abnorm, he'll be better at it."

An awkward silence fell. Ethan glanced at Jack, hoping the man would have a quick save, but his neighbor said nothing.

After a moment Ranjeet said, "I am an abnorm, Lou, but my gift is high-digit numerosity."

"What's the hell's that—"

"It means," Ethan said, "that he can instantly estimate high-digit systems. Leaves on a tree, matchsticks dumped on the floor, people in a stadium."

"I'm murder at county fairs," Ranjeet said. "That jar where you have to guess how many jelly beans? Whoo-eee." He flashed a smile, the white of his teeth dazzling against his dark skin.

Jack snorted a laugh, and it broke the tension.

They spent the next hour divvying up responsibilities. Talents were volunteered—who was a fair carpenter, who had first aid training—and cell numbers were exchanged. Then, as the windows darkened, men started to drift away. Most of them waved a generalized good-bye to the group; all of them took the time to shake Jack's hand. Ethan waited until he saw Ranjeet putting on his coat before he said good-bye to their host.

"Thanks for coming," Jack said.

"Sure."

Jack held the handshake, said, "Hey, how's Violet doing on that milk?"

Is that your way of reminding me I owe you one? "Great, thank you."

"Let me know if you need more."

"We'll be all right. Thanks, though."

The air outside was crisp and fresh after the humidity of the crowded living room. Ethan took a deep breath, let it fill his lungs. Twilight was surrendering to night, the sky a deep indigo smeared with charcoal clouds. He held the storm door for Ranjeet, then let it swing shut behind them with a bang. The not-quite-quiet of the city surrounded them, faint traffic noises and a distant siren.

Ethan said, "Wow."

Ranjeet nodded, reached into his pocket for cigarettes. He lit one with a yellow Bic, then offered the pack. Ethan shook his head. Up and down the block the houses looked warm and cozy, tri-ds flickering in living room windows, porch lights shining on well-tended yards.

"What that room needed," Ranjeet said, "was a woman."

"No kidding. One wife laughing and all that John Wayne machismo would have evaporated." He shook his head. "And that thing from Lou, Je-*sus*. He's the kind who when he plays basketball says he wants the black guy on his team."

"Ah." Ranjeet waved it away with a cigarette flourish. "Doesn't matter. We're toying with leaving town anyway. We have a timeshare in Florida and thought we might claim our turn."

"Amy and I have been thinking the same. Go stay with her mom in Chicago. Don't know why we haven't yet."

"Same reason we haven't. You go to bed deciding to do it, but when you wake up, the sun is shining, and you figure, no way this can go on another day."

"So how long do you keep doing that?"

"Until the freezer is empty, I guess." Ranjeet shrugged. "You know, it will probably blow over tomorrow. By next summer we'll have forgotten it. The Great Neighborhood Posse of 2013 will be a joke."

"No doubt," Ethan said. He was about to add, *Everything will be okay,* when in every house, every light went out.

Simultaneously.

CHAPTER 9

Air Force One was an hour shy of DC when the Secret Service agent told Cooper that he was wanted in the conference room.

Across a military and agency career, Cooper had ridden on posh private jets and rattling army transports, had soared in a glider over the Wyoming desert and jumped out of a perfectly good C-17 with a chute on his back. But Air Force One was unlike any aircraft he'd ever been on.

A customized 747, the plane had three decks, two galleys, luxury sleeping quarters, a fully equipped surgery, national broadcasting capabilities, first-class seating for the press corps and the Secret Service, and the capability to fly a third of the way around the world without refueling—which it could do midair.

Cooper unbuckled his seatbelt and walked fore. The agents at the door of the conference room nodded at him.

The room was a mobile version of the Situation Room, with a broad conference table and plush chairs. A holo-conferencing screen showed a sharp tri-d of Marla Keevers in her office at the White House. The president sat at the head of the table, with Owen Leahy at his right and Holden Archer at his left.

Archer glanced at him, said, "Tulsa, Fresno, and Cleveland have lost power."

President Clay said, "Marla, how bad is it?"

"Based off satellite imagery, we estimate that the entire metro area of all three cities has gone dark."

"Why based off satellite imagery?" Clay asked.

"Because engineers in charge of the power grid for each region report no unusual activity. All substations report back green."

"A cyber attack," Leahy said. "A virus tells the system to send massive amounts of power from the grid to individual transformers, blowing them out, while at the same time co-opting the safety systems so that there's no warning indicator."

"Yes," Keevers said. "That's what's got the engineers rattled. Work crews say there's no damage to the substations. The transformers are working. They're just not providing power to the cities."

"How is that possible?"

"The Children of Darwin," Cooper said.

Keevers nodded. "It would appear our protocols have been rewritten. It would take abnorm programmers to pull that off."

"So what you're telling me," the president said, "is that a terrorist organization has turned off three cities like they flipped a switch?"

"I'm afraid so, sir. With some anomalies. In each city, several regions still have power. Two in Fresno, three in Tulsa, and two in Cleveland."

The image of Keevers was replaced by live satellite footage. The view was haunting. Instead of the riotous glow of cities at night, the holograms showed deep black marked by faint ribbons of light that must have been highways. The only bright spots were in discrete blocks, roughly rectangular, where things looked normal.

"So the virus wasn't a hundred percent effective," Archer said. "It's a small comfort, but it's something."

Cooper leaned forward, staring at the maps. There was a pattern, he was—

Two areas in Fresno, three in Tulsa, two in Cleveland.

What connects them? Some are on major highways, some nowhere near. Some downtown, some not.

And yet this doesn't look random. The virus was too successful everywhere else to have failed completely in these spots.

These areas were left powered on purpose. Which means that they hold some value.

So what unites these seven areas?

—certain. "Hospitals," Cooper said.

Archer looked at the screens, then back at him. "What?"

"Those regions all contain major hospitals."

"Why would terrorists take out the power to three cities but leave hospitals functioning?"

"Because they need them," Leahy said. He turned to the president. "Sir, I've spoken to the director of the FBI and the DAR, as well as the head of the National Institutes of Health. They all believe, and I concur, that this may be the precursor to a biological attack."

"That doesn't make sense," Archer said. "Why leave the hospitals running if they're trying to release a biological weapon?"

"Because," Leahy retorted, "hospitals are the best way to spread one. People get sick, and they go to the hospital. While there they infect others. Doctors and nurses and receptionists and janitors and patients and families. With a really infectious biological agent, the number of cases can expand massively even under normal circumstances. But because these three cities are lacking food, and now power, the situation is far worse. Instead of resting at home, people will flee. They'll go to stay with relatives, or to second homes. And in the process, they'll swiftly vector the disease across the entire country. Sir, we believe the COD created this chaotic situation to mask their real attack."

"That's a huge stretch," Cooper said. "Abnorms would be just as vulnerable to infection. What good would a biological attack do the COD?"

"I don't know," Leahy said, with a hard look at Cooper. "But the COD are terrorists. We don't know what their endgame is."

"Of course we do. They're upset over the treatment of abnorms, and they want change."

"What are you basing that on, Mr. Cooper? Abnorm intuition?" Leahy smiled coldly. "I understand your sympathy for their situation, but that can't be allowed to color our response."

Would you count my response colored if I called you a close-minded bigot mired in old-world thinking? Instead, Cooper said, "Response to what? You're wasting time on a hypothetical situation when we have actual disasters in these cities. People are starving. With the power out, they'll be freezing, getting desperate, violent. Instead of worrying about phantom attacks, why don't we start getting them some goddamn food and blankets?"

On the screen, Marla Keevers coughed. Press Secretary Archer made an elaborate show of looking at his watch. Leahy fixed Cooper with an icy stare. "Mr. Cooper, your passion is quite touching, but you're a bit above your pay grade here. And you're not qualified to speak to what is or is not hypothetical."

"Maybe not," Cooper said. "But I can speak to what's right." He glanced around the room. *You guys don't get me, do you? I don't even want this job, so I've got nothing to lose by telling the truth.* "The people need food. They need medicine. They need electricity. That's what we should focus on. That's our job."

"It's also our job to protect them from attack," Leahy fired back. "Food and blankets in Cleveland don't protect people dying in Los Angeles."

Before Cooper could respond, the president said, "Owen, what exactly do you suggest?"

"Immediate quarantine of all three cities, sir. The National Guard has already been called up. Assume federal command, back them up with army troops, and shut these cities down completely. No one in or out."

For a moment Cooper thought the plane was banking wildly, until he realized that was just his head. "You've got to be kidding me."

"I don't find anything about this funny."

Cooper turned to Clay, expecting to see the same thought, the belief that this was beyond preposterous. Instead, he saw that the president was nervous.

Nervous.

"Sir, you can't possibly consider this. You'd be ordering military action on domestic soil. Turning three cities into police states, revoking people's basic rights. It will cause unimaginable chaos. These cities are already on the brink. Instead of helping, we're locking them up."

"No," Leahy said. "We're temporarily suspending freedom of movement for fewer than a million people. In order to protect three hundred million more."

"Panic. Hate crimes. Riots. Plus, if soldiers are busy quarantining the city, they can't distribute food. All based on nothing but a wild theory."

"Based," Leahy said, "on the collective analysis of the best minds in the intelligence and health services. A group that includes plenty of abnorms. Mr. Cooper, I know you're used to doing things your own way, but this isn't your personal crusade. We're trying to save the country, not play some moralistic game."

Cooper ignored the barb. "Mr. President, when you asked me to join you, you said that we were on the edge of a precipice." *You're an intellectual, a historian. You know how these things start. World War I was kicked off when a radical killed an obscure archduke. And nine million people died.* "If you do this, we step toward that precipice. Maybe over it."

"And if you're wrong?" Leahy asked. "You say the COD is interested in abnorm rights, but they've made no effort at dialogue. What if what they really want is to kill as many Americans as possible? There are a hundred biological weapons against which we have no ready defense—except quarantine."

The president looked back and forth between them. His hands were on the table, the fingers knit. His knuckles were pale.

Come on, Clay. I know you're scared. We're all scared. But be the leader we need you to be.

The president cleared his throat.

LIFE ISN'T EASY
But it's harder for our kind.

- For readers born knowing daddy's darkest secrets
- For eidetics reliving every humiliation
- For tier ones despised for being better

No matter what you're feeling, you are not alone. We've all been there. Literally—our suicide hotline is staffed entirely by brilliant volunteers.

Everybody gets blue.

But if you're thinking about hurting yourself, call us first.

1-800-2BRIGHT

Just because you burn twice as bright…
doesn't mean you should burn half as long.

CHAPTER 10

In DC, where scrabbling up greasy ladders was in everyone's job description, there were a lot of ways to gauge power. Budgets and staff were obvious ones, but Owen Leahy found it more telling to look at the trappings, the secondary signifiers. Office size, and which building it was in. If there was a window, or a private bathroom. How close that office was to the boss, senator, or president.

The ability to summon others to a meeting at ten o'clock in the evening.

As the secretary of defense, there were very few people who rated highly enough that *he* went to *their* office. And only one who could summon him straight from Air Force One in the middle of a crisis.

Terence Mitchum had moved from the CIA to the NSA, but Leahy would always remember him as the deputy director he'd approached twenty-five years ago. Every time he saw the man, Leahy remembered the nervous wait outside his office, the taste of salt and dirt from licking his fingers to clean off his shoes. Mitchum had made him, and Mitchum could break him, and they both knew it.

Technically, he was the number-three man in the National Security Agency, but org charts lied. If Mitchum wanted the top job, he would have had it two decades ago. Instead, he'd stayed in power while the men and women above him came and went with presidential administrations. From that position, he had directed the careers of countless people, cherry-picking those loyal to him and destroying those who resisted. Forty years of intelligence work, the latter half in an agency so secretive that not only its budget but even its size was classified. Forty years of collecting blackmail and withholding information and burying bodies.

Including 1,143 in Manhattan. The March 12th explosion at the stock exchange in Manhattan had been blamed on John Smith, but though he had planted the explosives, he'd intended for the building to be empty. Smith had even provided media outlets with advance notice of his intent. Leahy couldn't prove it, but he was certain it had been Mitchum who had squashed the advance warning, muzzling seven news organizations and ordering the detonation of the explosives when it became clear Smith wouldn't. A brutal, calculated move, like sacrificing a queen in chess. The attack had galvanized the country, and it resulted in the passage of a law that might save it.

"Hello, sir." Leahy took in the rest of the office, wasn't surprised to see the third occupant of the room. "Senator."

"I told you, call me Richard." The senator flashed one of his camera-ready smiles. "We're all friends here."

Mitchum pressed a series of buttons on his desk. The DC night outside the windows shimmered and disappeared as the glass turned black. A mechanical bolt on the door snapped shut, and there was a faint hum, some sort of anti-bugging technology, Leahy supposed. Then Mitchum steepled his fingers, looked over the desk, and said, "We're losing control of the situation."

"Sir, I advised the president exactly the way we discussed—"

"What I want to know," the senator interrupted, "is how the Children of Darwin attacks happened in the first place."

Richard was an ally, and useful. But sometimes Leahy wanted to strangle him. "That's complicated."

"Really? Because it seems simple to me." The senator shook his head. "I did everything you boys asked after the stock exchange fell. You have no idea how many favors I pulled to get the MOI not only passed, but in a landslide. Walker signed it. So what are you dawdling for?"

"Things have changed since the Monitoring Oversight Initiative passed." Leahy pulled out a chair. "You may have noticed."

"I have. Since we provided the legal grounds to microchip every gifted in America, abnorm terrorists have taken three cities hostage. Do I need to point out that if we had *implemented* that law, instead of just passing it, we'd know who was responsible?"

"You don't have to tell me how useful the MOI would be. I'm the one who suggested it in the first place. Everything we've done to date was building toward it."

"So why aren't you making it happen?"

"Clay isn't President Walker. It's going to take some time."

"Time," Mitchum said. The man said little, and yet those words were always carefully chosen, spoken softly and yet always heard.

"Yes, sir. President Walker was one of us from the beginning. He understood that protecting America would require unconventional means. Clay . . . he's a professor. His experience is theoretical. He's uncomfortable with this kind of reality."

"So, what," the senator asked, "he's going to put the MOI in a drawer?"

"That would be his preference. He knows he doesn't have the votes to repeal it, but he can stall it indefinitely."

"So how do we jump-start it?"

"We'll have our moment." Leahy turned to Mitchum. "Sir, can I ask you something?"

The director raised an eyebrow.

"The Children of Darwin. Are they by any chance a false flag operation?"

Before the director could respond, the senator interrupted. "False flag? What's that?"

Leahy fought a sigh. *Richard, you are going to find that the heights you've attained make for a long fall if you don't understand the mountain.* "A covert operation designed to look like its instigated by someone else in order to provide grounds for action."

"You mean like the bombing in the exch—"

"Senator." Mitchum spoke softly, but the word was a lash. Richard looked away. The director turned back to Leahy. "No."

"We're certain?"

"Yes. The COD are exactly what they appear to be, a group of abnorm terrorists."

"Good."

"Good?" The senator bristled. "Good? Terrorists have taken three of our cities, people are starving, and it's good?"

"Yes," Leahy said. "These terrorists may be brilliants, but I'm not sure how smart they are. They've got tunnel vision. They don't realize that every move they make is serving our ends."

"How?"

Leahy ignored the senator. Mitchum said, "Do we know what their next action will be?"

"The leading theory is a biological attack. But it doesn't matter. Even if they don't have anything else planned, what they've set in motion is enough. With every passing day, the public is howling for action. The president's hand is being forced."

"That doesn't mean it will play our way."

"Even an intellectual like Clay is going to have to make a decision at some point." Leahy shrugged. "When he does, it will be through me."

The senator cut in. "And you'll make the MOI a cornerstone of that response. I see the method in your madness, but there's too much madness in your method. We ought to go through channels. Bring it up on the Senate floor, hold Clay accountable in the media."

You mean make more headlines for yourself. "Too risky. It leaves the door open for people to claim that the MOI justifies the Children of Darwin's actions."

"Who would claim that?"

Jesus. Really? "The COD."

Richard scoffed. "You think they're going to issue a press release?"

"If they say they'll return everything to normal if we scrap the bill, do you think people in Cleveland or Tulsa or Fresno will say, 'No, thanks, we'll starve for our principles'?" He turned to Mitchum. "Sir, if we open the MOI up for discussion, that's the ball game. We're negotiating with terrorists, and from an inferior position."

Mitchum tapped two fingers on his desk. After a moment, he said, "You're certain of this, Owen?"

"Yes, sir. I've got this under control." The words were no sooner out of his mouth than he regretted them. *Under* control? *You're banking on a group of abnorm terrorists and a president with the fortitude of a noodle.*

The same thought seemed to be playing in Mitchum's mind. "All right, Owen," he said with the look of a lion eyeing a gazelle straying from the herd. "So long as you're sure."

Leahy nodded, forced a smile. *Mitchum made you, and he can break you.*

You better control this—or you're going to be dinner.

CHAPTER 11

There had been a time when Ethan could go on a two-week trip with a single carry-on bag. At twenty-two, he'd spent three months crisscrossing Europe with nothing but a backpack.

Now they couldn't leave town without jamming the Honda to the roof.

Their own luggage was the smallest part of it. The baby's suitcase was larger than theirs, and it was packed so full he'd had to sit on the thing to zip it: daytime diapers, nighttime diapers, wipes, onesies, pajamas, evaporated milk, burp cloths, swaddling blankets, a musical seahorse, picture books, baby monitor, on and on. Add to that the pack-and-play, the travel swing, the bright pink bathtub, and the play mat. Then a box of stuff in case the stay at Amy's mom's turned out to be longer than he hoped: d-pads and chargers, Amy's chef's knife and favorite pan, workout gear, medication and toiletries, winter coats. Ethan clenched the flashlight between his teeth to free both hands and cleared space for the cat cage. Inside, Gregor Mendel mewled pitifully, his eyes reflecting green.

"It's okay, buddy."

Atop the cage went a box of litter and a bag of Iams. Alongside it, a lockbox containing their passports, some jewelry that had belonged to Amy's grandmother, and a bundle of US Treasury bonds.

Ethan shook his head, then closed the rear hatch and threw his hip to slam it. He was glad they were going. Things were getting a mite too real in Cleveland. *And besides, someone kidnapped Abe. There's no way of knowing whether they're after you too, but if they are, better to be somewhere else for now.*

The house was already cold. Their furnace burned natural gas, but it took electricity to power the blower that moved the air. A pillar candle on the kitchen counter cast a soft circle of light on the empty cans that had served as dinner. No stove, no microwave, so Amy had ripped off the labels and heated the cans over the candle.

Clever woman. Lukewarm bean soup is nothing to shout about, but it trumps cold bean soup.

Amy came down the stairs, Violet in her arms. "I'm going to do a quick dummy check. Can you change her?"

"Sure."

The changing table was in the living room, and barely visible, but he could manage diaper duty with his eyes closed. Violet had recently started sort-of smiling, scrunching up her cheeks and sticking her tongue out. Once he had her clean, he spent a minute biting at her belly until she gave him that goofy grin.

"I think that's everything," Amy said.

"You sure? Grab me a wrench, I could disconnect the stove, strap that on top of the truck."

"Funny man."

At the front door, Amy turned to the alarm panel, started punching buttons. She made it halfway through the code before she laughed and shook her head. "Right. Never mind."

"It'll be fine." He tugged the door closed, then locked the deadbolt. Their block was eerie. No streetlights or porch lights, no glow of tri-ds in family rooms, no music on the edge of hearing. The flickering hints of candles and flashlights seemed tiny against the weight of blackness. Far away, he heard a siren wail.

Ethan strapped in his daughter, climbed into the driver's seat, and started the car.

"It looks so lonely," Amy said.

"The house?"

"The city." She leaned her head up against the side window. "Holy crap."

"What?"

"I can see stars." Her voice was bemused. "Lots of them. When was the last time you saw stars?"

Ethan had made the short drive to the freeway a thousand times, at every hour. But he'd never seen it like this. Every building was shadowed, the windows empty sockets. The trees, leafless and November-tossed, loomed ominously. The city wasn't just middle-of-the-night dark; it was Middle Ages dark. No porch lights, no streetlights, no floodlights on the billboards, no glow reflecting off clouds. The only signs of life were other cars, their headlights watery and weak in the darkness. It was a relief to merge onto I-90; the highway seemed almost normal, the westbound traffic moving well.

Amy twisted around her seat to look back at Violet. "She's asleep."

"Good."

"Are you okay with this?"

"No harm in waiting it out at your mom's. Use a little vacation time, burn a little gas, feign interest while your mom talks about gardening."

"She'll be really happy."

"She'll be happy to see the monkey. I'm not sure she'll be delighted about us sleeping on her pullout."

"We can get a hotel. And along the way we can stop at a grocery store, stock up on formula."

Ethan nodded. For a few moments they rode in silence, just the hum of concrete beneath the tires. They passed office parks and big-box stores, a huge McDonald's sign, the golden arches black.

"Ethan." Amy gestured with her chin.

He followed her gaze. There was a spill of light on the horizon, a brilliant pool that underlit the clouds. He couldn't make out the source, but the glow was hot white, an oasis of light. Ethan felt something in him release that he hadn't realized was clenched. Light meant power, and power meant normalcy, and they could sorely use some normalcy right now.

"This is the mall exit, right? I wonder why they have power."

"Seems like the light is coming from . . ." Amy trailed off. "Something's wrong."

Traffic was compressing in on itself, everyone merging over to the right. The light grew brighter and brighter. A minute later he saw why.

Heavy concrete barriers blocked I-90, two rows of them placed at angles. A battery of sodium lights blasted the night to harsh noon. Alongside them, Humvees idled, the big trucks looking like construction equipment, only with machine guns mounted on the back. Ethan could see soldiers manning those guns, little more than silhouettes against the glare of light. He could hear the generators even through the glass.

A flashing sign with an arrow showed the way—all traffic to exit. Ethan glanced in his mirror, saw cars lining up behind him. He looked at his wife; she said nothing, but the tiny creases around her clenched lips spoke volumes.

Ethan joined the line for the exit. It took five minutes to funnel in. At the top of the ramp, the road north had been barricaded. A tank was parked in the center of the intersection. Soldiers stood alongside the treads, watching the flow of traffic.

A tank. In the intersection.

The traffic flowed south across a bridge over the highway. On the other side lay Crocker Park Mall. He remembered the first time he and Amy had come here, how surreal the experience had been to a couple of urbanites: an outdoor mall pretending to be a village, a theme park of commercialism at its most vulgar.

It was considerably more surreal now.

The mall had been commandeered by the National Guard, with rows of Humvees parked beside a half dozen more tanks. Soldiers scurried to set up tents in the midst of the parking lot. Generators roared, powering floodlights that colored the sky.

"They're turning us back," Amy said. She pointed to the opposite on-ramp, back toward Cleveland. More barricades and soldiers, and another flashing arrow. The same cars he'd been following westward were obediently queuing up to return to Cleveland.

"You think there's been some kind of attack?"

"Or they're expecting one."

"So what now? Should we go home?"

He sucked air through his teeth. Thought about their dark house in its dark neighborhood, growing steadily colder. About the freezer that was nearly empty of meat, the fridge that had no fruit or vegetables.

"No," he said, and spun the wheel.

"Ethan, what are you—"

He pulled out of the line for the highway and aimed to the right, around the barricade at the road going to the mall. He passed four cars, five, and then the Humvee. A flash of the soldiers in and around it: digital camouflage and assault rifles and helmets with headgear. He'd always thought the National Guard was sort of the light beer version of the army, but those men had looked anything but soft.

"I don't want to be one of those wives," Amy said, "who says 'be careful,' but please be careful. Our daughter is in the back."

"I'm not going to do anything stupid. But they have to let us by."

At the entrance to the mall parking lot, two soldiers carrying machine guns stood beside a wooden barricade. Ethan pulled up to it and rolled down his window.

"Sir, do you have authorization to be here?"

"Can you tell me what's going on?"

"Sir, I'm going to need you to turn the vehicle around."

"I've got my baby daughter with me," Ethan said. "We're almost out of food, have no baby formula, and now no heat. We're just trying to get to Chicago to stay with my mother-in-law. Is there someone we can talk to?"

The soldier hesitated, then pointed. "My CO."

"Thank you."

Ethan drove where the man indicated. A handful of civilian vehicles and an eighteen-wheeler were parked in a cluster. He pulled up alongside and killed the engine. Turned to Amy, saw her look, and said, "I'm not going to do anything stupid. I just want to see if they'll let us past."

She took a breath, held it, and let it whistle out. "Okay. Talk good."

He smiled, leaned over, and kissed her quickly.

The night was colder than he'd expected, his breath turning to frost. The makeshift command center was lit by headlights and pole-mounted floods. He heard arguing and followed the sound of it to a group of people in civilian clothes, facing a soldier with ramrod posture and an implacable expression. An aide stood beside him, holding a rifle. Beyond them were more vehicles, a Humvee and a tank and, wow, a couple of helicopter gunships bristling with weaponry. Ethan joined the crowd.

"—you don't understand, my wife needs insulin, we used the last of it this morning, and without it, she's going to—"

"—packed rig due in Detroit tomorrow morning—"

"—there's no heat, no food, come on, show a little—"

The soldier raised both hands in a *calm down* gesture. When everyone quieted, he said, "I understand your concerns. But my orders are explicit. No one is to pass this checkpoint. For those of you with medical emergencies, we have rudimentary capabilities here, and the hospitals in Cleveland are operational. For everyone else, all I can say is that every effort is being made to supply food and repair the power grid."

"Can you tell us what's going on?" Ethan asked.

The officer gave him a quick evaluative glance. "The DAR believes the leadership of the Children of Darwin are here. There are missions underway to capture them. Our job is to ensure that none slip past. Which I'm afraid means that no one can leave Cleveland."

"That's insane," said a goateed kid in front of Ethan. "You're locking down the whole city to catch a couple of terrorists? That doesn't make any sense."

"Listen, man." A burly guy in a John Deere cap stepped forward. "I'm a truck driver. Bad enough people are burning us alive, but if I don't get my load to Detroit on time, I get stuck with the whole bill. That ain't gonna happen. So how about you let me past?"

"No one gets past."

"Now you listen to me—"

"Sir." There was a way soldiers and cops could say "sir" and mean, "I'm inches from beating your ass," snapping their voice like a broken cable. "Get back in your vehicle right now."

This is a waste of time. Ethan was about to leave when John Deere grabbed the officer's arm.

Oh, don't do that, that's a very bad—

The floodlights seemed to flare in the officer's eyes. His aide stepped forward and snapped the butt of his assault rifle into the trucker's face.

The sound was an egg thrown against concrete. The man collapsed.

Ethan saw motion behind the two soldiers, on the Humvee.

The .50 caliber machine gun swiveled over to aim at them. Maybe twenty feet away, and even from this distance the barrel seemed a hole big enough to crawl into.

Ethan stared past it, to the man pointing it. He was good-looking in that blond sort of way, cheeks ruddy beneath his helmet, gloved hands on the weapon, finger on the trigger. He looked all of nineteen years old, and scared.

What was happening? How and when had things slipped into this strange new place? A world where the grocery store didn't have groceries, where the power vanished, where terrorism wasn't something happening to someone else. A world where the line between this moment and utter disaster was so slender as to be defined by the fear in the heart of a nineteen-year-old boy.

The other civilians seemed frozen. On the ground, the trucker made a wet sound.

Slowly, Ethan raised his hands. Keeping his eyes locked on the soldier behind the gun, he began to back away. One step, and then another, and then he was apart from the group, and then he was turning around and walking back to the CRV where his wife and daughter waited. He opened the door and got in.

"Any luck?" Amy looked over at him, read his expression, and he could see it mirroring on her face. "What? What happened?"

"Nothing," he said, and started the SUV. "We're going home."

Here's the thing about freedom: Freedom is not a couch.

It's not a television, or a car, or a house.

It's not an item you can possess. You cannot put freedom on layaway; you cannot refinance freedom.

Freedom is something you need to fight for, not once, but every single day. The nature of freedom is that it is fluid; like water in a leaking bucket, the tendency is for it to drain away.

Left untended, the holes through which freedom escapes widen. When politicians restrict our rights in order to "protect us," freedom is lost. When the military refuses to disclose basic facts, freedom is lost. Worst of all, when fear becomes a part of our lives, we willingly surrender freedom for a promise of safety, as if freedom weren't the very basis of safety.

There's a famous poem written about the complacency of the German people under Nazi rule; today, it might read:

First they came for the revolutionaries,
and I didn't speak out because I wasn't a revolutionary.

Then they came for the intellectuals,
and I didn't speak out because I wasn't an intellectual.

Then they came for the tier ones,
and I didn't speak out because I wasn't a tier one.

Then they came for the brilliants,
and I didn't speak out because I wasn't a brilliant.

Then they came for me,
and there was no one left to speak for me.

—From the introduction to *I Am John Smith*

CHAPTER 12

It didn't look like much from the outside. But in Shannon's experience, the truly scary places never did.

The first thing she saw was a low granite wall bearing the words DEPARTMENT OF ANALYSIS AND RESPONSE. Beyond that, a dense line of trees screened the compound from view. She signaled, waited for an opening in traffic, and then steered the sedan up to a security gatehouse. It was a bright fall day, and the two men in black body armor looked alien against the cloudless blue. They moved well, one of them splitting off to circle the car while the other approached the driver's side. Both had submachine guns slung across their bodies.

Shannon rolled down the window and reached in her purse. The ID, scuffed and faded, identified her as a senior analyst; the picture looked like it was a few years old. "Afternoon," she said, polite and bored at once.

"Good afternoon, ma'am." The guard took the ID, his eyes flicking between it and her face. He swiped it against a device on his belt, which beeped. He handed it back to her. "Beautiful day, isn't it?"

"One of the last," she said. "S'posed to be colder next week." She didn't look behind her, didn't check the mirror for the armed man examining the back of her car.

The guard glanced over the car roof at his partner, then nodded at her. "Have a good day."

"You too." She put the ID in her purse. The metal gate parted, and she drove through.

And into the lion's cage we go.

No, that wasn't really it. This was more like walking into the lion's cage, strutting up to the beast, and jamming her head between its jaws.

The thought sent a shiver of adrenaline. She smiled, drove steadily.

The DAR grounds were nice enough, in a lethal sort of way. The road meandered in curves that seemed senseless, but would keep a car bomber from gaining speed. Every fifty yards or so she felt her tires hum over retracted spike strips. The landscape was green lawns and carefully pruned trees, but tall towers were dotted amidst them. No doubt snipers were tracking her progress.

The building itself was bland and sprawling, looking more like a Fortune 100 office than the nation's largest spy agency. At the west end, a construction crew worked on a five-story addition, welders on the beams sending showers of sparks. Apparently business was good at the DAR.

Shannon found an empty parking place about halfway down a lane, turned the car off, and flipped down the visor to look in the mirror. She could never get used to herself as a blonde. Odd how many women dyed their hair that color. In her experience, being a brunette hadn't turned men away.

It was a good wig, though, the highlights layered well to blend with a hint of root. The makeup was heavier than she preferred, but that was the point. She put on a pair of plastic-framed designer eyeglasses. An affectation in this era of easy surgery, but that was what made them fashionable.

"Okay," she said, then shouldered her purse and left the car.

It really was a beautiful day, the air cool and tasting of fallen leaves. One of the things she loved about being on a job, it heightened her awareness of everything. Every taste sweeter, every touch electric. On the walk in, she could just make out the tips of anti-aircraft batteries mounted on the roof of the building.

The lobby was marble floors and tall ceilings and armed guards. One line broke into several, each leading through a metal detector. Cameras stared unblinking from every corner. She joined the queue, looked at her nails, and thought about John.

■

When he had first proposed this little adventure, her response had been, "You want me to go *where*?"

"I know." John Smith wore a gray suit and a clean shave, and he seemed taller than she remembered. Healthier. The benefits of not being on the run, she supposed, not having that 24/7 paranoia pressing down. "It sounds crazy."

"Crazy I'm okay with. This sounds like suicide. Besides, I'm tasked out. All my attention is focused on West Virginia. I've got sins to make up for."

"I understand," he'd said, with that smile of his. A good smile, he was a handsome guy, though not her type. Too conventional, like a real estate agent. "But I wouldn't ask if it weren't worth it."

"Why?"

He told her, and the more he talked, the more incredible the tale seemed. Coming from anyone else, she wouldn't have believed it. But if John was right—a safe bet—then this could change everything. Shift the entire balance of power. Recalibrate the world.

Of course, first they had to find it. Which was where robbing the DAR came in. Why dig through a haystack yourself when someone already had the coordinates of the needle?

"Thing is, we can't just hack in. The DAR knows any data connected to the Internet is vulnerable. They keep their most precious secrets on discrete networks inside the compound. The computers are connected to each other, but not to the world, so the only way to access them—"

"Is to go into the compound itself."

He'd nodded.

"How would I even get through the gate?"

"I'll take care of that. The ID won't just get you in, it'll confirm your whole life. Redundant records backfilled into their system. Payroll data, employee reviews, work history, the whole bit. I've got my very best on this. It should be simple."

"If it's so simple, why do you need me?"

"In case it turns out not to be. Look, I'm not going to lie to you, Shannon. If you get caught, there won't be a trial. They probably won't even acknowledge they have you. You'll end up in a maximum-security cell where they will spend the rest of your life trying to break you, and there will be nothing I can do to help."

"You really know how to tempt a girl."

"But that's not going to happen. You can do this, I know you can." He leaned his chin on his hand, the drink untouched in front of him. "Besides, there's more. While you're in there, you can get everything there is to know about West Virginia. The complete security package. You'll be able to wash away your sins without risking lives."

She'd weighed that. "What if I say no?"

"Then you say no. It's always up to you, you know that."

■

The line moved well, and within a minute she was walking to a metal detector. She took off a delicate silver necklace shaped like three icicles and coiled it beside her purse in a bin on the conveyor belt.

The fear hit as she was walking to the metal detector, armed guards on either side, DAR agents behind and beside her. A sudden heavy thump in her chest like a double-kick drum, and a dump of chemicals into her bloodstream. It was nothing new, nothing she wasn't used to; it happened every time. But this time the fear was sharper, more intense.

More fun.

Shannon smiled at the guard as she walked through the metal detector. He waved her along. She waited for her bin to come through the conveyor, put on her necklace, grabbed her purse, and headed into the headquarters of an agency that had maintained a kill order on her for years. John hadn't been kidding; whatever brilliant had coded the ID truly was good.

He damn well better be.

As if in response to her thought, the glasses flickered to life. The inside of each lens was lined with a monofilament screen, the display visible only from this angle. The left showed a 3-D wireframe map of her position in the building; on the right, the words GOOD HUNTING appeared. She kept her smile internal.

Shannon strolled down the hall, the heels of her boots clicking on the tile. Once past the security, the Department of Analysis and Response resembled nothing so much as a large corporation: offices and cubicles, elevators and employee washrooms. It made sense. The department was split into two parts, and this was the analysis side. It was larger by far, employing tens of thousands of scientists, policymakers, advisors, headshrinkers, and stat-counters.

The other section was response, a different creature altogether. A creature that planned kidnappings, arrests, and assassinations. That had a governmental mandate to murder. Nick's old department.

This facility had been his office once, the source of his power. He'd been the top gun of its most secret division. How many times had he strutted these hallways? What had he been thinking when he did? Back then he'd drunk the Kool-Aid, believed in everything the DAR stood for. She pictured him, that almost cocky calm he wore like a tailored suit.

Speaking of her type.

She'd hated him the first time they'd met. Nick had killed a friend of hers, a brilliant who had started robbing banks. A sad and damaged boy, broken by the academy, lost in the world. It wasn't his fault that he'd gone so wrong, and while she agreed that he needed to be stopped—innocent people had been killed—that didn't mean she was okay with his murder, or prepared to forgive the soulless assassin who had committed it.

Thing was, Nick turned out to not be that at all. He was warm and passionate and smart. He was dedicated to his children and willing to do anything for them. In truth, they were actually a lot alike, both of them fighting to make a better world. They just had different ideas of how to accomplish it.

Shannon wished she could have told him what she was doing today. His first reaction would have been fury, but once she'd explained the reasoning, she was pretty sure he would come over to her side.

Pack that all away. Telling him was too big a risk, and this place is too dangerous to be thinking of anything but the job.

She walked down a long corridor, took an elevator up three flights into a broad atrium. People passed, looking at d-pads and talking about meetings. At thirty years old, Shannon had never been in a meeting, liked it that way. An aerial walkway with glass on both sides gave her a view of the complex. Enormous, with that rabbit-warren look of constant expansion. She reached the end, turned left.

Twenty yards away, a door opened, and a man and woman walked out. She was small, maybe five-one, but strutted with a screw-you spitfire energy. The man was fit, medium height, wore a shoulder holster. She recognized him. They'd brought down a presidential administration together. Bobby Quinn, Nick's old partner, the planner with the dry wit. A funny guy, good at his job, she'd liked him.

She had no doubt, none at all, that if he recognized her, he would take her.

Don't kid yourself, sweetie. There's no "if." You think fake blond hair, high-heeled boots, and a pair of glasses is going to protect you from Bobby Quinn?

He was talking to the woman as he walked, his hands out and gesturing. He would reach Shannon in seconds, and if he saw her, she would never see another autumn afternoon.

She didn't need to think. Didn't need to look around. The trick to doing what Nick called "walking through walls," and what she called shifting, was that it wasn't about studying the world and then making a decision. The only way to be invisible was to know where everyone was all the time, where they were looking, and where they were going. Every room, every minute. On bad days she got wicked migraines from the data overload, like sitting too close to the tri-d.

Data. Like:

The analyst in the bad tie digging through a file cabinet, actual printed papers, trust the government to be running behind.

The FedEx guy pushing the trolley, whistling, the stops on his route clear to her as a diagram.

The administrative assistant stepping from the break room with a coffee in her right hand and her eyes on the d-pad in her left.

The flirting couple almost-but-not-quite touching, his hand about to reach for her arm.

Quinn turning from the woman, the trust in the move; they were teammates.

The water fountain compressor kicking on.

Shannon shifted.

Slid into the path of the delivery guy, paused, opened her purse like she was looking for something, cut across the hall past the assistant with the coffee, slipped the toe of her boot forward just enough to catch the heel of the woman's shoe, the assistant stumbling, not falling but making a panic clench, keeping her grip on the d-pad instead of the coffee, now into the break room, opening a cabinet so her back was to the hall, the coffee cup arcing, hitting the side of the FedEx trolley just as Quinn and the woman reached it.

"Oh God, I'm so sorry," the assistant said, as Shannon stared into the cabinet and counted seconds. On three she closed the door and left the break room, not looking at the assistant and the FedEx guy assuring each other they were okay, not looking at Bobby Quinn and his friend, already past, both of them glancing back but at the wrong thing.

Always at the wrong thing.

Three minutes and five floors later, she was in a basement hallway lit by fluorescents. The air was chilly and quiet. In the left lens of her glasses, a dot began to blink on the map. It grew larger until she stood outside a metal-framed door. A camera was mounted to the ceiling above, and there was a swipe pad on the wall beside a big red button.

In the right lens of her glasses, a message appeared. Logs show no entrances since last exit. Should be clear.

Should be? That's comforting.

There was a long pause as the machine scanned her ID. This was the real test. There were probably fewer than a dozen people with the credentials to open this door.

With a click, the lock disengaged.

The room beyond was freezing, maybe forty degrees, and packed with neatly organized metal racks, each holding row upon row of wafer servers, computers a centimeter thick, each pumping and processing terabytes of data. Bundles of wires ran behind them in clusters as wide around as her arm. The hum of unseen fans filled the air.

The beating heart of the DAR. The facts and files of every covert operation, every secret facility, every profile on every target. She was in here somewhere; the details of her life, her childhood, her schooling, the things she had done and the people she had known. Shannon followed the map down the rows, the hair on her arms rising in the electrified air. Five aisles down and four over, she stood in front of a rack just like all the rest.

Shannon reached up to her necklace and twisted the central icicle. It unlocked, revealing a stamp drive insert. She ran her fingers down the I/O panel, found a connection, and slotted the drive. Nothing seemed to happen, but she knew the program was unspooling itself, sliding down the pathways of data, searching for the files they needed. A progress bar appeared in her right lens, slowly ticking up, 1%, 2%, 3%.

Nothing to do but wait.

It was always the strangest moment of a job. The nature of her skills meant that she often had to get into position and then wait. It was tense, and yet there was also something delicious about it, like that first drag of really good dope, like bouncing a glider between updrafts in the desert, like the clenching before orgasm. Her head served up a memory of a Washington, DC, intersection, the first time she'd seen Nick, she realized, almost a year ago. The DAR had managed to flip a defense contractor named Bryan Vasquez, and Nick had sent him back out to meet his contact, hoping to scoop them both up.

John had predicted the move, of course, and had a contingency plan in the form of a newspaper dispenser packed with explosives. Shannon was the one who'd triggered it, shifting past Nick's whole security team to stand next to Equitable Services' biggest badass as she blew the bomb and his operation in one.

Of course, at the time, she hadn't imagined she'd end up dating him.

Dating? Is that what we're doing?

The progress bar clicked agonizingly slowly. 63%.

It was reckless, getting involved with him. He'd left the DAR, but now he worked for the president, which was at best a lateral move when it came to the likelihood of a happy ending for the two of them. And she wasn't some teenage girl lost in a steamy fantasy. Two months ago, when Cooper had come after John Smith,

Shannon had pointed a loaded shotgun at him, and while she hadn't liked the idea, she could have pulled the trigger.

Of course, there was also a moment when the two of you sat in a basement bar in the New Canaan Holdfast, your thighs touching as he quoted Hemingway. There was also a moment when he trusted you with the lives of his children.

96% complete, but the bar seemed frozen, just a tiny fraction of an inch to go. She sighed, tapped her toes, and fought the urge to curse. No matter how far technology went, some things never changed.

Come on, come on.

97%. 98%. 99%. 100%.

The display vanished. Shannon unplugged the stamp drive, reconnected it to her necklace. If everything had gone as planned, the program would have downloaded every detail they needed, a mass of information on privately funded labs, underground think tanks, and black facilities doing cutting-edge research. The kind of place that didn't have stockholders and didn't pay an excessive amount of attention to government regulation. The kind of place where almost anything could be developed.

Even a magic potion that could change the world.

She turned and walked back to the entrance, her boots making a clonking sound on the hollow floor. Three-inch heels plus one-inch risers, ridiculous footwear, especially on a mission, but they served a purpose. At the door, she took a breath, blew it out, brushed her blond hair back, and stepped outside. She turned right and started back the way she'd come.

"Hey! You!"

The voice came from behind. Shannon thought about running, turned instead, pasting a *Me?* look on her face.

The guy was tall and pale, wearing jeans, a T-shirt with a logo, and a ragged cardigan. He had his ID in his hand, already stretched toward the door. A technician or a programmer. She began to audition lies, all of them thin to the point of transparency.

As it turned out, she didn't even get a chance to speak. As one of the dozen people who belonged in this room, he knew she didn't. His eyes widened, and then he slapped the big red panic button.

Nothing seemed to happen, but she knew alarms would be sounding all over the building, in every guard station. The whole of the DAR's security forces would be mobilized, hundreds of heavily armed soldiers.

There were no klaxons, no flashing lights, and somehow that only made it scarier.

Shannon turned and ran.

The hallway seemed longer and narrower, and the cameras more numerous. Her mouth tasted like copper, and her heart slammed in her chest. She rounded a corner, sprinted for the stairwell. The distance between her and safety was measured not in distance but in impossibilities. She was in the heart of a militarized complex, actively hunted by enemies. Not only that, but she was racing down an empty hall, an easy target.

Okay. Start there.

She slowed long enough to reach over and yank the fire alarm.

Now came the sirens, a loud repeating whoop and bleat of danger. Doors began to open behind her. She hustled into the stairwell, ran up the steps. Paused, then stepped out. The hall was filled with people. She could have kissed each and every one of them. Without people, she was exposed. But in a milling, confused crowd?

Shannon shifted.

Slid behind and between, paused and spun and dodged. Smiled and stopped to bend down as though her boot needed zipping. Stepped into open offices on the blind side of the people stepping out of them. *You move like water flows, kiddo.* Her dad's voice, years ago, talking about her on the soccer field. *Water always finds a way.*

Find a way.

Falling in behind a pair of burly executive types, she used a coded sequence of blinks to control the display of her glasses. The map zoomed out, then changed to a 3-D view, the hallways now laid out like one eye was playing a video game. She wished she could communicate with the handler on the other end of the lenses, could ask him—her?—to stream what she needed. But the link went only one way; an outbound signal from inside the DAR would have tripped all manner of alarms.

As if reading her thoughts, the fire alarm suddenly shut off. No surprise; security would have seen it for the distraction it was. It didn't matter. The hall was crowded now, people milling about, starting conversations. It had bought her the time she needed. She followed the glasses, shifting through and around and behind the crowd. The cameras would catch her, nothing she could do about that, but with this many cameras and this many people, so long as she wasn't drawing attention to herself, it would be a matter of luck for someone to be looking at just the right monitor.

There. A women's bathroom, right where the map said it would be. She pushed open the door and stepped inside. One mirror, two sinks, five stalls, and a faint odor of shit. She went into the middle stall and locked the door behind her.

Shannon sat on the toilet, then pulled off the boots and set them in front of her. The dress followed. From her purse she took a pair of light jeans and wriggled them up over her hips. The blouse was silk and wrinkled from being packed so tight, but it was okay. The best part were silver flats, which felt wonderful after the ridiculous boots. Shannon reached up to her hair, undid the plastic clips, and pulled the wig off. The blond hair and dress and glasses all got tucked into the boots; she'd drop them in the trash on the way out.

Now for the fun part. She unhooked one of the smaller icicles from her necklace. The tip of a hypodermic needle glinted in the overhead lights. Using a compact mirror from her purse, she moved it carefully up to her eyebrow. Needles were not her thing, but she ground her teeth and went to work. There was a tearing as the point penetrated. She squeezed gently, then pulled it out, moved it over, and repeated the process. Each injection pushed a few CCs of saline into her forehead. With bone on the other side, the liquid had nowhere to stretch the skin but outward. A larger amount would have looked comical, but the tiny injections just changed the lines of her forehead.

When she was done with her right eyebrow, she moved to her cheekbone. It hurt.

She was just finishing up the left side with the second icicle hypo when she heard the door to the bathroom open.

Be an analyst needing to pee, Shannon thought. *Be two assistants gossiping.*

"Ma'am?" The voice was female, brusque. "I'm going to need you to come out here."

Crap.

The good news was that it was just one guard, which meant they didn't know she was in here. This would be a routine check, security forces sweeping and clearing the building.

The bad news was that the guard would be armed and ready. Shannon could handle herself, but going toe-to-toe with a DAR commando wasn't a favorable-odds proposition.

Find a way, kiddo. Move like water flows.

"Excuse me?" Shannon said. "I'm using the bathroom." As quietly as she could, she spun on the toilet seat, the porcelain cold through her jeans.

"I understand, ma'am, but I need you to come out right now."

"Are you kidding me?" She planted a foot alongside the toilet, then another. "I'm in the middle of something."

The guard moved to the other side of the door. Shannon could see the tips of her combat boots, and then the door banged, hard.

"*Now*, ma'am."

"All right, all right. Jesus. Can I wipe?" She squatted beside the toilet, trying not to think about how often the floor got mopped, then rattled the toilet paper dispenser.

"Ma'am, if you don't step out in five seconds, I'm kicking the door open." She spoke from only feet away, and Shannon could picture her, standing at the ready, her weapon in hand but not raised. From that angle, the guard wouldn't be able to see anything.

"Five."

Shannon lay flat on the ground, perpendicular to the stall. Flexing one leg up, she hit the toilet handle with her toe.

"Four."

The flush was immediate, the leonine rush of water in a public bathroom. She took advantage of the sound to slide under the wall to the neighboring stall, her hands and face brushing along the tile.

"Three."

Well that was fairly disgusting. She rose silently.

"Two."

Shannon opened the stall door and stepped out.

The woman was built, strong muscles layered in bulky body armor. She wore a ponytail and a pissed-off expression, a fully automatic submachine gun slung on a strap around her shoulder, her right hand on the grip, her left reaching for the door. She looked extremely competent, and Shannon knew she'd been right, no way she could have handled this woman face-to-face.

But from alongside and by surprise was another matter.

Without hesitation, Shannon lunged forward and slammed the icicle hypodermic into the side of the woman's neck.

The needle was only half an inch long, and it caught in the muscle, but the intent wasn't to kill, just to shock and distract her, which it did, the guard yelping as she spun, her left hand going to her neck instead of to her gun, giving Shannon the opening she needed to throw a roundhouse kick into the commando's nose.

The guard collapsed. Shannon went with her, wrapped the gun strap against her neck. The woman tried to throw punches, but Shannon stayed close and kept the pressure on, twisting the strap tighter and tighter.

When it was done, she dragged the woman back into the neighboring stall and leaned her against the toilet. Searched for a pulse, found it strong. She'd have one hell of a headache when she woke up, but wake up she would.

Shannon closed and locked the stall door, slid under yet again, and then took a moment to look in the mirror. The guards would be looking for a five-eight blonde with a different outfit and a different face. It wasn't a perfect disguise, but it would do.

She washed her hands and stepped back into the hallway.

The odds of her getting out were no longer looking impossible. But it would still be a risk—security would be checking everyone thoroughly.

A bank of clocks on the wall showed the time in London, Chicago, Los Angeles, Singapore, and, of course, here in Washington, DC, where it was 16:45.

Shannon smiled. The DAR might be the biggest intelligence agency in America, but it was still a government office. Which meant that for most of the thousands of people who worked here, it was fifteen minutes till quitting time. Fifteen minutes until they flooded the exits.

She headed for the commissary. May as well have a cup of coffee while she waited.

THE UNREST INDEX

THE TREFFERT-DOWN SCALE

THE FACELESS
THE MONOCLE
MARCH 12

Overwhelmed by modern life? You're not alone.

Our grandparents had it right. Life is better without d-pads and 24/7 feedcasts. Better when you don't have to worry about political correctness. Better when your wife has a turkey in the oven and your dog is curled up at your feet.

And just because your wife can't cook and you don't own a dog doesn't mean you should be denied those pleasures.

The Tarry Program is about slowing down. Rewinding the clock to a simpler era, and experiencing life the way it was meant to be. Our seminars are a weekend away from the world—that will leave you ready to face it again.

Forget reality. Let's Tarry™.

> * Tarry Packages start at $1999 for three nights all-inclusive stay, non-intimate spousal companionship**, canine/feline rental, program materials and life coaching. Locations are secret, and emergency contact information is required. No gifted, please.

> ** Intimate spousal companionship packages available

CHAPTER 13

"Well diddle me sideways. Aren't you famous? BFFs with the president?" Bobby Quinn stood framed in the door of his apartment, a slow grin spreading across his face.

"That's right. Show some respect." Cooper puffed out his chest. "Genuflecting is preferred, but from my old partner, a deep bow will be sufficient."

"How about I turn around when I bow, so you can kiss my—"

"Yeah, yeah." Cooper grabbed his friend around the shoulders, pulled him into a bear hug. "It's good to see you. Let's grab a beer."

"Man, I'd love to, but I just this minute walked in from the airport, back from Cleveland. I'm whacked."

"Did I mention I was buying?"

"On the other hand, alcohol is part of a balanced diet."

The sign outside declared the bar was called Jack Chittle's; the interior was sunken booths and Christmas lights burning year round. Cooper's knowledge of beer ended with knowing he liked it, so he let Quinn order for them, a pitcher of dark stuff called milk stout. It was rich and delicious, with hints of chocolate and coffee, and it tasted even better after they added a couple of shots of Irish whiskey.

"So you're in from Cleveland, huh?" Cooper set down his shot glass. "The Children of Darwin?"

"Believe it or not, no. I've been working a subject there, a scientist. Guy decided to bolt, so I had to pay his protégé a visit, rattle his cage."

"He know anything?"

"Too early to say."

They caught up, Cooper letting the talk stay small for a while, not wanting to rush things. Bobby Quinn filled him in on the situation at the agency.

"It's a grade-A, top-shelf mess. Everybody playing duck and cover, tripping over each other to distance themselves. 'What? We track and kill bad people? Oh my. How rude.'" Quinn laughed. "And at the same time, we still have all these potential targets out there, so the same upper management yahoos that are wringing their hands on CNN are coming around and talking out of the side of their mouths, telling us to keep going, that things will get sorted soon."

"Will they?"

"Equitable Services is over. But yeah, sure. Give it a year to blow over, and we'll start back up under a new name. Everyone knows the work still has to be done. Meanwhile, the best and brightest agents in the DAR are in limbo. You know what else they've got me doing? I'm heading an internal fact-finding task force to support a congressional investigation. You want a good time some Saturday night, try writing a report on taking down a known terrorist without using the word *kill*."

"Terminate?"

"Neutralize. Makes it sound like maybe we pointed out the error of their ways and offered them vocational training." Quinn shook his head. "How about you? You're the only guy I know who can murder his boss and end up working for the president. Talk about failing upward."

"Wasn't my plan."

"You had a plan?"

Cooper laughed, gestured for another round of shots.

"Seriously though, Coop. You're a soldier, not a suit. What are you doing working for Clay?"

"Same as always. Trying to stop a war."

"How's it going?"

"Same as always."

Quinn took a pack of cigarettes from his coat, pulled one out, and spun it between two fingers. The bartender came over to pour their shots, said, "You can't smoke in here."

"Really? Is this a new public ordinance or just a personal policy?"

"Whatever." The guy set the bottle back on the shelf, wandered away.

"Yeah, whatever." His old partner tapped the cigarette, toyed with it. "Funny world. John Smith gets fat checks to speak at college campuses, but a guy who wants a cigarette can be killed and eaten."

"You don't even like smoking them. You just like thinking about smoking them."

"That's true. Delayed gratification, like tantric sex."

Cooper laughed. It felt good to be here, talking to someone who lived in the same world he did. But thinking that reminded him of why he was here, the fear that had been plaguing him. "Okay, full disclosure, this isn't strictly a social call."

"What's on your mind?"

"What do you guys have on the Children of Darwin?"

Quinn shrugged. "No record of them until about six weeks ago, then suddenly, poof, there they are, sneezing in everyone's sandwich."

"Any idea how they're being run?"

"We assume discrete cells, fluid command structure. Terrorist SOP. But with Equitable Services mothballed, nobody's been able to draw a bead on them."

"How is that possible? How can we know nothing?"

Quinn leaned back. "Is this the White House asking?"

"No," Cooper said. "I'm not fact-finding. I'm trying to work it out, and I need your help. You're my planner."

"Flattery works." Quinn sipped his beer. "Okay, between you and me? The whole idea they sprang up out of nowhere, it doesn't play. No one gets this organized this fast, not even brilliants."

"So you're saying they've been around awhile."

"Well, they know exactly how to hurt us, right? Before, most terrorists were planting bombs in post offices, assassinating minor officials, derailing trains. Bad, but essentially a nuisance. But these guys, they've got their shit together. Instead of attacking buildings, they hijack a couple of trucks and kill the drivers, knowing that insurance companies will pull their policies. Boom, they've starved the city."

"Same thing with the power," Cooper said. "I think they took down the grid hoping that we would react by enforcing a quarantine."

"Yeah, that was a terrible play." Quinn shook his head. "All it did was create chaos. We essentially just gave them those cities. How did you let that happen, man?"

"Wasn't my call."

"And the cover story, that we're locking down the city to capture the terrorists? Who is that supposed to fool, a ten-year-old with a head injury?"

"I know, I know. Honestly, I think Leahy believes you guys are going to come up with target coordinates for a missile launch."

Quinn shook his head. "No way. I'd guess the COD have no more than ten or fifteen operatives in each city. Discrete, no centralized command. And the grid probably got hacked by some teenaged twist in a Poughkeepsie basement."

"Why so few people?"

"That's all you need to hijack trucks and burn a depot. By keeping it that small, they're nearly impossible to find. Especially now."

"If that's true, then this was all planned in advance." Cooper chose his words carefully. He thought he was right but wanted to see if Quinn came to the same conclusion. "Not weeks ago. Years ago. Someone organized this, got people in place, funded them, and left them as sleepers for a time when the DAR was in chaos."

Quinn gave him a curious look. "You're saying John Smith."

"A plan like this would take an incredible strategic mind."

"You once told me that John Smith was the strategic equivalent of Einstein." Quinn sipped at his beer. "But . . . wait a second."

"A plan years in the making. A small, dedicated group who uses our systems against us. More than that, action timed at precisely the worst moment, when a strong if immoral president is impeached and facing trial, and the organization that would normally have protected the country is in shambles."

"If that's true, then it means—are you saying—" Quinn stared at him. "You realize what that means?"

"That's what's been keeping me up nights, Bobby. I just keep thinking it through and landing at the same place."

It was a place Cooper had never imagined ending up. When he'd gone undercover to hunt John Smith, he'd had no doubts about the man's guilt. But the journey to reach him had opened his eyes to certain facts he couldn't ignore. Facts like Shannon's abnorm friend, Samantha, whose gift for empathy could have made her a healer or a teacher, but who had instead been turned into a prostitute. Facts like a DAR tactical team arresting a family that had helped him, imprisoning the parents and putting the eight-year-old girl in an academy. Facts like the tenuous beauty of the New Canaan Holdfast in Wyoming, where a generation of optimistic dreamers were building something new and better.

By the time he'd finally found Smith, Cooper's faith had been strained. And when Cooper learned the truth about the massacre at the Monocle restaurant, his faith had snapped.

In a way, he had snapped.

Cooper remembered sitting on top of a peak in Wyoming, a thin finger of stone fifty yards high, watching the dawn. He and Smith had climbed it together, and as a bloody sun rose over the dusty landscape, they had talked. More than talked; traded truths. It had been a terribly surreal experience, conversing with his sworn enemy. It was that morning that Smith told him about the existence of the video showing Drew Peters and President Walker plotting the Monocle. Smith had claimed that they were the ones who wanted a war, that only people already in power would benefit from one.

While he hadn't bought everything Smith was selling, Cooper had believed enough of it to move forward. To find the video and kill Drew Peters and bring down a president.

And now he wondered if that had been Smith's purpose all along.

"Bobby," Cooper said, "I need you tell me the truth. Am I crazy? Or is it possible?"

His friend set down the pint glass. Picked up the cigarette, put it in his mouth, and then tapped at the bar with his fingers, his eyes down. Cooper let him think. Hoped against hope that Quinn would tell him that it was a paranoid fantasy. Cooper's gift for pattern recognition gave him huge advantages, but they were more tactical than strategic, more about the next moment than ten moves down the line. Quinn was the planner.

"It's possible." All the jocularity was drained from his friend's voice. "It is."

Cooper leaned back. His stomach went sour, and the back of his throat burned with bile. Possible was as good as certainty, if John Smith was the X factor. "He played us."

"But you realize what that means? All of it, everything we did, it was all part of his plan. When Smith told you about the video, sent us after Peters, it had nothing to do with his innocence or the truth. He did it because—"

"Because he knew that if I found that video, I would release it. And that would bring down the president and paralyze the DAR. He knew I would do the right thing, and he used that to make the situation worse." Cooper hesitated, tried to swallow the next words, found they tore his throat like razors. "It means that this is my fault, Bobby."

"Bull. You can't take that on."

"I have to. Sure, I was trying my best, but I played right into his hands. We all did. I thought he was using me to get exonerated and come out of hiding. But those were just fringe benefits. Crippling our response to the COD was the real goal."

"But why? I mean, if everything he did to bring you in and set you up was just step one, and he was already thinking of step ten, then what's the endgame?"

"War," Cooper said. "The endgame is war. I think that John Smith is no longer interested in equal rights for abnorms. I think he wants to start a civil war."

"And do what? Kill all the normals?"

Cooper said nothing.

"Jesus." Quinn rubbed at his eyes. "Wait. How does this get him what he wants? Things are worse now for abnorms than ever before. The microchipping, the hate crimes, hell, every third congressman holding press conferences to say we need to lock you all up."

"Exactly. Remember, it's not like abnorms are united. He can't just send us an e-mail. Most people, straight or twist, wouldn't have anything to do with him. They're just trying to live their lives. If Smith wants to take power, he needs an army. And since he can't start recruiting—"

Quinn's eyes widened as he got the whole scope of it. "He gets the government to do it for him. He goads them into getting repressive. People go from worrying about abnorms to fearing them. From there, it's a baby step to attacking them. Lynchings, riots. His army forms itself. After all, if everyone is trying to kill your people, you better get together and defend yourselves."

"And you'll need a leader to do it. A man of bold vision, one who promises you a world where you're not only safe—you're in charge. Not equal rights. Superiority for the superior."

The door to the bar opened, and a group of twentysomethings strolled in, laughing and joking. An icy draft flowed with them, and Cooper shivered. Quinn pushed his glass away. "Suddenly I'm not thirsty."

"Yeah."

"The DAR has been watching Smith as best we can. We haven't seen any sign that he's in contact with the COD."

"He wouldn't have to be. He could have made this plan two years ago, laid out a very specific set of instructions. Do this, then do this, then do that. Like you said, a small group who knows exactly how to hurt us."

"And meanwhile, he runs around the country giving speeches and signing books, going on tri-d, talking about how he's a victim. Whipping up support while pretending to be the voice of reason."

Fix it, Natalie had said. The thought almost made him laugh. Fix it? He'd broken it. True, his intentions had been pure, the kind of choices his father would have approved of. But they had served John Smith's goals regardless. Right had been warped to do so much wrong.

"You know," Quinn said, "some days I hate everybody." He shook his head. "Things are getting bad, aren't they? I mean, we've always been on the front line, and it always looks like it's about to go to hell. That's the game. But this is different." He looked up, met Cooper's eyes. "We really may be on the brink. The end of everything."

The end of everything. It was such a melodramatic statement, so huge and vaguely silly. The end of everything? Of course not. The cataclysmic never really happened. It just lurked out there.

Hurricanes didn't really destroy cities. Plagues didn't really ravage populations. People didn't really commit genocide.

Except . . . they did.

"Have you talked to the president?"

Cooper shook his head. "No one wants to hear it. They're all too sure that everything will be okay."

"You could be wrong about Smith."

"Nothing would make me happier. But I don't think I am. Do you?"

"No."

"So what are we going to do about it?"

Quinn sucked air through his teeth. "With the situation right now, there's no way the DAR will take any action against Smith. In the public's eyes, he's become a white hat. The victim of a repressive government. We couldn't arrest him if he was shooting strangers with one hand while jerking off into the American flag with the other."

"That's vivid."

"Thank you. What about President Clay?"

"Nope, no chance," Cooper said. "John Smith is untouchable."

"Completely off-limits."

"One hundred percent." Cooper picked up his napkin, tore a neat strip off of it, and another, and another. He looked up at his friend. "Want to go get him anyway?"

Quinn smiled. "Oh, hell yes."

RiNGO'S ARMY-NAVY
WE HAVE WHAT YOU NEED
OUR C.O.D. SURVIVAL KIT INCLUDES:
• BUTANE STOVE
• COLLAPSIBLE COOKPOT
• WATER PURIFICATION
• ALL-WEATHER BLANKET
• HAND-CRANK FLASHLIGHT
• MULTI-TOOL
JUST $999.99!
(SUPPLIES ARE LIMITED AND GOING FAST)
REMEMBER, ONLY YOU CAN PROTECT YOUR FAMILY!!
DEAD D-PAD BATTERIES? Recharge off our Generator! ($50.00 /

CHAPTER 14

Breath blowing white, Ethan sorted cans.

Their kitchen had a pantry, a fact that still blew him away. A room specifically to store food? What a novelty! What a luxury! In Manhattan, the pantry would have been rented out as an efficiency apartment. He was pretty sure he'd lived in one.

The power had been out for twenty hours now, and the house was cold. He wore two sweatshirts and fingerless gloves. It was funny how few cans of food had actual food value: tomato paste and pineapple slices and water chestnuts and chicken broth. All things a cook might need, and none of them a meal. He reorganized, putting the most useful on one shelf. Black beans, cannellini beans, lima beans. Soup, especially the heartier varieties. A couple of cans of coconut milk; not exactly haute cuisine, but each one packed almost a thousand calories, and the high fat content would help keep them warm. Below that went the pears and fruit cocktail and green beans. Fewer vitamins than fresh produce, but better than nothing. Pasta and rice. Finally, baking supplies, flour, sugar, cornmeal. Without power they couldn't bake, but they could mix a cold gruel from them if things got tight.

"She's down," Amy said from behind him. "I'm going to start with the water."

Ethan stood, stomped his feet to get some circulation moving. "Okay. Fill everything we've got. Glasses, vases, buckets, empty cans—"

"The bathtub. I got it."

"Thanks."

Ethan spotted a pack of birthday candles and added them to the pile on the counter. A box of tapers, three half-burned pillars from the bedroom, and eleven, no, twelve birthday candles. Three flashlights and a handful of batteries. Best not to waste them; they'd have to start keeping sunlit hours. No reading before bed.

They'd built a small fire in the fireplace, and he knelt to warm his hands, flexing stiff fingers. Debated tossing on another couple of logs and decided against it. They didn't have much firewood.

There's always the furniture.

Next up, the fridge. They were both foodies and usually had it well-stocked. But it had been six days since the stores were cleaned out, and they'd run through most of their fresh food already. The crisper had a couple of apples, a grapefruit, and half a bag of arugula, the bottom leaves already slimy. Normally he'd have tossed it all out; now he just picked through it, keeping all but the worst pieces. There was some leftover pad thai, two inches of orange juice, and a whole lot of condiments.

The freezer had already lost most of its chill, the ice sloshing in the trays, packages of hamburger and chicken softening around the edges. A couple of no-longer-frozen pizzas. Ethan sighed, started pulling it all out.

Filling glasses at the sink, Amy said, "We could put the food outside."

"How cold you figure it is?"

"Maybe forty-five?"

Hmm. That was probably about the temperature of a working refrigerator. Putting the meat outside would buy them a couple of days at best. "It'd last longer if we could cook it."

"I told you we should have gone for a gas stove." She smiled, then said, "Hey, wait. The grill."

Ethan laughed, then swept her into a hug. "Good thinking."

He was a purist when it came to grilling, charcoal or nothing. It was an easy argument to make when life was normal, but now he really wished he'd gone for propane. He dug around in the garage, found half a bag of Kingsford. He poured it all in the chimney, packed the bottom with newspaper, and set it aflame. A chilly wind blew from the west, sending white smoke in his face, but the charcoal caught.

Back in the kitchen, he cut open the packages of meat. Two pounds of flank steak, four chicken breasts, a pound of hamburger. He formed the ground beef into patties, then started to cut the steak into quarter-inch strips.

"Stir-fry?"

"Jerky," he said. "I'll boil water for the pasta, then cook the chicken and burgers, and finally do the pizzas. That'll about finish the charcoal, but if we hang these strips on the rack, they'll still dry out in a couple of hours. And jerky lasts for weeks."

"Nice." Amy straightened, put her hands on her lower back, and leaned, the vertebrae popping. "Man, what I'd give for a hot shower."

"Don't even," he said. Out the window, the afternoon was fading. Clouds hung low and oppressive, and wind tossed the trees.

Inventoried, the food seemed like plenty to keep them going. But he knew that if they ate normally, it would be gone in no time. He thought of the grocery runs they used to make, the cart filled to the brim, a dozen bags to unpack, and yet they'd visited the store almost weekly.

We'll have to start rationing. Stretch it out, drink a lot of water. Ladies and gentlemen, the American way has been temporarily suspended.

Which was fine. One of the benefits of living in the richest country in the world, there was a wide margin between normalcy and starvation. But still, what happened when they ran out? Could things go on that long?

And what about the people who don't have even this much? Somehow he didn't think they would quietly starve.

"I don't believe them," Amy said.

"Huh? Who?"

"The soldiers. You said they were locking down the city so the terrorists couldn't get out. It doesn't make sense."

"No."

"There's something they're not telling us."

Before he could reply, there was a knock at the door. The sound made them both jump. He'd never realized how noisy American silence was until all the gadgets died.

"Stay here," he said, then walked to the front door. Ethan put a hand on the knob, then caught himself. *It's a new world.* He glanced through the peephole.

Jack Ford stood on the porch, along with two guys from the neighborhood watch meeting. The engineer, Kurt, and Lou, the guy who had asked what his problem was.

He opened the door. "Hey."

"Hi, Ethan." Jack smiled, held out his hand, and they shook. "How are you?"

"Oh, we're taking stock."

He meant it with multiple layers, but Jack heard it literally. "Smart. Important to know how your provisions hold up. Hey, did I see you packing the truck last night?"

"Yes." An image popped in his head, Jack walking window to window, a shotgun in one hand as he peered through the blinds. Keeping an eye out for bad characters. "We were headed to Chicago to stay with Amy's mom. National Guard turned us back."

"I've heard. I've got a generator, been running it in intervals to charge our electronics and watch the news. They're saying that the city is locked down while the government hunts the Children of Darwin."

Ethan nodded. Waited. The three men looked at each other.

Jack started to speak, but Lou beat him to it. "You know that Ranjeet pretty well?"

"Sure, we've had dinner a couple of times. Nice guy."

"We were thinking we might go talk to him."

"About what?"

"Government says that they're looking for abnorm terrorists. Thought we might help out."

"Come on. Ranjeet is a graphic designer."

"No, hey, you misunderstand," Jack said. "We know he's not a terrorist. But he is an abnorm."

"So he probably knows terrorists?"

"Maybe he knows someone who's been acting weird."

"Abnorms hang out together," Kurt said. "I'm an engineer, believe me, I know lots of them."

Jack ignored him, said, "The government has a tip line for people to call in with anything suspicious. And since there's really nothing else to do right now, we figured, what's the harm?"

Sure. What's the harm in a whole city of hungry, scared people deciding to go terrorist hunting? "I don't think so."

"Forget it," Lou said. "I told you he wouldn't be up for it." The man cleared his throat, turned, and spat into the bushes. "Let's go."

Jack didn't move, just stood there with his hands at his sides. Ethan had the sense the man was trying to make a point, to let him know something. Jack was the de facto leader of the neighborhood now, the guy everyone turned to. Was he asking Ethan to join? Threatening him, vaguely? Or just suggesting that if people like Ethan weren't in, it made people like Lou all the stronger?

"Why don't you go with them, hon?"

Amy was out of sight of the men on the porch, and her concerned expression belied the lightness in her voice as she spoke loud enough for them to hear. "Go ahead, I can handle the grill. Just give me a hug first." She raised her arms.

Ethan glanced at Jack, then at her, then stepped into her embrace. In his ear she whispered, "Ranjeet has two little girls."

Of course. He whispered, "I love you."

"Ditto. Be careful."

He nodded, stepped back. "Let's go."

■

The Singhs' house was painted a cheerful yellow and fronted by flowerbeds lying fallow in the November cold. The walk there had taken only a minute, but it had seemed longer, dynamics bouncing invisibly between the group. Lou had led the way, a sense of purpose to his stride that made it almost a stomp. Jack and Ethan walked just behind, and at one point his neighbor had looked over at him, another inscrutable glance like he wanted to say something, though he didn't. Kurt had trailed like an eager puppy.

They paused on the sidewalk in front of the house. Lou shifted from foot to foot. Ethan pictured the scene from Ranjeet's perspective: four men clustered ominously outside, exchanging glances. Imagined how he would have felt, the subconscious middle-school certainty every person had that any group was looking at them, that every laugh was directed at their weakness. *This is a bad idea.*

Forcing a light tone, he said, "What are we waiting for, guys?" He started up the walk. He pressed the bell—nothing, right—then knocked. After a moment footsteps approached, and then the deadbolt snapped.

Ranjeet saw him first and smiled, the expression calcifying when he saw the other men. "Hey," he said. "The neighborhood watch. You catch any bad guys?"

Lou bristled, but Ethan said, "Nope, all clear. How are you doing?"

"Wishing we'd left for Florida."

"I hear you. We tried for Chicago, got turned back."

"Strange days." Ranjeet's eyes skipped past him to the others, then returned. "So what's up?"

"We come in?" Lou asked.

Ranjeet hesitated, his hand still on the doorknob. "Yeah, sure." He stood aside and gestured them in.

A short entrance gave way to the living room, a stylishly decorated space painted a precise shade of white. Two modernist couches were arranged on a yellow shag rug, and a book lay open atop a delicate glass table. There were toys scattered across the floor like they'd rained from the sky, stuffed animals and stacking cups and a xylophone. The sight of them gave him a flash of their future, Violet someday tottering around the house leaving a trail of toys in her wake, and the thought made him glow. "Where are the girls?"

"Upstairs. Eva is trying to convince them that it's nap time."

Ranjeet didn't offer them a seat, just put his hands in his pockets and waited. The four of them stood uncertainly in front of him. It was as cold inside the house as out, their breath fogging.

Ethan caught Jack looking at him, shrugged. *This was your idea, man.*

"Your place is really nice," Jack said, a bit awkwardly. "Sharp."

"Thanks. What's up?"

"I don't know if you've heard the news lately, with the power—"

"We've got a radio and batteries."

"So you know that the government is asking all of us to pitch in. There's a tip line to report anything."

"Like what?"

"You know." Jack shrugged. "About the Children of Darwin."

Ranjeet made a sound that wasn't a laugh. "Are you kidding me?"

Jack spread his hands in a conciliatory gesture. "We're not saying anything like that. We just wondered if maybe you'd—"

"Hung out with terrorists?"

"No, just . . . had any friends that were acting strange."

"Yeah," Ranjeet said, looking at Ethan. "You four."

"Listen, I know how this sounds," Jack said, trying for a conciliatory smile. "I'm sorry to ask, but we're all worried. Things are getting bad."

"Really, genius? What tipped you off?"

"Now I don't mean any offense—"

"You don't mean any offense? You come to my house with a posse and ask if I know terrorists, but you don't mean offense?"

"Ranjeet—" Ethan started, but his friend interrupted him.

"No, it's okay. You got me. I'm a criminal mastermind. My cover story is that I design corporate logos, but really I spend my evenings hijacking trucks. It's easier for me, you know, the dark skin. I'm half invisible at night."

"Let's stay cool," Ethan said. Ranjeet seemed oblivious to how tense everyone else was, how tired and scared. It was one thing to put on a brave face when the supermarket shelves were empty, but when there was still no food a week later, and the power was out, and the army had quarantined the city, and the weather was growing colder, and Thanksgiving dinner would be canned beans, that was something different. The social contract was straining at the seams, and righteous as Ranjeet's anger might be, it was the wrong response right now. "No one is making any accusations. We're all—"

"Why do you have this?"

Lou had gone to the coffee table and picked up the book Ethan had noticed earlier. He held it up so they could all see the cover. *I Am John Smith*.

Ah, shit.

"Excuse me?"

"Why do you have this?"

"You want to borrow it?"

"Last time I'm asking. Why do you have this?"

Ranjeet gave a thin smile. "I told you. I'm a terrorist."

"Lou, it's a free country," Jack said. "It's just a book."

"Yeah, a book by a murderer."

"He was framed," Ranjeet said. "If you caught the news every now and then, you'd know that. The government has dropped all charges against him."

Lou started reading where Ranjeet had left off. "'Here is a simple but ugly truth. Our politicians see us as little more than a medium to maintain their power. We are gasoline for an engine of corruption and selfishness. The men steering the nation care no more for us than you care for the gasoline you put in your car—gasoline which is consumed without a thought, so long as it gets the driver where he wants to be.'" He shut the book. "That sound American to you?"

"Yeah," Ranjeet said. "It sounds right on the nose."

Lou shook his head in disgust. "I was a marine. My father was a marine. He fought in Vietnam to keep this kind of crap out of our country."

Ranjeet laughed. "Is that why you think we were in Vietnam?"

"What are you saying?" Lou stepped forward.

"Guys." Ethan looked at Jack. His neighbor didn't move. "This is ridiculous—"

"You saying I'm stupid? That my father was stupid?" The man was squaring up, his gaze hard and chest out. He was four inches shorter than the abnorm but sported the barrel chest and thick arms of a weightlifter. "Is that what you're saying?"

Ranjeet's eyes darted, but he stood his ground. "Enough. It's time for you to leave."

"You people." Lou sucked air through his teeth. "You all think you're so goddamn smart. So much better than us."

Ethan stepped forward. "Come on, man." He put a hand on Lou's shoulder. The man shrugged it off.

"Which people?" Ranjeet asked, fire coming into his own voice. "Brilliants? Indian-Americans? Graphic designers?"

"Such a smart-ass." Lou held the book in one hand and tapped it against the abnorm's chest. "So tough." He tapped it again.

"I mean it. Get out of my house."

"Or what?" Another swing of the book.

Jack said, "Lou—"

Ranjeet slapped the book out of his hand. "I said, get out of my *house*." He stepped forward, put his hands against Lou's chest, and shoved.

Surprised, Lou staggered back. His foot came down on a toy truck and his leg flew up in front of him and his body canted, arms pinwheeling, and then he was falling. Ethan watched, his body frozen as his mind drew a line between Lou and the floor that went straight through the glass coffee table, and he thought that he should try to stop the fall, but thinking it was as far as he got.

The man hit the table backward, his weight smashing through, fragments of glass exploding outward as his body crashed through the top and then the shelf before hitting the shag carpet with a thud.

Ranjeet stepped forward, said, "Oh shit, I'm sorry—"

Lou gasped. He coughed, then rolled to one side. Glass crunching underneath him as he reached into the back of his waistband—

And came out with a gun.

The pistol was big, chrome, and the hand that held it was speckled with blood swelling from a dozen cuts. The barrel trembled, but it was aimed at Ranjeet's chest. The world had become a strange and terrible tableau that Ethan could see complete: Kurt with his mouth hanging open, Jack with hands on the sides of his head, Ranjeet frozen with one arm out, and Lou on the floor, curled up like he was doing crunches, the pistol in his right hand.

"You son of a bitch," Lou said.

As often happened, Ethan found himself watching with the eyes of an academic, noting the classic battle for tribal dominance as it escalated from threat to violence. One of the things that was beautiful about evolution was that it was at once messy and neat— messy in that it depended upon the randomness of mutation, a million false starts and blind alleys unguided by an architect's hand; neat because the rules were applied with inviolate certainty and brutal simplicity, genes and species tested against each other not on God's chalkboard but on the bloody battlefield that was life, in situations just like this one—

All of a sudden he realized that Lou's finger was tightening on the trigger. He was going to shoot a man over a disagreement and a flare of temper, shoot him dead in his own living room with his little girls upstairs.

Without giving himself time to think about it, Ethan stepped in front of Ranjeet.

Physically, he'd only moved three feet. But the shift in perspective was massive. Ethan found himself staring down the barrel of the gun. A view he'd seen in movie posters and the covers of mystery novels, but reality was very different.

Lou stared at him, his eyes narrow and nostrils flaring. "Get out of the way."

He wanted to, he really did, but all he did was shake his head. Afraid that any move too sudden or forceful might shatter the situation, might cause this hothead to do something truly stupid.

"Daddy!"

The cry came from the hallway. A pretty child in polka-dot pants and a sweater with a dolphin on it stared at them, something breaking in her wide, scared eyes.

"Baby, go upstairs," Ranjeet said. "Everything's okay. We were just talking, and Mr. Lou tripped."

"Is he okay?"

"Yes, sweetheart. Everything is fine."

Ethan stared at the dark perfect circle of the gun barrel, and beyond it, at the man's face, angry and scared and in pain and ashamed all at once.

Lou lowered the gun. Jack and Kurt hurried over, bent to help him up. He moved gingerly and groaned. Shards of glass tinkled against the carpet.

Ethan opened his mouth to apologize, to say the whole thing was a mess, an accident, but his friend spoke first.

"Get out of my house." Ranjeet cut his eyes from one of them to the other, landed on Ethan. If he was grateful, it didn't show in his eyes. "All of you. And don't come back. Ever."

The liberals and the intelligentsia and the media believe they've won. Together they brought down a president. And in order to do it, all they had to do was play a video. Well, bravo.

Do I deny that I authorized the attack at the Monocle? No. But defending a nation of three hundred million people requires tough decisions.

The murder of those people was morally reprehensible . . . and I would order it again. I stand before you as an American, as a patriot, as a president, and I tell you that the actions of that night saved lives.

I have committed sins. I have done terrible things, and I have ordered others to do them in my name. I have spilled blood, some of it innocent.

But when I stand before God Almighty, I know that he will look upon my actions and judge them righteous. For every life it was necessary to take, thousands were saved.

Protecting America is not a job for the squeamish.

I have done wrong, and I would do it again. For you and your children.

God bless you all. And God bless the United States of America.

—FORMER PRESIDENT HENRY WALKER,
TO THE FRIENDS OF THE NRA BANQUET

CHAPTER 15

"You look good," Cooper said. "This government agent thing doesn't work out, I think you've got a future as a rent-a-cop."

"Screw you." Quinn adjusted the blazer they'd boosted from the university security office half an hour before. "A polyester tie? Really?"

"That reflective strip down the side of the pants really brings the ensemble together."

"And once again, screw you."

The elevator stopped with a jolt, and the doors rattled open. They stepped into a concrete antechamber. A flyer taped to the wall had a profile shot of John Smith, chin up and staring into the future, the colors posterized into iconography, an illustrated style that made him look part politician, part rock star. The text read, "GWU WELCOMES ACTIVIST AND WRITER JOHN SMITH, AUTHOR OF THE *NEW YORK TIMES* BESTSELLING *I AM JOHN SMITH*."

Cooper and Quinn exchanged a smile, and then the two of them stepped into the underground parking garage. The deck was full, packed with economy cars sporting rusty side panels and bumper stickers for bands he'd never heard of. A few Volvos and Buicks bore faculty tags. They started up the ramp. Quinn pulled a black box from his pocket and took out two earpieces. Cooper tucked the tiny plastic in his ear. Two beeps sounded as the device synced. "Ladies?"

"Got you, boss," Valerie West said in his ear.

"Clear as a cock in the face," said Luisa Abrahams.

Quinn snorted a laugh. "As ever, you're a delicate flower." His voice was in stereo, the real man and the one in Cooper's ear.

"Hey, you want delicate, I'm sure some of these coeds could help out."

"I'll pass. Anything unusual?"

"I'm monitoring all activity from his team," Valerie said. "All SOP on their end."

"Good," Cooper said. He and Quinn parted ways as they rounded the corner, his partner walking up the center lane as Cooper moved to the front of the parked cars. It felt right to be back in action, relying on people he could trust with his life. The four of them had once been the top team in Equitable Services. Luisa was field ops, a five-foot-nothing who had faced off against men twice her size and possessed the most poetically filthy mouth he'd ever encountered. Valerie was a data rat who manipulated the stream of code that made up modern life. With Equitable Services on hiatus, they'd been reassigned to separate posts inside DAR, but both were too senior and too accomplished to be microman-aged; a short off-the-books gig should go unnoticed.

"Thanks again for the help," Cooper said.

"Anytime, boss. None of us ever doubted you, no matter what they said about the stock exchange."

Warmth bloomed in his chest. "Thanks. That means a lot."

"Hey, it's nice to have the band back together," Luisa said. "I'm going quiet; sing out if you need anything."

"Roger."

Cooper stepped up on a narrow curb and crouched low, slid-ing past the cars. Fifty yards ahead of them a black SUV was double-parked facing the exit. The engine was running, exhaust fogging in the cold. The windows were tinted, but they'd watched Smith arrive, seen his second security guard get out with him. It would be just the driver in the car. Armed, no doubt, and probably very good.

Cooper almost felt sorry for the guy.

Quinn strolled up the ramp with the bored ease of a campus security guard. Cooper moved in step with him but six cars back, staying down. Stealth wasn't his great strength, but the guard would be focused on Quinn. *Too bad you couldn't ask Shannon to help; she could sneak into Fort Knox.*

The thought sent a pang through him, and a memory of her body, naked and lithe, framed against the light of his refrigerator last night as she twisted the top off a beer and drank deep. As usual, she'd shown up without warning, and after the sex—he seemed only to get more hungry for her every time they touched, a kind of intoxication he thought had vanished with his teenage years—they'd talked. She had been circumspect with her language, but Cooper could tell that she'd been in action. It had stung a bit to realize she had no intention of telling him what she had been doing.

Of course, you're doing the same right now. This op will almost certainly mess up your relationship.

He'd almost told her. Last night, stroking her hair as they both drifted off, Cooper had almost told her that he believed John Smith was trying to start a war. After all, he'd trusted her with his life, with the lives of his children. But could he trust her to side with him instead of with her old friend and leader? He wasn't sure.

That's the trouble with dating a terrorist, Coop. So many tricky breakfast conversations.

He put her out of his mind. No time for distraction. Whatever was between them, whatever he hoped might be, he had a job to do.

Fix it, Natalie had said.

Quinn reached the driver's side of the SUV, rapped on the window. It slid down, and his partner said, "Excuse me, you're Mr. Smith's driver, right?"

Cooper dropped to his hands and knees, hurried past three more cars, and then crawled alongside the SUV. He'd be visible in the side mirror, but keeping the driver focused was Quinn's job.

Cooper slid the remote from his pocket and pressed the button. Newtech that Quinn had brought, an RFID decoder that quick-scanned through millions of codes. Funny, back in the days when cars had keys, they were a lot more secure. Now that everything worked at the touch of a button, all you needed was a master button.

"I understand that, sir, but you can't park here," Quinn said, the very model of disinterested officiousness.

With a click, the SUV's doors unlocked. Cooper yanked open the door handle and slid into the passenger's seat in one easy move.

The guard was good, already had his pistol in his lap. He spun, started to raise it, Cooper reading the move easily, the play of muscles in shoulders and chest. He didn't waste time struggling for the gun, just locked three fingers and stabbed them into the man's neck, spearing the carotid artery where it branched. The guard went instantly limp, the sidearm falling to the floorboards. Quinn leaned in the window with the hypodermic, jammed it into the guy's arm, and depressed the plunger. Pressure point knockouts didn't last, but the sedative would.

Together they dragged the guard out of the driver's seat. Quinn opened the back of the SUV, and they hoisted the guard inside and dumped him behind the seats. Cooper pulled up the cuff of the man's right arm, found the tight bracelet encircling his forearm.

"Valerie," he said, "he's got a biometric alarm."

"Yup." Her voice soft in his earpiece. "Just like we thought. I already hijacked it; it's broadcasting healthy vitals."

"You're a marvel."

Quinn walked to the front of the truck and hopped in the driver's seat. He picked up the guard's pistol, fluidly disassembled it, and tossed the pieces in the glove box. "You're on, Coop."

"Moving." He headed for the stairs. "Luisa, how's it going inside?"

"They're wrapping up. The target is modestly enduring a standing ovation."

"His body man?"

"Stage right, calm."

"Roger." He hurried up the back stairs of the subterranean parking deck and came out behind the auditorium. Even from outside he could hear the muffled roar of applause. The alley was cracked concrete and cigarette butts, the rear door rusted metal. There was another of the flyers taped to it. Cooper smiled, took a position leaning against the wall on the blind side of the door. In his ear, Luisa said, "Okay, we're wrapped in here. Elvis has left the stage."

Quinn said, "Are you sure he'll go out the back? He's an attention whore. Why not head out the front, soak up more adulation?"

"Easy," Cooper said. "He glad-handed for an hour, signed books for two, then did an hour on stage."

"So?"

"So, he's a chain-smoker. At this point he's jonesing for nicotine more than attention. Ten bucks says he'll be lighting up as he steps through the door."

"Seems thin—"

"Hold." The metal door started to open. Cooper moved with it, using it as—

The body man will come out first, check the alley, and then signal the all-clear.

Take him fast.

Spin around the door, grab Smith, yank him out, drop him.

—cover.

A chop across the windpipe, pulled just shy of fatal, staggered the burly guard, his hands flying to his throat. Cooper ignored his gasps, slid past him into the auditorium loading dock, and came face-to-face with a man with easy good looks and a cigarette in his lips, his hand holding a lighter flame an inch from the smoke.

"Hi, John," Cooper said, and then threw a right hook that snapped Smith's head sideways and sent the cigarette flying. He grabbed the man by the lapels of his expensive suit, turned, and hurled him into the security guard, both of them tumbling to the ground.

He bent, picked up the smoke, then stepped outside and let the door close behind him.

"Target acquired. Come pick us up."

■

The room was a portrait of urban decay, peeling walls covered in graffiti, the air thick with urine and rot. Cooper took a metal folding chair from the side wall and plunked it down in the center of the room. They undid the cuffs, then maneuvered Smith to the chair and forced him down. Quinn yanked off his hood.

John Smith blinked. He looked around the room, at the two of them. "This isn't a government facility."

Cooper locked eyes with him, smiled slightly, and shook his head.

The fear that flashed across the man's face came and went quickly. "You're not arresting me."

"No."

Cooper could see Smith processing the new data, reanalyzing. Wondering what was happening. He was, Cooper saw, living the kind of moment that happened to him exceedingly rarely—one he hadn't planned.

"You should know," Smith said, "that my security team will be here in seconds. I'm constantly monitored via biometric alarm."

"Like this one?" Cooper held up the bracelet he'd taken from the second guard, now sedated atop his buddy in the back of the SUV. "It's a good system. If you were to travel with a team of twenty people, you'd look like a third-world dictator. This way you can seem like a man of the people."

"Problem is," Quinn said, "it depends on your alarm sending accurate information."

Smith nodded. "So you've co-opted the signal. A good move. But one I anticipated, I'm afraid. My team has to communicate an all-clear code every—"

"Twenty minutes. We know."

The man's face tightened. "And that code changes every time."

"Yeah, a five-digit numeric that evolves algorithmically. It makes sense—you can't expect that a team will memorize a day's worth of codes every shift and never make a mistake, so instead you give them one code each day and a formula to apply. We're sending those okays," Cooper glanced at his watch, "right about now. Your bracelet is telling your security that you're still at the auditorium. In the can."

"And when I don't leave the bathroom? You don't think that will trigger—"

"You'll leave in a couple of minutes, and your bracelets will move around the theater. To your team, it looks like you decided to stick around and kiss babies." He leaned in, stared the man in the face. "No one is coming to save you."

Again, the flash of fear, again, mastered quickly. He might be a terrorist, but he wasn't a coward. Smith nodded. "It's good to see you, Cooper. Been a while."

"Three months. You've been busy, haven't you? I read your book."

"What did you think?"

"Specious self-aggrandizing nonsense dressed up in pompous prose. Tell me, did you already have it written when we sat on that peak in Wyoming and watched the sun rise?"

"Of course."

"All but the last chapters. The ones where you talk about the Monocle video and the president's involvement."

"No," John Smith said. "I had those written too."

Cooper laughed. "I appreciate you skipping the part where you pretend to be baffled and claim that you didn't send me off to serve your own agenda."

"I was perfectly honest with you. You knew that I had reasons."

"Right. You wanted to turn a pawn into a queen."

"Which I did." Smith rubbed at his wrists, then touched his cheek gingerly. It was swelling badly, the purpling already starting. "So. It's your meeting. What do you want?"

Quinn snorted, then moved behind Smith. Standard interrogation technique, let the man sweat the guy he couldn't see. Cooper said, "I want you to know that I can get to you. Anytime. There is nowhere that I can't find you, no security you can cloak yourself in, no rhetoric that will protect you. You're mine now. You belong to me."

"Huh." Smith reached slowly into his suit jacket, pulled out the cigarettes. Put one in his mouth and lit it with shaking hands. "Funny."

Cooper reached forward and plucked the smoke from his lips. He dropped it, then twisted his toe over the burning ember. "What is?"

"I expected more from you than a Gestapo routine. You just another bully in a suit?"

"I'm not the terrorist."

Smith shrugged, glanced over his shoulder, then back again. "I don't know what you're talking about. I'm an author. A teacher."

"Save it." Cooper leaned in until he could smell the man's sweat. "I know better. Let's put aside all your old sins, the bombings and assassinations. I know that you're behind the Children of Darwin." He spoke calmly and focused on details. Let his eyes soak up all the tiny clues, every tremble of muscle and pulse of blood. "I know that you ordered those trucks hijacked. That you ordered your soldiers to snatch innocent men and women, handcuff them on the side of the road, pour gasoline on them, and set them on fire."

On cue, Quinn leaned in and held his d-pad in front of Smith's face. Cooper couldn't see it from this side, but he knew the image, had stared at it for hours. The burned corpse of a thirty-nine-year-old truck driver named Kevin Temple, blackened skull locked in a scream, ruined arms still bound behind him.

Cooper never let his eyes move from Smith's face. He saw the pupils dilate, the orbicularis oculae tighten, the sudden flush of blood as the brain dumped adrenaline into his system. He imagined the other sensations the man would be feeling, the pressure at his bladder, the sweat soaking his armpits, the tingle in his fingers.

He saw it all, and in that moment, he knew that he was right. Smith had planned the attacks, had ordered the burnings. Had paralyzed three cities and left millions cold and hungry. He wanted a war.

John Smith said, "Got proof?"

Cooper smiled.

Then he clocked Smith in the other eye hard enough to knock him out of his chair. Before the terrorist hit the floor, Cooper leaned forward and slid the sidearm from Bobby Quinn's holster. The weapon felt right in his hand. A flick of the thumb disengaged the safety.

Smith moaned, then rolled onto his side, his eye squinted shut. "Because you need that now."

Cooper straightened his arm, aimed at center forehead.

"You're not a secret policeman anymore, Nick. You don't work for the DAR. You can't just murder anyone you want." He blinked, groaned again. "You shoot me, and you'll spend the rest of your life in prison. Once a month you'll see your children through plexiglass." Despite his obvious pain, Smith smiled. "Pull that trigger, and you prove the truth in everything I've said, everything I've fought for."

He's right. But what choice is there? Someone needs to stop him.

You may not have legal authority. But there's such a thing as moral authority.

Quinn said, "Boss—"

Cooper pulled the trigger.

The pistol bucked in his hand, that good firm punch. The shot was deafening in the small room, echoing off the crumbling walls and fading graffiti. John Smith lay on the broken concrete floor. The bullet had torn the smile right off his face.

Cooper squatted. He paused for a long moment. Then he said, "It's something, isn't it? A bullet missing your head by an inch, you never forget it. You'll feel that wind in your dreams."

He stood up, handed the pistol back to Quinn. "You're right. I'm not a midlevel government employee anymore. I'm the special advisor to the president of the United fucking States. I know what you're trying to do, and I won't allow it." He turned and started for the door. Over his shoulder, he said, "I'm coming for you, John."

Quinn snickered, said, "Enjoy the walk home, asshole."

Outside the burnout, the sun was shining on a cold blue afternoon. Broken glass tinkled under their dress shoes. Quinn side-armed the keys to the SUV into the sewer grate as they walked to the sedan they'd left waiting. Quinn started the car, and they pulled away, driving through the decay of Anacostia, DC's blighted southwestern section.

"Well," Quinn said, "that was bracing."

"Yeah." Cooper stared out the window, watching the blur of rundown houses and abandoned businesses. "You know, I almost didn't release it."

"Release what?"

"The video from the Monocle. After we took down Peters, I sat on a bench near the Lincoln Memorial. I had the footage of Peters and President Walker planning the attack on the Monocle. The leaders of the free world agreeing to murder seventy-three Americans. I had it loaded on my d-pad, ready to send, but I just . . . sat there. Trying to decide."

Quinn glanced over, said nothing.

"I knew what was right," Cooper continued. "The storybook kind of right, the things my dad taught me. That truth is its own reward, and honesty is always the best policy. But I kept thinking, what if I'm wrong? What if by sharing this, I make things worse?" He shook his head. "I don't know, Bobby. It's getting harder to tell which way is north. On paper, I did the right thing. But because I did, three cities are under terrorist control. Because I did, twenty men and women died screaming, burned alive."

"You can't take that weight on, man."

"Maybe. Or maybe I better learn from it."

They hit a stoplight, and Quinn took the moment to pull out a cigarette. He tapped it, spun it, and then slid it between his lips without firing it. "I'm not gonna lie, I'm glad you didn't shoot him back there. I'm not fond of prison." The light turned green, and he accelerated. "But there's no reason we couldn't find a way to do it so we don't get caught."

"No," Cooper said. "He's got us in check there. Even if we got away with it, he'd become a hero, a martyr. It would make things worse. No, what we need to do is expose him. Beat him without killing him."

"Outstanding. How?"

Cooper shrugged. "Still working on that part."

But I will find a way, John.

I know what you're trying to do. I'm certain of it.

And I won't allow it.

LIVE FEED FROM THE STREETS OF CLEVELAND!!

1:13 PM, THANKSGIVING DAY

Susan Skibba here, your favorite intrepid columnist, always up-to-the-minute wherever the scene is hottest.

I'm typing from the heart of the rock-and-roll city, where regular news is afraid to venture. Treading the mean streets to keep you up to date.

And dear readers, I have to tell you, it's getting ugly.

Today may be Thanksgiving, but this ain't no parade. It's been a week since the Children of Douchebags shut down the supermarkets, and by the look of this crowd, no one thought to buy a turkey in advance. And with the power out for a second day in a row, the thousands of people mobbing the streets all look cold, hungry, and pissed off.

I'm going to city hall to talk to the mayor. Wish me luck, kids!

1:48

Do you know the difference between a national guardsman and a Nazi?

Me either, dear reader, me either.

It took me twenty minutes to fight three blocks, and you all know Mama Sue can throw an elbow. Once I made it to City Small, I was shocked to see the whole building surrounded by armed soldiers. These aren't the "yes, ma'am, no, ma'am" soldiers Sue likes to get behind—or under, if the circumstances are right—these are storm troopers with automatic rifles and no discernible sense of humor.

I politely requested an interview with Mayor McCheese and was told to move along. Move along! As if the press could be stymied by a pimply teenager with a machine gun.

The scene here is grim. A sea of hungry people have surrounded the building and are yelling slogans and demanding food. Let's do a little man-on-the-street, shall we?

2:11

SUSAN SKIBBA, Intrepid Feedcaster: Excuse me, sir, tell me, how long have you been here?

Handsome in a Grungy Sort of Way: Since morning.

SSIF: And have you heard anything from city hall?

HGSW: The soldiers keep trying to break us up. But I'm not going anywhere. They want us to leave, they better give us some answers.

SSIF: What do you mean by "break you up"?

HGSW: Pushing, waving guns. I heard there was tear gas, but I haven't seen that.

SSIF: Is there anything you'd like to say to your government?

HGSW: Yeah. My family is out of food. My neighbors are out of food. It's cold. We need help. Now.

2:43

The air is chilly, but the body heat rising off this crowd must be changing weather patterns. There are thousands of people, but no apparent leaders. Everyone is surging and pushing against each other and the wall of soldiers. Still no word from—

Wait!

The front doors of city hall are opening, and someone is coming out. It looks like . . . it appears to be more soldiers, dressed differently. They are carrying heavy riot shields and wearing . . . oh shit, gas masks. Several of them are pointing devices at the crowd. Some sort of weapon?

They're firing . . .

2:49

Tear gas, it turns out, is painful. Luckily clever Mama Sue was near the back of the crowd and suffered only a whiff of the stuff.

I've climbed onto a planter outside an office building, and from my undignified perch I can see the gas swirling around the street. People are running in every direction, and those who fall are being trampled by the people behind them.

A group of tough-looking fellows wearing bandanas over their faces and carrying baseball bats and tire irons are pushing back toward the building. The soldiers have locked shields and are preparing to repel them.

Oh—oh God.

2:53

What started as a peaceful demonstration is becoming a bloodbath. People stagger around the streets, bleeding. Fist-fights are breaking out, people are stealing jackets. A woman lies in the gutter, not moving.

The little girl beside her is screaming, "Mommy!"

2:57

The crowd has blocked a police car. The officers are yelling through their speaker, telling everyone to back away.

Now a group of men have begun to rock the car, bouncing it on its axles, each bounce going higher.

The car just tipped onto its side. One of the officers has opened his door and is trying to crawl out—

Oh *shit*, the crowd pushed the car onto its roof. The officer who was escaping is—my God, it looks like his leg was caught under the car. He's screaming.

Men are surrounding him, they'll pull him free. Or—

JESUS!

3:02

Chaos. Smoke rising, can't see from where. People howling. They've become a mob, it's gonr crazy here, no one actng like people, they've become animals, throwng rocks and bottles. There's no aim or purpose just people falling apart, angre turning to rage.

father is holding boy and running, boy crying, terrified.

Woman with torn blouse, blod on her face.

Rock shattering window in cty hall

What was that sound?

Not gas. That sounded like

CHAPTER 16

Gunfire. Not sure from where. But more than one.

I'm scared.

i'll try to get out of here. So many peple, all the hate.

How can ths be happning here?

If I don't make it, tell my mother I love her.

Tell peopel about ths. Don't let it be covred up. don't let them—

Ethan's d-pad went blank.

He jerked, blinked. He'd been staring at the screen so intently that his eyes were dry.

He pressed the button to turn it back on—nothing. Out of juice. Funny, he couldn't remember the last time he'd actually run the thing down to nothing. It felt strangely crippling, his connection to the world reduced to a useless piece of composite fabric.

A boom like a crack of distant thunder came and went.

The writer had said everything was happening around city hall. That was only a mile and a half away. Ethan folded the d-pad and slid it in his pocket. It was cold in the house, and his limbs were stiff. He walked to the front door, stepped onto his porch. Bleak gray skies. Thanksgiving weather, perfect if there was a fire burning and a house full of family and the smells of cooking food.

Less perfect wearing three sweaters over an empty belly. Less perfect when columns of smoke rose in dark curls to the east. Less perfect as military helicopters hovered like hummingbirds above the downtown area.

Strange. He'd been plugged in, reading about things that were happening just up the road. Modern living right there.

"What was that sound?" Amy had joined him on the porch, Violet in her arms.

"A car blowing up, I think. There's a riot downtown."

"Over food?"

"Over everything."

Amy nodded. One of the things he loved about his wife, she didn't panic, didn't go silly over bad news. She just worked the problem. He could see her doing that now, the gears of her head turning. "It's been a week. If they were going to get food in, it should have been here by now."

He nodded. They stood and watched the smoke rise. Another boom sounded. Violet stirred, moaned softly, and then went back to sleep.

Amy said, "Remember that time we were driving to California? We were in one of those boring states where nothing changes, losing our minds, and we played that game."

"Sure. The zombie apocalypse." Amy had looked over at him and said, *So what do we do when the dead rise?* They'd spent hours talking about what to pack, where to go. How they'd want to hit a camping store, load up: water purification tablets, first aid supplies, matches, good knives, a tent, a shotgun and ammo if possible. Whether an isolated farmhouse would be ideal, or whether it would be better to steal a boat. How the key would be to act fast, to recognize that things had changed. It was a universal fantasy, a game everyone had played to while away the hours.

"Well, it's not zombies. But it's time to start thinking that way."

He looked over at his wife, their daughter in her arms, standing on the porch of their lovely home, the first they'd owned together. A place they'd bought for Violet before she even existed, imagining her playing in the backyard, walking to school. Their little slice of the American pie.

"Cleveland is not Manhattan," he said, slowly. "You can't hold a couple of bridges and tunnels and lock everyone in."

"Right. Before we tried the highway. Probably the first thing they closed. But they can't watch everything all the time."

"They can watch the streets."

"Then we get off the streets. They can't lock arms around the whole metro area."

"I saw helicopters," he said. "They probably have more now. They'll be using them to watch for people leaving."

"It's a lot of space. And helicopters make noise. We pack light, drive as far as we dare, and then we walk."

"You know what we're talking about, right? Abandoning everything. Becoming refugees."

"Better that than waiting for the riots to reach us. 'Normal' is gone, hon. We're on our own."

He thought of the day before, the insanity of it. How a conversation had turned to violence over a few words and a book.

Mostly he thought of Lou, lying in a halo of broken glass, a gun in his hand.

"Let's get packed."

■

He'd have laughed if he had the heart.

When they'd tried to leave a couple of days ago, they had crammed the Honda to the roof. Two suitcases filled with clothing and luxuries, Violet's travel swing, a lockbox of documents, on and on. All things that seemed necessary.

Funny how flexible a standard "necessary" was turning out to be.

They'd culled all the obvious stuff quickly. If they had any chance at getting out, it would be on foot, and that meant none of the plastic crap, the baby accessories that had taken over their home. No pack-and-play, no bathtub. No picture books, no monitor, no musical seahorse.

Food. Water. His tent, musty from disuse. Winter jackets and good walking shoes and a couple of changes of clothes. Matches and a flashlight and batteries. A first aid kit. Diapers and wipes and rash cream. Sleeping bags.

He found his old backpack in the basement, the same one he'd worn across Europe two decades before. It took three minutes to realize it was too small.

Okay. No spare clothes, just socks. The bulk of the diapers went next. They were light, but they took up a lot of space. He kept twenty, which was maybe three days' worth. Batteries were the opposite problem, little space but too much weight, and he swapped the big flashlight for a small Maglite and AA batteries.

The canned food would last but weighed a ton. He trimmed it down to the remaining evaporated milk for Violet, the jerky, a few cans of soup, and a container of peanut butter. A can opener.

One sleeping bag; they'd have to share, use the winter coats as blankets.

Amy joined him as Ethan was hoisting the pack onto his back and tightening the straps. Forty pounds, maybe? A solid load, but doable. It would be better if they could both manage full packs, but one of them needed to be wearing their daughter.

"What about Gregor?"

"Shit." Ethan looked at the cat, splayed out on an easy chair, oblivious. His buddy for years, lap-warmer and near-constant companion. "We can't take him."

"We could try," she said, her voice empty of conviction.

For a moment, he considered it. Bringing the little guy, bearing him in their arms as they walked. Packing food for him.

The key to surviving the apocalypse is to recognize that things have changed.

Ethan knelt down beside the cat, rubbed his head. "I'm sorry, buddy. I'm afraid you're going to have to take care of yourself for a little while." Whenever Gregor saw birds and squirrels, the cat went nuts. He'd finally get his chance at them. Ethan stood up before emotion could paralyze him, opened the back door and the screen, and left them agape.

"Is that everything?"

"Almost." Amy held up the gun.

He looked at her, at it. Nodded. "Let's go."

They threw the bags in the back of the Honda, strapped Violet into her car seat, and then got in themselves. Ethan stared out the driver's side at the house. *Normal really is gone.*

"Ethan." Amy pointed.

Jack Ford was walking toward them. Lou was two steps behind.

Something cold settled in his belly. For a moment, he just stared. Then he reached over to the glove box and withdrew the pistol. He set it on his lap as he rolled the window down.

His neighbor stared at him, a haunted look in his eyes. "You guys are leaving?"

"No. Just going for a drive." The lie coming awkwardly. "See if we can find some food."

Jack's eyes flicked to the back of the truck; he must have seen them putting the backpack in. Lou moved up alongside, all tension and clenched muscles. Ethan's hand on the gun felt wet.

"Listen," Jack said. "About yesterday."

"We've got to go." He put the truck in reverse.

"Wait." Jack put a hand on the doorframe. His other hand was behind his back. Ethan tensed. Voices screamed silently in his head.

"Here," Jack said, and raised his other hand, revealing a small cardboard box. He held it out. "Just in case."

Ethan looked at him, then at Lou, the man's face expressionless. The same face he'd seen on the other side of a gun barrel.

Then he reached out and took the box of ammunition. "Thanks."

"Thank you," Lou said. "I almost. Yesterday."

In the backseat, Violet let out a sudden startled cry, and all four of them jumped. Ethan said, "We've got to go."

"Good luck," Jack said. "We'll watch your house."

"Keep an eye out for my cat, would you?"

"Sure."

Ethan rolled up his window and pulled away. The two men stood in his rearview mirror, and beyond them, columns of smoke rose while helicopters darted between them.

Was I just prepared to shoot my neighbor?

Yes. Yes, he had been.

No more normal.

CHAPTER 17

On the monitor, Cleveland was burning.

Cooper watched the president watch it. Lionel Clay's face was drawn, his shoulders tight beneath his dress shirt. He stood like a man caught in a spotlight.

"The situation's getting worse." Owen Leahy pressed a button, and the image shifted, an overhead view of a government building. Cold stone and columns, it was a gray island encircled by a sea of people, thousands of them, a mass of rough currents that formed no pattern. The secretary of defense continued, "City hall is surrounded. The national guardsmen who were already on scene have secured the building, but they're having trouble getting reinforcements in. Cleveland PD has a riot team en route, but the mob is making it slow going."

"Where did the fire start?" The president spoke without looking from the screen.

"The east side, 55th and Scoville. A tenement building, but it's spreading fast. There are twelve square blocks burning, another twenty at risk in the next hour."

"Fire crews?"

"They're spread thin, and they're tired. There have been multiple fires every day for the last two weeks. This is the first that's gotten out of control. Crews are focusing on containment, with every station sending men, but the mob is—"

"Making it slow going."

"Yes, sir."

"Get the mayor on the phone."

"We've been trying." Leahy left the rest unsaid.

"The Children of Darwin are behind this?"

"They're certainly involved. But there are thousands of rioters. It's out of control." Leahy pressed another button, and the angle shifted, zooming in.

A camera drone, Cooper figured, unmanned and circling a mile above the scene. The video showed the front line of a pitched battle, men and women screaming at each other, whirling, spinning. A man in a leather jacket swung a baseball bat. A teenage girl, her face a bloody mess, leaned between two people pushing to get out of the fray. A white guy stood over a black man, kicking him savagely. A group rocked a car, bouncing and shoving and bouncing until it tilted up on one side, held for a moment, and toppled.

"The whole city is like this?"

"A lot of people are out protecting their property; others are just watching. But everything within half a mile of Public Square is a mess. Intelligence estimates there are as many as ten thousand rioters in the downtown area. And the power is still out. It will get worse when night falls."

"Why didn't the mayor call in more police right away?"

"We don't know, sir. But at this point, even if riot squads make it to city hall, they won't be able do much more than protect the staff. The mob is just too big."

"The Democrats are going to have a field day with this," Marla Keevers said. The chief of staff had a way of turning the word *Democrats* into an obscenity. "You're going to take a huge—"

"I don't care about politics right now, Marla. One of my cities is on fire. Is this part of a larger attack?"

"We don't know, sir."

"Why not?"

"It's chaos down there, Mr. President." The secretary of defense paused, then said, "Sir, it's time to take aggressive action.

We should assume that this is the first step in an attack, maybe a national one."

The president said nothing.

"Sir, we need to act."

Clay stared at the screen.

"Mr. President?"

And as Nick Cooper stood beside a glowing Christmas tree in the Oval Office of the White House, watching the world begin to fall apart, he found himself thinking of something his old boss had said just before Cooper threw him off a twelve-story building.

"Sir? What do you want us to do?"

His one-time mentor had said, *If you do this, the world will burn.*

"Mr. President?"

The monitor had shifted back to a wide aerial view. The fire had spread, and thick smoke blotted out half the city.

"Sir?"

President Clay just stared at the monitor. Cooper could sense the tension in him, the fear. The man was staring like everything was a dream and if he concentrated hard enough he might wake up.

"All right." Owen Leahy turned to Marla Keevers. "The National Guard isn't enough. I'm ordering all military forces to active alert, and pulling secondary divisions from overseas to reinforce positions across the country. We need to be prepared to apply overwhelming force."

Keevers nodded.

"We should immediately arrest John Smith, Erik Epstein, and any other known leaders. Also, detain all tier-one abnorms who are under surveillance by the DAR—"

"I'm all for arresting Smith," Cooper said. "But you're talking about thousands of people."

"There are protocols in place to establish regional internment camps." Leahy turned back to Keevers. "In addition, effective immediately, we're activating the Monitoring Oversight Initiative. We can't wait until next summer. If we had done it when the measure passed, these cities might not be under attack. Begin with tier ones and move down the ladder. I want a tracker in the neck of every abnorm by Christmas."

Cooper couldn't believe what he was hearing. Not just the content, but the fact that Leahy was making these decisions on his own. "You can't do that."

"It's already law, Mr. Cooper. We're just moving up the timetable."

"No, I mean *you* can't do that." Cooper stepped forward, purposefully too close. "Unless you're launching a coup d'état."

The secretary bristled. "Watch your tone."

"Watch your own." He stared the man down. Knew he was being insubordinate and offensive and didn't give a shit. Some moments a person had to stand up. "I haven't heard the president give any of these orders."

"This nation needs strong leadership right now. Any more delay and things are going to get worse."

"I agree. But you're not the president." He turned to Clay. "Sir, if you think things are bad now, just wait. Rounding up citizens and activating the MOI means declaring war on our own people."

"We're already at war." Leahy gestured to the screen.

"That's a riot, not a war. And you can't save America by imprisoning all the Americans." He wanted to yell, to slap the desk, to grab them by the shoulders and shake them and make them wake up. "This will galvanize the terrorist cause. It will turn everyone against each other. This is what will lead to war."

Leahy said, "I've had enough. We appreciate your service, Mr. Cooper, but it's no longer necessary. You can go."

"I don't work for you."

As if on cue, Clay coughed and stirred to life. He tore himself from the monitor. His eyes darted back and forth between them. "Nick—"

Cooper cut him off. "Sir, this is a bad idea, and I think you know it, and I think that's why you recruited me in the first place. You knew that someone would be standing here telling you to start a civil war. And you weren't sure you'd be strong enough to say no."

"*Hey.*" Keevers's voice cracked like a whip. "Enough."

"It's all right." Clay's voice was weak. "Go ahead, Nick. Say what's on your mind."

"Sir, we all agree something has to be done. But not this. I'm not being idealistic, I'm being practical. We'll lose. We'll lose everything."

"So what do you suggest?"

"We shift our focus. Instead of dealing with the terrorists, we deal with the gifted." He'd been wrestling with the problem ever since he and Quinn left John Smith in the burnout. If he couldn't just kill Smith—and he was starting to regret that he hadn't—they needed a way to cut him off at the knees. To change the game so that it wasn't Smith against the repressive government, but Smith against Americans. That meant bringing in another player. Someone with clout and influence and money. "We go to Erik Epstein."

Marla Keevers scoffed. Leahy said, "Are you serious? The man doesn't even exist. He's just an actor. John Smith and the Children of Darwin might be pulling his strings. There is no Erik Epstein."

"Yes," Cooper said. "There is. I've met him."

All of a sudden, the room was very quiet. Clay and Leahy and Keevers all stared.

Cooper said, "In the New Canaan Holdfast in Wyoming three months ago. Erik Epstein is very real, and very much in charge. He's just private. The man you called an actor is actually his brother Jakob. The two of them faked Jakob's death a decade ago so that he could become Erik's public face."

President Clay sat down on the edge of his desk. He rubbed at his chin. "Well, Nick. You are full of surprises."

"He trusts me." That was a lie of epic proportions; he'd betrayed Epstein. Cooper had agreed to kill John Smith, and instead he'd not only spared him, he'd unwittingly served Smith's agenda. Because of Cooper's decisions, the New Canaan Holdfast was in greater danger than ever before, and there was nothing in the world that Epstein cared about more than his little realm in the desert.

Still, not much mileage in them knowing the world's richest man is pissed at you. "Let's reach out to him. Ask him to join us in calming the nation."

Leahy said, "What possible good would that—"

"It would reframe the discussion. In the 1960s, the government legitimized Dr. King's movement by bringing him into the discussion. That put radicals like Malcolm X and Huey Newton on the outside. Suddenly it wasn't blacks against whites, it was pacifism against violence. You were a history professor, sir. You know that this has to be the way."

Clay stared at the Christmas tree, a Victorian mess of bows and baubles.

Marla Keevers said, "Something else it does." She turned to the president. "It gives us a target."

Cooper said, *"What?"*

"We don't have any way to reach the Children of Darwin. But if we were to work with Epstein and the NCH, to offer them support on the condition that terrorism cease . . ." She shrugged. "It's a win-win. Either they get the situation under control, or we have legitimate reason to strike the stronghold of abnorm power."

"Wait, that's not what I—"

Clay stood up. "All right. Nick, pack your bags. You're going to New Canaan as our ambassador. Convince Epstein to join us, help stop these attacks, and return our cities to us."

"Sir, I'm not a diplomat. I don't know the first thing—"

"You know Erik Epstein. He trusts you."

"I—yes, sir." Cooper felt dizzy.

Clay moved around the other side of the desk. "Meanwhile, Owen, make the troop deployments. Bring nonessential military home, and reinforce all domestic bases. And just in case, prepare a plan for concerted military action against New Canaan Holdfast."

"Sir, what about the Monitoring Oversight Initiative? We should still move that—"

"We're going to try this way first."

Leahy started to argue, caught himself, and swallowed the words with a visible effort. He shot a look of purest poison in Cooper's direction. "Yes, sir."

Clay turned to him. "It's on you now, Nick. You had better succeed."

The president was too gentle a man to add the unspoken next sentence, but in Cooper's head, Drew Peters's voice finished it for him.

Because if you don't, the world will burn.

CHAPTER 18

"So now you're supposed to save the day?"

Natalie had an unsarcastic way of saying things that made the bald fact of the statement itself seem ridiculous. Usually Cooper enjoyed it, but after standing in the Oval Office watching a city burn while the president sat idle, it irked.

"It's not like that. It's not me against everybody. I'm just . . ."

"Putting on a cape and flying in?" She stacked dirty plates, piling silverware atop. The smell of turkey and stuffing and cranberry sauce made his empty stomach tighten.

"Trying to do what you said. I'm trying to fix it."

She turned and walked for the kitchen, and he followed. "Oh, Nick," she said over her shoulder. "No pressure, huh?"

"Look, I'm not asking you for anything. I'll handle it by myself."

"You're kind of proving my point, hon."

"Natalie . . ."

"When are you leaving?"

"Tomorrow. I'll come by in the morning to say good-bye to the kids. I figured I would—"

Natalie set down the plates with a thump. "Tomorrow."

"Yes. I figured I'd make pancakes—where are you going?"

She didn't answer, just left the kitchen, went through the dining room, and opened the hall closet. Stretching, she pulled down a suitcase.

"Natalie?"

She ignored him, just slung the suitcase and climbed the stairs. At a loss, he followed.

The bedroom had once been theirs, a place they'd read books and made love and talked about the kids. But since the divorce, he'd been in it only once, to help her move a dresser. She'd shuffled and redealt the space, putting the bed under the windows and repainting. His ex-wife had the suitcase open on the bed and was piling clothes beside it.

"What are you doing?"

"Packing."

"Look, that's sweet, but I'm going alone."

"Like hell you are." She spoke mildly, but as a woman who rarely swore, her word choice had power.

"Natalie—"

"Nick, be quiet." She turned to look at him. He could see her wanting to cross her arms, see her making the choice not to. "Tonight was Thanksgiving dinner."

"Hey, look, I'm sorry I missed it, but it's not like I was drinking at a bar. My job—"

"I know," she said. "I'm not mad. In fact, I'm proud of you. I'm just saying, tonight was Thanksgiving, and you couldn't be here. That's one less Thanksgiving Todd and Kate will have with you."

He hadn't thought about it in those terms. Cooper leaned against the wall.

"The last time you went away you were gone for six months," Natalie continued. "I know it was for the best possible reason, but the kids are just now getting used to having you back in their lives. They deserve not to have their dad vanish again. And you deserve to get to be a father."

"You know I want that."

"I do," she said. "That's why we're coming with you. This is something we can do. You're not going undercover to kill someone. You're the ambassador for the president of the United States. That means that there will be protection. It will be as safe as anywhere else is right now. Plus, it will be good for the kids. Kate will get to be in a place where she doesn't feel different than everyone else. And Todd will experience the other side of things, to see that the world is bigger than the schoolyard. We're coming with you."

Cooper knew his ex-wife. She was kind and smart and gentle, and her words were more aligned with her intent than most anyone he'd ever met.

She was also as moveable as the Rock of Gibraltar when she set her mind to something. No argument, no stormy sentiment, no tidal pull could shake her. Short of cold-cocking her, there was no way to make her stay.

"People ask too much of you. Your father, the army, Drew Peters, now the president. Even me. You don't always have to be the lone wolf. It will be good for the kids to see their dad trying to save the world. It will be good for us as a family."

There was a slight emphasis on the last word, a tiny inflection that most people might have missed. One with a world of possibility behind it. He remembered sitting inside the fort they'd built in the living room when Natalie had kissed him. That hadn't been a friendly peck. It had been . . . well, maybe not a declaration of intent, but certainly a statement of possibility.

When it had been good, their marriage had been very good. And he'd always been proud that when it stopped working, they had both recognized it. Had been able to acknowledge that though they loved each other, they were no longer right together, and they'd been able to part without rancor. He loved her, always would. But there was love and there was being in love.

Has something changed for her?

It was odd to think that the things he had done in the last year might actually have drawn her closer to him. They had been apart most of that time, and there had been the horrifying night that Drew Peters had kidnapped her and the kids. On paper, it should have pushed her away.

But in reality, all of the things he'd done had been to protect his children. Plus, he had made the choices she would have wanted him to make, right down to revealing the truth, despite the cost of that action.

Cooper had a theory about personality. Most people considered personality to be a singular identity. Malleable, sure, but essentially cohesive. But he tended to see people as more of a chorus. Every stage in life added a voice to that chorus. The different iterations of himself—lonely military brat, cocky teenager, faithful soldier, young husband, dedicated father, relentless hunter—they all existed within him. When he saw a ten-year-old girl, there was a ten-year-old boy inside him that thought she was pretty. Just one voice in a chorus of dozens, which was what marked the difference between healthy people and broken ones; in the broken ones, the inappropriate voices held an inappropriate number of spaces.

And the man who had been in love with Natalie had added a lot of voices to his personality. In moments like this one, that segment of the choir sang loudly.

He realized that he was staring into her eyes, and that she was staring back. He thought of that night in the space station, the way her lips had felt against his, the wine-sweet taste of her tongue—

THUD, THUD, THUD.

They both jerked upright. "Are you expecting—"

"No."

He stood, moved swiftly down the hall. Another THUD, THUD, THUD at the front door. His sidearm was in a lockbox in the car, too bad. He moved down the stairs lightly, heard Natalie following him. What was this? Someone from the White House? Something worse?

"Cooper! I know you're in there." The voice was muffled, but perfectly recognizable.

Yep. Something worse.

He unlocked the door, opened it. Shannon stormed in, poking her finger into his chest. She wore a leather jacket and an angry aura, the muscles in her neck bunched. "You're a colossal prick, you know that?"

"What's wrong?"

"What's *wrong*? I spoke to John, that's what's wrong, you fascist—" She stopped, her glance going over his shoulder, to the dining room table, the remnants of Thanksgiving dinner spread out across it. Her posture tightened. "Shit."

"Shannon," Natalie said, her voice level. "Are you all right?"

"Yes, I'm—I'm sorry, I forgot it's Thanksgiving. I didn't mean to intrude."

"You're always welcome here. Come in."

"I don't mean to—"

"It's fine. Really." Natalie turned to him. "Why don't you guys talk in the living room? I'll give you some privacy. I've got a lot to do if we're leaving tomorrow." Her smile was as perfect and chilly as if it were carved from marble. She turned and went back up the stairs.

"Shit," Shannon repeated.

"Come on." He let go of the door, walked into the other room. "You want some turkey?"

"No. I don't know what I was thinking, banging like that." She shook her head. "I totally forgot it was Thanksgiving."

"It's okay," he said. "So did I." Funny how the life they lived made it easy to forget the things that defined everyone else's. It was one of the reasons he and Shannon had the connection they had. They both lived apart.

She followed him into the living room. "Where are they going?"

"What?"

"Natalie said she had a lot to do if they were leaving."

Actually, she said "we," which was a little stiletto on the way out. The brutality with which women waged war always surprised him. "I'm going to New Canaan tomorrow to talk to Erik Epstein. Natalie and the kids are coming with me."

Shannon said, "Oh."

"So." He flopped down in an armchair. "You were calling me a fascist?"

Her eyes flashed, and whatever social awkwardness she'd been feeling fell away. "You kidnapped him? Put a gun to his head? Beat him up?"

He met her eyes. "Yup."

"That's it? '*A-yup*?'" she said in her best hick voice. "That's all you have to say, honey?"

"No, dear. You want to hear something funny? Yesterday I sat in a meeting about a massive security breach. A terrorist snuck into the DAR and stole a huge amount of data. Most of it about genetic research centers and bio-labs, the kind of privately funded, quasi-legal places that develop chemical weapons and customized viruses." He leaned forward. "And there I am, thinking, 'Huh—the terrorist on the security cameras looks just like my girlfriend.'"

"Oh Jesus, Nick, I wasn't after bioweapons."

"What were you after?"

"A magic potion."

He shook his head. "Cute."

"I was working. You know the kind of work I do."

"For terrorists."

"For my cause."

"Goddammit, you can't put me in that position!"

She regarded him coldly. "Just because we've had sex a couple of times doesn't mean I owe you anything."

"And it doesn't mean I can't bring you into the DAR in handcuffs."

"That's great. So when you need my help, it's all love and trust. And the moment you don't anymore, you're ready to arrest me?" She crossed her arms. "I saved your children's lives, Cooper. Don't you ever forget it."

He started to retort, caught himself. Took a breath. "You're right. I'm sorry about that last bit."

"I knew us dating was a bad idea. But I told myself that even though we were on opposite sides, I could trust you to do the right thing." She shook her head. "But you're still a storm trooper at heart, aren't you?"

"No." He felt silly sitting in the chair and wanted to stand up, but thought it would look even sillier. "No, I'm just a guy trying to stop a war."

"Nick Cooper, one-man army. Judge and jury."

"Said the woman who stole government secrets. Tell me, Shannon, what are you blowing up today? How many innocents are going to die in your next adventure?"

She stared at him, a storm raging inside her. He could see the fire and fury of it, the lightning flashes and howling winds. "I'm going to West Virginia. I'm going to do the best thing I've ever done. And you know the funny part? If you'd asked me about it this morning, I would have told you everything."

"What's in West Virginia?"

"Watch the news." She spun on her heel and stalked out. "And fuck off."

Before he could respond, he heard the door open and then slam shut.

Shit. He hadn't meant for things to get that far; angry as he was about what she'd done, she had the same reasons to be angry at him. They had both been keeping secrets, and he'd expected a fight about it. Just not right now, not here. He rubbed at his eyes. *Shit, shit, shit.*

After a moment, he heard Natalie enter the room. She leaned against the wall, a dish towel in her hands and the ghost of a smile on her lips. "Oh, Nick."

"What?"

She shook her head. "You haven't lost your touch with women, have you?"

EDUCATING THE GIFTED CHILD: A TEACHER'S MANUAL FOR ACADEMY INSTRUCTORS

Section 9.3: On Pity

Being an instructor at a tier one academy is a privilege for which few are qualified. It requires not only the most advanced educational training, but also a sense of mission rooted in unshakable personal discipline.

Humans are conditioned to love children. It is difficult to see a child suffering, whether the harm is physical, emotional, or psychological. That is natural and right.

However, a child who has been burned in the past will not reach for a flame. A minor injury prevents major ones.

In other words, pain is a teaching tool.

Pity undercuts that education. Short-sighted and destructive, pity trades a brief benefit for long-term damage. When we see a child reaching for a flame, pity tells us to stop him. To protect him.

Instead, we must stoke the fire. We must encourage the child to burn himself. If need be, we must manipulate him into doing so.

How else will he learn that fire is not for him?

For the good of the academy, for the good of the world, and for the good of the children themselves, it is your duty to purge yourself of pity.

CHAPTER 19

The sun was setting, and it made no difference at all.

Heavy clouds quilted the world as Ethan turned off the Honda. For a moment they sat in silence, just the ticking of the engine and the quiet rasp of Violet's breathing in the backseat. The parking lot was half full; he wouldn't have guessed that Thanksgiving was a big day for church, but it seemed the good people of Independence felt differently. Or maybe it had nothing to do with the holiday; maybe it had more to do with what was happening to the world.

He looked over at Amy. "Zombie apocalypse?"

She nodded.

"Okay," he said, and opened the car door.

Independence Presbyterian was a funky A-frame shingled in brown, with an old-fashioned spire rising from one side. Located just off the square of the quiet suburb—Independence called itself a town, but seriously, come on—it seemed a good place to leave the CRV. Who messed with cars in a church parking lot?

Ethan's best guess was that if the government wanted to quarantine Cleveland, they would use the highways as rough boundaries. I-80 was ten miles south, but since he didn't know exactly where the cordon would start, it was boots and backpacks from here. Twenty-two miles, much of it through national park land, with Cuyahoga Falls as the promised land.

Now there's *a phrase that may never have been uttered.*

Ethan shouldered the backpack and cinched the waistband tight to distribute the weight. Muscle memory gave him a flash of strolling through Amsterdam, bicycles and cobblestones, the sun glinting off canals four thousand miles and a million years away. He tucked the pistol into his belt.

Violet was awake, the straps of her car seat tight across her little round chest. "Hello, my love. Want to go on an adventure?" If she had any feelings about the idea, she kept them to herself. Ethan hoisted her out. For a moment he held her to his chest, the sweet weight of her, the steady breathing and milk smell, and when he slipped her into the carrier Amy wore, her absence made him colder.

He and his wife looked at one another. Her smile was taut, as if she were trying to convince herself. Ethan stepped forward and wrapped his arms around her, around both his girls, Violet the center of their sandwich, and for a moment they stood and breathed.

It would be dark soon.

"Let's go."

Hand in hand, they started walking.

■

Twenty minutes later, they left the road.

A dense forest of pine trees backed up to a row of two-story houses, their neatly mown lawns tapering into dirt and soft needles. He led his family along that terminator, skirting the edge of backyards. The sky's bruised glow made silhouettes of the houses. He saw candles inside some of them, could imagine families huddling around fireplaces. The temperature was falling, but the effort of humping the pack kept him warm.

"Twenty-two miles," he said.

"Nothing," she replied.

"A little stroll."

"Not even a marathon."

A high privacy fence on one of the properties forced them farther into the forest. He walked ahead. The trees were dark geometries against the fading light. The needles stuck to his down jacket, and a sap smell rose. They walked in silence, just the sounds of their footfalls and the susurrus of branches swaying in the wind.

When it grew too dark to see, he took out the flashlight. The stark light blanched the trees. He cupped his hand around the head of it to muffle the beam, fingers glowing Halloween red.

A shift in the wind brought a distant siren's wail. Nightfall would have made the riots worse. He could imagine cars burning on Lakeside Avenue, the smell of scorched rubber and the crash of shattering windows and the screams of the wounded.

■

The forest grew denser. Ethan bushwhacked through pine boughs, holding them for Amy and Violet to walk past before he let them snap back. He relied on the compass to keep them heading south. It would have been easier to follow the line of houses, but with tensions running so high, he was afraid someone might take a shot at people creeping their backyard.

Violet woke with a cry, not loud, but startling. Amy rubbed her back through the carrier, whispered, "Shh, it's okay, go back to sleep," but instead his daughter sucked in a breath and released it as a howl.

"She needs a change," Amy said.

Ethan unslung his pack, then spread out his jacket as a changing table. "Come here, little one."

Amy held the flashlight while he swapped the diapers. Violet's poop was the color and texture of mustard, and smellier than usual from the condensed milk. She gurgled as he worked.

When he finished, he straightened, let his daughter lie on her back and kick. Funny, all he knew about evolution and the life cycle, and he had still been caught unprepared by the reality.

It was one thing to know academically that it took years for the brain and body to develop, and another to witness the slow progress of her eyes focusing, her muscles gaining control. He felt sometimes like a gym teacher substitute-teaching a biology class; he was reading the same book as his pupil, and only about a week ahead.

Amy had a hand planted against her lower back to stretch. The flashlight beam wobbled as she moved, a tiny circle of light surrounded by crushing darkness. "How far do you think we've come?"

"A mile and a half, two, maybe. Are you getting tired?"

"No. It's just we're going so slow."

"Better to be safe."

"I suppose." She shrugged, then smiled at him. "Hey, something I meant to say earlier."

"What's that?"

"Happy Thanksgiving."

■

An hour later, as he looked over his shoulder to check on his girls, something grabbed Ethan's foot. He stumbled, yanked, tried to bring his other leg forward in time, but the weight of the pack threw him off. He fell, and his knee slammed into a rock. The flashlight skittered off into the woods.

"Ethan!"

"I'm okay," he said between gritted teeth. He cursed, sucked in a breath, cursed again. His fingers explored his knee, every touch sending a zing, though the bulk of the pain was already receding to a hard ache. It didn't feel like his jeans had been torn, but he couldn't be sure in the dark—oh shit.

"The flashlight. Where did it go?"

"Oh shit." Amy was just a dark shape amidst darkness as she shuffled around, kicking at the needles with her feet. After a moment he heard the sound of the metal body off her shoe, and she bent down, then sighed.

"Broken?"

"Looks like. How about you?"

"Just banged up." He planted a hand and rose slowly.

"Can you walk?"

He nodded, then realized she couldn't see him. "Yes." Ethan looked around, saw nothing but shades of black. The sky was only slightly brighter, the thick clouds hiding the moon and stars. "But I don't think we can keep going this way."

"We could camp here, start again in the morning."

"It will be easier to sneak past the cordon in the dark."

"So."

"So."

■

The office park was squat and bland. After the quiet isolation of the forest, it seemed alien and surreal, as though the world had been abandoned. The whole zombie apocalypse metaphor was starting to get to him.

Still, it had a broad drive they could follow easily, and though his knee twanged a bit, it felt good to move at a normal pace. He shrugged to shift the weight of the backpack and led the way.

They found themselves on an east-west street, three lanes and no cars. He flicked the lighter and held it as close to the old-fashioned paper map as he dared.

"I think we're here," he said. "Pleasant Valley Road." There was no valley, and it didn't strike him as all that pleasant. He found himself wanting to zoom in and switch to satellite mode. When he'd been a kid, he'd known the phone numbers of all of his friends, could dial them from memory; now, thanks to d-pads and mobiles, he barely remembered his own number and hadn't navigated on anything but an interactive GPS display in a decade. Technology made life so much simpler.

Yeah. Tell that to Cleveland.

Amy said, "It looks more populated to the west."

"Right. East it is. Then we can pick up . . . this one, Riverview." The street was illustrated with the thinnest line and ran a meandering course through the national park. It changed names a few times but led more or less directly into Cuyahoga Falls.

They set off down the middle of the lonely street.

■

It was almost nine when they saw the first of the others.

Sweat soaked his back, and his hips had started to burn. Twenty-two miles was a day's march for a soldier, a reasonable hike for an experienced backpacker. But working as a research scientist didn't offer much in the way of physical conditioning. Both he and Amy hit the gym when they could, but since Violet's arrival, that had meant a half an hour snatched here and there.

At least they were making better time. Riverview Road turned out to be a narrow two-lane stretch of cracked blacktop with fields on one side and forest on the other. Skeletal towers strung power lines along the west side, and they passed the occasional rural driveway, just a mailbox and a dirt path.

Ethan was looking at his feet—not counting steps so much as feeling the rhythm of them like a drumbeat—when Amy put a hand on his shoulder.

Something white bobbed ahead of them, and by the time he'd realized it was a flashlight, the beam had splashed over them. It was maybe forty yards ahead, and all he could see was the pinpoint of light itself. A heaviness sank through him.

"Ethan—"

"No sudden moves," he said. Slowly he extended his arms and turned them palm up, remembering the nervous teenager behind the gun turret on the Humvee. *Caught is bad, but panicking them is worse.*

As suddenly as it had hit, the light flicked away. It whirled in an arc that threw strange shadows off the trees until it pointed at the chest of a man. The barrel of a rifle stuck up above one shoulder, but he was dressed in hunter's flannels, and beside him were two other figures: a woman and a boy of eight or so.

The light lingered for a moment, and then it swung forward and once again began to bob, heading away. Ethan released a breath he hadn't realized he was holding.

"They're like us," Amy said. "Trying to leave."

Ethan nodded. They started walking again themselves, following the will-o'-the-wisp of the flashlight. "I wonder how many other people have the same idea?"

■

An hour later, there were dozens. Each group walked apart from the others, strung along the road like beads on a necklace. Most had flashlights and made no effort to conceal them. Some talked. Up ahead, someone sang "Auld Lang Syne."

"I love that song," Amy said.

"I know."

"Kinda fitting, huh?" She broke into soft song. *"We two have run about the slopes, and picked the daisies fine; but we've wandered many a weary foot, since auld lang syne."*

"My feet are weary," he acknowledged.

They were passing a development suburb, one of those strange neighborhoods in a box plunked down in the middle of nowhere. A dozen houses were under construction, the steepled framework dark against the sky. There was a sign by the entrance he could just make out: THE BEST OF NATURE WITH THE MOST MODERN CONVENIENCES. DREAM HOMES STARTING IN THE LOW THREE HUNDREDS! Next to it was a completed model home, and Ethan saw a man standing on the front porch, watching the slow trail of refugees. He nodded at the guy but got no response. Out in the woods, a bird shrieked. The sound was unmistakably predatory, and Ethan wondered what had just died. A mouse, maybe, clutched in the talons of an owl.

"'For auld lang syne' means 'for the sake of olden times.'" Amy's voice was soft. "I wonder if that's our life. Olden times."

Ethan glanced sideways, caught by the sadness in his wife's voice. She wasn't one of those aggressively cheery people, but overall, Amy saw the existence of the glass itself as pretty amazing, whether half-full or half-empty. More than what had happened to their city, to their neighborhood, more than the terrorism or the riots, more than becoming refugees, that note in his wife's voice brought home the weight of circumstances. Not just what was happening to them, but what was happening to the world.

He flashed back to something he'd heard on the radio the night the supermarkets had been stripped. The guy had been talking about the way stores were supplied, how everything happened in real time. Ethan could imagine the system to make that work, the scanners and computers and inventory management and logistics and shipping. Just one of a million plans that kept the world turning, a scheme as intricate and efficient as the vascular system that supplied a human being with blood.

But for all the efficiency of the vascular system, cut an artery and the body died.

Is that what the Children of Darwin had done? Was it possible that the madness engulfing Cleveland would spread, that power would fail widely, that food wouldn't move from farm to store, that the police wouldn't protect nor the hospitals heal?

Could life be so delicate?

You know that it can. The world worked because people agreed to believe it worked. He could hand a piece of paper to a clerk and walk out with clothing because they agreed to ascribe value to the paper. He could interact with people thousands of miles away and call it chatting. The d-pad in his pocket could access the sum total of accumulated human knowledge, from setting a bone to building an A-bomb.

And none of that was real. It was a shared and beneficial hallucination.

What happens when we can't believe anymore?

"Everything will work out."

"You don't have to keep saying that for me," she said sharply. "I don't need to be managed."

He started to protest, caught himself. "You're right. Sorry."

She softened, said, "Me too. Just tired."

"Yeah. Your mom's pullout couch never sounded so—" He broke off and stopped moving.

"What is it?"

"Do you hear . . ."

Engines. The sound, faint at first, grew rapidly louder. The night was quiet; they should have been able to hear a car for miles. Instead, it was as though . . .

As though they had been parked and waiting.

"Run!" Ethan grabbed Amy's hand and pulled her off the road. Others had heard the sound too, and their flashlights whirled as they scattered, spots of brightness and blurs of color. The heavy pack bounced on his shoulders, and talons of fire clutched his knee as they sprinted up the entrance to the complex.

Humvees ripped around a bend in the road, their mounted spotlights turning night to day. A voice boomed over a loudspeaker, the words lost in screams and the roar of engines. Ethan didn't waste any time trying to listen, just made for the cover of the model home, Amy half a step behind. His heart thumped his ribs as they pounded up the gravel drive and slid into shadow against the wall.

Violet had woken and was crying, and Amy's face was pinched as she murmured, "Shh, no, not now, please, shh."

Now what?

Peering around the edge of the building, he could see that the Humvees had split up, one holding the base of the road, two others swinging out to corral the refugees. The swiveling spotlights were blinding, and people froze in their beams.

"Do not run. We will fire. Get down on your knees and put your hands on your head."

Would they really shoot? He didn't know. If the government actually believed they might be terrorists, or infected with something . . . it was possible.

On the road, people were complying, setting down packs and blankets, kneeling on the blacktop. As the spotlights swung back and forth, they framed the huddled figures in light, throwing twisted shadows.

"Dr. Ethan Park. A drone has identified you on this road."

His mouth fell open, and icy panic drenched his body. His hands tingled and itched.

A *drone*?!

Why in the name of everything holy would a drone be looking for him? Why would anyone?

"Put your hands on your head and walk slowly toward the vehicles, Dr. Park."

"What?" Amy's eyes were white with reflected light. "Why do they want us?"

He flashed back to the DAR agents who had come to see him, Bobby Quinn and Valerie West. The two of them asking about his research. *That can't be. It's silly.* "I really don't know."

"Should we turn ourselves in?"

He peered back around the edge of the house. Soldiers had dismounted the trucks, transforming the cheerful column into a huddle of terrified prey.

Near the middle, one man was still standing. It was the one they'd seen before, wearing flannels and carrying a rifle. His son knelt on one side of him, his wife on the other, her hands tugging his pant leg. Instead, he reached down and pulled her to her feet.

"Put your hands on your head, Dr. Park."

"I'm not him," the man yelled back. "We're not him."

"Get down on your knees."

"I'm an American citizen. And I am not going back to Cleveland." He started forward, ignoring his wife pulling at him.

"Sir! Get down on your knees, now!"

"We're not who you're looking for."

"Drop the weapon and get down on your goddamn knees!"

"I have rights," the man shouted. "I'm not a terrorist. You can't do this."

"Stop, you idiot," Ethan whispered. "Get *down*."

The man took one step, and then another.

A short series of detonations, flashes of brilliant light and booms that ricocheted through Ethan's stomach like fireworks, only that couldn't be, fireworks were in the sky, not on the road, and then the hunter's back exploded.

For a second, the only sound was the echo of the gun blasts reverberating through the trees. Then the screaming started.

"Ohmygodohmygodohmygod," Amy said, "ohmygod."

People were standing now, starting to run. The loudspeaker boomed again, told everyone to stop, but hysteria had replaced fear. Ethan had a terrible image of the guns opening fire, strafing the crowd, but it was the spotlights instead, the soldiers hopping off the trucks and yelling.

Ethan grabbed Amy's arm, squeezed hard. The woods were—

A sudden tapping sound made him jump. His first thought was that he'd been shot, but there was no pain, and the sound was too quiet.

It was the window of the model home, the one they were hiding behind. A woman held a flashlight in one hand as she opened the window with the other. "Quick," she said, with a *come here* gesture.

He looked at her, a stranger in a tank top, her face twisted with urgency. Ethan grabbed Violet, pressed her into the woman's arms, and then half boosted, half shoved Amy through the window. He gripped the edge of the windowsill and pulled himself up and over, the backpack making it awkward.

More gunfire sounded on the road.

■

The woman turned out to be named Margaret, and she was the wife of the guy Ethan had seen on the front porch, who now put out his hand. "Jeremy."

The five of them were in the basement of the model home, a finished space designed to be a family room, though at the moment it held just a couple of folding chairs and a conference table. Outside, the loudspeakers boomed commands. He could imagine the scene, people being rounded up and zip-tied, loaded onto trucks. The soldiers would be ID'ing each of them, looking for him.

But why?

He didn't know. Maybe it was the DAR; maybe it was whoever kidnapped Abe; maybe it was a mistake. Regardless, it seemed best not to be the name read over the loudspeakers. Hoping his wife would pick up on what he was doing, Ethan said, "I'm Will." His middle name. "My wife Amy. And this is Violet."

Amy didn't miss a beat as she said, "Thank you for letting us in."

"Of course, sweetheart." Margaret shook her head. "I don't know what those boys were up to, shooting at people, but I couldn't let you stay out there. Not with the little one." She cooed down at Violet, now back in Amy's arms. "My lord, she's precious."

"You think the soldiers will search the house?"

Jeremy shook his head. "Wouldn't think so. The doors and windows are locked, so no reason for them to think people are here."

"We're sort of caretakers," Margaret said. "Watch over the place, make sure kids don't come out to party, that kind of thing."

Ethan said, "We won't stay long. Just until they leave."

"Nonsense. We've got plenty of room. It's too late at night to be wandering around, especially with those soldiers all wound up."

"You know the guy they were looking for?" Jeremy asked.

"No. We didn't know any of those people. Just trying to get out of town, go stay with Amy's mom in Chicago."

Jeremy swiveled a toothpick from one side of his mouth to the other. They seemed to have run out of things to say, and in the silence, a Humvee engine revved. They all listened, heads cocked, as the sound grew fainter.

"We've got some food," Ethan said. "It's not much, but are you guys hungry?"

■

It was the strangest Thanksgiving he could remember, although there was something wonderful about it, too. Margaret and Amy worked together over the camp stove, heating cans, while he and Jeremy set the table. Paper plates and plasticware, a Coleman lantern in the center of the table. The man wasn't much of a talker, but Ethan learned that they had two kids upstairs—"boys'd sleep through Judgment Day"—and that Jeremy also worked as an electrician, wiring the housing development.

Dinner was an odd mix: Campbell's soup, black beans, jerky, peanut butter sandwiches. They all held hands as Jeremy said grace, and then everyone tucked in. Margaret kept up a steady stream of talk, all of it pleasantly inane. The food tasted better than it had a right to, and there were moments when Ethan forgot that they were huddled in a basement on the outskirts of a paralyzed city under terrorist attack and hunted by drones.

Afterward, while Amy checked on Violet and Margaret cleaned up, Jeremy cocked his head at Ethan in a *come with me* gesture. They went out to the front porch. The street was abandoned, no sign of the chaos that had taken place just hours ago. Almost no sign: Ethan thought he could see a dark stain on the concrete.

Amy was right. The life we knew was olden times.

"Listen, I want to thank you again," Ethan said. "You saved us there."

Jeremy nodded. "Wife's got a big heart."

"So do you. Thanks."

The man stepped off the porch and reached behind a drain pipe. He came out with a pint bottle of whiskey, unscrewed the cap and took a pull, then sighed. "Margaret doesn't like it, but sometimes a man needs a drink."

"Amen." Ethan took the offered bottle.

"She your first?"

"Violet? Yes."

"Changes you, don't it?"

"Changes everything."

For a moment they stood listening to night sounds, rustling trees and the sigh of the wind. Ethan took another swig and passed the bottle back.

"It's a good thing," Jeremy said. "Fatherhood. I used to do roofing, up spreading tar in the heat of summer, no shade. By June my neck would have cracked and peeled and burned again. I was eighteen, thought that was hard. Then I had children."

"It's crazy, isn't it? You think you know what you're getting yourself into, but you have no idea. None at all. Everybody talks about all the overwhelming love, and that's true, but that's not really it. It's the overwhelming everything. The idea that for every second of the next eighteen years, you're responsible."

Jeremy took another tip of the bottle, offered it. Ethan shook his head. The man capped the whiskey, then returned it to its hiding place. He stepped back up on the porch and put his hands in his pockets, looked up at the sky. "These are strange days, Will.

Maybe the last days." He turned. "You take care of that little girl, you hear?"

"I will. I'll do anything I have to."

"Hear that." Back inside, Jeremy left them the Coleman, and everyone said their goodnights.

The moment Jeremy and Margaret were out of sight, his wife spun on him. "Okay, what the hell is going on?"

"Amy, I swear to God, I have no idea."

"They knew your name. Knew that you were a PhD. They said there was a *drone* looking for you."

"Yeah." He bent to spread out the sleeping bag. Amy had already made a nest for Violet, and his daughter lay splayed on her back, arms and legs out, head to one side. "All I can think of is that it has something to do with Abe going missing."

"So it was the DAR?" She frowned. "But if they wanted to talk to you, why wouldn't they have just knocked on our door?"

"I'm wondering if they were watching the house, hoping whoever took Abe would come after me." He sat down, unlaced his boots. "Only, we left, and that surprised them."

Amy considered it. "But a drone? They must really want to talk to you."

"I guess," he said.

"You think they're after your work."

"Yeah."

She settled onto her sleeping bag. "I know how much it means to you, baby. And I know how strict Abe is about his nondisclosure. But this is the government. The DAR. Maybe you should—"

"Right now," he said, "all I care about is getting us somewhere safe. We'll deal with the DAR after that."

She nodded slowly, but she didn't seem entirely convinced. He didn't blame her. He wasn't entirely convinced himself.

Ethan turned out the lantern, then crossed his arms behind his head and stared upward. Thinking of burning cars and a line of refugees. Thinking of fireworks and a spatter of blood. Thinking of how close he and Abe were, and whether their own government intended to steal their work from them.

The pistol in his waistband was heavy but strangely comforting.

For the sake of olden times.

CHAPTER 20

The guard was young, with all the screw-you swagger that implied. Which was impressive considering he was kneeling on the floor with a gun to his head.

"You're both dead." His voice had a thick West Virginia drawl. "This is a DAR facility. We'll know who you are, where you live. You may as well give up now."

"Sweetie," Shannon said, "I promise you. The DAR already knows who we are."

She nodded at Kathy Baskoff, and the commando jammed her submachine gun barrel deeper into the guard's neck. His swagger disappeared. After all, he'd watched Kathy kill his partner without hesitation.

And you have no idea how much she'd like to do the same to you.

Shannon took a roll of silver duct tape from her kit bag and yanked the end free. She wrapped a dozen loops around his wrists, then another dozen across his chest, binding him to the chair.

"We're go," she said, then stepped over the body of the other guard and into the cold predawn.

There were engine sounds, and the headlights of four trucks rolling up the hill. Light splashed across the heavy sign that read DAVIS ACADEMY, carved in granite and sitting there like it should have read YALE.

"This was my academy," Kathy said. "From age eleven to eighteen."

"I know," Shannon said. "That's why I picked you."

In the dark, the commando's thin-lipped smile looked carnivorous.

A Jeep and three heavy trucks pulled forward, engines chugging. Shannon waited for them to line up. "All of you, listen." She had the urge to yell like William Wallace urging the Scots to battle, but she knew the earpiece would carry just fine. "You all know why we're here. No matter what they call this place, no matter what they pretend so they can sleep at night, every academy is a prison. Some of you, like Kathy, spent time in them. Some of you didn't. That doesn't matter now. What matters is that tonight the first is falling. We're done playing nice."

She heard whoops through the truck walls.

"Every adult here is complicit. Guard or janitor, they all sat by and watched children be brainwashed and tortured. If they surrender, fine. If not"—she shrugged—"even better."

The whoops were replaced by laughter.

"But remember. Our first goal is to get every single kid out of here. So check your targets. Don't pull the trigger unless you're sure." She walked to the passenger side of the Jeep, pulled herself up. "Let's roll."

"Where to?"

"Administration. There's someone there I want to talk to."

■

Shannon had been planning the attack on Davis Academy for two months. Her penance, a way of making good on her sins. She'd pored over satellite photos, memorized reports written by former "students," analyzed the list of attendees. She'd even spent a week camped out in the woods near the perimeter, watching vehicles come and go, and she was not a camping girl. After all of that, the inescapable conclusion was that there was simply no way to do it that didn't put her team—and the children they were rescuing—in serious danger.

For a while, she'd even wrestled with bringing Cooper in on it. His knowledge of DAR systems would be invaluable, and together they were pretty unstoppable. Besides, the sin was his too.

It had seemed such a minor thing at the time. Three months ago, when she was delivering Nick to John Smith, they'd been on the run. They'd been in Chicago, hunted by the DAR, and when they needed a place to sleep, Shannon had suggested a friend's apartment.

She just hadn't thought it through, that was all. Hadn't realized the massive force arrayed against them. How far the government would go to catch them, and what it would do to anyone in its way.

Tonight you wash those sins away.

In an ironic twist, it was John and his crazy mission that had made this possible. She'd agreed to rob the DAR for him, but in trade, his programmer had to make sure they lifted the things Shannon needed, too.

Like the bypass code for the alarm system.

Like the duty roster and guard post locations.

Like detailed maps of the administration building, including the residence.

Information is usually more dangerous than bullets.

The most dangerous part had been sneaking up on the outer gate post. Low profile was the way to go, so dressed in tactical blacks and night vision goggles, she and Kathy had crept in alone. Taking their time, staying down, branches snagging at clothing, animal sounds magnified.

When they'd reached the guard booth, Shannon eased alongside the door and knocked. Things had gone fast after that, Kathy coming in hard as Shannon shifted into the guard hut, blocking the panic button.

One guard had gone for his weapon. Kathy's silenced submachine gun had made a single *whoomp*, and he was down, a hole in his forehead, which bled surprisingly little.

The other had decided to settle for talking tough. She hoped he was enjoying the show on the monitors.

Now, rolling through the night in an open-topped Jeep, the air cold, she felt a crystalline clarity. Most times on a job she was surfing adrenaline, getting off on the rush of whatever ridiculous stunt she was pulling. But this was different. She wasn't working solo tonight, for one thing. Instead of a spy or a scout, tonight she was a soldier, and she knew that some of her fellow soldiers might die.

But it had more to do with a fear of what she might find. A fear that all of this might not grant the absolution she was looking for. The redemption for her terrible error.

You couldn't have known. There was no way to predict that spending a night in your friend's home would mean their daughter was shipped off to an academy.

Besides, it's going to work. In fifteen minutes, you'll be leading 354 children out of prison.

Including her.

In the distance, she heard faint thumps, the sound of silenced gunfire. Suppressors didn't work as well in real life as they did in the movies; bullets were propelled by explosions, and there was only so quiet you could make those.

By now, academy security would know that they were under attack. They'd be following protocol, retreating to checkpoints, tripping panic signals that were supposed to bring down the might of the US military. Under normal circumstances, special forces teams in attack choppers could land within seven minutes of the first alarm.

But not tonight. Tonight, you guys are the defenseless ones.

■

Something woke him.

It had been a disheartening thing to realize, as he grew older, that a solid night's sleep was the province of children. Rare indeed was the evening that he didn't get up thrice to use the restroom.

But it wasn't his bladder that woke Director Charles Norridge. It was a sound, a loud crack that had snapped through his dreams. Fireworks? Perhaps some of the older kids had snuck out, were playing at homegrown terrorist again. If so, there would be boys in the stockade come 9:00 a.m. A crude device, but effective. Far more useful than the physical discomfort was the shame; at this age, there was no more effective teaching tool than humiliation.

"Hello, Chuck."

With a click, his bedside lamp turned on, revealing a slim woman with dark hair. Behind another woman, bigger, stared at him with unmistakable hatred—and a large gun in her hands.

"Who are you?" His voice came out weaker than he hoped, and he coughed, summoned an imperious tone. "I don't find this funny."

"Really?" The slender woman smiled. "I think it's kind of hilarious."

More cracks in the distance. Gunfire, he realized, not fireworks. "What's the meaning of this?"

"What's the meaning?" She brushed her hair behind her ears. "That's a tricky question. Like, politically? Ideologically? Morally?"

How dare she. "This is a school. I'm an educator."

"This is a prison. You're a warden."

"I never hurt anyone," he said. "I love my students."

"I wonder if they'd say the same of you?"

He started to slide out of bed, froze when she said, "Uh-uh." She sat on the edge of the mattress. "I'm going to give you a present, Chuck."

"Do I know you?"

"My name is Shannon. You've known plenty of my friends."
She gestured at the woman by the door, the one carrying the gun.
"Like Kathy."

Norridge looked. The woman had a restless energy to her;
even standing still, she seemed to be fidgeting. "I've never seen
you before. Who are you?"

"My name is Kathy Baskoff."

"I don't know any Kathy Baskoff."

"Sure you do. You just called me Linda." The woman smiled
without warmth. "Linda Jones."

Until that moment, as frightened as he'd been, it had all felt
at a remove, too. The aftereffects of a bad dream, nothing to be
taken seriously. Now his bladder hit, a sudden icy tightness. "I
never hurt you."

"You don't even remember me. How many Linda Joneses have
you had at this school? A hundred? A thousand?"

Shannon said, "Kathy, what was the worst part about being
here?"

The dangerous-looking one paused. "It wasn't just that you
took us from our families. That you renamed us. That you turned
us against each other and poisoned our minds." She raised the
gun, stared down the barrel at him. "It was living in fear. Every
single minute, in fear, and knowing we were trapped. That there
was nothing we could do about it."

Suddenly the one called Shannon gripped his forearm.
Charles tried to pull away, but she was surprisingly strong. She
snapped something around his wrist, cold and metal, and then
jerked his arm up and fastened the other end to the bedpost. Norridge yanked, and the handcuff bit into his skin.

Shannon said, "Listen."

He waited for her to speak again; when she didn't, he realized
she meant it more generally. "I don't hear anything."

"That's right. No gunfire." A pause. "Your guards are all dead.
No one is coming to save you."

Something wet coated his thighs, and Norridge realized he'd lost control of his bladder. The shame that washed over him felt hotter than the urine.

"Right now, our people are planting explosive charges. In the classrooms, the dormitories . . . the administrative residences." She smiled. "In five minutes, this facility will be a smoking hole in the ground."

"My God. You can't!"

"It's done. But here's the good news. You have a chance to survive."

He gulped air, strained against the handcuff, feeling weak and old. "You can't do this," he repeated.

"Chuck," she said. "You're not paying attention. You have one chance to live, one. All you have to do is answer a question."

He tried to gather wits scattered like frightened rabbits. "What?"

"You have a student here named Alice Chen." She leaned forward, her face inches from his. "How old is she?"

Norridge stared. His legs wet, his eyes crusted with sleep, his hand cuffed to the metal post of the bed he'd slept in for two decades. "I . . ." He fought to think, to conjure the records of his students. This woman was wrong. He knew his students, knew them all. He could look at a child and remember their transponder number, repeat every detail of their file, all their secrets. He just . . .

Didn't know their names.

As though she could read his mind, the woman shrugged. "Too bad." She stood up, and the two of them walked to the door.

"Wait!" His voice was as fearful and querulous as a child's. "You can't do this."

Kathy Baskoff stopped at the door. "In five minutes, you're going to die. And there's nothing you can do about it." She smiled. "Live with that."

The bedroom door shut with a click.

CHAPTER 21

Soren smiled.

Books he loved. Movies and tri-d and stage plays and dance and comedy and sports and music were all torture. No matter the intelligence of a screenplay, no matter the elegance of a joke, at his timescale they were endless. Each note of a Bach concerto was drawn out until all meaning and emotion were lost.

But a book. He'd learned long ago how to widen his eyes to take in the whole page, focusing on individual words with his mind rather than his pupils. A good book was close to personal nothingness, a place the self could be lost. He often read five or six books between rising and sleeping.

John Smith had been thoughtful in furnishing the apartment in New Canaan. It was quiet, tastefully lit, and walled floor to ceiling with bookshelves. Soren found it a touching gesture, this reminder that his friend knew him in a way no one else did.

John said, "Iwillneedyousoon."

"To?"

"Kill. Willyoukillforme?"

"Yes."

"Myplansarelaid. Butthingsarefluid."

Things are fluid. Yes, that was certainly true. "And?"

"You'retherook. Overlookedonthebackrow."

A reference to their childhood at Hawkesdown Academy, play-ing chess in the cafeteria. Soren always lost, but it hadn't mattered. The games had been periods of simple pleasure and engagement spent in the company of a friend. Maybe the first time in his life when time had passed too quickly.

His role was plain to him now. Smith would have spent years preparing for this moment, but strategies always changed in execution, always. So Soren would be the asset his friend's enemies didn't know about. The solution to problems yet undiscovered.

"I understand."

"Ihaveasurprise."

Soren followed his friend through the apartment to a closed door. John gestured to it, smiled, and left.

Soren opened the door and saw her waiting for him.

The only woman in the world. Tiny and blond and perfect. The one who understood what he needed. Not just understood it. Became it. That was her nature, her gift and her curse; she could transform herself into what others needed. Could sense and embody the desires people didn't dare speak.

Samantha was naked, pink tulips and fresh cream, and her arms were open. "My love," she said. "I've missed you."

•

Bliss. Not an instant's worth, the way normal people experienced love, but complete and lasting. Bliss like warm water he swam languidly.

His curse could be a gift, too. With her.

In Hawkesdown they had found each other, perfect Samantha. When they were fourteen, she had come to him and touched his cheek and begun without a word spoken, and every touch lasted minutes. The caress of her tongue, the softness of her hair trailing down his body, the grip of their clenched fingers, all threatened to overflow him with fullness. When it finally came, the orgasm was a long, slow freefall down the curve of heaven.

Then she had vanished from the academy, stolen away by her mentor, and he had never seen her again.

Soren had tried with others, but failed miserably. Women wanted to banter and share and be charmed, to know and feel known. He understood that, but the rituals of the mating dance were unbearable to him. Jokes drained of all flavor, small talk lasted days.

There had been a prostitute, one time. An expensive call girl he paid in advance. He had given explicit instructions in an e-mail: she wasn't to speak, wasn't to delay. All he wanted was her perfumed warmth writhing above him.

She had done as he asked. But there was a moment as she moved on him when the expression on her face flickered, the mask slipping. Just an instant for her, but he had been forced to stare for long seconds at her boredom and hatred and contempt even as he was inside of her. Unable to turn away, to shut his eyes. He still burned with shame to think of the moment.

He and his love slid together, parted, and rejoined. She was his need. And he knew that for her he was the safest, purest thing she would ever know. She was an addict to her own self, and he let her be that with purest gratitude.

When at last they were done, she curled into the hollow of his arm and laid her head on his chest, and he basked in the afterglow of their bodies' desire with perfect peace.

Thank you, John. A surprise indeed.

And another debt.

Will I kill for you?

God himself.

CHAPTER 22

"Wake up."

Ethan's eyes snapped open.

A shotgun was pointed at his head.

His brain was still swimming up from sleep, and his first thought was, *Jesus, not again with a gun pointing at me.*

He moved without thinking, starting to sit up.

Jeremy racked the shotgun.

It was a horrifying sound, one he'd never heard in real life, and it made his fingers tingle and his belly go cold. Beside him, Amy gasped.

"Quiet." Jeremy swiveled the shotgun to her. His face was tight, lips squeezed white.

"What is this? What are you doing?"

"Get up."

"Jeremy," Amy said, "what's going on?"

"I said get up. I don't want to shoot you, but I will."

Slowly, Ethan slid a hand down to his waist, touched the butt of the pistol. It was warm from contact with his skin. He thought, *Ease it out, aim upward through the sleeping bag, and . . .*

What? Blast away like a gangster? He'd never fired a gun in his life. The inaugural occasion was going to be at a human being, one who seemed quite comfortable behind the shotgun pointing at Amy?

What if you miss?

He let go of the gun. Nodded. "Okay. Easy." Ethan stood slowly, making sure the hem of his shirt draped to cover the gun. He reached down and helped Amy to her feet.

Violet made a snorting sound in her sleep, and they all jumped.

If he so much as glances in her direction, pull out the pistol and fire.

"Now what?"

"Get your girl and go."

He had a moment of pure relief. "Okay. Give us one minute to pack our gear, and we'll be out of your life forever."

"No."

"What?"

"Leave everything. Just walk out of here."

"You're . . . this is a robbery?"

"Told you, these are the last days. World's falling down around us. Money, sleeping bags, a tent, whatever else you have, it might save my family's life."

"You're not serious," Amy said. "Where's Margaret?"

"In the morning I'll tell her I found you looting our cabinets, ran you out."

"What will you tell her if you shoot us?"

The man's expression hardened. He turned and spat the toothpick. "Same thing."

"You're a piece of shit, Jeremy." Amy's eyes blazed. "A coward. You're what's wrong."

"I'm a man looking out for his family, that's all."

"No," Amy said. "My husband is a man. You're a—"

"Honey," Ethan said gently. "Let's go."

She looked at him, fury shining in her. Ethan flicked his eyes downward to where Violet slept. Amy caught the gesture and swallowed whatever she'd been about to say.

"Can we put our shoes on?"

"Coulda. Before you mouthed off. Now you just get your little one and get out."

Amy shook her head, then bent down and picked up their daughter. She squirmed and started crying. Ethan's right hand tingled, the gun seeming to pull at it.

You're not a criminal. All the man wants is stuff. If you can walk out of here without violence, do it.

Jeremy followed them up the stairs, the shotgun leveled.

At the front door, Amy turned to him. "You said grace last night."

"So?"

"So God damn you." She turned and strode out the door. Ethan wasn't sure if he'd ever been more in love with her than he was at that moment. It made him want to yank out the gun and blaze away, to shoot until he was out of ammo and then stand over Jeremy's body and keep pulling the trigger.

Instead, he followed her into the night. Thinking, *It's not about you. It's not about feeling like a man. It's about being one.*

That means doing whatever it takes to protect them. Whatever it takes.

CHAPTER 23

It was no Air Force One, but Cooper had to admit the diplomatic flight was a pretty nice ride.

It had been a fun morning, lit with a simple sweetness. Apple pancakes in the skillet, the Stones on the stereo, his children spazzing, high on sugar and excitement. They'd gone to bed expecting the dawn to bring a day like any other, and instead, hours later, here they were playing tag in the sky. The jet had leather seats, integrated tri-d, a fighter escort, and a steward happy to bring them all the Coke their parents allowed.

"Hey, Todd," Cooper called. "C'mere."

His son dashed down the aisle, sweating and smiling. Cooper tapped the window. "Check it out."

Obligingly, Todd pressed his face against the glass. They'd started their descent, and from this height, Wyoming looked like cake left too long in the oven. Near the horizon, almost out of view of the window, something glowed silver and white. "What is it?"

"That's Tesla. The capitol of New Canaan. It's not the only city, but it's the biggest. It's where Erik Epstein lives."

"Is he really that rich?"

"Yup."

"Everything looks like it's made of mirrors."

"That's solar glass. It captures energy and keep the insides cool."

"Oh." Todd looked up at him with a grin. "Too bad. A city of mirrors would be cool."

It was one of those weird moments of discordance, a sense of greater meaning. Cooper found himself staring at his son, a thought rising unbidden. *A city of mirrors. He's not far from right. If ever there were a place that reverses everything, this is it.*

■

Their reception in Tesla was certainly a different experience than the last time he'd arrived, three months ago. That time he and Shannon had snuck in with false papers, worried every moment they'd be caught.

This time there was a motorcade waiting, guarded by a security team. Instead of the heavy limousines favored everywhere else in the world, the motorcade was made up of tear-dropped electric vehicles and sleek ATVs. Gasoline was one of the many things the Holdfast had to import, and it was correspondingly expensive.

As for the security team, they were young even by military standards, ranging from sixteen to maybe twenty-two. Their light-weight desert fatigues were made of active camouflage, the fabric patterns shifting and morphing as they moved. Despite their youth, he could tell they were good; they moved as a single unit, covering every angle without needing to speak to one another. He didn't recognize the assault rifles they carried, some sort of NCH newtech with rounded curves and plastic stocks. *When did you start manufacturing weapons, Erik?*

"Ambassador Cooper." The woman who met them had the willowy beauty of a runway model but not so much as a whiff of sexuality. "I'm Patricia Ariel, Mr. Epstein's communications director. On behalf of Epstein Industries, welcome to the New Canaan Holdfast."

Ambassador. That'll take some getting used to. "Thank you," he said. "This is Natalie, and our children, Todd and Kate."

"Welcome. If you'll follow me, I'll see you to your residence in the city."

Cooper said, "Epstein couldn't make it?"

"He thought you'd want to get settled first. Shall we?"

Hmm. Cooper hadn't expected the real Erik Epstein—he probably never left his cave—but his brother Jakob should have been here. It was a snub, and a bad sign.

The car wasn't as heavy as President Clay's ride, but it was comfortable, with leather seats and broad windows. A privacy shield separated them from the driver. The motorcade started rolling immediately, engines humming softly.

"Mr. Ambassador, this isn't your first visit to the Holdfast, correct?"

Cooper shook his head. "But my family hasn't been here before."

"Well, as you know, we're corporate-held land, custom designed from the ground up . . ." Ariel continued talking, and he patterned her while his family enjoyed the tour. She was smooth and polished, but every so often a rounded consonant crept in, and he figured her to be from the Boston area. Probably a tier two, he suspected memetic based on her speech patterns, and definitely not academy-raised. He imagined her parents were loving and still married, proud of their daughter but not residents of the NCH. Sunday phone calls and e-mails about seeing her on the news, polite inquiries into her social life met with polite deflections.

Once he had figured her out, he turned his attention to the view. The airport was small, two runways for jets and a handful of glider paths. Todd oohed as one took off, a hydraulic winch a mile away yanking the carbon-fiber plane into the sky. Cooper remembered riding in one with Shannon, felt his stomach lurch. He didn't mind heights, but airplanes without engines were another matter.

Outside the boundaries of the airport, they passed a huge solar array, tens of thousands of black panels stretching into the distance, all of them perfectly aligned and bathed in sunlight. Traffic was light, and though the motorcade moved without sirens, they rarely slowed down. One of the benefits of building a world from scratch, traffic patterns could be anticipated, roads built wide enough to avoid congestion. He wondered if Ariel ever thought of Boston, the antithesis of everything here: an old city by American standards, confusing and crowded, horse paths turned into streets, winding mazes instead of neat grids.

"What's that?" Todd pointed at a complex of domed structures on a ridgeline, the silver sides open to the wind.

"Moisture condensers," Ariel said. "We harvest water from the wind. This is the desert, after all, so water is always a concern. You may find showers a little strange . . ."

He tuned back out, his mind returning to the Oval Office. Last night had been close. Cleveland on fire, and the president comatose while his secretary of defense practically staged a coup. If Clay hadn't snapped out of it, this morning abnorms all over the country would be getting shipped to internment camps as troops descended on the Holdfast.

Cooper's last-second save had bought a little time, but only a little. Now he somehow had to convince Erik Epstein to abandon his deliberately neutral posture and throw his support fully behind the US government—a government that was at that moment drawing up plans for an attack.

Maybe that's your angle. Carrot and stick in one.

He tapped at his teeth with his thumb, watched Tesla unfold around them. Low-rise buildings of stone and solar glass, fronted by broad sidewalks and charging stations for electric vehicles. Signs for restaurants and bars, holographic arcades and coffee-houses advertising brands of marijuana. The people on the street favored rugged, practical clothing, jeans and boots and cowboy hats. There was a genial air, people smiling at one another as they passed, stopping in small groups to talk.

He imagined US Army Seraphim drones circling above, raining down finger missiles. Vehicles exploding, walls cracking and collapsing. Or worse, bomber-dropped incendiaries; in the dry climate, the heat would reach levels hot enough to shatter stone and boil solar glass.

"Everyone is so young," Natalie said.

"Youth is strength," Ariel said without hesitation. Definitely memetic. Professional communications had always been about the attempt to generate memes, to make a message viral; abnorms just took that to a higher level. Back when he'd been a DAR agent, Cooper had read a brief arguing memetics was the most dangerous gift. As politicians had long known, people preferred short, catchy answers to complex ones, even if the short answers were oversimplified to the point of ridiculousness. Phrases like "old-world thinking" could be as devastating as a bomb, and much farther ranging.

After all, remember how many times you saw "I am John Smith" scrawled on a wall.

And now he's a hero, and that's the title of his bestselling book.

"Youth is being young," Cooper said. "Strength is something else."

Ariel smiled politely, continued the tour. "The average age in the Holdfast is 26.41, although that's misleading; the number of parents and grandparents who move here with gifted children skew the math. The median is closer to sixteen."

"A city of children," Natalie said.

"Not a city, a new community, united in a common purpose. When people are invested in what they're doing, biological age is less important than energy and focus. Look at Israel's growth after the Second World War. A generation of passionate Jewish youth transformed a desert into a global power." The motorcade purred to a halt outside a gracious brick building on a neighborhood street. "And here we are."

Cooper had been expecting traditional diplomatic quarters—a luxury hotel, one floor cordoned off for them, agents posted everywhere. Instead, Ariel led them into a lovely three-story apartment, tastefully decorated in Western style, tile floors and sheer drapes. The back half of the house looked out onto a public square surrounding a tall tree with thick rubbery leaves, no doubt a genetic variant that required minimal water. Despite the cold, men and women chatted on benches, read d-pads in the sun. A group of boys kicked a soccer ball. Todd pressed against the window, his breath fogging the glass.

"Your security detail is quartered on the first floor; if you need anything, just pick up the phone."

Todd said, "Can I go play?"

Cooper hesitated. He wanted his children to experience this world—that was one of the reasons he'd agreed to bring them—but this was more exposed than he'd imagined. As if reading his thoughts, Ariel said, "The security team can accompany him if you'd like, but it's not necessary."

"Why's that?"

Ariel smiled. "You're in New Canaan. Approximately fifteen percent of our police force are readers; they move through the cities looking for dangerous personality discrepancies. Pedophiles are screened out, as are those with violent tendencies."

"You have tier-one readers wandering the streets?"

"Of course not. There are tier-one readers in the Holdfast, but mostly they choose to live in special facilities where their needs can be met by automation so they never need to see another human being. They'd go mad wandering the streets. The readers in the police are generally threes. They can sense imbalance, sociopathy, psychopathy, but they're still able to function in human society. The system has been exceptionally effective there hasn't been a child hurt by an adult anywhere in the Holdfast in years."

"What about terrorists?"

"Not a threat. These being diplomatic quarters, that protocol is expanded to include political insurgents. Your children are safer here than they are in your front yard in Washington."

New-world thinking. Gotta love it. He caught Natalie looking at him, shrugged. She said, "Sure. Be home by dinner."

Todd whooped and streaked for the door.

"If it's okay with your mom and dad," Ariel said to Kate, "there's a sandbox and swings, other kids your age."

His daughter wrapped her arms around herself. "I don't really like playing with other kids."

"That's because you're gifted." Ariel smiled. "I know how you feel. I used to feel the same way. Normal kids can be so mean. Trust me, it's better here."

Kate looked up at Cooper, a question in her eyes. A hope, he realized, and remembered his own childhood. He'd been a military brat, and so always an outcast, but that had been made far worse because he was gifted. It seemed like he'd had to fight for his place every day of his life.

Imagining his beautiful baby girl feeling that way broke his heart.

He squatted down in front of her. "Mom will go with you, sweetheart. You don't have to play with the other kids unless you want to." He put a hand on her shoulder. "It's up to you."

Kate bit her lip. Then she nodded. "Okay." Natalie held out one hand, and Kate took it.

"Now, Ambassador Cooper, we have a dinner planned this evening. The car will be back to pick you up at seven, if that's all right."

"It's not." He stood and turned to the communications director. "I want to talk to Epstein."

"Mr. Epstein is engaged—"

"Now."

■

Ariel was considerably cooler on the ride away from their apartment. After she had realized that he wasn't kidding, there had been a hushed phone call, a lot of *yes, sirs* and sideways glances. Like any official, she didn't like having her legs kicked out.

Cooper didn't care. If Epstein was hoping he'd play the polite diplomat, the man had lost his touch.

Though Epstein Industries was officially headquartered in Manhattan, the real power center was here, in a complex of silver cubes that shimmered with reflected sky. The tallest was a six-story building topped with a bristling array of equipment. Satellite dishes and climatic trackers and scientific gear, he knew, but also laser defense shields and antiaircraft batteries and surface-to-air missiles. Gear that should never have been okayed for a private corporation. However, $300 billion bent a lot of rules. The gerrymandered whole of the NCH proved that, the nested sieves of legal loopholes that turned the Holdfast into something like a private nation-state.

Flanked by four security guards, he and Ariel walked to the building. Cooper imagined an Avenger missile streaking toward it. Extremely low-altitude trajectory, remote guided, stealth build, integrated ECM, hypersonic. When it came to stopping an Avenger, the countermeasures on the roof would be as effective as a kid's slingshot. Cooper imagined the building vaporizing, a shock wave rolling out, pushing glass and stone in a lethal globe.

The atrium was broad and sunlit and backdropped by the skyline of Cleveland, columns of smoke rising from the city center, a news ticker five feet high scrolling. A massive tri-d screen with spectacular resolution. Apparently President Clay had formally declared martial law in the city; regular army tanks were rolling down Ontario Street.

Ariel led him to an elevator, the doors whisking open at their approach. She started to board, and he said, "No."

"I'm sorry?"

"I'm going alone."

"I'm sorry, sir, but Mr. Epstein asked that I join this meeting."

"I'll explain why you're not there."

She hesitated, then said, "Regardless, the security team—"

"Can wait down here." He adopted a bland smile. "This is still American soil, Ms. Ariel, and I'm here at the personal request of the president. Believe me when I say now is not the time to start a turf war."

The word "war" seemed to hang in the air. After a moment, Ariel said, "As you wish."

Cooper smiled, then boarded the elevator. There were no buttons, but he wasn't surprised that it slid immediately into motion.

He shouldn't have been surprised by who was waiting on the other side, either, but he was. A ten-year-old girl with electric purple hair and clenched shoulders, eyes that wouldn't meet his own. "Hi," she said. Then, "Oh God. Really? They're going to attack?"

Cooper sighed. "Hi, Millicent. Dyed your hair a different color, huh?"

■

"Nick Cooper. Welcome back to the NCH." The man wore a five-thousand-dollar suit and the easy grace of someone who dined with presidents and golfed with oil barons, who bantered on CNN and spoke on the floor of the Senate. The world knew him as Erik Epstein.

The world was wrong.

"Hello, Jakob. Nice to finally shake your hand." The last time Cooper had been here, Jakob Epstein had appeared as a fully dimensional hologram, a stunning reminder of how far advanced technology was in the NCH. That had been the Holdfast's real defense these last years; not legal wranglings or massed billions, but simply the fact that there were more brilliants here than anywhere else, that they were working together, and that the results of that work were astonishing. *The best way to protect your country,* Cooper thought, *is to create things people desire more than they fear your ability to create them.*

"Our deal. You didn't honor it. Statistically, that was unlikely, 12.2 percent." The real Erik Epstein slumped on a couch, blinking like an animal ripped from its den. It wasn't entirely inaccurate. The last time Cooper had been here, he'd seen Erik's inner sanctum, a digital Xanadu below the building. A cave of wonders, he'd thought at the time—a solemn, dim space, lit entirely by projected data. Within it, Erik worked his gift, finding patterns in seemingly unrelated things and using them to expand his empire. It was there that Erik had predicted that John Smith represented the greatest threat to the New Canaan Holdfast; Epstein believed that his actions would drive the United States government to grow increasingly repressive against all abnorms, and specifically against the NCH.

And he was right.

"Our arrangement," Erik continued, "was that you would kill John Smith. You didn't."

"You didn't tell me the truth about him," Cooper said. There was no point in being anything but open so long as Millie was in the room. She was one of the most powerful readers he'd ever come across, a gift that was in practice a terrible curse. Readers didn't have a filter, couldn't choose to turn away from what their gift offered. Tier-one readers saw everything, every hint of darkness in a person's soul, every fractional flicker of cruelty and evil. Starting with Mommy and Daddy.

Poor Millie had never known peace in her own mind, never known trust or faith. Would never believe in love, because she saw clearly the parts of themselves people never showed the ones they loved. She would almost certainly kill herself before she was twenty.

"It's okay," she said. "Don't feel sorry."

"I can't help it."

"Be afraid instead."

The words were ice down his spine. He looked at her, then at Erik and Jakob. "I am afraid."

"These are fearful times," Jakob said, sitting on the edge of his desk. "And you betrayed us."

"Prior chance of the US military attacking New Canaan: 53.2 percent." Erik spoke with his eyes closed, one hand in his lank hair. "Current chance, given impeachment of President Walker, deactivation of Equitable Services, and the emergence of the Children of Darwin: 93.2 percent within the next two weeks."

"Three things which are all, by the way, your fault, Cooper." Jakob smiled thinly. "More or less."

"You didn't tell me the truth," Cooper repeated. "You manipulated me the same way Smith did."

"Truth is relative. Data is absolute."

"Okay, well, you didn't give me all the data, then, did you?" Cooper hadn't known what to expect out of this meeting, but it hadn't been this. "You didn't tell me that Smith wasn't behind the massacre at the Monocle. You didn't tell me that President Walker and Drew Peters were. You didn't tell me that there was evidence of it."

Erik waved his hands. "Irrelevant. You came to New Canaan to kill John Smith. That was your mission. His death would have stabilized trends. Helped protect our art. We made a deal. You broke it."

"And then you made things worse," Jakob said, "by releasing that video."

Cooper struggled for words. None of this was a surprise. It was the reason he had joined Clay in the first place, the reason he had kidnapped John Smith, the reason he was here right now. *Because in your heart, you know that what you did, while morally correct, was a mistake. The world would be in better shape if you had used the Monocle video to blackmail President Walker. The Children of Darwin would never have been this successful if the DAR was strong and Walker was still in charge. You could have put yourself in a position to shape policy and improve lives.*

True, he would have to become corrupt himself. But did his personal values count more than the lives at stake?

Somehow doing the right thing was wrong. Dad never covered that eventuality, did he, Coop?

Millie said, "He understands."

"I'm sure he does," Jakob said. "But understanding doesn't fix anything, does it?"

"Maybe not. But that's why I'm here. Do you want to know what would be happening right now if I weren't?" Cooper was about to continue, but instead he turned to Millie. Put all the events of the last days in his eyes and his bearing. Remembered standing in the Oval Office last night watching Cleveland burn. "Tell them."

She cringed, dipping her face to her lap, hiding behind a shield of purple hair. Erik and Jakob both looked at her, staring intently. Cooper felt another flash of sympathy for the girl. Ten years old, and grown men were looking to her for information that would decide the fate of the country.

Finally, she said, "They want to attack. Not just the Holdfast. Brilliants."

"By 'they,'" Cooper said, "she means the most powerful people on the planet. Last night Defense Secretary Leahy gave orders to arrest all known tier ones, start the microchipping program, and move military forces to your borders in preparation for an invasion. None of which happened—because I stopped it. So how about you two drop the tough-guy act and we work the problem together?"

A long moment of silence fell. Jakob turned to face the floor-to-ceiling windows. The city of Tesla spread out around them, orderly and neat, a new world sprung from desert soil. A world that Cooper had to admit he quite liked. More than that—admired. Ever since the emergence of the gifted thirty-odd years ago, most of the world had been turning inward, becoming destructive. His own government had focused on containment and control, on smashing anything deemed dangerous.

Funny, there had been a time when building things was what America did. From massive dams to towering skyscrapers, from mechanized factories to moon rockets, the nation had *created*, had viewed that as part of the national identity. Being an engineer or an architect had once been high aspirations.

Now everybody wanted to be musicians and basketball players, and America didn't build squat.

But out here, in the least hospitable place, the Epsteins had. The NCH was a dream made real. A beautiful place that he would very much like not to see obliterated, both for its own sake and for what would happen to the country afterward.

"You want our support." Erik crossed his leg at the knee. The richest man in the world wore threadbare Chuck Taylors. "For the NCH to join forces with the government. Against the Children of Darwin."

"Against every terrorist. Against John Smith. He's behind the COD, isn't he?"

"The data is inconclusive—"

"You're lying," Millie said. "I hate it when you lie."

Erik Epstein winced. It wasn't, Cooper realized, because she had contradicted him. It was because of what she had said. Clearly, he cared for Millie. Understood her.

"Yes," Jakob said. "Smith is behind the COD. He set up the organization years ago as sleeper cells with a very specific set of instructions. They were to activate once he was cleared of the charges against him."

Cooper stared. His legs felt wobbly, and he steadied himself on a chair. On one level, he'd known it since he and Bobby Quinn had confronted John Smith. But it felt different to have it confirmed—and to learn that his actions had been the trigger for everything. *All those people. All that chaos.*

All your fault.

He took a deep breath, blew it out. "Okay. You said there's a 93 percent chance of a military attack in the next two weeks."

"93.2 percent. Not enough time. Not enough time."

"For what? There's no magic potion that will fix this."

Abruptly, Millie started laughing. It was an eerie sound, like she had only heard laughter described to her. Cooper stared, a little creeped out. After a moment, she stopped as abruptly as she had begun.

Unsettled, he said, "If you want to know if I would make the same choices now, I honestly don't know. And frankly, if your crystal ball is so goddamn clear, then you should have been making other plans. You shouldn't have gone all-in on one angle."

There was a half second hesitation before Jakob—

You're missing something.

These are very smart people, with enormous resources.

What are the chances that they bet their entire survival on you? A rogue agent working as an assassin in a situation he didn't, couldn't, fully comprehend?

They do have other plans. There's something else.

And why did Millie start laughing just then?

—replied, "You're right. Erik?"

"Fluid situation. Too many variables. The patterns are indefinite."

"That's why we need to act," Cooper said. "I understand how awkward this is for you. But if you don't come out right now in defense of the government, if you don't denounce the Children of Darwin and dedicate the full resources of the Holdfast to ending terrorism, you're slitting your own throat. I'm not posturing here." He glanced at Millie, who said nothing, just continued playing a game on her d-pad. "This is what I believe. Something I believe in so strongly that I came here myself, with my family. If we work together, right now, we have a chance to save everything."

Jakob cleared his throat. "We can see the advantages to President Clay. And to your country."

"*My* country?"

"But like Erik said, the situation is fluid."

"What does that mean?"

"You want me to put it bluntly?" Jakob shrugged. "We're no longer sure that the United States of America will survive."

"That the—what are you talking about? Are you saying that—"

"We don't want to back the losing side."

Cooper barked a half laugh, involuntary and not funny. "You're considering siding *with* the terrorists?"

"An appellation," Erik said to his lap. "A name given to a vector. There is no morality in the data."

"What my brother means is that John Smith would call himself a freedom fighter. And unlike your government, he has a plan. Allying with him might be better for the NCH."

Cooper couldn't believe it. He could not fucking believe what he was hearing. How could this be happening everywhere? All of them: President Clay and his staff running electoral math; John Smith trying to start a war; the Epsteins caring only about their own interests. Could it really be that everyone in power, on every side, was blind to the larger stakes?

The Civil War had been the bloodiest conflict in America's history. Three-quarters of a million dead, cities burned, infrastructure destroyed, disease run rampant—and that was all before Seraphim drones and Avenger missiles. Could positions be so hard-line, so intractably personal, that the people who held them were willing to risk the entire world?

"Yes," Millie said.

Erik looked at her. "Yes what?"

She shook her head.

All right. If they won't listen to reason, if terror of the consequences won't work, maybe something else will. "You said the data was unclear."

"Fluid."

"There must be something that would help solidify it." Cooper paused. "Something that we can offer you."

Erik and Jakob shared a look. To a normal person, it might have seemed they were considering his words. But to Cooper, the meaning was clear. They had already decided what they needed. There was a price for their help.

And it took all of three seconds for him to work it out.

CHAPTER 24

Soren read.

Cooper: Sovereignty. They want sovereignty for the NCH.

Clay: The hell you say.

Cooper: In return for which they'll denounce the COD and all other terrorist organizations, and dedicate the full resources of the Holdfast to eliminating them.

Clay: I will not go down in history as the president who allowed half of Wyoming to secede.

Cooper: Sir, we need to consider this. Erik and Jakob confirm that John Smith is behind the Children of Darwin. We can't act on that information without proof. But with their help, we could capture the COD and the most dangerous man alive in one move.

Clay: In trade for which we have to create a new nation within our own borders and accord them diplomatic rights and privileges. Not only that, but a nation of gifted, the first in the world. That's a deal with the devil, Nick.

Cooper: When the devil is the only one dealing, sir, you look at his wares.

Clay: I know you disagree with Secretary Leahy's approach, but the Monitoring Oversight Initiative, combined with targeted arrests, may offer a chance—

Cooper: Excuse me, sir, but it's not that simple. If we don't allow the NCH to secede, I believe that they'll join the terrorists.

Clay: They wouldn't dare. Epstein knows we can reduce the Holdfast to rubble.

<2.9 seconds of silence>

Cooper: Is that really what you want?

<4.2 seconds of silence>

Clay: Start the conversation. But we're going to need their full and unequivocal support. Not just on the COD, but into the future. A new special relationship.

When the file arrived on his d-pad, Soren had been in the middle of a novel, a baroque historical packed with architectural terms. It wasn't very good, but he found it impossible to be nothing here. Too many sounds from too many people coming through the walls. Too great a sense of the weight of humanity around him. Even a poor distraction was better.

There was a knock on the apartment door, the handle turning at the same time. John, knowing that the greater courtesy was respecting his time rather than his privacy.

John Smith said, "Youreadthefile?"

"Yes."

"Youunderstand."

It wasn't complicated. If the Holdfast allied with the American government before the jaws of John's trap closed, the revolution would be over before it began. "Yes."

"He'spowerful."

Soren had read files on the new ambassador, had watched footage of his arrival. "Yes."

"Canyoudoit?"

"Yes."

"Willyou?"

When John had pulled him from his retreat, led him into the world with all its pressures, he had explained why. Everything hung in the balance. A war was likely. Millions would likely die. But things would be forever changed. The gifted would assume dominance in America, and from there, the world.

Soren didn't care. The barriers that separated him from the world would never be toppled. Social change was irrelevant; prejudice had never been his problem. The revolution meant nothing to him.

But it meant everything to John, and to Samantha. The only two people in the world Soren cared about.

"Yes." He set aside his novel and looked his friend in the eye. "I'll kill Nick Cooper for you."

(AB) NORMAL

FROM CREATOR MAX VIVID

THE FIRST AND ONLY SHOW THAT PITS GIFTED INDIVIDUALS AGAINST
TEAMS OF NORMALS IN DANGEROUS COMPETITIONS

"ENTERTAINMENT'S A BLOODSPORT, BABY"

MAX VIVID

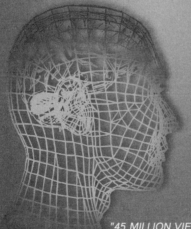

"45 MILLION VIEWERS A WEEK"

ENTERTAINMENT WEEKLY

"Follow the money," Quinn deadpanned over the video link. "Just . . . follow the money."

Cooper rolled his eyes. "Really?"

"Hey, it won an Oscar."

"I think it won them all. Do you have the files or not?"

Quinn said, "Sending." The projection went half-transparent as he leaned too close to the camera.

Cooper sat in the office Epstein had provided, across the square from the apartment his family was staying in. It was stylish, modern, and no doubt bugged from floor to ceiling. While it might be possible to keep secrets from Erik Epstein, he didn't imagine it was possible to do it in the New Canaan Holdfast.

It didn't matter. Let him watch.

Cooper glanced at his d-pad. "Receiving."

"For all the good it will do you."

"Epstein has a hole card. Something we don't know about."

"My friend, he has dozens. We've had teams of lawyers and forensic accountants working full-time to decrypt Epstein's finances for years. A third of a trillion dollars spread across hundreds of shell corporations in scores of countries. If you were to print out all the data I just sent you, you know how tall a stack it would be?"

"No, how tall?"

"Really tall."

Cooper laughed. "As ever, I feel safer knowing you're involved, Bobby."

"I'm not involved. The special advisor to the president asked for a favor, and the DAR was happy to help."

"Good, because I need another. I want you to link my d-pad to Daria."

"No way. She's an agency resource."

"And I work for the White House."

"Cooper—"

"Bobby, please. With sugar on top. And presidential authorization."

His friend blew a breath. "Fine."

"Thanks." Cooper tapped a button, and the projection of Quinn vanished. His d-pad showed that less than twenty-five percent of the file had been transferred. Considering the bandwidth available in the Holdfast, that was saying something. Maybe Quinn was right. How much could he expect to accomplish in the face of all of that information?

Cooper sighed, leaned back. There were three tri-ds mounted on the wall, and he had them all on, all tuned to news, all muted. The most interesting by far was the pirate station out of the NCH that hacked into the datafeeds to broadcast a distinctly partisan take on world events. Right now it was showing an image of former President Henry Walker, and as the host talked, someone doodled on the video, drawing a Hitler moustache and horns on the man. Not sophisticated, but kind of funny.

Okay. What are you doing?

On one hand, the answer was simple. He was using his gift for pattern recognition to sort through the finances of Epstein Industries, looking for anomalies that might give him a window into Erik's intentions.

On the other hand, that was ridiculous. $300 billion was an incomprehensibly huge amount of money. If the Coca-Cola Company merged with McDonald's, their combined market

227

capitalization would still be $20 billion less than Epstein's personal fortune. Cooper could stare at spreadsheets for a year and never see the same one twice, and he didn't have a year.

So do it your way. Forget a brute-strength approach. Trust your gift. Look for the sharp edges and knotty corners. The parts you can catch on.

When he'd met Erik Epstein months ago, the abnorm had asked Cooper to kill John Smith. It wasn't personal; Epstein wanted Smith dead because he believed that the terrorist leader posed a threat to New Canaan. A belief borne out by recent events.

Okay, fine. But Cooper couldn't possibly have been Epstein's only plan to protect New Canaan. In fact, talking to Erik and Jakob earlier, it had been clear that while they'd hoped he would succeed, they hadn't gone all-in on that notion. Why should they? They were intelligent men running a complicated empire. He had probably been a long shot.

There it was. The first clue. If he had been a long shot, that meant they had other plans in action as well. Plans that predated his arrival and that would have continued after he left.

Now you just need to figure out what they are.

His d-pad pinged softly, showing the connection had been established. Cooper switched to verbal control, and said, "Daria?"

"Hello, Nick. Department of Analysis and Response Inquiry Assessment, ready." The voice was female, but the force behind it wasn't a person. DARIA was a research tool, a personality matrix used to sift data.

"Sort largest expenditures, by category, in Epstein Industries and all subsidiaries, 2010 to 2013."

"Complete."

"Remove everyday costs of doing business."

"Nick, I'll need more precision."

"Take out stuff like maintenance and legal fees, but leave in things like, I don't know, product development."

"Complete."

"Display."

A list scrolled. And scrolled, and scrolled. What had Bobby said? A third of a trillion dollars, spread across hundreds of companies.

"Filter for anomalous results."

"Nick, anomalous in what way?"

"As compared to—" A flicker of motion caught his eye. Something was happening on the tri-d. All of the news stations were showing the same footage. "Um, other multinationals."

"Nick, that will take several moments."

"What? Fine."

He tapped buttons on the desk, and the screens unmuted, audio pouring out from three sources at once, as the video showed . . .

Shannon?

Just flashes of her, moving fast. Dressed in black fatigues and carrying a submachine gun. She was racing down a hall somewhere, a dozen similarly dressed people behind her. The hall was painted a sad shade of green, and the windows were narrow. It looked familiar.

The announcers were talking over one another, and he muted two of them, left CNN running.

"—a terrorist attack on Davis Academy, an institution for advanced study located in West Virginia. The academy is an elite facility for the most powerful gifted—"

Davis. No wonder it looked familiar. That was the academy he had visited last year. The one where he had seen children manipulated into brutal fistfights. Learned that the kids were bugged so that their deepest secrets could be used against them. Where names were taken away and identities destroyed and personalities turned more docile, more fragile, and more compliant.

Where his daughter, Kate, would have ended up.

Holy shit. Shan. I should have trusted you.

"—terrorists stormed the gates and subdued the personnel, killing an undisclosed number of guards and teachers, including Charles Norridge, the facility director. Whereabouts of the more than three hundred students of the school are unknown at this time."

Cooper's hand flew to his mouth, a laugh bursting free. He remembered the anger that had pumped through his veins the day he listened to Norridge, the fantasy he'd had about hurling the director through the window. That was the day his eyes had started opening, the day he'd realized that the DAR wasn't all he had hoped it might be.

He swapped the audio feed from CNN to the Tesla pirate station.

"—liberating more than three hundred kidnapped children before planting explosives and blowing the shit out of the symbol of horrific oppression that was Davis Academy. The chief torturer, Charles Norridge, was killed in the attack, and we all feel real sad about that. Bravo to the brave freedom fighters who pulled this off. You'll never pay for a drink again. Mama! Daddy! Your babies are free!"

As a representative of the government, he knew he was supposed to be horrified. Knew that this was an attack on the status quo. An act of terrorism that would further upset the already delicate balance of the country.

And he just didn't care. The Tesla pirate station had it right: bravo. And it was Shannon's doing. What had she said last night, in the midst of their fight? *I'm going to West Virginia. I'm going to do the best thing I've ever done.*

My God. What a woman.

Right, Coop. But remember what she said next? "Watch the news. And fuck off."

The first reaction was bile in his throat and an *oh shit* feeling, a sense that he'd screwed up. But the second was—

Before that. You were accusing her of trying to steal bioweap-ons—which, by the way, you know Shannon wouldn't do—and she said she was there for something else.

A magic potion.

The phrase must have stuck in your head, because that's what you said this afternoon.

That was what made Millie laugh.

—more important. He muted the news.

"Daria. Retask. Do you have access to the information stolen from the DAR earlier this week?"

"Nick, I have a topical list, but no details. That information was sequestered—"

"Yeah, I know. It was primarily information about research facilities, right?"

"Nick, that's correct."

"Run a correlation pattern against all Epstein Industries expenditures. I want to know if Epstein was funding any of the labs that Shan—that the terrorist stole information about."

"Nick, there's one match. The Advanced Genomics Institute."

He leaned back, feeling that tickle in his brain that told him his gift was close to finding a pattern. "Tell me more."

CHAPTER 26

The last time he'd been in New Canaan it had been the height of summer, and even so the evenings had been chilly. Now, midnight in late November, it was twenty degrees. Even standing in a crowd, the wind on the airfield cut through the leather jacket he'd brought, and he stomped his feet and blew into his hands.

Too bad you ditched your security detail. They probably could have lent you a proper coat.

It had not been the most diplomatic move, slipping out the second-story window of his loaner office and hailing an electric cab. But he wasn't on the airfield as an ambassador.

With a last roar, the 737 came to a stop on the runway. Ground crew drove a stair car up to the side of the plane as the engines wound down. Around him, the crowd surged with barely restrained desire.

"Can you believe it?"

The man who'd spoken was in his midfifties, his face leathery and lean. No one had water fat in Wyoming, but it was more than that. The guy looked like someone who had fallen asleep and woken up in misery every day for a long time. Cooper said, "Son or daughter?"

"Son," the man said. "Peter. He'll be fifteen now."

The more Cooper looked, the more he realized he'd been wrong about the man's age. Biologically, he was probably forty. It wasn't hard to figure out why he looked so ragged. The Treffert-Down test that identified abnorms was administered at age eight. The man hadn't seen his son for seven years.

"We never gave up. Every year on his birthday we'd have a cake, try to sing. Last year my Gloria died." The guy's voice was soft. "After that, it got harder to believe."

It got harder to believe. Truer words. Seven years ago, Cooper had just been promoted to agent status in Equitable Services. He had been a believer then, eager to hunt the targets Drew Peters had given him. While he'd never been affiliated with the academies—hadn't seen one until last year—it would take the worst kind of self-deception to suggest that his work hadn't landed children in them.

For all Cooper knew, he had been instrumental in stealing this man's son.

The thought was a railroad spike of guilt. For a moment, Cooper's defenses fell away, and he realized the full weight of the stakes he played for. Even striving every day to do the right thing, working to create a better world for his children, he had made unforgivable mistakes, caused unimaginable pain. And meanwhile, despite his best efforts, every day the world had gotten more complicated, the solution farther out of reach. It was, indeed, getting harder to believe.

With a clunk, the door of the 737 opened. The crowd chatter died, leaving just the whine of the dying jets and the howl of the wind.

A figure stepped out onto the stairs. Shannon wore the same black fatigues he'd seen in the news footage and held a little girl in her arms. Even from a distance, something about her looked different. When he saw the girl's face, Cooper understood.

It might be getting harder to believe, but Shannon had found a way.

■

The scene was happy chaos, and even desperate as he was to talk to Shannon, Cooper waited. Children streamed off the plane, the little ones first. Their reaction was uniform; they froze at the doorway of the jet, staring, hoping, straining. Some of them saw parents in the crowd and raced down the stairs into their arms, mothers and fathers openly weeping, crushing their stolen children to their chests, swearing never to let go.

Others milled, the hope in their eyes draining slowly. Of course—not every parent would be here. At least, not yet. Cooper had a feeling several hundred families were about to uproot their lives and join the NCH, and screw the consequences.

It was the older ones he really felt sorry for. The teenagers had spent half their lives in that academy. It had become their reality, and they had the darty eyes and nervous bearing of felons released from prison.

Except felons are allowed to keep their names.

Cooper caught a glimpse of the man he had been talking to, a scrawny kid almost hidden in his embrace, the guy squeezing so hard it was like he was trying to push his son inside his own chest.

Amidst the crowd, armed commandos became the eyes of miniature hurricanes, people crowding around them to slap their backs and shake their hands, women kissing them, people offering them money, love, faith. But Shannon waited atop the stairs until the last child had disembarked.

Then, staying out of the fanfare, she strolled down, skirted the edge of the crowd, and started to move away, the little girl in her arms. No one seemed to notice them.

Cooper dug out his phone and dialed.

■

The girl squirmed in her arms. "You can put me down now, Aunt Shannon."

"I know, sweetie," she said, but didn't. Even tired as she was, the weight was sweet.

But man, was she beat.

Honey, you've been beat before. This is different.

Bone-weary. No, not just bone—soul-weary. It wasn't simple exhaustion, although she had that in spades. Shannon was going on forty hours awake, some of that high-adrenaline time, and the world was bleary; her muscles ached, and her head hurt, and her eyes felt like sandpaper.

All of which she'd expected. She'd just also expected to feel . . .

What? Redeemed? Cleansed of your sins?

Well, yeah.

Killing people is a strange way to accomplish that.

Whatever. They were bad people, and Charles Norridge hadn't been her first. If there was an afterlife and the people you'd murdered were waiting, she was going to have a pitched battle to make it through the gates.

No, it wasn't the killing that was bugging her. It was something more abstract. A feeling of . . .

Pointlessness?

There it was. All the time she'd been planning this up, she'd imagined the moment when they returned triumphant, and in that imagining she'd been at the center of the celebration, champagne spraying and everyone laughing. But when the moment had arrived, she'd just stood at the top of the stairs and watched.

It didn't matter. Thread through the airport, snag a cab, find a hotel. Sleep for a week. Then dig into the problem of finding—

"Hey."

The voice froze her. She set the girl down, then turned slowly.

Nick stood ten feet away. He looked a little haggard, but still good. Homey, which was a strange way to think about a man she barely knew. Shannon stood locked for a moment. So many things she wanted to say, but she didn't trust herself to speak. He was a government man, and she had just led an attack on a government building. She knew the raid had been right, but she was so tired. If Nick started a fight, she might just lie down on the concrete and weep.

"I'm sorry," he said. "I'll never doubt you again."

It was the last thing she'd expected. She felt her throat tighten, and just nodded.

"Hi, Alice," Nick said. "I don't know if you remember me. I'm Cooper. We met at your parents' house a couple of months ago."

Oh, don't say that. A squad of soldiers stormed their building because we were there. Alice spent the last months being called "Mary" and crying herself to sleep because we were at her parents' house . . .

"I know you've had a long day," he said, "but I've got someone who wants to talk to you." He held out his phone. Alice Chen stared at it, her expression blank.

"Go ahead. It's okay." He put it in her hand. Slowly, she lifted it to her ear. Said, "Hello?"

And then, "Mommy?"

And, "Daddy!"

Something in the girl gave, and she started crying and babbling, a mix of Chinese and English, and even the words Shannon couldn't understand she understood. And for a second, just a second, she felt the emotion she had imagined she would in the first place, a pure joy thumping in her chest like a kick drum. There was the meaning she'd been missing, and Cooper had been at the heart of it.

"When I saw the news," he said, "I woke Bobby up and gave him a direct order from the office of the president to find and release her parents. Lee and Lisa are being processed now. They'll be on the first flight in the morning."

"You can do that?"

"It's done."

"Won't you get in trouble?"

"I'm going a little bit rogue." He shrugged. "Are you okay?"

"I'm fine. Tired."

Nick stepped closer. He needed a shave, and his eyes were red, something manic in them. He cast a quick glance over at Alice— sitting on the cold ground clutching the phone in both hands and cry-talking—then said, "I need to clarify something."

"Yeah?"

"I was wound up last night. Saying things I didn't really mean. You and me, we may not see things the same way. But I know you don't want biological weapons. I was being stupid." He reached for her hand, and she let him take it, warm against the cold. "I know the things you won't do."

She didn't trust herself to speak, just nodded.

"Listen," Nick said. "What I want more than anything right now is for us to check into a really expensive hotel and spend a week talking." He smiled. "And not talking."

"But?"

"*But* right now we can't. And I need to ask you about something."

She sighed, pulled her hand away. "Come on, you know I'm not going to—"

"Wait," he said. "Just hold on. I'm going to tell you what I know. After that, speak, don't, it's up to you. Okay?"

She rubbed at her eye with the heel of one hand. "Sure."

"You broke into the DAR to get classified information on bio and genetic research labs. But you didn't take information on one place or one project; you took most of what we had nationwide. That means John Smith believes that a laboratory is creating something he wants, only he didn't know which lab. I bet he does now: a place called the Advanced Genomics Institute, run by a scientist named Dr. Abraham Couzen.

"Couzen is by all accounts a genius. His work has offered new ways to look at the genome. Which means new ways to look at humanity." He cocked his head. "Last night when I asked what you were after, you said a magic potion. I thought you were being a smart-ass. But you weren't, were you?"

She kept her gaze level and her breath steady.

He gave her that smile, soap-opera scruff, the one he knew was charming. "You're not going to help me here?"

"Your rules."

"Right. Okay. I'm guessing here. But I've been patterning it, and I can only find one thing that fits. Only one thing important enough for you to risk breaking into the DAR; only one thing that Dr. Couzen could develop that John Smith and Erik Epstein would both want desperately." Cooper paused, laughed. "God, this sounds crazy."

"So go crazy."

"I'm thinking that Dr. Couzen has figured out what makes people abnorms."

It was a struggle, but Shannon kept her poker face up. *You wouldn't have gone for the guy if he were dumb.*

"He's discovered the genetic basis behind the gifts," Cooper continued. "Not only that, but he's found some way to . . . to . . ."

Say it, Nick. Say the thing that no one dared hope.

"Shannon, has he found a way to give gifts to anyone? A magic potion that turns normal people into abnorms?"

It was her turn to watch intently. She wasn't a reader, had no gift to tell if someone was lying to her, to cobble together their unspoken thoughts. But it wasn't hard to see the incredulity on Cooper's face. She remembered having the same feelings herself when John had told her why he wanted her to break into the DAR.

But what does it mean to you, Nick? Is it exciting? Or terrifying? Because your answer determines so much.

Picking her words carefully, she said, "If that were true, what would you do about it?"

"The opportunity for anyone to be gifted? It would be a hundred thousand years of evolution in a blink. The status quo would vanish. All our systems, our beliefs." He shook his head. "The government would want to keep it quiet, control it."

"Yeah," she said. "But I asked what *you* would do."

"What you're really asking," he said, "is whether I would do the same thing I did last time. Because when I shared the truth behind the Monocle, behind President Walker and Drew Peters and Equitable Services, it had massive consequences. I was trying to do the right thing, and in the process I pushed the world closer to disaster. And you want to know if I would do the same thing again."

She waited.

"Absolutely," he said. "Without hesitation. This can't be a decision made behind closed doors, by people who have agendas. This belongs to all of us."

A glow started in her chest and spread out through her body, a tingle of warmth that the cold Wyoming night couldn't touch. She stepped forward, put a hand on his cheek. Looked him in the eyes. "Good answer."

He sagged, not as though weight had landed on his shoulders, but rather like something rigid within him had fallen away. Like he could breathe for the first time in a long while. "It's true, then? It exists?"

"Yes."

"My God."

"Yes."

"This changes everything."

"Yeah," she said. Then smiled at him. "Don't think it means I'm done being pissed at you yet, though."

Nick laughed. "Never dreamed of it."

We are plugged in all the time now. As we work, as we drive, even as we read a book or watch the tri-d. Our lives are partially virtual, lived in the digital space.

It's the great equalizer: black or white, male or female, norm or abnorm, the first thing most people do in the morning—before they even brush their teeth—is reach for their d-pad.

You want to change the world? Forget politics. Learn to code.

—Jennifer Laurens, CEO of Bridgetech,
   to MIT's graduating class

CHAPTER 27

The woman in the projection field was slender, and the tactical blacks made her seem even smaller. But she carried herself with the grace of a ballet dancer, each gesture assured as she slipped past a guard, the man's eyes elsewhere, his weapon coming up. There was a muffled bang, and a hole appeared in the center of his head. He had barely crumpled before a second commando stormed in. She forced the other guard to his knees and dug the barrel of a submachine gun into his neck.

Leahy said, "Pause."

The two women froze, their expressions locked in the in-between of an awkward photograph.

"That's Shannon Azzi," Leahy continued. "Her friend is Kathy Baskoff. They're both abnorms, known terrorists with strong connections to John Smith."

Senator Richard Lathrup stepped into the display field, his body casting shadows as he blocked the projectors. "This one doesn't look like a soldier."

"Shannon's not, usually. A spy and an assassin. She's the one who broke into DAR headquarters last week."

The senator whistled. "And now Davis Academy. Busy girl." He turned. "Taking out the guards I can understand. But how did they disable the security protocols?"

"Part of what she lifted from the DAR was the academy IT package. They used it to put the alarms in a loop and black out the facility."

Mitchum said, "Another failure."

"Yes, sir," Leahy said. "Worse, while ordinarily we could have kept this quiet, the terrorists released the footage to the media. Our presumption is that the public impact was the real purpose; freeing a few children has no tactical value."

"This plays into our hands, doesn't it?" The senator gestured at the frozen footage. "Attacking a government facility, killing teachers and administrators, blowing up buildings. It's a clear indicator that the gifted can't be trusted and a perfect reason for the president to move up the timetable on the Monitoring Oversight Initiative."

Leahy shook his head. "When Cleveland rioted, I pushed Clay to do just that. He refused."

"That's not all he did," Mitchum said, "is it?"

"No, sir." Leahy took a breath. "Clay wants to deal with the gifted directly. He hopes to broker a deal with Erik Epstein, a full partnership between the NCH and the United States to end terrorism, starting with the Children of Darwin."

"That's correct. And as an envoy, he sent Nick Cooper, the DAR agent who killed Drew Peters and released the evidence against President Walker. Evidence that could lead back to our involvement." Mitchum paused. "Would you say the situation is under control, Owen?"

Leahy forced himself not to wince. *You knew he was going to make you eat that.* "Clay has turned out to be weaker than I thought."

"A dangerous miscalculation. And now we have an abnorm of uncertain loyalties negotiating with Erik Epstein."

"Yes, sir." He gritted his teeth, said, "I admit, the situation is out of my control."

The senator said, "Is it such a bad thing that Clay is talking to Epstein? Cleveland, Tulsa, and Fresno are under siege. Maybe Epstein can end this."

Good Christ, man. Are you even clear on what we're trying to do here? The senator was a useful ally, no question. While the Monitoring Oversight Initiative had been Leahy's idea, it was Richard who had proposed it in the Senate and served as the public face. But at the end of the day, he was a politician, not an intelligence agent. Leahy said, "I'm concerned about how far Clay will go to be liked."

"You should be," Mitchum said. "Yesterday our president authorized Nick Cooper to offer the New Canaan Holdfast the opportunity to leave our fair nation."

Leahy's mouth fell open. "Secession?"

"Indeed."

"My God. How do you know?"

Mitchum didn't respond, and Leahy cursed himself. A boneheaded move, admitting surprise. Secrets were power. *Worth noting, though, that even the* president *can't keep secrets from Mitchum.* He said, "Clay is losing it. That will never work."

"My concern is what happens if it does."

The senator looked puzzled. "Why? Surely ending terrorism, not to mention the siege of three American cities, is worth some scrub land in Wyoming."

Leahy was about to respond, but to his surprise, Mitchum wheeled on the man, all the careful meter gone from his voice. "'Scrub land in Wyoming'? Senator, we are talking about sovereign territory of the United States. Our job is to protect our country, not give it away."

"Yes, but—"

"Dreaming of a better world is for poets. Men in our position can't afford to think that way. Surely you wouldn't want your constituents, not to mention your caucus, to know that you're willing to parcel out America as party favors."

The senator paled. "No, sir. Of course not."

Leahy almost smiled. *Nice of Richard to step up to the whipping post, take some of the heat off you. But don't get complacent.*

"I think we have to acknowledge that the Monitoring Oversight Initiative is dead. Events have spiraled past that point."

Mitchum said, "Resume, full mute."

The two terrorist women slid back into motion. Shannon Azzi pulled out a roll of duct tape and began to bind the guard with it. Leahy had seen the footage more than once, and so he turned his attention to Mitchum. For twenty-five years he had worked for Mitchum in one capacity or another, sometimes directly, sometimes simply because he owed his position to the man. He knew how Mitchum's mind worked, and admired it.

Intelligence work was about collecting mountains of information. There were three components to success. The first was spotting which minor detail was the important one. The second was deciding what to do about it. The third was having the stomach to carry out those actions ruthlessly.

Mitchum was very successful indeed.

In the footage, Shannon Azzi patted the guard on the cheek, then pushed his chair toward the bank of monitors and walked out. The view jumped to the area outside the guard hut, heavy trucks rolling into sight.

"People who disparage the status quo have never experienced the opposite," Mitchum said. "Maintaining order, keeping the system running, flawed as it may be, is a sacred duty. It's not about words on a piece of paper. It's about our children. America may not be perfect, but it's closer than anywhere else, and preserving it for my children is my highest calling."

Leahy had never heard Mitchum wax so poetic. The senator was doing the sycophantic thing, nodding sagely, but Leahy knew better. Terence Mitchum didn't need to be loved, didn't rationalize his actions. *That speech was a message.*

He flashed back to that moment, more than two decades ago, when he had sat outside Mitchum's office, holding the study announcing the arrival of the gifted. His hands sweaty and his thoughts scattered. It had been a bold, even reckless maneuver, and it had made him. If he hadn't caught Mitchum's eye, Leahy would probably be a midlevel manager at some private military contractor instead of the secretary of defense.

Perhaps it's time for another bold maneuver.

"One of the things I've always found concerning," Leahy said slowly, "is that the New Canaan Holdfast is quite peaceful. There's no greater refutation of the argument that abnorms are a threat than that happy little enclave. Normal and gifted coexist there. It's a problem."

Richard looked at him. "Son, you have a strange worldview."

"I'm not your son, Senator. I'm the secretary of defense of the United States of America."

"I didn't mean—"

"It's a problem because it's false. The NCH is about as self-sustaining as a two-week-old puppy. They are able to function as a city on a hill because of us. We shield them and support them. And meanwhile, abnorms work together there, with limitless funding and little regulation. They pile advantage on advantage, leapfrogging science and technology, and then doling it out at a pace that pleases them."

On the projection floor, Shannon Azzi hoisted her gun into the air. Leahy said, "Freeze."

He'd timed it perfectly, caught her just in the moment of exhorting her troops, weapon high, face wild, the stock pose of every third-world rebel commander. "That, Senator, is what the gifted represent. We are protecting an environment that harbors terrorists and drains our resources while creating advancements we cannot hope to match." He turned to Mitchum. "Sir, if we don't act, I believe that we are fostering our children's future masters."

Mitchum rubbed his chin. His eyes were unreadable.

Leahy thought of last night in the Oval Office. Thanksgiving, and the president sitting catatonic as he watched Cleveland burn. There had been a chance to save the country. To take the kind of strong action that could turn things around.

Nick Cooper's misguided policy of appeasement had put an end to that. But Marla Keevers had raised a point that had been bouncing around Leahy's brain ever since.

"Sir, I'm wondering if we haven't been thinking too small." He thought of adding more, then decided against it. Let them work it out themselves.

After a moment, Mitchum said, "Can it be done?"

"With Clay's policies of compromise and discussion, there are certain to be more attacks. More destruction in American cities. More of"—he gestured—"her. Instead of trying for the MOI, what if we thought bigger?"

"My God, man," Richard said. "Are you really talking about—"

"Senator," Leahy said, "shut up." He stared at the man, put the threat in his eyes.

Mitchum walked over to stand in front of Shannon Azzi. For a long moment he stared thoughtfully into her holographic eyes. Finally, he said, "Play for all the marbles?"

"This is our moment, sir."

"Maybe." Mitchum turned. "Of course, Clay is unlikely to launch an attack."

"Yes, sir, he is." Leahy slid his hands in his pockets. "That's why he'll just have to trust his advisors."

CHAPTER 28

Cooper was having a hard time keeping his mind on his breakfast.

In an hour he would be sitting down with Erik Epstein to negotiate the terms of the New Canaan Holdfast's secession from the United States. An enormous political maneuver with consequences so far-ranging they boggled the mind.

And it didn't matter, because what they would actually be talking about was the biggest development in human history since . . . fire?

When the gifted had first appeared thirty or so years ago, scientists and philosophers alike had wondered what they meant. Why some people had amazing abilities and others did not. But after decades of research and thousands of theories, no answers had been found. As the ramifications of that dichotomy had grown, the *whys* and *hows* had started to seem less important as people focused on the question of what the world was going to do about it.

And now, suddenly, all that was wiped away. There would be no more "us" and "them"—no more divisions. There would be questions and fears and a million decisions to be made. But at least there would be options. The growing tension that was pitting the country—the world—against itself would ease. Instead of terrorism, there would be debate. Instead of genocide, there would be choice.

And humanity would never be the same. In a very real way, humanity as it had been would cease to exist, replaced by something better.

All of which made it hard to concentrate on breakfast.

For now, be here for your family. You've lost enough time with them already.

The restaurant was bright and airy, tastefully designed, and alive with chatter. One of the guys on their security team had recommended it; apparently the chef was famous in the NCH, a brilliant who ran a string of places. Cooper largely avoided abnorm chefs; maybe his palate wasn't sophisticated enough, but he just didn't need his breakfast "deconstructed":

Steamed egg cut into a cube, the yolk removed and the hollow stuffed with spinach and goat cheese; kelp protein extruded and dyed to look like rib eye, served atop a smear of braised beet puree; rutabaga tater tots served with crystallized ketchup.

"How do they turn ketchup into crystals?" Todd poked at his plate suspiciously.

"I gotta say, Toddster, I think the more important question is why." Cooper glanced around, taking in the room, old habit. It was busy, a crowd of people waiting, but a table had been made for them the moment they arrived. One of the benefits of being an ambassador. Thankfully, the security team was keeping things low profile; most of them were outside, and the two guards in the restaurant wore plainclothes.

Soon we won't need guards, won't fear terrorists.

"I like it," Kate said. Her crepes were folded into origami animals and covered with freeze-dried berries. He'd stolen a strawberry off her plate; it tasted sweet but had the texture of a cheese puff. "I like it here."

Natalie shot him a quick look over the table, a smile in her eyes. "You do?"

Kate nodded. "It's nice. Everything is new."

"It's stupid," Todd said.

"Come on," Natalie said. "Why would you say that? You've only been here a day."

"They screwed up *soccer*."

How did it work, turning a normal into a gifted? Probably it amplified latent tendencies; if you had always been good at guessing how other people were feeling, you would now be a reader. If you had always had grace on the athletic field, now you would be able to sense the others' moves before they made them.

My God, though, what a change that would bring. The Children of Darwin thought they had caused some chaos? Their little insurrection was bush league compared to the upheaval that would flow from Erik's pet project. A magic potion indeed.

Be here *now.*

He turned to his son. "What do you mean, they screwed up soccer?"

"I played with some kids yesterday. They have all these stupid rules 'cause they're gifted."

"Like what?"

"One kid can do the thing you do, where no one can touch him, so to get a goal he has to score and then take the ball back and score again. This other girl just sits in the center of the field. She doesn't even move, but they picked her *first*. A *girl*. Plus, one kid is allowed to use his hands, because he's seeing math."

"He's seeing math?"

"That's what he said. Angles and stuff, and he needs to be able to pick up the ball and throw it. Then when he does, it does crazy trick stuff and bounces off things and people and no one can get it and it just, like, rolls past you."

Cooper fought an urge to laugh. *Remember when you said a city of mirrors would be cool, kiddo? Welcome to a world of them.* "So they're changing the rules. No one says the rules have to be the same all the time."

"They *do*. That's what rules means."

"You're just mad because you lost," Kate said.

"I didn't lose. They cheated."

"I like it," Kate said. "Nobody here thinks it's weird that I organize things."

"That's not weird, sweetie. You're not weird."

"I'm weird at home. Can we stay here?"

Cooper laughed. He was about to reply when a knife slid across the throat of one of his bodyguards, and a fountain of sudden blood sprayed across three tables.

■

Soren rode.

Passenger side, the backseat of the cab. The driver had a mole on his neck, a hair growing out of it. Out the window, momentary flashes turned into still life paintings. A man and woman walking hand in hand. Look at it slow and notice that her hand clutches harder than his, that his eyes are on a display window, that her neck showed age ten years past her makeup, and his belt was buckled but pants unbuttoned. Grace, permanence, purity—they were illusions. People were just fluids and flesh, meat and hair and bone.

The weapon was what he had asked for, a Fairbairn-Sykes. A fighting knife, dagger-tapered and razor-sharp, thin enough to slide between bone. Made famous during World War II, although those had been steel and this one was carbon-fiber. The edge wouldn't hold, but it was so light he could move it without any momentum at all, just an extension of his hand. A knife good for killing and little else. His fingers rested on the pommel.

The car began to slow. It would be almost a minute before it stopped. Soren used the time to read the security outside the restaurant. As John had predicted, it was a diplomatic protection team, all gifted, all armed, all wired via earpiece. Guards used to escorting high-value assets, attuned to threat at all times. They would have constant situational awareness, evaluating everything in terms of risk.

So he became a tourist from Missouri, wide-eyed and unthreatening. He had all the time in the world to slip into character. He paid the driver with the mild excitement of someone for whom a cab ride was a novelty, something more often seen on tri-d. Told the driver to keep the change, a buck too much, exactly enough to be appreciated and forgotten. Stepped onto the sidewalk and looked around, trying at once to pretend that he belonged here— keep the muggers away—while simultaneously taking everything in. After a minute and a half that was eight seconds to the rest of the world, he turned and walked into the restaurant, consciously putting a little pleasure in his step, anticipating a meal unlike any he could get in good old MO.

The team registered him, watched him, and dismissed him. Even the reader by the door. Readers amused him. They were so attuned to everyone else in the world, yet his gift meant that to them he was like the optical illusion of a tire rim spinning backward as it sped along—an incorrect approximation based on flawed perception.

Inside, the restaurant was chaos and noise. So many people, all being. Just sitting there being, and so loud about it, volume and intensity. But he was ready, became nothing at all as he walked to one of the two bodyguards and slit his throat, the blade's edge so sharp that the skin sprang apart at the touch, the carotid neatly bisected.

Arterial spray gushed out in an arc. It was rather pretty, the fluid dynamics of it, and he spent a few seconds admiring it before heading for the other guard. That one was drawing his gun, a smooth and practiced move, and Soren took the time to look at the angle of the man's arm, the way his left hand was bracing his right, and positioned himself so that the man's own momentum brought his inner elbow into contact with the blade, the force of the guard's motion driving the knife through cloth and flesh and muscle and tendons to sever the brachial artery.

There was screaming, but not in his nothing.

For some reason, Soren found himself thinking of the spider, the one he had spent time being when John came to get him. Why? Ah. The calm immobility that preceded lethal motion. Yes.

He turned. The two bodyguards crumpled at about the same rate, as if they had choreographed it.

Soren took in the still life. Nick Cooper was on his feet, his eyes appraising. No hesitation or paralysis. Interesting.

It wouldn't be enough, of course. But it was interesting.

■

Cooper was on his feet without thought, reflex taking over. But by the time he had stood up, the second bodyguard was done, a textbook-perfect slice splitting the inner bicep to the bone. He'd have a few seconds of consciousness before the long fall into darkness.

The man with the knife turned, his face calm. Behind him, the two guards collapsed, not clean and quick like on tri-d, but messy, arterial spray lashing like a hose each time their hearts beat. A woman coated with blood screamed a ragged, inhuman sound.

Cooper took in the scene in an instant, his mind patterning for the fight to come. The killer was lean and slight, the knife he carried modeled after the old British commando daggers. He looked at Cooper, and then—

His knuckles aren't white. His breathing is steady. The pulse in his neck is maybe seventy beats a minute. He just murdered two highly trained guards in three seconds, and he is perfectly calm.

This isn't an abnorm with a grudge, the brother of one of your old targets. This is an assassin.

Which means he was sent for you. Probably by John Smith.

And your children are here.

—started walking toward the table.

In one move, Cooper spun, grabbed the back of his chair, circled back around, and hurled it at the assassin, an easy throw at ten feet, the chair not heavy but massy enough to tangle the guy up, lessen the advantage of his knife. Cooper kept the momentum going and hopped right up on the table, the shortest distance between a killer and his children being a straight line. He dropped down the other side, following the chair, thinking, *Go low, sweep his leg, then stomp his wrist, groin, wrist, neck—*

Only when he got there, the chair had flown through space undisturbed, the man somehow standing calmly to one side of it. Not even blinking as a chair missed him by a fraction of an inch.

Fine. Cooper slid into a fighting stance, light on his feet, knees bent, arms up to block. The trick to facing an opponent with a knife was knowing you were going to get cut, period, and maintaining an attack despite that. Act like prey and you became prey.

The assassin's face was composed. He seemed barely awake. Cooper shifted his weight, watching the man, gauging his next move . . .

And getting no sense of it. Nothing. It was like the man in front of him had no plan, no intent. He was a void.

It didn't matter. Cooper faked a jab, then put his weight behind a devastating hook to the man's left kidney, followed it with an uppercut that caught his chin and snapped his head back, exposing the neck for an elbow strike that crushed the assassin's trachea.

Only the man didn't react to the fake, and when Cooper threw his hook, instead of flesh, he found himself punching the edge of the dagger, the thing held parallel to his knuckles so that the edge slid right between his second and third fingers and split his hand halfway to the wrist.

Oh.

Shit.

He took a half step back, his arms up to guard, only his right hand was a mess of gore, half of it sort of flopping, no pain yet, the edge of the knife too sharp, and shock setting in so that for a fraction of a second all he could do was stare at his hand, thinking, wow, how weird was that.

Still no expression on the man's face, just the flicker of his eyes to one side as—

He's immune to your gift. Exempt from it.

He can't be. Everyone shows intention. Our bodies betray our minds. But somehow his doesn't.

Which means that your gift won't help you. This fight isn't like any you've ever had.

And what's he looking at?

Oh. No.

—Todd, somehow on his feet, ran at the man.

No!

It all slowed down then, not an effect of his gift but the by-product of a massive spike of adrenaline and terror, Cooper thinking faster than he could move, and harder than he could bear, trying through sheer force of will to make the universe not allow what was happening, his son yelling as he ran at the man who had hurt his dad. Ten years old and tall for his age but a boy, just a boy, skinny legs and skinny arms and good intentions but no business doing what he was doing, and Jesus oh Jesus no, don't let this happen, Cooper trying to block Todd with one arm, an arm hurled with all his force, better to knock the kid back and take the breath out of him and maybe even bang him up than let him anywhere near this empty-eyed killing machine who even now was spinning with terrible force, arm up and elbow out, no no no not my son you bastard, me, take me but not my boy—

The assassin's blow was square, the arm locked, the elbow conveying all the force of the move directly into Todd's temple. His son's head snapped too far sideways and his eyes went glassy.

Cooper screamed as he threw himself at the killer, ready to strip the skin from his body and tear the tissue from the bones as, moving like he had all the time in the world, the man continued his turn and buried the dagger in Cooper's chest.

Slick cool plastic parted skin and muscle, slid between his ribs, and pierced his heart.

He knew he was dead then.

Tried to fight anyway even though he couldn't move his arms, but it didn't matter because the guy was already turning and walking away, his mission accomplished, his target assassinated.

Cooper fell down.

Natalie was suddenly there, her face filling his vision, black spots dancing, holes in her head, and she was yelling something, couldn't hear, the blood coming fast and on the floor he landed beside Todd, his beautiful boy, the son he and Natalie had made, and it couldn't be that his son was on the ground, that he wasn't breathing, and this couldn't be the last thing it couldn't it can't remember instead a whirl of green and your kids clinging to each arm as you spin them on the front lawn of the house you'd shared with Natalie all of them smiling and laughing and the world a whorl a whirl a beautiful world

CHAPTER 29

It wasn't that Ethan was tired, though he was. Exhausted, in fact, walking-dead tired—there were the zombies again—bleary-eyed and wasted, his arms leaden from holding Violet. Twelve pounds didn't seem like much until it was sagging deadweight carried for miles.

And it wasn't the pain, although there was plenty of that. His hips and back felt like hot steel rods had been inserted into them. His knee had swollen up. Worst were his bare feet. Before bed, Amy had taken off her socks with her shoes, and so once they'd left Jeremy's, he'd peeled off his own and insisted she take them. Hours of walking through the darkness across fallow cornfields and state park land had cut his soles ragged, and he tracked blood with every step. It would have been easier on roads, but they were done with roads.

Still, it wasn't any of that. What was killing him was the help-lessness. He'd never felt so goddamn *useless.*

Violet had woken up an hour ago and had been crying ever since, piteous, confused howls of hunger, and he had nothing to feed her.

A man had pointed a shotgun at the people he loved, and he hadn't been able to do anything about it. Even with a gun in his belt, he hadn't been able to do anything. His belly still burned at the memory of that. He knew he had made the smart move, knew that what he was feeling was just leftover monkey stuff, but it didn't matter.

He was supposed to protect his family, and instead they were wandering the countryside with nothing, no food, no shelter, no money. Not even much of a plan.

Dawn had broken on the three of them hiking a back road, fleeing a burning city. Refugees, simple as that. They must have crossed the quarantine line sometime during the night without even knowing it. They'd seen a helicopter a while back, at a distance, but it had passed without incident.

Not the most empowering feeling, though, to be huddling under a bush with his family, watching a helicopter circle.

Last night you swore you'd do anything to protect your family. And you meant it.

So take another step. And then another. And another.

He switched Violet to his other arm, took the steps, and then more after them.

"Hey," Amy said.

Ethan had been staring at the ground so intently that he was almost surprised to see the rest of the world was still there when he looked up. "What?"

Amy pointed.

A couple of hundred yards away, at the edge of the field, stood a gas station. Cuyahoga Falls.

"We made it."

■

They used the gas station restroom to clean up as much as they could. Washed the dirt off their hands and faces, the blood off his feet. Changed Violet, although with no diaper to put her in, the term felt hollow. They'd ended up wadding up about ten feet of toilet paper as a makeshift diaper.

While Amy used the bathroom, Ethan held his daughter, cooing to her as he paced the inside of the gas station. A minimart, just candy and soft drinks and the essentials.

Including packs of Huggies and tubs of formula. He stood in front of them, staring.

After a moment, he heard a cough. The clerk leaned on the counter, eyes alert. A bulky guy with grease stains under his fingernails.

"I'm not a shoplifter," Ethan said.

"Good."

"Listen." He opened his mouth, willed words to come, better ones than those that presented themselves. He was a first-rate scientist at the top of his field. Sought after by universities and research laboratories. A man who had always prided himself on finding a solution, who had always believed that if fortune turned on him, he would still manage, still be able to provide. That he would find a way.

And what he was left with was begging.

You promised the universe you would do whatever it took.

"Listen," he repeated. "We got robbed last night. My wife and I are okay, but my daughter is starving." He picked up a tub of formula. "Is there any chance—"

"Sorry about your trouble, but nope."

"I'm not a bum or anything, I'm just a guy having some bad luck."

"And I'm just a guy pulling a double."

"I'll pay you back. Plus twenty bucks for the kindness."

The clerk yawned, looked back at a magazine on the counter.

Ethan said, "She's three months old. Come on. Be a human being."

Without looking up, the guy said, "Move along, buddy."

There's another way. You still have the pistol in your waistband.

The thought felt so good that he let himself indulge in the momentary fantasy of how much fun it would be to watch the clerk's expression change as Ethan pulled out his gun.

It felt good, but it was crazy. They'd have money again in a few minutes. Load up on diapers and food—somewhere else, no chance he was giving this gas station a cent—and then rent a car. Worst case, catch a Greyhound. Strange and bad as things had gotten, they were almost over. The three of them had made it out of Cleveland, had escaped the National Guard and faced down a shotgun and walked across a quarantine line, and they'd made it.

Just get cash and get on the road.

■

His bank looked the same in Cuyahoga Falls as it did in Cleveland. Blue and gray carpet, fake wood desks, bulletproof glass, a security camera over the door watching the tellers, eighties pop music playing in the background. He didn't know how people worked in banks. Nothing wrong with it, just, how didn't they go out of their mind?

"Can I help you?" The greeter's tone was polite but circumspect, her eyes sliding down his ragged clothes and bare feet. He was glad Amy had decided to wait outside with Violet; the three of them would have looked like a Dorothea Lange photo.

"Yes," Ethan said. "We got carjacked. Two guys with guns."

"Oh my God!" Her eyes wide. "Here?"

"A couple of miles up the road."

"What did the police say?"

"My next stop. Is the manager around?"

He was. A jocular guy in an off-the-rack suit, he introduced himself as Steve Schwarz, and led them into his office. "So sorry to hear about what happened to you. Is everyone okay?"

"Yeah," Ethan said. "Just rattled. And broke. They took everything. Our phones, wallets, everything."

"We'll get you fixed up. Did you open your account here?"

"Cleveland."

Schwarz cocked his head. "You coming from there?"

"No," Ethan said. "We've been on vacation."

"Do you know your account number?"

Ethan slid into a seat opposite the man's desk. "Never memorized it."

"Ah, me either. How about your social security?"

He rattled off both his own and Amy's. Schwarz typed away. "Since you don't have ID, I have to ask a couple of security questions."

"Shoot."

They went through PIN numbers, the location of their preferred branch in Cleveland, recent charges, the rough total of their monthly mortgage payment. The manager was quickly satisfied, said, "We'll get you new debit cards right now. Credit cards will need to be mailed, I'm afraid."

"Sure. Some cash too, please."

"How much?"

"Say five thousand?"

"No problem, Dr. Park." More typing. "You got lucky, you know."

"How's that?"

"They didn't take your wedding ring."

Ethan had been relaxing in the chair. He looked up to see Schwarz staring at him, a question in his eyes. *Let him wonder.* "Guess you're right, we got lucky."

The man looked like he was about to say something else when the phone on his desk rang. "Excuse me," he said, and picked it up. "Steve Schwarz, branch manager."

Ethan couldn't hear the voice on the other end. But whatever they said, Schwarz hadn't been expecting. He stiffened, his hand tightening on the phone. His eyes jumped to Ethan and quickly away again. "I understand."

Then he held the phone out. "For you."

What the—? He looked around; the office walls were glass, and he could see the rest of the bank, everything looking just as it had. But what had seemed comforting in its familiarity now seemed pregnant with menace. Ethan took the phone.

"Hello, Dr. Park." A man's voice, assured and smooth. "This is Special Agent Bobby Quinn of the Department of Analysis and Response."

"Quinn?" It didn't make any sense. That was the name of the agent who had come to his house, who had told him that Abe had been kidnapped. "What are—how did you know I was here?"

"That's not important. Listen, Doctor, I know we didn't part on the best terms, and I apologize. But it's crucial that we talk."

"I don't understand."

"I know that, sir, and I'm sorry. I'll explain everything."

"Am I in trouble?"

"No, no nothing like that. We need your help, Ethan."

"With what?"

"I can't explain over the phone. A matter of national security."

National security? What is he talking about?

Then, *Does it matter? He's a government agent, and you're an American citizen.* "When?"

"Just sit tight. I'm in DC, but I'll requisition a jet and be there in two hours. If you'd like, I can bring fresh clothes and some shoes."

Ethan started to thank him, and then thought, *Shoes?* A tingle slid down the back of his thighs. Slowly, he turned.

The security camera by the door had rotated to point into the bank manager's office.

Behind the counter, two more gazed unblinking.

Out the window, a camera on a telephone pole stared at his wife and child.

"My God."

"Dr. Park, we've taken control of every closed-circuit camera for a two-hundred-mile radius. That's how important you are right now."

"The drone," he said. "The National Guard."

This man has gone to enormous trouble to find you. A man you didn't trust when you met him before; a man who lied about the reasons he was there.

"That's right. You're starting to understand."

"No," Ethan said. "I'm not. Why aren't you having the police pick us up?"

"I told you, I'll come myself."

"But you said that time is a factor. And you're in Washington, DC. So why not have the police meet us?" He shifted the phone to the other ear. Stared at the security camera. "Is it because you don't want them involved?"

The thoughts coming fast and hard now, dots connecting. True, the serum was years away from being publicly available. But it worked. They could give normal people gifts.

Which was revolutionary in every sense of the word. Not just get-astonishingly-rich revolutionary; change-the-world revolutionary.

Maybe the DAR doesn't want the world to change. Not this much.

"If local police picked us up," Ethan said slowly, "there would be an arrest record. Processing. A trail. Not to mention a number of cops who knew we had been taken."

"What difference do you think that would make?"

"If there are no witnesses, it's easy for us to just disappear."

"Disappear?" The agent laughed. "Dr. Park, you're being paranoid."

"In the last few days, my boss has been kidnapped, my city quarantined, my house put under surveillance, and military drones tasked to search for me. I've had four guns pointed at my head, two of them by soldiers, and been robbed of everything down to my shoes. Last night I watched the National Guard kill an innocent man. Guardsmen you just admitted you sent for me. I'm starting to think I'm not being paranoid enough."

"Ethan. Listen—"

And then another connection. Abe. Dr. Abraham Couzen. A genius. A massive pain in the ass who had found the answer to a question the whole world had been asking for thirty years. A question that had shaped everything, changed everything. That had given rise to the DAR—and to the Children of Darwin. And now he was gone, his work missing, blood in his lab.

Ethan said, "Agent Quinn? Where's Abe?"

There was a long pause. When the government man spoke again, what he said was, "Dr. Park, what you're thinking of doing? Don't."

But by then Ethan had already dropped the phone and started running.

CHAPTER 30

He'd never wanted this job. Hadn't, in truth, wanted the vice presidency either. The Senate had been the limit of Lionel Clay's political ambition: a place where he could craft the laws and dialogue of the nation, where a strong argument and a persuasive voice could still change the world the same way Cicero had in Rome.

The first time the RNC had come to him to feel him out on the idea of running as Walker's vice president, Clay had said thanks, no. Henry Walker wasn't his taste, and that was more limelight than he needed. But they'd kept coming, with charts and stats, with arguments about the social importance and need for an academic perspective and, finally, with the honest truth, which was that he won Walker the South, and that was the ball game.

Even as he'd agreed, he'd known that accepting the position was a mistake. And now, walking into the Situation Room, he was more certain of that than ever. Everyone stood as he entered, and he waved them down. "What happened?"

Leahy coughed. "Sir, about twenty minutes ago, at 9:43 local time, Nick Cooper was assassinated in Tesla, New Canaan."

Clay had been about to sit down, and the words froze him. He took a deep breath, then lowered himself to the chair. "He's dead?"

"Yes, sir. An abnorm named Soren Johansen entered a restaurant where Mr. Cooper was having breakfast with his family, killed two plainclothes bodyguards, and then stabbed Cooper in the chest. The blade punctured the left ventricle of his heart. He was rushed to Guardian General but pronounced dead on arrival."

"His family?"

"His son Todd was wounded in the attack. He's in critical condition."

"And this assassin, Soren Johansen?"

"We're still getting a clear picture. But it appears that he escaped."

"My God." Clay leaned back. "How did this happen?"

The chairman of the Joint Chiefs, General Yuval Raz, exchanged glances with Jen Forbus, the director of the DAR. Mentally, Clay sighed. So much of politics was a matter of everyone covering their collective asses. After a moment, General Raz said, "Our information at this moment is very preliminary."

"Understood."

"We haven't intercepted any evidence of a conspiracy. However, Johansen walked past a team of Epstein Industries diplomatic security. He killed the two inside the restaurant, but . . ."

"Epstein is complicit in the attack?"

"His team at least failed to prevent it."

"That may be because of the nature of our assassin," Forbus added. "Soren Johansen's gift is temporal, with a T-naught of 11.2, an exceptional rate. That means that what we experience as one second, he perceives as slightly more than eleven. With that much difference, it's possible he simply had time to do everything right."

"How do we know that?" Clay asked.

"He was academy-raised. At Hawkesdown."

"Hawkesdown Academy?" Clay steepled his fingers. "The same as John Smith."

"Yes, sir, and at the same time, although Smith is two years older. However, after graduation, Soren disappeared. If he's political, he's been very quiet. There's no evidence tying the two together. But my gut says that John Smith is involved."

"Mr. President," Leahy said, "we'd like to detain John Smith for questioning."

Marla Keevers, quiet until now, said, "That's a political nightmare. He's got enormous goodwill following the Monocle revelations. He's been on the talk shows, the speaking circuit. His book has been a *New York Times* bestseller for weeks. Arresting him will have major blowback."

"We're past that point," Leahy said.

Clay studied the man. A former soldier, Leahy had spent the last three decades in the intelligence field, rising to run the CIA before being appointed secretary of defense. To say that his résumé prepared him to view the world militaristically was an understatement of massive proportions.

That doesn't mean he's wrong. After all, Owen was against sending Cooper in the first place.

"Detain John Smith," he said.

Leahy nodded to General Raz, who picked up a phone and began to speak into it quietly.

"In addition, sir, we need to move forward with a military response against the New Canaan Holdfast."

"Why? If we believe that Smith—"

"Cooper was an ambassador for the United States. His assassination has to be treated as an act of war."

"What does Epstein say?"

Leahy looked around the table. "Sir, we haven't been able to reach him."

"Excuse me?"

"It could be that things are just happening too fast. But ultimately, there are two possibilities here. Either Epstein and the NCH are themselves acting as terrorists, or their government"—Leahy said the word with distaste—"is riddled with them. Either way, an American advisor was murdered on a diplomatic mission during a time of unprecedented unrest. Three cities are under martial law, without power or food. We can't afford to consider our options." Leahy paused. "Sir, it's our recommendation that you order preparations for a full-scale military invasion of the New Canaan Holdfast."

Clay glanced at Marla. She shrugged, said, "People are scared. Calling in the cavalry demonstrates that the government of the United States is still in charge."

"General Raz, what would an invasion look like?"

"We'd establish air superiority with F-27 Wyverns operating out of Ellsworth Air Force Base. Ground all but humanitarian flights in the region. Units from the Fourth Infantry Division, First Armored Division, and 101st Airborne would then seize Gillette, Shoshoni, and Rawlins, the entrance points for the NCH, cutting it off."

"How many troops would be involved?"

"Approximately seventy-five thousand."

"*Seventy-five thousand?* That's almost equal to the entire population of the Holdfast."

"Yes, sir. It's important to bring overwhelming force to bear. We're not proposing a fair fight," the general said, "we're demonstrating that we can annihilate them. It makes the idea of resistance ridiculous. Ultimately, that will save lives on both sides."

A dozen faces stared at him. Men and women in uniforms heavy with medals, the commanders of every branch of the military and intelligence community. Lionel Clay took pride in having lived an honorable life. He had been a teacher and a leader. But he had never been a soldier.

And my God, did I never want to be the person making this decision.

"You're talking about a military attack against American citizens."

"We're talking about preparing for one," Secretary Leahy said. "Moving troops into position. It's a reminder to our enemies that they are facing the combined might of the finest fighting force the world has ever seen."

"What's the endgame?"

"Sir?"

"If I give the order to attack. What happens after we take the NCH?"

Leahy looked around again. "That's up to you, sir. But our recommendation is that all leaders and tier-one and tier-two abnorms be held in temporary internment camps. The NCH itself should be evacuated and destroyed."

What had Cooper said?

You knew that someone would be standing here telling you to start a civil war. And you weren't sure you'd be strong enough to say no.

A second civil war, only this time, not between states, but between a majority and a minority, with all of the potential horrors that entailed—up to and likely including genocide.

"Sir, you don't have to decide to attack yet. But moving troops into position gives us the option, while also sending a message to the enemy and reassuring the public."

A thought hit him. He could stand up and walk out of the room. Then out of the building. He could go to the corner and hail a cab to the airport and book a ticket back to Columbia. He could just quit and go home.

It was an absurd fantasy. But tempting.

Lionel Clay stared at the table. At his fingers spread on the polished wood. "Dictators ride to and fro upon tigers which they dare not dismount. And the tigers are getting hungry."

"Winston Churchill," Leahy said. "But we're not dictators."

"I wonder if history will agree."

"Sir?"

"Order the army into Wyoming."

CHAPTER 31

He'd hit the door to the vestibule at a sprint, adrenaline overriding the pain from his bare feet. Burst out into the parking lot under bright blue skies and saw his wife staring at him.

"Ethan?"

"Run!"

A thousand questions in her eyes, but she packed them away and started running, their daughter clutched to her chest. They raced out of the parking lot and onto the sidewalk, heading north, a direction picked at random. Cuyahoga Falls was one big strip mall, a town sponsored by chains. A drugstore up ahead, a restaurant to the left, the logos for both familiar. State Street was four lanes, traffic in both directions. No sign of police, but that would come next.

As they ran, Ethan counted cameras. They were everywhere. Cameras on traffic poles, cameras in parking lots, cameras on the corners of buildings. He'd never realized how many there were.

And all of them were pointed at his family.

Every single camera swiveled to follow them as they ran.

His skin tightened and shivered.

"Ethan," Amy said, punctuating the words with pants, "why, are, we—"

"Trust me."

She nodded, and they continued north. It would take at least a few minutes for the DAR to reach out to the local police. They'd have to pull rank, tell them a fugitive—*my God, we're*

fugitives—was running up State Street. Another minute or two for
a cruiser to get here.

Still. How far could they make it? And what difference did it
make if the cameras tracked them?

"This way." He turned down a side street. His breath came fast
and hot, and every step pounded up his skeleton. They ran past
a broad parking lot, dodged around two staring kids on skate-
boards. Another block and they were on a strip of small homes,
bungalows and frame houses nestled close together. Lawns gone
to yellow-brown and faded American flags. A dog barked and
snarled on the opposite side of a fence. Ethan turned right arbi-
trarily, went another block, then went left, deep in a neighborhood
now. Hardly safe, but at least away from the cameras.

Amy said, "I have to stop." She was pale, clutching Violet in
both arms. Their daughter was bawling, not loud howls but steady
unhappiness that rang through his core. He nodded, dropped to
a fast walk.

"What's going on?"

"Amy, I know this sounds crazy. But I think the DAR is trying
to arrest us because of my work."

"You're right. That's crazy."

"Is it? Remember the drone? The National Guard?"

"Yeah, but . . . come on."

"When I was in the bank, the phone rang. It was Quinn, the
agent who came to our house. He was watching me on the security
camera." He turned to look at her. "Why would he be doing that?"

They passed a series of faded brick houses, the lawns growing
wider as they went farther from town. It wouldn't be long before
they were back on golf courses and forests. Cornfields. He winced
at that, his feet bleeding again.

After a long pause, Amy said, "You know, for more than a
year I respected your commitment to the nondisclosure agreement. I thought it was silly and excessive, but it mattered to you,

so I accepted it. But it's time you told me what you and Abe are working on."

He looked over at her. It had killed him not to be able to share the project with her, not to be able to tell his wife about their success. But Abe had made it clear: no one, absolutely no one could know. Anyone who broke that policy was done. Fired, stripped of patent rights, blacklisted, cooked.

Ethan had thought the old man paranoid, but he'd gone along to get along. If that was what it took to work in a private lab with limitless funding alongside the greatest genius in the field, well, cost of doing business. Now he was starting to wonder.

Was it someone telling their wife that led to the DAR finding out?

And do you give a crap anymore?

"We figured out how to turn normals into brilliants."

She stopped like she'd run into a wall. Stared at him. "Are you kidding me?"

"No. And the DAR doesn't want that to happen. I think they kidnapped Abe, and they're after us."

"So—what do we do?"

The billion-dollar question.

And then, up ahead, he saw the answer.

"Wait here."

■

A digital bell binged as he walked into the place. Candy and soft drinks and the essentials, the same as before. Ethan walked to the middle aisle, picked up three packs of Huggies and both tubs of baby formula. He set them on the counter. The clerk looked at him, ran his hands through his hair. Lank strands of it fell around his neck. "You again?"

Ethan turned and went back to the aisles, loading his arms. A flashlight and a pack of D batteries. All the jerky on the rack. Band-Aids and ibuprofen. Added it to the pile.

The clerk said, "Come on, man."

Next was a box of Snickers.

A carton of eggs and two gallons of milk.

Eight liter-bottles of spring water.

Four lighters from the display by the register.

A roll of duct tape.

"Dude, I have to put this all back."

"No, you don't. Bag it."

"Fine. You want to do it like that?" The clerk reached for the phone. "I'll call the cops."

"Don't worry," Ethan said, "I'm leaving. Just one question first."

The guy stared at him with the wary expression of someone being panhandled. "Yeah?"

Ethan reached into his waistband and pulled out the revolver. He raised it and pointed it right at the clerk. Watched the guy's expression change just the way he'd thought it might. It felt as good as he'd imagined.

"What kind of car do you drive?"

Precision Aerospace Industries™, the world's leading developer
of multiple-launch-environment missiles, proudly presents:

The Avenger (BGM-117)

Conceived and designed
by Academy-trained brilliants,
the Avenger is:

FAST

The first multiple-launch missile to achieve hypersonic speeds
up to Mach 5.3, or more than 4,000 mph

UNDETECTABLE

Our next-generation stealth technology ensures invisibility to
early warning systems

UNSTOPPABLE

Integrated electronic countermeasures demonstrate a 97.8%
success rate against defense systems

FLEXIBLE

Capable of carrying either conventional or nuclear payloads, the
Avenger can hit as hard as you need.

THE AVENGER MISSILE

Vengeance is yours.

CHAPTER 32

The air was cool and smelled faintly of ammonia.

There were sounds. There had been for some time, he realized, although he hadn't been conscious of them. Just drifted in their currents. A hum and beep.

He opened his eyes. Light. Painful and purest white, no shapes or definition, light like the pearly gates, like the one at the end of the tunnel.

Is this heaven?

An image flashed across his memory. Todd's face, inches away, his eyes blank and staring.

Hell.

Cooper sat up with a gasp. The world canted and wobbled, and he reached a hand out to steady himself, banged his right hand on something, the hand clumsy, and agony flashed up, slammed into the bubble-wrap feeling of heavy narcotics and punched right through. Searing pain dilated the world and took away everything but the throbbing.

Breathe, just breathe, breathe through it.

Slowly his vision widened again. A room, a bright light, hard surfaces and an ugly chair. He was in a bed, high, with rails. His right hand was a mass of bandages, and there were IVs running into his arms and a cable snaking into his chest.

It was real, then. It had happened. That man had come out of nowhere, a demon in the shape of a man, and had killed the guards and stabbed Cooper in the chest—a fatal wound, no way

around that, so how was he alive?—and worst, worse than anything, had hit—

*Todd's head snapping sideways, too far, and his bright eyes
going glassy.*

Cooper gasped again, a sob coming from some deep place,
splitting him. He started to reach with his right hand, remembered the bandages, used his left to grasp the IV tubes, started
pulling them out. Next was the cable running into his chest, which
slid out with a weird, slick, sick feeling. At the end spidery robotic
arms no wider than a thread glistened and twitched. He fought
the urge to vomit, kept it down. The beeping sounds had turned to
shrieks. Tangled in blankets and drugs, he spun. Managed to get
one leg out of the bed, then the next. Stood, wobbling.

The door opened. A woman in green scrubs hurried in. "What
are you—"

Cooper staggered forward, grabbed the woman's bicep with
his left hand. "My son."

"You need to get back in bed—"

"My son! Where is my son?"

The door was open and through it a hallway, and Cooper
pushed past the nurse, barely on his feet. A hospital, yes, but not
like any he'd seen, the hall too nice and too short, only a few doors,
no nurses' station, a side table with flowers, a chair, Scrubs coming
behind him trying to grab his shoulders, and Cooper shrugged
her off and pushed open the next door.

Another room like the one he had just left. Hard surfaces,
bright light, beeping machines. A woman standing beside the bed,
whirling at the sound. Natalie, her eyes red and cheeks wet, and
in the bed . . .

In the bed, his son.

Natalie said, "Nick?" and there were volumes in that one
word. It started with surprise, and he could imagine it from her
perspective, the door banging open and a madman in a hospital
gown staggering in, and then the pleasure at seeing him, at the fact

that he was alive at all. But that was quashed by fear, fear for their son, fear that the gods were watching and any happiness tempted them. And then, last, the questions, the same asked by any parent standing over a child in a hospital bed:

How did we get here?

This can't really happen, can it?

Will you take me instead?

He stepped forward and swept her into his arms, wrapped them around her slightness and squeezed, the two of them holding onto each other as though against gravity. Her body trembled, and her face was wet against his neck.

"Is he—will he—"

"I don't know, I don't know, they don't know."

The words hurt more than the dagger had. He leaned into her, and she leaned back. Behind them the nurse started to say something, then thought better of it.

After a long moment, he released her. "Tell me."

Natalie wiped at her eyes, smearing tears around. When she spoke, he could hear the quaver in her voice. "He's in a coma. There was internal bleeding."

"Do they know when he'll wake up?"

She shook her head. "They don't know for sure if he will. Or if . . . if . . ."

He closed his eyes, squeezed them hard. The nurse said, "Mr. Cooper, please." He ignored her, stepped forward. Todd looked tiny in the big hospital bed, his limbs slender under the sheet. Tubes snaked into his arms. Bandages wrapped his head, and they'd shaved the hair on one side. Todd would hate that, the weird haircut, would worry about what other kids would say.

Cooper reached out and took his son's hand in both of his, the physical pain that rocketed up from the right nothing compared to the howling inside him. Then a thought hit. "Wait a second, where's Kate? Is she—"

"She wasn't hurt. She's sleeping, finally."

"Finally?" Of course. The cable in his chest, the elaborate bandages on his hand, the drugged feeling. He glanced at the clock on the nightstand, saw that it was five in the morning. Twenty hours since they were attacked. "Did they get him?"

Natalie shook her head.

The nurse said, "Mr. Cooper, it's amazing that you're even alive. The left ventricle of your heart was torn open. The surgery that saved you is beyond radical. You *have* to go back to bed."

"No."

"Sir—"

"I'm not leaving my son."

There was a long pause and then a dragging sound, Scrubs bringing a chair from one wall. "At least sit. Please?"

Without taking his eyes from Todd, he sat. Natalie stood beside him, one hand on his shoulder, one on Todd's shoulder.

The machines beeped and hummed.

■

He sensed them before he heard them. A tingle in the back of his mind, his gift patterning relentlessly away, even as he did little but stare at the rise and slow fall of his son's chest while thoughts brittle and dry as autumn leaves chased themselves in pointless circles. Prayers and bargains and threats, but beneath it all—and he hated himself for this—his mind patterning away.

It wasn't long before he heard the nearly imperceptible sounds of elite security personnel, rubber-soled boots and efficiency. A trained voice, vaguely familiar; Patricia Ariel, the NCH's communications director. From unseen staff, the murmured tones of sycophancy. And finally, two pairs of shoes: the click of Italian oxfords counterpointed by the squeak of Chuck Taylors. He listened to them walk down the hall, listened to them step into the room and stop.

Without turning around, Cooper said, "Give me one good reason I shouldn't break both of your necks."

"Your son."

He rose fast to face Erik and Jakob Epstein. "Are you threatening—"

"No," Jakob said, his hands up. "We're not. But the most advanced medicine on the planet is being practiced here. You want that for him."

Natalie said, "Nick, calm down."

"Calm down? I brought you here. I trusted the security of our family to these two. And some asshole waltzed in and . . ." He saw the point of the man's elbow driving into the soft hollow of Todd's temple, lost his breath. "I don't think I'll be calming down anytime soon."

"Good," Erik said. "Your efficiency is improved when angry." He pulled a d-pad from his pocket and uncrumpled it with a flick of his wrist. A photo filled the monosheet, a plain man with hollow cheeks and dead eyes. "Soren Johansen, tier-one temporal."

"Which is how he waltzed in," Jakob added. "Point of interest, John Smith once referred to Soren as the only person he'd ever met who truly understood him. The d-pad has everything we have on him, which includes everything the DAR has on him. We're pursuing him ourselves, of course, as is your government. But we had a feeling you'd want the information yourself."

Cooper balled the pad and jammed it in his pocket. Didn't say thanks, and didn't plan to.

"As for your son, I'm sure you've spoken to the doctors. I won't go back over it. What I will say is that there is literally nowhere in the world where people can do the things we can here. And your son arrived in far better shape than you. After all, he was alive."

Cooper had been preparing a response, found it withering on his lips. "Huh?"

"The actual time between Soren hitting Todd and stabbing you was 0.63 seconds," Erik said. "To a T-naught of 11.2, that means he had 7.056 seconds to position his attack. The wound was perfect, tearing open the left ventricle of your heart. Death was almost instantaneous."

"You're saying . . ." He glanced around. "What, I was dead and you brought me back?"

"Nick," Natalie said, "it's true."

He turned to her. "Yeah?"

She nodded. "I watched you die." Like most things Natalie said, the statement was bald and direct. She didn't play games, didn't obfuscate or work agendas. Which didn't mean that that simple statement wasn't shaded with meaning. Beyond the fact, he heard the pain, the loss, the regret—and the joy and hope of his impossible reprieve. She continued, "This isn't a hospital. It's their private underground clinic."

"There are advantages," Jakob said, "to living in a place with more brilliants than anywhere else. Especially if you're in charge of it, and you couldn't give a shit for FDA policies and ethics review boards."

"Greatest danger postmortem is cellular damage due to lack of oxygen," Erik said. "Solution is obvious: reduce metabolic demands to near zero, suspending patient. Then repairing the damage is a matter of tissue engineering using adipose stromal stem cells harvested from fat."

"You mean I have a . . ." He looked down at his chest, remembered only in that moment he was wearing a hospital gown. Shit. Hard to look dignified in one of them. Gently, he eased the neckline out. A small shunt rose out of the puckered scar in the center of his chest. Fluid had leaked from when he pulled the cable out. He remembered the robotic arms, and panic rose quick, a feeling of being too deep underwater with no air. He paused, took a breath, then another. "What, a mechanical heart?"

"Of course not," Jakob said. "What do you think this is, 1985? Your heart is still your heart. We didn't even have to cut you open. Our doctors used the wound as an entry point, injected your own harvested stem cells to seal the tear in your ventricle. Like patching a leaky tire."

"But . . . they've tried that at Johns Hopkins, at the Mayo. They've never been able to get the cells to—"

"This isn't Johns Hopkins," Erik snapped. "This is new. Your rules don't apply here."

Cooper stiffened. He'd gotten in the habit of thinking of Erik as a lovable nerd and Jakob as the real power, when in fact the opposite was true. Jakob was a good talker and a smart guy, but everything around them—including the black clinic that had brought him back from the dead—began and ended with Erik.

And now your son's life is in his hands.

Slowly, he said, "I need to talk to the president."

"Shortly after he heard that you had been assassinated," Jakob said, "President Clay ordered the military into Wyoming. They've seized the towns of Gillette, Shoshoni, and Rawlins, effectively cordoning off the NCH. The air force is flying patrols over every city. More than seventy-five thousand troops are involved, from every branch of the military."

"Seventy-five *thousand*?" Cooper rubbed at his eyes. "But once the president knows I'm not dead—"

"He still has to act the same way." Jakob shook his head. "Clay doesn't have any choice."

"Storm clouds," Erik said. "Birds of prey. Vectors with mass. Frightened people want action more than they want correct action. It's in the data. Clay has no choice."

Cooper said, "Why are you still lying to me?"

That caught Erik off guard, so he followed the jab with a hook. "I know that you've found the source of the abnorms. That you've even developed a serum that can give normal people gifts."

Natalie said, "What?" She'd been staring at Todd, but Cooper's declaration had caught her. "Is that true?"

Cooper looked at the Epsteins. After a moment, Jakob nodded. "There's a lot to iron out, but it works."

"That's the real protection for the NCH," Cooper said. "Not me killing John Smith or sovereignty or their billions. So I'm asking again. Why are you lying to me?"

"What do you mean?"

"You talk about people being terrified, about Clay not having a choice, but you don't mention that you have a magic potion that changes the world. Most normals don't want a war; they're just scared that they're being made obsolete. This changes that, or at least gives them the option. So all you have to do is . . ." He trailed off, because it hit him that—

Jakob's arms are crossed; Erik is biting the inside of his cheek. Negative reactions. Why?

They can't be holding out for financial gain; they have more money than anyone alive.

Besides, they're facing a full-scale attack. Sharing the truth about the serum is the only thing that might prevent the destruction of the Holdfast. Not to mention stopping a civil war.

And yet they've gone negative.

—he'd been missing something.

"Wait. Yesterday when we talked, you said there wasn't enough time. You were talking about this, weren't you? Even your bid for sovereignty was calculated to buy you more time." He stared back and forth, brother to brother. Both smart, both well-meaning in their own way, and the three of them somehow responsible for saving the world, and how exactly that had happened didn't matter anymore, because his gift had jumped ahead and answered the question for him. "Which means"—he rubbed at his forehead—"you don't have the serum, do you?"

"The scientist behind it is a difficult person," Jakob said. "Dr. Couzen would only accept our funding if he had complete autonomy. He shared progress reports, test results, but never the formula itself."

"So?"

"Dr. Couzen was kidnapped a week ago," Jakob said.

"By the DAR," Erik added. "Your government wants a war."

Revolution? You're an idiot. You don't even know what that word means. Forget your precious Mao and Che and Fidel. If they've appeared on a T-shirt, they haven't changed shit.

You want revolution, look at Alexander Fleming. Penicillin transformed the world in ways Lenin and Washington only dreamt of.

Now sit down and shut up, you autocratic frat boy. It's adult swim.

—Dr. Abraham Couzen, answering a student question at What's Next Next: The Future of Futurism conference Harvard University, May 2013

CHAPTER 33

The pond was shallow, the edges rimmed with toppled cattails, their stalks broken. The water smoothly mirrored the hazy November sky, and the air was crisp with the scent of pine and a promise of the snow the winter would bring.

A muffled boom rolled in from the distance, some hunter's shotgun, and Ethan tried not to read omens in that.

"What do you think, chunks? Pretty, huh?" His daughter squinted up and flopped her arm. The scientist in him imagined the scientist in her; he sometimes pictured Violet as a tiny being in the cockpit of a vehicle she didn't understand. Row upon row of dials and switches and knobs, and no instruction manual. Nothing to do but stab and twist at random and see what happened. *Punch that button, this appendage flaps. Interesting.*

Amy said, "She's cold."

Ethan jumped. It was the first thing she'd said to him in almost twenty-four hours, and though he was pretty sure the blanket he had wrapped around his daughter was keeping her plenty warm, he nodded, wrapped it tighter, and then turned back to the cabin.

His wife was still pissed off. Not that he blamed her.

Yesterday, after taking the clerk's keys and duct-taping the man's hands and feet, he'd carried the bags out of the gas station. Amy had looked at him, confused, as he'd led her around back to the battered pickup parked there. He put the bags in the bed, next to a battered toolbox.

"What's this?"

"Our new truck. Come on."

"Ethan, what did you—"

"What I had to. Please, Amy, trust me."

She started for the truck, then said, "There's no car seat."

"We're not going far."

She stared at him, and he had one of those moments when he realized the difference a baby made. Turn refugee and flee their city? She was game. Believe him when he said to run from federal agents? You got it. Drive a couple of miles without a car seat? Houston, we have a problem.

"Baby, please, we have to go. I promise I'll drive carefully."

Reluctantly, she had climbed in.

His every instinct was screaming at him to hit the open road, to put distance between himself and Cuyahoga Falls. But he had to be smart. They were being tracked by an incredibly powerful governmental agency. It wouldn't take long for them to discover the hogtied clerk, learn the make and model of the truck Ethan had stolen. And while he supposed he could swap license plates, somehow he didn't suspect that would fool an agency that could co-opt security cameras at will.

No, much as he wanted to run, it was smarter to hide. If they were lucky, the DAR would start looking hundreds of miles out. Maybe lose track of them altogether. *For a while.*

"Where are we going?" In the passenger seat, Amy was clutching Violet with all her strength.

"I'll know it when I see it."

"Honey, I love you, but I'm about to kick your ass."

"I'll explain everything once we get settled." He'd tried a smile, gotten nothing in return. "Look, right now we have to concentrate. This will only work if we don't pass any cameras. Can you help me?"

She grimaced but leaned forward and stared through the windshield. They'd stuck to back roads and residential streets, wending their way to the national park, the same one they'd just trekked through. The first couple of houses hadn't looked right—too close to the street, or with cars parked in front. After another few moments, he spotted a hand-painted sign that read THE HENDERSONS' HIDEAWAY beside a dirt driveway. "This might do."

"Do for what?"

He steered the truck up the drive, wound forty yards through faded pines. The Hendersons had the right idea of a hideaway: a cabin in the woods, tastefully sized and out of sight of the neighbors. Add the pond out back and you had the perfect spot for summer weekends. "Yeah. This will work."

"Ethan . . ."

"Two minutes."

He hopped out of the truck and went to the front door. Banged on it, got no response. There was a big bay window in front, and he tented his hands over his eyes to look inside. The furniture inside was covered with sheets. Perfect.

There wasn't a crowbar in the toolbox, but he found a tire iron with a tapered point for popping off hubcaps. He walked back to the front door, slid it into the jamb. Hesitated for a moment, then thought, *Hey, you're already a fugitive and a car thief. In for a criminal penny.*

A fast, sharp jerk and the wood gave with a splinter, the door swinging open.

Ethan turned, found his wife holding their daughter and looking at him like he'd lost his mind. He smiled, said, "Welcome home. Want to get a fire going?"

■

"Start over."

"From where?"

"From, you know, over."

"Okay." Ethan used the iron poker to jiggle the logs in the fireplace. Sparks danced upward as the wood cracked. "So the first gifted were recognized in 1986, right? That means that for the last twenty-seven years, pretty much every geneticist on the planet has been trying to figure out how they came to be. The first step, and maybe the most important, was mapping the human genome. If the brilliants hadn't come along, that wouldn't have gotten a tenth of the funding or attention. Hell, I bet we wouldn't have finished mapping the genome until, like, 2003."

"And instead it was done in 1995."

"Right. Now we had a benchmark. Everybody figured it would be easy after that—compare enough abnorms to norms, and we'd be able to spot the gene for brilliance. Of course, that takes a lot of computational power and time, so it was years before everybody accepted it wouldn't be that simple."

"There's no gene for it."

"Correct. So everybody fans out in different directions. Some people start looking at causes and working backward—was it pollution, growth hormones, the ozone layer, nuclear testing, et cetera. Others decided it must not be genetic at all, but some sort of a virus or prion, a structure that infected a percentage of people. Abe and I and others like us, though, we still believed DNA was the key—just not one gene. Like intelligence."

"Intelligence *is* genetic."

"Sure, right, but there's no single gene for it. We still don't know exactly how it works, but the research coming out of Stanford and Tokyo suggests that it's actually dozens of genes, maybe hundreds, that in conjunction determine baseline intelligence. And it turns out the same is true of the brilliants. Only it's even more subtle."

Violet gave a short cry, and they both paused, looked over at her. The scene was cozy: mom and dad by a flickering fire, baby tightly swaddled and napping. All they were missing was eggnog and it could have been a Christmas card.

If you left out the fact that federal agents might kick in the door at any moment.

"So what is it?"

"Epigenetically associated telomere lengthening."

She gave him a look, and he said, "Right. So telomeres are these nucleotide sequences at the ends of chromosomes that protect them from unraveling. Like the plastic caps at the end of shoelaces."

He walked her through it as best he could, how telomeres varied in length, how they'd discovered that longer telomeres at the end of certain chromosomes were tied to cellular lifespan. Ethan's conviction was that it wasn't the genes themselves that were different, but rather their interactive mechanisms. An epigenetic solution explained why the answer was so elusive. The root cause had occurred not to the brilliants themselves, but to their ancestors two or three generations back. Not only that, it hadn't altered their DNA sequence—only the way in which those genes were regulated.

"Think of it like cooking. The DNA sequence provides the raw ingredients. But the way those ingredients interact, the order they're added to the pan, the temperature used, that all changes the final result.

"Only here, it's not a handful of ingredients; human DNA has more than twenty-one thousand genes, and they interact in very subtle, complex ways. Still, once we started looking at epigenetic alterations in gene expressions, specifically as they relate to telomeres, we found the pattern."

"Simple as that."

He smiled, cocked an eyebrow. "Pretty sexy, right?"

"So what was the root cause?"

"Hmm?"

"You said that something had happened to their ancestors that created the brilliants."

"Oh, that." He shrugged. "No idea. Science tends to be about stumbling onto the *what*, then spending decades understanding the *why*. My guess, there is no single cause. For a hundred and fifty years humanity has toyed with the planet. We've poisoned the seas and damaged the food chain and tested thermonuclear weapons and introduced mutated crops and just basically been mucking with things we don't fully understand. And one of the results of that is the gifted."

She stared at the fire, the light tracing the fine features of her face, making her eyes glow. "So you figured out what makes people brilliant. Why not share it?"

"Once we understood the pattern, it occurred to Abe that it might be possible to recreate it. That it might actually be pretty easy."

"Easy? People have been working on this for thirty years."

"Right. Locating the cause was hard. But replicating it isn't. Call it the three-potato theory." He saw her look and laughed. "A phrase of Abe's. Say that the cause of the gifted is eating three potatoes in a row. Figuring that out, given the entire range of human experience, that's hard. But once you realize it—"

"All you need to do is eat three potatoes."

"Or in this case, design a target therapy using non-coding RNA to regulate gene expression."

"And it works? You can make people brilliant?"

"Our proof-of-concept work was wildly successful. We were just trying to figure out how to move into phase one trials on human beings when Abe disappeared."

Amy stood up and stalked away. The move was so sudden that his first thought was maybe she'd heard something, and he stood quickly. "What is it?"

She was staring out the window, her hands clenching and unclenching.

"Baby?"

His wife whirled. "You stupid, stupid little boy."

Her words caught him like a sucker punch. It had been such a relief to talk to her, to tell her about his triumph. To sit in this stolen moment of comfort and show off for his wife. "I don't—"

"What did you think would happen?" She hissed the words, and it was worse than a yell. "*Did* you think?"

"What are you talking about?"

"Are you really that blind?" Amy stepped forward, and the firelight that a moment ago had made her so lovely now only underscored her fury. "You and Abe. Two dumb geniuses."

"Look, I know it's off-the-reservation, but you have to understand, we were onto the biggest discovery since, I don't know, splitting the atom."

"That's right. That's exactly right. And what did they use that for?"

He opened his mouth, closed it.

"You have a *family*, Ethan. A daughter. And you and your buddy cook up this little science project—"

"Hey—"

"—that will change the whole world. I mean, change everything. And it didn't occur to you that people would want to take it from you?"

"I." He blew a breath. "I'm a scientist. I just wanted to know."

"Well, congratulations. You've made history." The scorn in her voice was shocking. The two of them were good liberal intellectuals, they talked, they listened. They fought, sure, but didn't go for blood. In the years they'd been married, he'd never heard her speak this way.

That's not true. It's just never been directed at you. But you heard it last night, when she called on Jeremy's god to damn him.

"Amy . . ."

"Be quiet, Ethan. Just. Be quiet."

And he had, the rest of the day. He'd hoped a night's sleep might clear it all up, but though they'd shared the master bed, she'd slept huddled up on the far edge, her body angular with fury even in her sleep. This morning he'd made breakfast, cooking eggs and brewing coffee.

She hadn't said a word. Hadn't, in fact, said anything to him until just now, when she suggested Violet was cold.

They started back toward the cabin. The boom of another shotgun rang out, closer this time. He wanted to talk to her, to beg her to talk to him, but he forced himself to stay quiet.

And at the back entrance to the cabin, she turned and held out her arms for Vi. Ethan passed her over in silence. Amy clutched their daughter and started away, then changed her mind. "Ethan, I love you. You know that. But I don't know if I can forgive you."

"Amy . . ."

"If it was just us, that would be different. But someone kidnapped Abe, probably killed him. Those same people are after you. Maybe that's federal agents, maybe not, but it doesn't matter because the DAR is chasing you too. You robbed a gas station yesterday—"

"I had no choice!"

"And all of that, all of it, is going to come down on us." She hoisted their daughter. "On her. Think about that."

Then she walked inside and slammed the door.

CHAPTER 34

He was a dead man, haunted by the words of another dead man.

"If you do this, the world will burn."

Had it only been three months since Drew Peters had said that to him? Three months since he'd sat on a park bench outside the Lincoln Memorial with a bomb in his hands, deciding whether to set it off. Deciding that the world deserved the truth, no matter the potential costs.

You pitiable fool. What naïveté, what blind optimism, to tempt the universe.

As a direct result of his decision, Equitable Services had been shut down, and the DAR's teeth had been pulled. John Smith had been exonerated in the court of public opinion and given free rein to act. President Walker had resigned and was facing trial, making room for a good man without the will or wisdom to be president, a man who was about to plunge them into the civil war Cooper had spent his whole adult life fighting to prevent. The mailed fist of the United States government was clenched just outside the city walls. And his son lay in a coma, lost in a world of nightmares for the sin of trying to protect his dad.

Yet again, his children were suffering for his actions. Not in some metaphoric way, but literally. The d-pad on his lap played the video again and again. The whole nightmare was only ten seconds long: Soren entering the restaurant, cutting the throat of one guard and the brachial artery of the other before turning. Cooper throwing the chair, leaping onto the table, attacking. The dumb look on his face as he stared at his hand cut near in half. Todd charging. The assassin spinning with his elbow up. His son's eyes gone glassy and his body limp. Cooper hurling himself onto the dagger, the knife spearing him through the heart. Falling beside his son as Soren walked away.

Freeze. Skip back. Soren entering the restaurant . . .

He'd made himself watch it over and over, the impact never going away, the images never losing their horror.

Cooper rubbed at his eyes with his good hand. In the hospital bed, his son lay still, breathing and little else. Tubes running into his arms. A mass of bandages around his shaved head.

After the Epsteins had left, Cooper had convinced Natalie to lie down. She'd been reluctant, but exhaustion finally won over, and she'd curled up with Kate in the next room. Cooper, meanwhile, didn't think he'd ever sleep again. His meds were wearing off, and it felt like talons were digging into his chest while a red-hot chainsaw spun in his hand. The pain was good, the tiniest penance for his hubris. Like watching the video again and again. Like picturing the troops massing outside New Canaan. Seventy-five thousand troops, a ridiculous excess of force. It wasn't about subduing the Holdfast, it was about obliterating it. Even in this subterranean space, he could hear jets streak by overhead.

If he could give back the life that had miraculously been returned to him in trade for Todd to be up and playing soccer, he'd do it without hesitation. But even that felt like it would be just a reprieve. John Smith would have his war, and the world would burn. No one was safe.

And here you sit, helpless to do a thing about it. Hell, you couldn't even protect your son.

He could feel a scream building inside him and pictured it like a blast wave, a force that would sweep outward and flatten the world. But if the last months had taught him anything, it was that he was only a man.

For lack of anything useful to do, he stabbed at the d-pad, shutting down the video and opening the file on Soren Johansen, the man who had tried to take his son.

The file was extensive. Information on Soren's birth, his early diagnosis. Every note from Hawkesdown Academy, where he'd grown up. Detailed analysis of his gift.

Tier-one temporals were extremely rare, even amidst the rarified numbers of gifted, and Cooper hadn't dealt with any personally. Philosophically, they presented a fascinating notion; like relativity, they proved that the very things people thought of as constants were in fact anything but. Of course, temporals didn't actually bend time the way velocity did. It was entirely a matter of perception, and for most of them, it was a very slight variation. In the lower tiers, fours and fives, the difference might not even be noticed. An individual with a T-naught of 1.5, after all, might simply seem particularly quick-witted.

But at 11.2, Soren's T-naught was the highest Cooper had ever heard of. How strange the world must appear to him, every second stretched to agonizing lengths.

Good. I hope your whole life has been misery.

It also explained why his own gift hadn't been of any use. Cooper read intentions, built patterns based on physical cues and intuition. But Soren hadn't possessed any intention. He didn't plan to swing here or stab there; he simply waited for his opponents to move and then took advantage of their molasses-slow crawl to put his knife where it would do the most damage. In fact, he'd made only two real attacks: the first security guard, whose throat he had cut, and . . .

Cooper saw the moment again, squaring off against the guy, and in that time getting just one flicker of intent, one moment when he knew what was going to happen, the fucker spinning with his elbow up and arm locked.

Todd's breath caught for a second, and Cooper jumped, filled at once with unbearable hope and unimaginable terror. But then the breath rattled out again in a snore. A tiny biological hiccup. Even so, Cooper watched unblinking for another twenty breaths.

The explanation of *how* he'd been beaten so handily did little to help. Okay, fine, Cooper read intentions, and the guy had none. But how that translated into practical action was less clear. How did you beat a man who used you to defeat yourself?

Stand in front of him and stare him to death?

The truth was, everything in life came down to intentions and results. Cooper's intentions in killing Peters and releasing the video had been good; the results had been a disaster. Did that make his intentions wrong? If so, that meant morality was really only a way of talking about how we wished things were. Hope, empathy, idealism—maybe they didn't matter. Maybe the only thing that counted was results.

A cold pragmatist's way of looking at the world, and he'd always felt Ayn Rand was a humorless hack. Intentions had to mean something, had to—

Wait a second.

He caught his own breath. Stared straight ahead, mind running in overdrive. Not patterning, not his gift, just *thinking*, and if he was right, then . . .

Cooper dumped the d-pad from his lap and stood up. The move sent a spike of pain through his chest, and his head went wobbly, but he didn't let that stop him. A quick look around the room, and there it was, in the corner of the room, a tiny bump about the size of a marble. He moved to the camera and started waving his arms. "Erik! Erik! I know you hear me, you bastard, this is your little world, come on—"

The phone on the side table rang. Cooper moved to it, snatched it before a second ping. "Erik, I need data."

"Data. Yes. What?"

"You said that Dr. Couzen was kidnapped by the DAR."

"Yes, statistical projection based on multiple variables—"

"Yeah, I don't care how you know. What matters here is intention."

"Statistically speaking, intention is rarely relevant—"

"If the DAR took Dr. Couzen, then someone had the intention of seizing his work. We're not talking about statistics, we're talking about people."

A pause. "Explain."

Use Erik-speak. "I know President Clay. You'll posit what I mean?"

"Your gift for patterning. Yes. Posited."

"Clay is a good man. He doesn't want a war; he's being pushed into one. It's the extremists on both sides. They're trying to remove all options for compromise, for discussion. But Clay would seize on any reasonable way to avoid a disastrous conflict."

"Posited."

"Dr. Couzen's work offers such a way. The fact that Clay hasn't used it means that we can presume he's not aware of it. And yet the DAR is a government agency. Which means?"

"Forces within Clay's administration have concealed it from him. Presumably the same forces that are pushing for war." A beat. "And if you are able to prove that—"

"Then in one stroke we can neutralize the hawks surrounding the president and foil John Smith's plan for war. Because not only can we show him that he's being played, but we can also give him the good doctor—*because Couzen is already in government custody.*"

Cooper could picture Epstein in his cave of wonders, that darkened amphitheater where he danced with the datastream. Imagined him gesturing for charts and graphs, bright holograms of information that no one alive could interpret the way he could. Knowing that the man would be checking Cooper's work, correlating it against a hundred other factors. He held his breath. So much came down to the next thing Erik said.

When the man did speak, there was something like excitement in his voice. "Your theory is statistically valid. I'll send all data on Dr. Couzen's abduction to your system."

Cooper didn't say good-bye, just hung up the phone and returned to his datapad. His chest felt like molten steel had been poured on it, his hand throbbed with every beat of his repaired heart, and it didn't matter, because there was a way to make things right. To fix it, like Natalie had told him to. There was a way, and he had figured it out, goddammit. *Not so helpless after all.*

He dropped in his chair, set the d-pad on the bed to free his good hand. The screen showed a massive file transfer in progress, but the most important pieces had already arrived. Cooper could feel his pulse, the rasping of his breath, and a joy that made his fingers tremble as he began to read, looking for the proof that he needed.

It took five minutes to realize he was wrong.

Five minutes to realize that things were even worse than he had imagined.

CHAPTER 35

Natalie said, "I don't understand."

They were in the hallway of the subterranean clinic, Cooper pacing, feeling the weight of the earth above them, the weight of the world about to crack. He'd been so sure he was right, so sure he'd found a way out. For a moment life had seemed like it was supposed to, like if he fought the good fight and didn't quit, maybe things would turn out all right.

He'd imagined that it would take hours, that he would have to pore over personality profiles and arm-twist Bobby Quinn and maybe get Epstein to hack into privileged government systems. But all it had taken was five minutes of looking at the crime scene photos.

"There is no way that the DAR kidnapped Dr. Couzen."

"How can you be so—"

"Because it's what I do, Nat. You know how many operations I've run for the DAR? How many times I've sent teams to arrest a target, or tracked one down myself? I know what our protocols look like. The DAR has some of the best tactical assets in the world."

"So?"

"So, the window beside Couzen's door was broken so that someone could reach in and unlock it. The DAR would have used a ram or a Hatton round, a specialized shotgun shell meant to breach a door. The neighbors reported hearing gunfire; the agency would have used suppressed weapons. There was furniture overturned, evidence of a struggle, but how does a 150-pound egghead make that kind of mess against a tactical team? And there was blood all over his lab; if the department wanted him alive, then that's how they would have taken him."

"Maybe he had a gun. Maybe he saw the agents coming, and he—"

Cooper shook his head. "It wasn't the DAR. Trust me."

"Okay," she said. "But what difference does it make who kidnapped him? Nothing has changed."

"Everything has changed."

"Why?"

"Because he wasn't kidnapped at all."

It was the blood that gave it away. He wasn't a forensic expert, but you couldn't do what he had spent a decade doing and not pick up a few things. *If* Couzen had been attacked by the DAR, and *if* he had fought back hard, and *if* they'd been forced to use a weapon that caused blood spatter at all, it would have been a firearm.

The blood from a bullet wound sprayed in tiny droplets, what was called high-velocity impact spatter. Yet the blood on the wall was densely packed and medium size. The kind of pattern that occurred with brutal blunt force, like a lead pipe hitting the head. The kind of weapon the DAR would never use.

But exactly the kind of pattern that might result if someone took a small container of their own blood and flung it at the wall. There was more, but that was when he'd known.

"He faked it." Cooper stopped pacing, leaned against the wall, his eyes closed. "He faked his own kidnapping. No one came for him."

Natalie paused, thinking it over. "But if that's true, it means—"

"It means that he's running. That for some reason he decided to vanish and wanted to buy himself time. Maybe someone made him a better offer than the Epsteins. It doesn't matter." He rubbed his eyes. "All that matters is that the one man who has a solution to all of this madness has gone AWOL."

"I still don't understand. Why is that worse?"

"Because it means he's *hiding*. Actively hiding."

"So find him."

He laughed. "I can barely move without seeing spots. My right hand is utterly useless. We're ten minutes from a civil war, and the only guy who can stop it has a huge head start. My son is in a hospital bed." Cooper slid down the wall and sat on the floor. "What do you want me to do?"

He knew how everything he'd just said sounded, and he didn't care. The floor tile was comfortingly cool through his hospital gown. He'd been running so hard for so long, and all that he'd accomplished was to make things worse. Enough.

Natalie walked to the wall opposite him and sat down herself. Her hair was bundled back in a tight ponytail, and coupled with the dark circles under her eyes, it made her look drawn and pale. She said, "You think you're the only one?"

"No. I know that you—"

"I'm the reason Todd is here. Me. It was my dumb idea, remember? I wanted us to be together, as a family. For the kids, and also"—she shrugged—"if I hadn't had some romantic notion of all of us being together, of what it might mean for us, you and me, Todd would be back in DC right now. Instead, he's in a coma. So don't start with me, okay?"

"Natalie—"

"You don't see it. You never did. In your head, it was always you against the world. You, personally, were going to be the man to save it." She laughed coldly. "What would you even do if things did get better? Tell me, Nick, I'm curious. What would you do if suddenly the world didn't need saving? Take up golf? Become a CPA?"

"Hey," he said, "that's not fair."

"Fair?" She snorted. "You're the only man I've ever loved. And we were so good together, we were happy, we made beautiful children. But somewhere along the line it stopped working. Maybe it was your job, maybe it was that you're gifted and I'm not, maybe it was just that we fell in love too early, burned out on each other. Not fair, but, fine. Life happens, you move on. And we did, and that was okay too.

"And then it turns out that Kate is an abnorm, and not only that, but she's tier one. They're going to take her from us.

"Instead, you do this amazing thing. You go undercover and risk everything for her. Not fair. And the way it ended, not fair either.

"But life starts to go back to normal. Maybe better than normal. And part of me starts to wonder, were we too quick before? Should we have stuck it out? And because I'm wondering that, and because I want you to know that you're not alone, we come here, and—" She sucked in a deep breath. "'Fair.' Fuck you."

The words were a slap, and he jumped. "Natalie—"

"You're hurting, I get it. And things look bleak, I get that too. But don't talk to me like that. Did we make mistakes? Sure. No doubt. But we were fighting on the side of the angels. I know it, and you know it too. And now you've got a choice. You can sit on the floor outside your son's hospital room and wait for the bombs to start falling. Or you can take one last shot, no matter how slim the odds are, to make a better world. It's up to you, Nick, it really is. No one could blame you no matter what you decide. But either way, don't talk to me about fair."

As suddenly as she'd started, she stopped, and the silence felt like the aftermath of a thunderclap, the air electric. Cooper stared at her and felt a pain in his chest that had little to do with the knife wound. He tried to think of what to say, how to answer. Where to start.

Finally, he said, "Couzen is a genius. He knows he'll be pursued. He won't go anywhere people would look for him. Nothing he owns, no family or friends, no research facilities."

Natalie gazed at him, that cool, level look that always matched her thoughts. "So how do you find someone if all you know is that he won't go anywhere you expect?"

He stared down at his hands. One in ruined agony—

Time is against you. War will break out any moment.

Dr. Couzen may be the only person on the planet who can stop it. His research could change everything. Even in this desperate hour.

Only, he's hiding, and the chances of you finding him are slim to none.

The data Epstein gave you said that though Couzen was a genius, he didn't work alone. He had a team of the best and brightest.

Including a protégé.

Where are you, Ethan Park?

—the other still strong. He rose, then leaned over to offer his good arm to Natalie. She took it and stood opposite him. Their faces were close.

Cooper leaned in and kissed her, and she kissed back, both of them hungry. After far too short a moment, he broke it, leaned back. "You'll tell the kids I love them?"

Natalie bit her lip. He could see the realities hitting her, the consequences of her speech, and see that even so, she didn't regret it, and he loved her for that. She nodded. "Where are you going?"

"To convince Erik Epstein to loan me a jet. But first"—he smiled—"I'm getting out of this goddamn dress."

CHAPTER 36

The sound of a low-flying plane pulled her from the deep black.

Shannon blinked, rolled over. The hotel bed had half a dozen pillows on it, and she'd used them all. Her cocoon was warm and soft, and her body felt heavy in that good way. She yawned, then glanced at the clock.

10:12 a.m. Good lord. She'd slept for . . . eighteen hours?

Being awake for two days straight will do that to you.

After Nick had left last night—well, the night before, she supposed, but not to her—she'd waited in the Tesla airport for Lee and Lisa to arrive. Molded chairs, bad music, her body aching and her eyes grainy, she'd sat vigil as her goddaughter slept. Shannon had stroked the girl's hair and watched people walk by and waited out the gray hours.

It had been almost dawn when she saw two figures running down the concourse. She hadn't seen Alice's parents in months, not since the night she and Cooper had stayed at their Chinatown apartment. A night that had ruined their lives, had landed them both in prison and their daughter in Davis Academy and Shannon in the emotional purgatory she'd been dealing with ever since. The two of them had aged years in those months, deep circles etched beneath Lisa's eyes, a stoop to Lee's shoulders she'd never seen before.

But when they caught sight of their daughter, it was like the moment a campfire caught, a sudden flare of warmth and light. Shannon had shaken the little girl in her lap, said, "Sweetheart?"

Alice opened her eyes, and the first thing she'd seen had been her parents racing toward her. She'd leapt up and hurled herself at them, and the three had collided in a group hug, arms entwining, words flowing, love and loss and joy. They had all been crying, and Shannon, standing there feeling useless, had clenched and unclenched her fists.

Finally Lee Chen had turned to her. Shannon had dreaded this moment, the first look from her old friend; she had been devastatingly careless, and he had paid the price. She deserved every hurtful thing he was about to say to her.

"Thank you." His face was wet, his nose red. "Mei-mei. Thank you."

And at that she'd lost it too, had joined the hug, all four of them crying and laughing.

Shannon yawned and stretched, then flipped the covers aside. Padded to the bathroom, peed for half an hour, splashed some water on her face. Her cheeks had pillow lines. *No kidding, lazy girl,* her dad said in her head. She smiled.

One of her favorite things about hotels was bathrobes, and the one hanging beside the shower was a beaut, thick, soft terrycloth. Even better, there was a coffeemaker in the room. She put two packets of coffee into the machine, stood waiting while it gurgled and hissed, remembering the warmth of Alice's head in her lap, the feel of the girl's hair between her fingers.

She'd splurged on the suite, and the décor showed it. The room was a study in minimalism, the walls white, the furniture low profile. One wall was solar glass, the surface mellowing the harsh winter glare. Shannon took her coffee out to the balcony, shivering and tightening the belt of the robe. Wyoming in November, no thank you. *You need to find a revolution based out of San Diego.*

Still, cold as it was, it felt good, bracing, and the contrast made the coffee taste even better. Tesla spread out below her in all its blocky, preplanned glory. The mirrored walls of the Epstein Industries complex reflected cold desert sky. There was a growling roar coming from somewhere, traffic probably. She wondered how Nick's meeting with Erik had gone, whether the billionaire had admitted what his scientists had created. The thought of the serum still blew her mind, a feeling like the morning after she'd had sex for the first time, the way the whole world looked the same and yet different, and what was that roaring, because it sounded an awful lot like . . .

The sound was suddenly more than a sound, it was a presence all around her, full and huge, strong enough to lean against, growing fast and all-consuming, a blasting howling wail coming from not one or two but three fighter jets streaking overhead, a formation of predatory triangles flying low enough that she could make out missile clusters hanging beneath the wings.

What the hell?

Shannon gripped the balcony railing, watched the planes kite through the gray sky, the roar echoing and bouncing. She didn't know much about military aircraft, couldn't have said what make they were, but she had been a soldier her whole adult life and recognized a threat when she saw one.

She hurried back into the suite, leaving the door to the balcony half-open, a chill wind creeping in. The tri-d was sleek and stylish, more modern art than entertainment center, but all she cared about was finding the damn power button and the controls to jump the channels. The faded kitchen of a faded sitcom, the hyperkinetic animation of some kid's show, a commercial for a personal injury attorney, and then, finally Fox News, the middle of a flashy graphics package. Bombastic music played in the background as three-dimensional letters tumbled in to spell AMERICA ON THE BRINK, then the letters exploded, replaced by a stylized map of Wyoming on fire behind the title SHOWDOWN IN THE DESERT. A fast serving of patriotism bouillabaisse: flag, stars, White House, eagle's screech, fighter jets.

The package cut to an aerial shot, moving slowly, a news drone. A military encampment of prefab buildings buzzing with activity. Rows of tanks and trucks. An airfield packed with helicopter gunships. And thousands and thousands of soldiers.

The landscape was dusty brown and cold-looking, the sky the same color as the one out her window, and if it looked familiar it was only because she'd been through it half a hundred times: Gillette, the eastern gateway of the New Canaan Holdfast. Shannon gasped, not believing what she was seeing.

American troops occupying an American city.

The newscaster's voice, saying, "Military forces continue to gather in Wyoming in what the government is describing as 'anti-terrorism exercises.' There is no word on whether these exercises will involve entering New Canaan Holdfast land."

The shot switched to a map of Wyoming, the gerrymandered blob of the NCH shaded a bloody red. There were only three routes into the Holdfast, massive highways flowing from Gillette, Shoshoni, and Rawlins. All three cities were marked with stars that looked rather like bullet holes.

"Army spokesmen confirm that a joint force of as many as seventy-five thousand troops are involved in these maneuvers."

Cut to a shot of a runway somewhere, a military base, jets streaking away.

Cut to a line of tanks, huge metal monsters surrounded by soldiers loading ordnance.

Cut to a barricade across a freeway, Humvees angled to block it. Men leaned on heavy machine guns. A snarl of semis ran to the horizon.

"Access to the New Canaan Holdfast has been suspended, against the complaints of local government, who note that most basic necessities must be shipped in."

Cut to a foppish man in a good suit and glasses, behind a podium. The crawl read HOLDEN ARCHER, WHITE HOUSE PRESS SECRETARY, as the man said, "All efforts are being made to ensure a swift and peaceful solution to this situation. Meanwhile, let's remember that three American cities are still without power and food as the direct consequence of terrorist actions—terrorists we believe to be harbored by the NCH."

On cue, the screen cut to a photograph. A handsome man with a good jaw standing beside a podium.

"Senior White House sources confirm that orders have been given for the arrest of activist and public speaker John Smith. Once considered a terrorist leader, Smith was exonerated of his crimes in dramatic fashion when evidence surfaced of former President Walker—"

From outside, the roar grew again, louder and louder. At first it sounded like a stereo turned to maximum; then thunder rolling overhead; then the howl of the crowd in a stadium. Finally the sliding sound of the jets blasting by. The hotel windows shook.

The newscaster continued, "While tensions have been running high since the initial attacks by the Children of Darwin, the Unrest Index currently stands at an unprecedented 9.2 . . ."

There was a knock on the door, and Shannon about jumped out of her robe. Coffee sploshed onto her hands. "Crap." She muted the tri-d, yelled, "No housekeeping, thanks!"

"Shannon?"

She froze in the process of wiping her fingers on her robe. She knew that voice, though she wouldn't have expected to hear it under these circumstances. Setting the coffee on the table, she walked to the door. A mirror over the side table bounced her reflection back, and she grimaced. There were lines on her cheek from the pillow, and, yikes, her hair. She ran a hand through it, accomplishing nothing at all. Then she took a breath, straightened her shoulders, and opened the door. "Hello, Natalie."

Nick's ex-wife looked pale and tired. "Hi."

They stood like that for a moment, either side of the door, and then Shannon said, "Everything okay?"

"Can I come in?"

"Oh, yeah, sorry." She held the door open, gestured. "The coffee hasn't kicked in yet."

Natalie walked into the suite, turned slowly, taking in the modern décor, the view, the obvious expense. Shannon could almost see her appraising it, imagining Nick here, judging the woman he had chosen instead of her.

Stop that. She's never been anything but gracious. It's not her fault that you're falling for her ex.

The thought caught her, and she did a mental double take.

"Falling for"? When did "dating" become "falling for"?

The answer was obvious. Last night at the airport. Not because of what he did for Lee and Lisa, and not because he'd given her the right answer about the serum. She was glad of both, but grand gestures and political conscience were not the bedrock of love.

Nope. You started full-on falling for him when he apologized. When he said he would never doubt you again.

It was that last word that really did it. The semi-stated promise of a future that means something.

She realized she'd been standing blankly, and she shook herself. "Can I get you anything? Some coffee?"

"Listen," Natalie said, turning to face her. "I don't know where things stand between you and Nick. Or for that matter between me and Nick. But you saved my children's lives. I'll never forget that. And even if you hadn't, I'd still be here, because you deserve to know that he's alive."

What do you mean, between you and Nick? I thought you two were—wait a second. "Who's alive? What are you talking about?"

Natalie said, "You know, the first time he killed for Equitable Services, we sat up all night talking. I'm not some movie wife who doesn't know her husband is a secret agent."

"I—what? I never thought that."

"I can't do kung fu, and I can't help him find terrorists. But we've made dinner together a thousand times, made love a thousand more. He fed me ice chips and rubbed my back while Todd was born. I held him when his father died."

Shannon had been in a car accident once, gotten clipped from behind and spun into traffic, only an oncoming truck had kicked her car back around the other way, just in time to be hit again. Standing here in a hotel bathrobe, she was feeling that same dizzy vertigo. Fighter jets, mustering troops, cryptic proclamations, and now whatever this was. "Natalie—"

"Just let me finish, would you? I need to get this out."

Shannon tightened the bathrobe, nodded.

"What I'm trying to say is that I'm not an idea, a concept of an ex-wife. Nick and I, our history, it's real. He was my first crush, and he's the father of my children."

Oh God.

She's still in love with him.

Astonishingly, the idea had never occurred to her. She and Nick hadn't had a typical courtship, hadn't faced the everyday awkwardnesses of a couple coming together. Hell, they'd barely had much that counted as a date: dinner, a bottle of wine, small talk. All things that Nick must have done with Natalie years ago. She knew Cooper loved his children, but she'd always assumed that, romantically, he and Natalie were done.

"I'm not telling you what to do," Natalie said. "Honestly, I don't even know what I want. And you can't claim a person like calling shotgun." She paused, as if reconsidering, pondering doing exactly that.

And if she does, what then? Badly as you want Nick, are you going to get in the way of a woman trying to put her family back together?

Before Shannon could answer that question, something on the muted tri-d caught her eye. It wasn't the speed and efficiency with which the paramedics were working on the figures on the floor. Nor was it the fact that she thought she recognized the restaurant. It wasn't even the security team holding back a screaming woman.

It was that the screaming woman was Natalie.

Nick's ex-wife followed her gaze, saw the video. She winced. "I need to get back. My son is still—"

"Natalie," Shannon said, "what happened?"

"A man attacked us yesterday morning at breakfast. He was after Nick, but Todd got in the way."

"Oh my God." Her hand flew to her mouth. "Is he—"

"He's in a coma, but they say he's going to be okay." Natalie said the words steadily, facing them. She was strong, no question about that. "We were lucky. If this had happened anywhere else, Cooper would be dead."

Natalie told the story in clipped sentences: The assassin taking down the guards like they weren't there. Stabbing Nick. His heart stopping. The medics, not regular first responders but elite doctors in Epstein's employ, somehow suspending his fading metabolic processes, then transporting him to a clinic for a surgery that sounded like science fiction. Nick waking to find his son in a coma and his country tearing itself apart. All of it happening while Shannon was unaware, while she tramped back from the airport and booked this suite and collapsed into bed.

"Can I see him?" Shannon started for the bedroom. "Let me get dressed."

"He's gone."

She paused, turned slowly. "Gone?"

"Epstein is arranging a jet for him. He's trying to get to Ohio."

"He's . . . what?"

Natalie's exhale wasn't quite a laugh. "Yeah."

"Why?"

"There's a scientist who has developed something extraordinary. Something Nick thinks might be able to prevent war."

"I know," Shannon said, "I'm the one who told Nick about it." Not a jab, she told herself, not an attack, but there was nothing wrong with claiming her space. Natalie had history with Nick; she had this, this strange, intense life they both lived on the edge, and it wasn't nothing.

"Right." The other woman's lips thinned slightly. "Well, Dr. Couzen has gone missing. Nick is trying to find him."

"Yesterday morning he was having heart surgery, and today he's going to Ohio?"

"You know. He's trying to save the world." She made a gesture something like a shrug. "I have to get back to my son. I just thought you deserved to know he was alive."

Shannon nodded, walked her to the door. "Thanks."

"Yeah. Take care."

"You too."

And then she was walking away, a woman in a ponytail and a borrowed coat, her shoulders up despite the weight on them, and Shannon watched her go. The jets screamed by once more, and Natalie was still in love with Nick, and Nick had been dead and now reborn, and if there was a pattern here that was better than everything circling the drain, she wasn't seeing it.

Shannon shut the hotel door and went to the bedroom. Her phone was on the night table. She typed a sequence of digits she'd never used before. Hesitated over the wording of the message, decided screw it, be blunt.

I NEED ANSWERS. RIGHT NOW.

She pressed SEND, then went to the bathroom, spun on the shower tap. The hotel was lux indeed, and instead of the navy shower she was used to in the NCH, the water ran consistently and hot. When she stepped out, she saw the response on her phone.

THOUGHT YOU MIGHT. 44.3719 BY -107.0632.

■

The rental was an electric, but she managed to get a pickup with decent tires. The GPS coordinates demanded it; not backcountry by any means, but more than a mile off the road, bumping and bouncing up an old streambed gone dry. The landscape ran the spectrum from tan to ocher: dust, rocks, even the twisted little bushes were shades of brown. Her tires kicked a haze of dust behind her, a gloomy brown line back to the highway.

Shannon spotted the meet location before she got there, an empty ridge maybe fifty yards high. She parked the truck at the base, next to a Humvee, an actual gas-guzzler, dusty and weathered. The man who leaned against it held his assault rifle with the loose calm of a professional. His fatigues had no flags on them, no rank, but his belt held two spare magazines and an eight-inch knife. "Hey, Shannon."

"Bryan VanMeter," she said. She flashed back to a job in Boise a year or two ago, doing a scout on a bank that he and his team later robbed. One of the forgotten details of revolutions was that they required money, and she'd pulled more than one heist for the cause. She and VanMeter hadn't worked together since, but she'd been impressed; he was competent without being macho, able to work without her worrying that he might start shooting strangers. "That's serious kit. You invading something?"

"President Clay"—he hawked and spat—"gave the order yesterday. Feds are looking to arrest John."

She caught the use of his first name, thought, *Smart move. Make this guy your friend, not your employee.* Then she remembered that she called John by his first name too.

Sure, but with you it's different.

Was that true? It was hard to be sure. Bryan VanMeter wasn't just muscle—he'd been an Army Ranger before he saw the light—but Shannon had never thought of him as someone who kept counsel with Smith. *I wonder if VanMeter thinks the same of you?*

"Where is he?"

"Up top. Watch your footing, some loose stuff."

She nodded and started up the path. It was steep but simple enough. The day was raw and cold, angry clouds whipping along, a figure silhouetted against them. If he heard her approaching, he showed no sign of it, just kept staring out at the horizon. John Smith had traded in his suit for rugged work pants and a long-sleeve shirt with a down vest, a knit gray skullcap. Both his eyes had big ugly shiners turning yellow and green—*courtesy of Nick, those*—and coupled with the outfit, he looked different. Less a politician and more a battle-scarred warrior.

She said, "Tell me there's a reason."

"Hello, Shannon."

"I saw the news. I know it was your old academy buddy who attacked Nick and his family. The time freak. Don't tell me you didn't send him."

"His name is Soren. And yes, I sent him." His tone was matter-of-fact.

She clenched her fists, released them. "You know that Nick is a friend of mine—"

"A friend?"

"—and you sent someone to kill him anyway."

"Yes. I'm sorry, but it had to be done. This is bigger than personal feelings."

"It better be," she said. "Because putting aside my relationship with Cooper, what I can't understand is *why*. He was an ambassador to the president of the United States. He was here to make peace. And even if you didn't believe that, you had to know that murdering him might start a war."

John's laugh had no humor in it. He gestured with his chin. "Might?"

Out across the barren scrubland, five miles away, stood the skyline of Tesla. It looked pitifully small from this distance, a spread of low buildings expanding out from the silver towers of Epstein Industries. A city of unarmed dreamers huddling beneath angry skies. And even from here, she could see the jets circling. See helicopters buzzing low. See Humvees bouncing around the desert floor. An arc of troops longer than the city itself, poised and ready.

"Look at their army," John said. "Statistically, about seven hundred and fifty of them are gifted. Want to bet how many are officers?"

"You think I don't know that? But starting a war to fix it is insane."

"I agree," he said. "I was an activist, remember? I tried to change the system. Well, the system doesn't want to change. It will fight to the death to destroy anything that tries to change it."

"Save that act for the coeds, John. Tell me there's a reason for all this."

"There is," he snapped, and turned to face her. "Shannon, they enslave children. They want to microchip our friends. They murdered families at the Monocle to make people fear abnorms, and they blew up the stock exchange with eleven hundred people in it to fan the flames. They've quarantined their own cities, and when their citizens begged for food, they tear-gassed and shot them. They will never, ever, let us be equal. The only world they can conceive of is the one they have, and they will do anything, spill any blood, to keep it."

"So you play into their hands by trying to kill a peace envoy?"

He started to respond, stopped. Reached into his vest and took out his cigarettes. "Trying?"

Oh shit. "You know what I mean. How could murdering him help us? How can it lead to anything but an attack on the NCH?"

He looked at her appraisingly. Opened the pack, shook out a smoke, and lit it with a Zippo, his eyes never leaving hers.

The truth sank in. "You *want* them to attack."

"They will. And when they do, they'll doom themselves."

"How? There are seventy-five thousand troops out there, one armed soldier for every man, woman, and child in the NCH. And millions more where they came from."

John took a deep drag. Smiled. "Shannon, this isn't something I came up with in the shower this morning. I've been planning for *years*. I crippled an agency and took down a president to do it. If war is the only way for us to get what we deserve, then by God, they'll have their war."

Shannon stared at him, wondering, whirling. She'd known John for years, and for him she'd risked prison and faced soldiers and killed more than once. But while she knew he wasn't afraid of conflict, she'd never imagined that he wanted open war. Good God, what would that even look like? Brilliants were outnumbered ninety-nine to one. There was no way, shy of genocide and slavery, for them to take what John believed they deserved. Equality would have been fine by her, a world where the government tried to serve the people, all of them, instead of manipulating the truth to serve those at the top.

And there was something else.

"The serum," she said slowly. "Dr. Couzen's work on replicating abnorm gifts. When you sent me into the DAR to find out about it, you never intended to share it, did you? To make it public."

He didn't respond, just held her gaze.

"I ask because I believed in you."

"Shannon—"

"There's a way out of all of this. And you aren't using it." She stared at him, seeing it all now, the whole ugly mess. All the things she had let herself ignore. "You want this war as badly as they do, don't you? You want to march at the head of an army and conquer the world. No matter how much blood is spilled in the process."

His eyes hardened. "I care about our blood. Not theirs."

"Blood is blood."

"No," he said. "It's not. And I won't be the one starting this war. They're the ones who will use military force."

"They haven't yet."

"They will. Someone on their side will be so sure of the need to kill abnorms that they'll launch a concerted strike against their own people. Maybe Clay, maybe someone on his staff, maybe some eighteen-year-old kid who gets nervous behind a trigger. They'll attack, and when they do, they'll unite the brilliants." He glanced at his watch. "It's happening. You may as well accept it."

"I won't."

"You better. I understand that you had some notion of us all holding hands and singing 'Kumbaya' while we penned a new constitution, but it doesn't work that way. Building a better world is a bloody business. And you better decide who you really care about." He flicked the cigarette off the edge of the ridge. "Because you're either us—or you're them."

CHAPTER 37

Soren aimed.

Through the telescopic sight, he watched the woman argue with John. Soren was four hundred yards out, but the scope had a magnification of twenty, and with the crosshairs on her forehead, it was easy to read her lips. He didn't care for handguns; the recoil, magnified by his time sense, made for inelegance. But a sniper rifle was a matter of pure mechanics. Brace it, breathe properly, squeeze rather than pull the trigger, and it was just a projection of will across distance. Still, he was pleased not to have to kill her; John had told him she was close to Samantha.

After she got in her truck and left, he swiveled the scope back to John. His friend had an intense expression he remembered well from their games of chess. Lost in the permutations, following a chain of probabilities.

Finally, John looked directly at him and spoke. He used a normal speed this time, guessing—wrongly—that the distance would require it. "Cooper survived. That's a problem."

In the distance, the streaking jets sounded like angry insects.

"Everything is going as planned." Smith rubbed at the back of his neck. "Only one thing can stop it now."

Soren waited to hear what his friend needed.

"Dr. Couzen has a protégé named Ethan Park."

The rest was obvious. Soren stood up and began walking.

CHAPTER 38

Cooper had been expecting a corporate jet. Something sleek and fast with leather seats and tri-d streamed to the headrests. "No, sir," the pilot had laughed. "Not while the good men and women of the United States Air Force are paying us a visit. All private craft have been grounded. Only things cleared to be in the sky are cargo transports with high-priority freight. Some of the ballsier smugglers are making runs, but there's a good chance of getting exploded, so Mr. Epstein suggested this route."

"This route" was a cargo-modified Boeing 737, seats removed, windows plugged, and a big red cross painted on one side. Cooper had looked at it, shrugged. "So where do I sit?"

"Well, you can pick any crate you like." The pilot grinned. "But it might get kinda cold at thirty thousand feet."

"Right. Copilot it is." He'd strapped in, ready to rock and roll.

Three hours later, they were still waiting on the runway. Cooper had railed and cursed, but the pilot had just shrugged. Nothing to be done about it; according to him, it was a lucky thing they were taking off at all.

When they finally did get clearance, Cooper had looked out the window at the troops below and felt his stomach fall. It was one thing to *hear* the numbers and another to *see* it. A wide arc of military force aimed right at the heart of the Holdfast. Quick-fab barracks and hangers, row upon row of heavy equipment, a mass of ant figures moving. It'd been almost a decade since he'd left the army, but he could imagine the activity on the ground, the tension growing in every chest, the nervous energy that made you wish the worst would happen just so you could stop waiting for it.

The soldiers might look tiny from this height, but that was an illusion; the truth was that he was the tiny one. One man barely out of a hospital bed heading off to search a country of three hundred million for one genius who didn't want to be found. As wild a goose chase as the world had ever seen.

How about instead of feeling sorry for yourself, you get to work?

He had flicked open his d-pad and began to read.

If there was one thing Epstein had, it was information, and the time had passed quickly as Cooper tried to absorb everything about Ethan Park. His parents, his childhood, his itinerant academic's pedigree, his work on epigenetics, his relationship to Abraham Couzen. The guy was clearly a brilliant scientist, but to Cooper's eye, it looked like he was one of those who inspired and supported others, rather than led the way. A catalyst, a protégé, destined to be near greatness. That was useful; the difference between someone like Ethan and the guy accepting a Nobel was likely a raging ego, an important variable when it came to predictability.

All the while, something nagged at him. There was a clue here, some piece of data that he hadn't yet assembled. He knew better than to try to force it, just acknowledged it and let his mind spin, fed it the data that served as gasoline to the engine of his gift.

Cooper was unsurprised, but not at all pleased, to learn that Ethan Park was on the run himself. Good news was that though Park had been visited by DAR agents, that didn't appear to be why he had left his home. Instead, it looked like it had been the situation in Cleveland that had driven him out of town. A risky play, but one Cooper approved of; better chancing a difficult journey than waiting until there was no way out at all. An especially tough decision for a new father to make; Cooper found himself admiring the guy for his chutzpah.

The pilot spoke into his headset, and then as he came in for his approach—

Wait. Park had been visited by DAR agents. Why?

The DAR would have seen through Couzen's faked kidnapping as quickly as you did. But why would the DAR even hear about a simple kidnapping, unless . . .

They knew what Couzen was working on. And when he vanished, the agent in charge took the logical next step, the one you're taking right now.

He went after Ethan Park.

—the landscape shifted.

"Son of a bitch," Cooper said.

"Sir?"

The nagging clue came into sudden sharp focus. *Unbelievable.* The answer had been in front of him before he even knew to look for it. Been in front of him the night he'd gone out for a beer with his old partner.

"When will we be down?"

"About three minutes."

"Okay." Cooper tried to flex the bandaged wreck of his right hand. The palm felt like it might split, and ribbons of flame shot up his fingers, but he gritted his teeth and did it anyway. "I'm going to need two things."

"Name it. Mr. Epstein said carte blanche."

"First, I need a secure telephone line the moment we land."

"And second?"

"A really fast car."

■

It was a tribute to the sheer muscle of billions that despite the fact that they were in Akron, Ohio, at a small airport Cooper had never heard of, fifteen hundred miles from New Canaan, a man in a jumpsuit was hustling across the tarmac holding a bulky phone before their engines had even spun down.

Cooper unbuckled himself from the copilot's seat and met the guy at the top of the rolling stairs. He started to reach for the phone with his right hand, caught himself just in time. "This is secure?"

"Yes, sir. Epstein Industries executive-level encryption."

Which is probably safer than anything the DAR has. Cooper looked at the pilot until the guy said, "Right. On my way." He closed the cockpit hatch behind him.

Cooper dialed the number, one of a few he had memorized. There had had been a time he called it a dozen times a day. It rang twice, three times, Cooper thinking, *Come on, pick up,* and then there was the sound of connection and a familiar voice.

"Quinn."

"Bobby, it's me."

Silence. A long beat of it. Then, an edge to his voice, Quinn said, "Whoever this is, you should know that I have initiated trace algorithms. Enjoy whatever cute little game you're playing, because in a few seconds, when I find you, I'm going to direct a drone strike."

What? Oh. Right.

"Bobby, I'm not dead. Erik Epstein pulled a medical rabbit out of his hat, an illegal newtech surgery, saved my life."

"Keep talking, asshole. How long do you think your encryption can hold up against the DAR?"

Cooper sighed. "You're divorced. Your daughter's name is Maggie. Three months ago, you, me, and Shannon threw Director Peters off a roof in midtown DC."

A pause. "Cooper and I went out for drinks not long ago. Where did we go?"

"I don't remember the name of the bar, but it was a dim place, Christmas lights. We drank beer and whiskey and talked about kidnapping John Smith."

"Jesus Christ! Cooper? Is that really you?"

"It's really me, man."

"Oh God. Oh shit." The man's voice was fast, relieved, an overflow of emotion. "What the hell, Coop? I thought you were dead. We all did."

"I was."

"Huh?"

"Apparently, medically, I was. They did some kind of suspended animation thing, repaired my heart. Something to do with stem cells, I don't know, but listen, I really don't have time—"

"What about Todd?"

A rush of warmth for his friend hit at the same time as a terrible stab of guilt and pain. "He's . . . they say he's going to be okay."

"Thank God. I was so scared—my God. Coop! You're alive."

"Hey, keep your voice down, would you?" He pictured Bobby's office, how many people might walk by at any moment. "That's not public knowledge."

"Why not?"

"There are advantages to being dead. If I'm alive, I should call the president and follow orders. But dead men can do what they want."

"Oh crap." Bobby was suddenly serious. "What are you up to?"

"Saving the world, same as always."

"How's it going?"

"Same as always. Listen, we're on the clock. That night in the bar, you said you'd just gotten back from Cleveland. That you'd been working a target there, a scientist who had run."

"Yeah?"

"It was Dr. Abraham Couzen, right?"

More silence. "I'm not sure I can confirm—"

"I know it was Couzen, and I know you were there to work his number two, a guy named Ethan Park. Right?"

A sigh. "Yeah."

"I know what Couzen developed. And so do you. He found the root cause of the brilliants, and he was working on a way to replicate it."

"You know I love you, man, but this is way, way above—"

"Bobby, no kidding, this is not the time. I can be your old boss, or a special advisor to the president, or just your best friend, whatever you need to cut the crap right now." He put steel in his voice, let Quinn hear the desperation. "Can you do that?"

A long pause. "What's going on?"

"Couzen faked his kidnapping. I was trying to figure out why he would do that, and it finally came together. He did it because the DAR came looking for him, right? Somehow you found out what he was working on, and you wanted it."

"Shit, man, everyone wants it. Thing like that could change the world. Maybe even stop what's about to happen."

"My thinking exactly. That's why I need to find it, and right now."

"Good luck. Couzen may not be much at faking a crime scene, but he's turned out to be aces at lying low. I've been running every protocol we have to catch the guy, but no luck."

"And now Ethan Park is on the run too. He's my target."

Another pause. "Is that right?"

Cooper hated the phone. In person, he could have read the layers of conflict behind what Bobby was saying, parsed it. But without the tiny physical cues, the twitches of muscle, the hint of nerves, his gift was useless. *Second time that's happened recently. Maybe you're relying on it too much, Coop.*

Maybe it's time you used your brain instead.

"In Cleveland, you said that you'd braced Park. My guess, you put him under surveillance, right?"

"Sure. But then things got stupid in Cleveland. When the riots hit, my men were pulled off to help. That's when he bolted."

"You think he knew about your team?"

"Nah. Just dumb luck. A lot of people tried to leave Cleveland then. Once I realized what had happened, we ran a video scan, found his car. I got drone surveillance on it, found him and his family hiking south. The National Guard was supposed to pick him up, but some hothead shot a refugee, and then it was chaos."

"You lost him?"

"For a while, then picked him up in a bank, lost him again, got him robbing a gas station."

"Seriously?" That was way out of character with the pattern he'd built. "I thought he was a geek. He turned criminal?"

"Yeah, well." There was a note of embarrassment in his friend's voice. "I took a risky play, called him at the bank and tried to talk him in. He panicked."

"Where was the gas station?"

"Place called Cuyahoga Falls, outside of Akron."

Cooper laughed. "You're kidding me."

"Nope. Why?"

"Guess where I'm calling from?"

"No shit? Huh."

"What does 'huh' mean?"

"Well, our boy Ethan is smart. He took the gas station attendant's truck, but he didn't try to run. Laid low instead. It took some time to scan satellite feeds, but we found him. He's in a cabin not far from there. I was just about to send cops in to pick him up."

"Local PD? No way. Bobby, we can't lose him. If some rookie sees he's got a gun and takes a shot—"

"Yeah, I know, but I got no choice, Coop. I have no resources, none. Have you turned on a tri-d? Everything is focused on Wyoming. Right now, I couldn't order a pizza."

"So sit on him. You've got him tagged; he can't go anywhere."

"That was the plan, until your playmate turned up in Ohio."

"My playmate?"

"Soren Johansen. You remember, asshole with a knife?"

"*Soren?* He's here? How do you know?"

"I know because I pulled every favor I'm owed to implement a nationwide random camera scan. Nobody kills my partner and walks away, I don't care if World War III *is* about to start. With everything as it is right now, I could only get public safety cameras, you know, government institutions, airports—"

"Airports?"

Quinn read his tone. "Where exactly—you said you were in Akron. Are you at Fulton International?"

"Couldn't get into Cleveland with the city shut down, so I came here."

There was a long pause. "I don't know how to tell you this, but so did Soren."

Cooper felt a tightening in his chest, a weird and sudden pressure. His heart seemed to stick, a beat and then nothing, like a burp that wouldn't come. An animal panic flooded him, fingers tingling, and then his heart jumped again, the beats coming, fast now. His vision went a little wobbly, and he leaned against the back of the pilot's seat.

"Coop? You okay?"

It wasn't fear, although that was there as well. It was something mechanical, like his heart had lost its rhythm. *I guess a patched tire isn't as strong as an undamaged one.* He took a breath, concentrated on smoothing out the beats. "I'm fine. Listen, if he's here, it's for Ethan."

"No kidding. That's why I've got no choice but to send the cops."

Cooper considered it. Why not let the police help? Surely he didn't have to save the world single-handedly. Especially now.

Then he remembered the scene in the restaurant. The ease with which Soren had murdered Epstein's highly trained guards. Add to it a scared father with a gun, a man who had no idea about the forces swirling around him. Stir in a handful of suburban cops thrilled to have a little excitement. It would be a disaster.

"Don't send the cops, Bobby. There's another option."

.

The car was a Porsche 911, one of the new models that on a government salary he'd never even allowed himself to look at. A rear-mounted, turbocharged engine capable of zero to sixty miles per hour in 2.9 seconds, set in a candy-apple red body that screamed sex.

Looks like Epstein took you seriously about needing it to be fast.

Bobby had taken convincing, but in the end, he'd agreed to give Cooper the address of the cabin where Ethan and his family were hiding, as well as a thirty-minute head start on the police. But Soren had a head start too.

Cooper got in the car, fired it up, and was about to blast off when he realized that with his hand in the shape it was, he couldn't use the stick shift. He pushed in the clutch, pinned the wheel with his right wrist, and then leaned across to shift with his left hand. A wave of exhaustion and frustration washed over him.

What are you doing?

Sitting in the hallway of Epstein's clinic, he'd heard the truth behind Natalie's words, good and bad. The truth was that as much as he loved his children, as much as he felt he should be sleeping in the chair next to Todd's hospital bed, he was too much of the soldier to believe that made sense. It was romantic to believe that he would go ten rounds with the Grim Reaper for Todd's life, but the truth was that sitting there would have been useless. The world was about to be at war, bombs were about rain on New Canaan, and he had a chance to stop it. So, yeah, better to go.

But the plan had been to find Ethan Park. To use his mind and his gift to track down a scientist and convince him to share what he knew. Not to go into combat. Not to face John Smith's best friend and best killer.

With every beat of his heart, pain coursed through Cooper, a throb that started in his chest, echoed in his hand, and grated through his head. His vision was a little jumpy—not blurry, but lagging half a frame behind. As he skipped second gear and jump-shifted into third, he remembered the fight in the restaurant. The terrible economy of Soren's movements, the way he danced around every blow like it hadn't even been thrown.

For the first time in a long time, Cooper felt real fear. Not nerves or tension or concern. Not panic at an unexpected moment or terror for the safety of those he loved.

The idea of facing Soren again scared him.

And yet, what choice did he have? If Soren got to Ethan first, any hope of the war being averted was doomed. The military would attack New Canaan. The fragile dream would be destroyed, along with tens of thousands of its young dreamers. And after that, America would be over. At least the America he loved.

Not to mention the fact that Natalie and your children are dead-center of the crosshairs.

Once again, it came down to everything. Just as it had in DC months ago, when Peters had kidnapped his family. Once again, Cooper's whole life lay on the table as fate's roulette wheel clattered and spun. Only this time, he could barely—

Enough.

Win here, or lose everything.

Let's see what you've got, soldier.

CHAPTER 39

As far back as she could remember, Holly Roge had wanted to fly.

Dad had been part of it, a navy man, a pilot who parked jets on moving aircraft carriers. When other little girls had been lulled to sleep with tales of princesses and unicorns, Dad had lain beside her in the dark and told her what it was like to scream in low and steep, dark water below, a tiny target ahead. How precise the angle had to be to catch the landing cable, how if you screwed up you could slide right off, bounce out into the ocean.

"Was it scary?" she'd asked, always.

And always he'd say, "Sure. But in the good way."

And after he had kissed her forehead and told her to have beautiful dreams, she'd lie awake staring at her ceiling, wondering what that meant, scary in the good way.

Now, suited up and sitting in the ready room at Ellsworth Air Force Base just east of the Wyoming border, she wondered what Dad would think of all of this. He'd died while she was still at the academy, an aneurysm that took him in his easy chair, fast as a missile with hard lock. He'd never seen her earn her wings, never known that she made top of her class. Never known that she'd been the first woman selected to fly an F-27 Wyvern, that gorgeous piece of $185 million equipment, her second true love. Sixty-seven feet and sixty-five thousand pounds of high-performance glory, capable of soaring eighteen miles high, of after-burner blasting at Mach 2.9, twenty-two hundred magnificent miles an hour. A machine so sophisticated that the computer in the helmet read her brain's alpha waves, allowing her to control the gauges and secondary systems just by thinking in coded patterns.

A fighter jet that she had been flying over American soil, buzzing low over a city of her own countrymen, carrying a full load of ordnance.

That was the part she didn't dig, and she didn't think Dad would have either. She was a warrior, had flown peacekeeping missions all over the world, been selected to fly in the honor guard for Air Force One on President Walker's trip to India. Her job was to protect America, not threaten it. And no matter what you thought about the abnorms, last she'd heard, Wyoming was still part of the fifty.

The fact that today's briefing was being given not by Major Barnes, as usual, but by the big dog himself, Lieutenant Colonel Riggs, didn't make her feel any better about the situation.

"—continued state of high alert. Now, you all know that the Holdfast has antiaircraft batteries." Riggs paused, a slight smile on his lips as twenty pilots chuckled. "And though it's true that they would be particularly dangerous to MiG-19s"—more laughter—"that doesn't mean I want any of you getting careless. Everything by the numbers, people. I want all of my pilots back without a scratch. You'll be carrying . . ."

Holly knew the load, the same she'd flown the last sorties with. Military life, though, never double-check when you could quadruple-check.

It had to be posturing, she figured. A message to the Children of Darwin and all the other terrorists out there. Sure, you may be able to take out a few trucks, but can you do *this*? There hadn't been a declared war since Korea, which meant that most of the time, military assets were more about communication than they were about offense. A way for the politicians to talk to one another, play their games of high-stakes poker.

Thing was, who were they talking to here? The Holdfast was a bunch of kids living in the desert, pretending it was a new world instead of a bunch of rocks. Fine with her, so why the full load? Each Wyvern carried enough ordnance to wipe out half of Tesla. Flying a full wing of them over the scrub town was like bringing an A-bomb to a backyard brawl.

"Any questions?"

Holly looked around. Wanted to raise her hand and ask, *Sir, respectfully, what the hell are we doing here?* She wouldn't, of course, but maybe someone would. The nineteen other pilots in this room were among the best in the world, and that came with a hot-shot sense of entitlement.

If it had been Major Barnes giving the briefing, maybe one of them would have. But the vice chief of the air wing was another matter. They all sat ramrod straight and steely-eyed, ready to snap salutes and mount up.

It was only ten minutes later, as the cockpit windscreen closed and her HUD glowed to life, that it occurred to Captain Holly Roge to wonder if that was exactly why it had been Riggs giving the briefing.

CHAPTER 40

Soren drifted.

He couldn't try for nothingness, not in a moving Escalade with the radio news in the background, announcers practically selling war bonds; not with three strangers checking their weapons and talking in rough voices. Nothingness would have to wait. For now, he simply leaned back in the seat and let his eyes go soft. Let the world wash over him, past him, a leaf on a river swept away in the current.

He understood John's decision to send Bryan VanMeter along. The situation was fluid, and if Ethan Park had moved, they would need to hunt him. Better to have a team that could talk to people, could persuade and bribe and convince, things Soren could not do. Still, he felt the presence of the three soldiers, the testosterone charge and rough competence grating at him, making the moments longer.

You need to go back into exile. All this noise. You're losing your nothingness.

Soon. John would have his war. The grand cause and glorious battle meant nothing to Soren, but he hoped that his friend was happy for it.

For himself, he hoped only that Samantha would come with him. There hadn't been time to say good-bye, the kind of irony that had never amused him. The flight here had been on a military jet, as fast an option as existed, but with his time sense, he had perceived it as more than thirty hours long. A day and a half on a plane, and yet no time to see his love.

You are a leaf, and the current will carry you away.

VanMeter briefed his team, and Soren tried to ignore it.

"Cuyahoga Valley National Park . . ."

"No neighbors in sight, but . . ."

"Tactical advance, two front, one rear . . ."

Out the window, faded pines scraped at a gray sky. The wind stirred dead leaves. The knife was so light that he had to concentrate to feel it, a good meditative exercise. Be the muscles of your chest, be the skin against your shirt. He wondered how Nick Cooper had survived. Remembered the look in the man's eyes as Soren's elbow met his son's temple, the raw agony in it, as damaging a blow as piercing his heart had been. Idly, he wondered what it would be like to have a child, to have created life. If that would be the thing that brought meaning to the endlessness, or if it would only make things worse.

"Okay," the one called Donovan said, "but why all the trouble? He's an egghead. Let's just roll up, do the thing, get out."

"You're a hump, you know that?" VanMeter grimaced. "We flew here on a *military* jet. That pilot was a sleeper, an asset, and John burned him to get us here. Hell, can you even imagine the amount of influence he's had to use to find this guy, with the DAR looking for him?" The soldier shook his head. "I don't know how he did it, and I don't know why John wants the guy dead. All I know is that he needs this done, so we're going to do it right, we're going to do it clean, and we're going to do it completely. You get me?"

"Completely? You mean—"

"Orders are to eliminate everybody there. Wife and baby too."

"Baby?" Donovan sucked air through his teeth. "Shit."

"Makes you feel better, they're normals, all three." VanMeter turned to Soren. "Sir?"

He raised an eyebrow.

"We're less than a minute out. Anything you want to add?"

The trees had grown denser, the driveways between them fewer and farther between. He could see the one where Dr. Ethan Park and his family waited.

Soren said, "You're weak."

Soon, this tiresome walk through the world would end, and he could return to his nothing.

"I'll kill the child."

CHAPTER 41

"You are my sunshine, my only sunshine . . ."

Late afternoon, and already the sky was starting to fade, cold clouds going fat and dim. They had a fire burning and news on the TV, an actual old-school television, not a tri-d. Ethan was splitting his attention between the horror show in Wyoming and the sight of his wife crooning lullabies to their daughter. It was a jarring juxtaposition, footage of soldiers and tanks and jets, of missiles being fueled and politicians thumping the podium, set against the two loves of his life, his daughter safe and warm and drifting off on a tide of song.

"You make me happy, ev-er-y day."

They did a lot of singing to Violet. Sang the "Naked Baby" song as they got her into her bath (to the tune of "Alouette": "Naked baby, naked naked baby, naked baby, naked baby time"). Sang free-form about toys and breakfast and pooping. And early on, Amy had declared that they would have their own version of "You Are My Sunshine," one that addressed certain thematic difficulties.

Now the news was showing footage of Cleveland. If it hadn't been identified, he wouldn't have recognized it. Fire had swept through most of downtown, and what was left was all gray people in gray clothes digging through rubble, ragged families on street corners, and squads of riot police locking shields.

"You'll never know, dear, how much I love you."

Ethan's eyes wandered from screen to family, family to screen, but a part of him, the part he would have pointed to as his real self if anyone had asked, wasn't really taking either in. It was thinking about what Amy had said earlier.

The fact that she was right was so obvious it didn't bear thinking about. He and Abe had rushed foolishly into places angels feared to tread, and while they had found answers there, they had also made enemies. Funny that the idea had never occurred to him before. Even when the DAR had shown up at his house about their research, he'd asked Bobby Quinn to leave like the agent was a census-taker. In hindsight, it was all so clear: the DAR must have been watching them, watching from before Abe disappeared. And they would never stop looking for him, never. Not with what he knew.

"No one can take my sunshine away."

And what if the DAR wasn't the only group who wanted the serum? Another thing he'd never thought of until Amy laid him out. The value of their discovery was literally incalculable. Controlling it would be like holding a patent on the wheel. No wonder Abe had been so rigid about his nondisclosures, his loose-lips-sink-ships policy. The problem was that Abe hadn't gone nearly far enough. They should have been operating in perfect secrecy on some remote Pacific island.

If the DAR knew about their work, maybe the Children of Darwin would too. Plus their mysterious backer, whose deep pockets had financed the lab in the first place. Ethan had always suspected that might be Erik Epstein—who else would benefit so highly?—which meant he and Abe had been working for a rogue state currently surrounded by American troops.

All those forces arrayed against him, and here he was huddling in a cabin, waiting for the sky to fall and crush him. Not to mention his wife and daughter. Because of what Ethan had done.

No, that was imprecise. It wasn't because of what he'd *done*. It was because of what he *knew*. The difference was important. The former was about punishment for a sin already committed. Nothing to be done about that.

But if people were after him for what he knew . . . well. That made things clearer.

Ethan focused on his wife and daughter. Amy was gazing down at Violet, a faint smile on her lips. A knit blanket draped her shoulders, and the fire wrapped them both in soft flickering light. His daughter's tiny hand clenched his wife's index finger. What wouldn't he do to protect them?

"No one can take my sunshine away."

He'd have to act soon. Every moment he stayed with them, he put them at risk.

If he was going to leave them, maybe forever, he'd have to act soon. Now.

Ethan was trying to make himself stand up and walk away from everything he loved when he heard a sound that didn't belong. It wasn't menacing in its own right, not something he would have noticed under other circumstances. But now it meant the world. Meant, in fact, that the world was ending.

It was the sound of a car door closing.

They were here.

CHAPTER 42

"I'm not convinced."

Secretary of Defense Owen Leahy stared across the coffee table at the president of the United States and thought, *This can't be happening again.*

"I understand," Clay continued, "that a military response may be necessary. But I'm not convinced I need to take that step now. Epstein and I are still in discussion."

"Sir, the situation in Cleveland—"

"I know what's happening in Cleveland. People are hungry and scared and angry, and they want a quick fix, want to know that payback has been doled out."

"It's more than that—"

"Luckily, we live in a republic, which means that they elect us for the exact reason that in a time of crisis, it probably shouldn't be the victims calling the shots." Clay stroked his chin. "Attacking the New Canaan Holdfast won't get blankets or food into Cleveland."

"It's not about food and blankets. It's about the fact that terrorists are operating with impunity on American soil."

"An attack on the NCH won't disrupt the Children of Darwin. Intelligence suggests that it's unlikely they report directly to anyone in the Holdfast."

All right, enough. Leahy said, "Sir, that's not the point, and I need you to stop acting like this is a graduate seminar and we're debating."

Clay's eyes flashed. "Excuse me?"

"This isn't the time for a lecture on the benefits of living in a republic. Do I need to lay it all out for you?"

"What you need to do is watch that tone."

Leahy almost laughed. For years, simply microchipping the gifted had seemed a difficult enough goal. Now there was the opportunity to do so much more. He had no intention of letting Clay's soft sensibilities get in the way of that.

And every normal in America should hit their knees and thank us for it. Because our work, unsavory as it may be, is all that is protecting their children.

"Now, if that's all . . ."

"It's not." Leahy leaned forward, enumerating on his fingers. "Here are the facts. Three cities are under terrorist control. Casualties are in the thousands, property destruction in the hundreds of millions. Faith in the government is the lowest in history. All over the country, people are stockpiling food, hiding in their basements." That was five, and he switched to his left hand, kept counting. "John Smith is at large in the New Canaan Holdfast. Erik Epstein is a puppet, and we're not certain for whom. Our intelligence shows that Holdfast technology already outstrips our own. We know they're manufacturing weapons and funding research labs developing God knows what. And now the American ambassador to the Holdfast has been murdered in public, in front of his family." He held up all ten fingers. "Do I need to go on?"

"Owen—"

"No, sir. No more discussion, no more thinking it over. For the good of the country, it's time to act. You have to give the order to attack. You have to do it right—"

"I don't have to do a goddamn thing." Clay leaned forward. "I'm the president of the United States. I decide when we attack. If you can't deal with that, I'll accept your resignation right now. Do you get me?"

The grandfather clock in the corner ticked off the seconds. Leahy shrugged, said, "I get you."

"Good." Clay rose. He turned his back and went to his desk, the dismissal evident.

Ah well. You knew it might come to this. Leahy said, "But you're only half right."

The man spun. "Owen, I swear to—"

"You are the president." Leahy flashed a thin smile. "But you're not the only one who can order an attack."

CHAPTER 43

Ethan leapt to his feet. In the opposite chair, Amy startled, joggling Violet. His wife read his face, said, "What is it?"

"Someone's here. Take Violet into the kitchen."

She didn't hesitate, and he loved her for that, for not wasting precious time. His wife was stronger and better than he was. She'd manage without him. He wished he could have told her he loved her, that he could have apologized for bringing this all down on them. But they'd survive, and that was the most important thing.

The revolver was on the side table. The weight that only a week ago had felt so strange in his hands was now comforting. He made sure all six chambers were loaded.

You keep telling yourself you'll do anything to protect them. Time to prove it.

He slipped to the front door and flattened himself against the wall beside it. The door had a small window with a dusty curtain. Through it the front yard looked as he remembered, dotted with thin trees and carpeted with pine needles. Their stolen truck was parked facing out, ready to bolt at a moment's notice. No sign of another vehicle. Had he been hearing—

Something moved behind the truck bed. Ethan's chest felt like there wasn't room for air, and his hands went sweaty. Best to do this fast. If he stalled, he might lose his nerve.

A sharp, short inhale through his nostrils, and then he yanked open the door and came out with the gun up. Cold air and the smell of pine sap, needles crunching underfoot, the gun shaking.

Two steps, three, and then he caught another flash of movement, from the other side of the truck; the guy had circled around. Ethan whirled and lined up the sights and pulled the trigger.

The gun jumped in his hand like it was alive, and the roar startled him. A flock of birds leapt from a nearby tree, cawing. The man was still on his feet and coming, just feet away, Ethan had just this one chance, and he leveled the gun and didn't flinch as he pulled the trigger again, only somehow the man wasn't where he was supposed to be. He'd stepped aside as if pulled by invisible strings, and his left hand flashed out to knock the pistol aside while at the same time he lunged forward, Ethan's world suddenly filled with the man's head, a crack and a whirl and an explosion of pain between his eyes, and the sensation of falling.

He landed on his back, the breath whistling out of him, and stared, coughing and squinting at the figure above him.

"Hi, Ethan," the man said. "I'm Nick Cooper."

■

The ground screamed beneath Holly Roge. She took the F-27 into a smooth pitch turn, the horizon falling fifteen degrees and spinning as she banked around the east edge of Tesla. From her altitude she had a clear view of the rest of the military presence, the ground troops and armored column just miles away. Domed prefab buildings and the glint of metal, helicopters buzzing like dragonflies. Her brothers- and sisters-in-arms, the coiled might of the United States military. A force that would have looked at home in a desert far away, ready to rock and roll.

Idly, she generated the alpha wave patterns to change the heads-up display to quarter-thermal. No specific reason, but Holly liked information, was constantly swapping displays to screen the ground and sky around her. Her baby made it so easy, this marvel of machinery, a chair strapped to a rocket managed by a computer she controlled with her brain.

With the partial thermal overlay, the city seemed to glow in gauzy yellows and oranges, heat sources marked out against the cold air. Squinting, it made it look like Tesla was on fire.

That's enough of that. She swapped the HUD back to standard, then did a reflexive positioning check. Her Wyvern was in perfect formation with the other two, five hundred meters apart and level. Just as they had been ten seconds before, and ten seconds before, and ten seconds before, and she took more than a little pride in knowing that the same would be true ten seconds hence.

Out the cockpit glass, the city slid by. Holly had spent a fair number of hours flying over it in the last few days, and she knew its topography, the shift and shape of buildings and boulevards. It wasn't a bad-looking little town, despite the lousy location; plazas dotted the landscape, and gene-modified gardens grew atop the buildings. The beating heart was a complex of more than twenty blocky cubes of mirrored glass that reflected the Wyverns' passage. The tallest buildings bristled with gear, satellite dishes and climatology equipment as well as surface-to-air missiles, the anti-aircraft weapons they'd all laughed about earlier. All of it would be utterly ineffectual against her Wyvern.

"Leopard One, we have new orders for you."

"Roger, Ground, ready."

A stream of text began to scroll across the cockpit glass. Standard operating procedure during a mission with combat potential, don't announce intentions over verbal transmissions, even coded ones, not when it was easy to send them—

Holy shit.

"Ah, Ground, I think we may have an error of some sort."

"Checking." A moment passed. "Negative, we're showing everything green on your bird, Leopard One."

Holly stared at the display. Hoping that somehow she had misread it. Knowing that she hadn't.

MISSION PROTOCOL DELTA ONE, and then a stream of familiar details. They reviewed all anticipated protocols before wheels ever left runway, and she knew what this one said without reading it, but words kept leaping at her: TARGET and COMPLEX and FULL PREJUDICE and AUTHORIZED.

"Ground, can you confirm this order?"

"Roger, proceed with Delta One."

"What? No." Her mind was racing, and yet it felt like she was lagging behind. This couldn't be happening. "Ground, this is an attack order."

"Roger." The voice cool and distant, and Holly wondered if she knew the person on the other end. "Proceed."

■

Cooper's forehead was throbbing from the head butt, one more part of his body that hurt. Pretty soon it was going to be easier to catalogue what *wasn't* in pain.

Up on his elbows now, Ethan Park said, "You're going to have to kill me."

"Huh?" He bent down and picked up the revolver with his left hand. Should've asked for a weapon in addition to a car. But it would have meant a delay, and Soren was on his way. "You've got the wrong idea, Doc."

"Who are you with?"

"I'm with the United States of Get Off Your Ass." He smiled. "Look, I'm here to help. You're in danger like you don't even know. Besides, there's a war about to start."

"I'm . . . what?"

"I realize head-butting you wasn't the best introduction. But then, you did try to shoot me." He slid the revolver into his pocket, the barrel warm through his pants. "I'll explain everything, but first, no bullshit, we gotta get out of here."

"Let my wife and daughter go, and I'll come with you."

"Okay."

"I mean it—wait. You'll let them go?"

"Sure."

Ethan Park stared up at him, distrust radiating from every muscle. But below it, fear, and not for himself. The man was scared for his family. Cooper could relate.

"Listen," Cooper said, "I'm one of the good guys. I'm not out to steal your work. I'm not after your family. I've got kids of my own. All I want is to stop a war. And the happy news is, we do it right, it gets you out of the crosshairs too. So please. With sugar on top." He reached a hand down. Ethan hesitated. Cooper said, "The other guy coming for you? He'll feel differently."

The scientist took his hand, and Cooper pulled him up. A twig cracked behind them, and his left hand flew to his pocket, fumbling awkwardly with the sidearm, stupid putting it away just to be able to help the guy up, but luck was with him and the gun didn't snag as he yanked and pointed in one clean motion, framing up his sights on . . .

"Jesus," he said. "You two are a pair."

He recognized Amy Park from photographs in her file. An attractive woman, fire in her eyes, ten feet away and cocking an axe like a baseball bat. The head was rusty and pitted, a woodsplitter. Cooper lowered the gun, said, "Doc, would you mind?"

"It's okay, babe," Ethan said, his voice only marginally convincing. "If he wanted to kill me, he could have already."

She hesitated, then lowered the axe. "You're not with the DAR."

"No."

"Then who?"

"Right now what you need to know is that people are on their way here to murder your husband. You and your daughter too, I imagine."

Her features tightened at that, a sudden ferocity. He didn't need to be gifted to recognize a mama bear protecting her cub. Cooper had to admit he was starting to like the Parks. "Your daughter is inside?"

She nodded.

"Go get her. Hurry."

Amy and Ethan silently conferred, their eyes locked. Then she dropped the axe and ran back around the house. Cooper turned to Ethan. "Anything here you can't live without?"

Ethan shook his head. "We got robbed."

"What about your research? Any notes or samples?"

"Abe kept all of that. What I have is in my head."

Cooper had expected as much, but it would have been nice to be wrong. While President Clay would listen to him, it was hard to say whether he would act on their word alone. Especially without any sort of data. Of course, Bobby and the DAR could corroborate to a point, but—

Don't get ahead of yourself. First get out of here.

The Porsche was pure sex, but it was also a two-seater. They'd have to take the pickup. He could call ahead, have a plane waiting to get them to DC. Time was running short.

God, he was tired. Cooper straightened and took a deep breath, drew it into the base of his lungs. The air was clean and cool, fragrant with the needles scattered on the ground. The bright cherry ember of a cigarette glowed near his feet, and he stepped on it idly, bad idea to be smoking out here with all this dry stuff, only the bright dot was on top of his foot now, weird—

Cooper whirled. A red dot darted up Ethan Park's chest, and then Cooper noticed the silence, hadn't there been birds before? He hurled himself at Ethan's chest, a graceless tackle that tangled them and brought them down in a heap as the woods around them exploded with machine-gun fire.

■

"What are you talking about?" President Clay's lips were twitching.

Leahy rose from the couch, walked to face the man. *What was Mitchum's phrase?*

Play for all the marbles.

"Right about"—he glanced at his watch—"now, three F-27 Wyverns are launching their ordnance at the Epstein Industries complex in New Canaan. I don't know how much you know about Wyverns, sir, but they're capable of carrying—"

"What have you done?"

"I thought that was obvious." Leahy shrugged. "I gave the order to level those buildings. In your name. We're at war."

Clay stared, hollow-eyed and disbelieving, like he was trying to convince himself it was a joke of some kind.

"If we're lucky," Leahy continued, "we'll get Epstein himself. But either way we'll cripple the governing body, not to mention set them back technically."

"No," Clay said. He reached for the phone. "I'm going to stop this."

"God, you really have no business behind that desk, do you?" Leahy laughed. "It's already done, Lionel. Three planes just launched a devastating attack on a civilian building, resulting in the deaths of thousands. And they did it on your watch."

Clay's skin went ashen. Slowly he sank down into his chair. "You'll hang for this."

"No," Leahy said. "I won't. Instead, you're going to pick up that phone and back my play. You're going to order a full-scale attack against the New Canaan Holdfast."

"I'll do no such thing."

"America just declared war. There's no going back. It's us versus them now. You can act, and secure a quick victory that saves countless lives. Or you can dawdle, and risk all-out genocide."

"I'll tell them it was you, that I didn't—"

"That you didn't order the attack? That the president of the United States can't command his own military?" Leahy shook his head. "None of the dead will care who ordered the strike, and none of their surviving family members will split that hair either. You'll have nationwide anarchy, riots that make Cleveland look pleasant.

Plus, you've never worn a uniform, so you might not understand this, but soldiers don't like it when their commanders abandon them. I wouldn't be surprised if you face a coup d'état. Regardless, America will be destroyed, and millions will die."

Clay stared across the desk, a desk that had seen the rise and fall of nations, that had been here when the atom was split, when the first gifted were born. His hands gripped it like he was trying to hold on, like the wood might provide a solution.

"I'm going to say it one more time." Leahy leaned in. "We. Are. At war. Your country needs you. What are you going to do?"

For a long, gut-churning moment, Clay just stared, and Leahy wondered if he'd pushed too hard, if he'd gone catatonic again.

Then, like a man in a nightmare, the president reached for the phone.

CHAPTER 44

Cooper hit the ground hard, the impact ringing his shoulder and sending a sick tearing sensation through his chest, a boiling-water shock of pain. Gunfire cracked the afternoon, three-round bursts like God stuttering. The window of the cabin exploded.

The pain was enormous, a razor-beaked creature inside his body, but there wasn't time, and Cooper forced himself to roll to his side and then into a crouch. They'd landed behind the pickup truck; Ethan Park lay prone with his hands laced over his head, but Cooper didn't see any blood. He pressed his back against the tire and craned his head up to peer over the hood of the truck. Bright flashes burst from the woods, and bullets pinged off the truck just as he yanked his head back—

Muzzle flashes from two positions about thirty degrees apart.

If the shooters were prone, the flashes probably wouldn't have been visible.

Ending up behind the truck was a bit of luck, but it won't hold. Assault rounds will punch right through sheet metal. The engine will absorb some of the fire, but not all.

You don't have to go home, but you can't stay here.

—then dropped to the ground with the pistol aimed in front of him. Took a deep breath, said a silent prayer, and rolled, trying to fix exactly where he'd seen one spot of brightness, pine needles poking through his clothes, the smell of dirt and the cold of the ground, the gun held in his left hand and braced on his right wrist, the truck bumper, the sky, trees, a line of dense bushes, a tall man duck-walking toward them with an assault rifle at his shoulder, the guy spotting him, tracking his motion, sighting, dirt exploding ahead, and then Cooper exhaled and double-squeezed the trigger, one-two.

Part of the man's head sheered away, and he spun as he fell, muscle twitches making the rifle fire another burst into the sky.

One down. Not bad for a righty.

Cooper scrabbled back to the cover of the truck as bullets tore divots in the spot where he had been lying. No surprise, but these men were good. And Soren was out there somewhere.

One thing at a time.

"Doc, are you okay?"

Still prone, the scientist gave a quick nod.

"You want to stay that way, do exactly what I tell you." Cooper wriggled his back up the truck, ready to move. "When I say, stand up, run for the house, and jump through that broken window."

"What about the door—"

"Too slow. Ready? Now!" He stood up, exposing his head and chest, but he was already moving along the truck from the front to the bed, three quick steps chased by bullets, the windshield shattering, side windows blowing out. When he reached the rear tires, he pointed the gun and fired twice, snap shots with no chance of connecting, but they had the desired effect, made the other guy take cover. Cooper risked a glance over his shoulder in time to see Ethan take a Superman through the bay window, arms in front of his face to protect from what glass remained.

He turned back, braced his hands on the lip of the truck's bed, aiming carefully. If the guy was macho and came out trying to aim, Cooper would have a slight edge on him. It was a terrible mismatch, a .38 revolver against a fully automatic assault rifle, but if there was a better move, he couldn't think of it.

Come on, come on.

The gunman leapt from behind his tree. Cooper aimed, but the guy kept moving, sprinting diagonally forward, daring Cooper to shoot. Thin trees screened his progress, and then he reached a towering pine, the trunk two feet across, good cover, only Cooper could read his intention, the strain of his muscles and his forward momentum, and he knew the man didn't plan to stop behind the tree but on the other side of it. *Gotcha.* He put the gun there, and when his gift told him to fire, he double-squeezed the trigger.

The hammer snapped back twice, but the revolver didn't fire. Oh shit.

Cooper was a professional, had been counting his shots, four fired. But in the pressure of the moment, he'd forgotten that Ethan had already shot twice at him. The gun was empty.

For an endless fraction of a second, he and the other soldier stared at one another. Gazes locked like lovers. The man was bearded and stocky, with thinning hair and thick eyebrows. Cooper watched as the man realized that he should be dead, and watched the beginnings of a smile pull at his lips. The barrel of his rifle came up. Cooper told his body to move, to read the vector of his aim and dance away, but he was so tired, his body so sore and beaten, and even if he'd been in perfect health and well-rested he doubted it would matter, because it was one thing to know roughly where someone was going to shoot and another to dodge bullets. A blur of red marked the laser sight, and Cooper could almost feel the dot on his forehead, and for the second time in two days, he knew he was dead.

He thought about closing his eyes, decided he'd rather go with them open.

A fast cluster of gunshots blasted, the weapon on full auto. He marveled that he could hear them before he felt them.

Then the bearded man collapsed like a giant hand had squashed him.

Cooper stood with his mouth open. Not processing. Behind him, someone laughed. Slowly, he turned.

Shannon stood at the edge of the cabin, the stock of a submachine gun braced against her shoulder. She quirked her half smile. "Hi."

■

Natalie wanted to scream.

The room was unlike anything she'd ever seen. The closest parallel she could think of was a planetarium, only bigger, and instead of stars, holographic images hung in space. Charts and graphs and rainbow-colored diagrams. Pictures replacing each other in a sequence that seemed nonsensical: a smiling blond child, a macro close-up of a flower petal, a bombed-out concrete structure in some gritty country. Live feeds from news drones throughout New Canaan showed the world outside, massing troops, people staring open-mouthed at fighter jets streaking above, a line of tanks rolling across the desert trailing clouds of dust. Information piled on information, all of it moving and changing, swapping in and out according to the whims of their strange ringmaster, Erik Epstein, the richest man on the planet dressed in a hoodie and sneakers.

The glowing light washed in pale colors across the pale skin of her only son, and Natalie wanted to scream.

Moving here from the clinic had been Erik's idea, no sooner voiced than a team of efficient techs were rolling the bed through the private clinic, Natalie trailing behind.

"Are we hostages?" she'd asked, and he'd reacted like she'd bitten him.

"No. Safer. The clinic is good, good walls, good security, but this is my world. The safest place."

From what Nick had told her, Epstein did nothing without calculation, and she wasn't sure that she believed that was the only reason for their presence. As a lawyer, she knew that negotiations weren't about what was said, but about the cards all parties held, played or not. If the war started, there might be some benefit to Epstein to have the ex-wife and children of an American diplomat close by.

In the center of the room, Epstein said, "Quads two to ten, nix. Replace. Video, Tesla drone composite," and the data wavered and changed.

In her arms, Kate said, "We don't have to be scared, Mommy."

Natalie had grown to accept that her daughter, like her ex-husband, was forever going to be able to know her mind before she spoke. Often there was something sweet in it, like the two of them shared a private language. But there were other times when being a parent meant not letting your five-year-old know that you were terrified. Terrified that her father was out somewhere, in danger, that her brother might not wake up, that your world had already fallen apart and that the rest of the world seemed like it was about to follow suit. That you wanted to scream.

"I'm not scared, honey. I'm just tired."

Epstein said, "Decode intercepted data packets from Ellsworth AFB to F-27s, Leopard Wing."

Kate wrinkled her brow. "We're safe here."

"I know, baby." *Except that I can see troops on a dozen different screens. Jets blasting over this city, bombs on their wings. Armored tanks rolling this way.*

And in the center of all of this destruction, my children.

"No," Kate said. "Of the soldiers. We don't need to be scared of them."

Epstein said, "Natalie? Listen to this?" in a voice like he was asking her to the prom.

"What? Sure." She shifted Kate to her other side.

Over hidden speakers came two voices in an argument:

"Ground, can you confirm this order?" A woman's voice.

"Roger, proceed with Delta One."

"What? No. Ground, this is an attack order."

"Roger. Proceed."

"Ground, I'm seeing civilians everywhere. Those buildings have not, repeat, not been evacuated."

"Understood. Proceed with attack protocol Delta One."

"There are thousands of people—"

Natalie said, "Is that—"

"Yes. The jets. Above. Your government has ordered them to destroy the complex we are in."

"What? You said we were safe!"

"Mommy," Kate said.

"One second, honey. Erik, you promised we were safe here."

"Yes." There was a note of something like sadness in his voice. "I wanted you to hear so you would understand."

"Understand what? Erik, my God, surrender, do it now, maybe you can—"

"Computer," Epstein said, "activate Proteus virus."

"Yes, Erik. Spectrum?"

"All of them." The words almost a sob. "Do it to all of them."

Before Natalie could ask what that meant, the voices from the speakers were back.

"Ground! Ground! I have lost instruments! I repeat, I have lost HUD. Ground, my computer is shutting—" The woman's voice cut off.

Motion in one of the screens caught Natalie's eye. A camera mounted on top of a building was tracking the three jets blasting over the city.

All three were spinning out of control, tilting at angles that couldn't possibly be intentional. As she watched, one of them did a lazy flip, spun too far, and crashed into another. They exploded in a rain of fire.

"See, Mommy?" Kate said. "I told you. You don't need to be scared."

■

Cooper stared at Shannon. "How?"

"Epstein. The phone he gave you has a tracker. I thought you might need a hand." She smiled, and he felt something stir in his chest that had nothing to do with his wound. He thought about storming over, putting one hand behind her neck, and pulling her into a kiss that would mash them together. But.

"Soren is still out there."

"*Soren?*" She jumped, spun a fast circle. "He's here?"

"Yes. Come on." Cooper turned and sprinted for the house.

He made it two steps before he fell down.

"Nick! Are you okay?"

"I'll live," he said, and pushed up. "Come on."

The door to the cabin was ajar, and he pulled it open, stepped in quickly. "Dr. Park?"

The television was on, scenes of troops in Wyoming. Ethan was picking glass out of arms streaked with red. There was a wail, and Cooper turned to see Amy Park holding a crying baby. A tiny thing; he'd forgotten how small they were at this age. The woman looked at him and asked, "Is it over?"

"No." He turned to Shannon. "Where's your car?"

"On the road. I heard gunfire, bailed, and ran through the woods."

Shit. "Okay. Everybody in the pickup truck. We're getting out of here." *That's assuming the old piece of shit will still run. It took a lot of rounds. And what if—*

"No," Ethan said.

Cooper and Amy said, at the same time, "What?"

The scientist looked at his wife. "I didn't have a chance to tell you before. We need to split up."

"Ethan—"

"They're coming for *me*. They don't care about you."

Cooper said, "Doc, that's noble and all, but we don't have time."

"This is my fault. My doing." Ethan turned to him. "You said it yourself. It's me they want. If we run, will they follow?"

Slowly, Cooper nodded.

"Fine. Get my family out." The man's voice was calm. "I'll stay here."

"Doc, the guy coming, he's not here to talk."

"I don't care." Ethan walked to his wife, put an arm around her, and pressed his forehead to hers. He whispered softly. Cooper couldn't hear him, but he could read her body language, her reluctance—

If he stays, you and Shannon can get his family out. And Soren will kill Ethan.

But what can you do about that? Sorry to be blunt, buddy, but Soren already kicked your ass once. And now your right hand is useless, you can barely stand up, and you're out of bullets.

What hope do you have against him? How can you beat a man who has no intentions for you to read?

Time to choose, Coop.

—and said, "He's right." He turned to Shannon. "Get Amy and the baby out of here. Go out the back, and be careful. Soren will come for us, but there may be more." When she hesitated, he said, "Shannon. Please. They're coming."

She grimaced, then hoisted the submachine gun and turned to Amy. "Let's go."

Tears streamed down Amy's face, and Violet was still screaming. "No, no, you can't—"

"For your baby." Shannon put a hand on her arm and pulled. "Come on." She tugged again, harder, and without taking her eyes off her husband, Amy moved.

"I love you," Ethan said.

And then they were gone. Cooper could hear them hustle through the next room, then the sound of a door opening.

Okay. Now what?

"You don't have to stay," Ethan said. "No point in both of us dying."

"I told you, Doc. I have children too." Cooper stalked around the room, looking for a weapon, an idea, a prayer. "Besides. Who said anything about dying? Maybe we'll win."

Now if only you believed that.

■

Sirens screamed as Holly Roge fought the controls. The stick was loose in her hand, the plane unresponsive. Outside the cockpit glass, the world flipped and twisted. Her stomach tightened like she was pulling a full-speed unloaded extension as the nose of the Wyvern dipped down. All the displays were gone, and ground control had vanished.

Her mind conjured a scene from the academy, an instructor explaining modern jet fighters. *The thing to remember,* he'd said, *is that they aren't airplanes. The wings won't hold you up. This is a rocket. It doesn't fly, it blasts, and you and your computer work together to harness that.*

Now, with her computer down, with control dead, her rocket was subject to the whims of wind and gravity.

They'd run a thousand simulations, including ones for failed computers, even though that was a practical impossibility. The systems were triple-redundant, and even if the advanced systems glitched, basic control was supposed to—

Out the glass, Leopard Two tipped into a nose-down kite, flipped over, and crashed into Leopard Three.

"No!"

She felt the collision as a wave of heat and a sudden kick, and then ground and sky lost all perspective, her jet completely out of control, sirens screaming, everything dead, and a building ahead of her.

Training took over. Holly crossed her left arm over her chest, tucked her head down, and pulled the eject.

An explosion beneath her, a blast of light and noise, her stomach yanking down to her knees, the wind hitting hard and cold, everything spinning, no horizon line, and then a jerk at her back and the woof and snap of the parachute opening above. She swung in a wide arc, momentarily level with her chute, and then swung back down as nylon caught the air.

Hyperventilating, shivering, she hung in the sky.

There was a crash beneath her, a crumpling and shattering louder than thunder, and she looked down and watched the tail of her Wyvern snap off in a gust of fire as it collided with one of the mirrored buildings, the one she had been heading toward. Flames blew out the side, a rippled shock wave shattering every window.

Breathe. You have to breathe. What's your situation, pilot?

She concentrated on drawing shivery lungfuls of air and tried to evaluate. Forced herself to be mechanical, not to think or feel, simply to collect data.

Explosions continued in the building below her, gusts of flame shooting out the windows.

On the ground she could see the twisted remnants of Leopard Two and Three strewn for half a mile. She scanned the sky, saw no other parachutes. She'd been friends with both pilots, had gone drinking with Josh and given dating advice to Taylor, and now they were both dead, burned or blown apart.

What about the rest of the troops?

She tore her eyes from the burning planes and looked to the horizon.

While the military forces had been split into three positions, by far the largest was near Tesla, an arc of forty-five thousand troops that spanned two miles.

Two miles where a pitched battle raged.

Smoke rose in billowing towers from a hundred locations. Explosions flickered like distant fireworks, constant and bright, the dull thump of the sounds coming seconds later.

The armored division was at the front, a ragged line of tanks and troop transports half a mile from the city. Tiny toys in the dust. As she watched, flashes of light sparked amidst them, over and over. They were firing.

But at what?

She couldn't see any enemy forces, no opposing line of armor. So what were they—

As she watched, a tank rocked up on its side, hung for a moment, and then toppled upside down. It took a moment before the sound reached her, a faint punch at this distance.

A troop transport exploded in a fireball, tiny specks riding the edge of the blast, specks she knew were soldiers.

The desert lifted up and consumed a formation of Humvees.

How? Where is the fire coming from?

It could be mines, or—

As she watched, one of the foremost of the tanks spun its barrel in a lazy arc. Light blew from its barrel.

And the tank next to it exploded.

My God. They're attacking each other.

Somehow the machines have been compromised. Like your Wyvern.

And now they are killing your comrades.

Freezing, lost, Holly Roge hung helpless three thousand feet above a view of hell.

CHAPTER 45

Shannon glanced out the open door at the landscape beyond, a thin swath of gray-green grass leading to a small pond. The same medium-dense forest crawling up low hills. It looked peaceful enough, but that just made her more nervous.

She'd never met Soren, but she'd heard plenty. Samantha had loved him, probably still did, but in a way that set Shannon's teeth on edge. A relationship like a short circuit, their mutual frailties feeding each other. Samantha needed to be needed, and no one could need her as intensely as a man for whom one minute seemed like eleven.

As for John, he'd told her that Soren was the closest thing he had to a twin, but darkly mirrored; where Smith lived entirely in the future, plans within plans that stretched out years, Soren dwelled in an endless present layered just as densely. When Smith had talked about his old friend, there had been warmth in his voice, but also a healthy respect, the mix of emotions a zookeeper might have for a rare and particularly lethal snake.

And if you were said snake, where would you be?

It had probably been less than a minute since she dropped the guy who was aiming at Nick, but that was an eternity in a fight, and longer to Soren. He might have been willing to hang back initially, let the tactical team do the work. But now that they were down, he'd be moving in himself.

Let him. Better he come after you and this lovely H&K 9mm than Nick in the shape he's in.

Enough. If he was out there, she'd deal with it. Shannon stepped outside, pivoting back and forth. No motion. Behind her, the baby continued to cry, while the woman—Amy?—tried to shush and rock her.

So much for stealth. Let's try speed.

"Come on," she said, jerking her head toward the nearest hill. "Let's go."

She was afraid Amy would hesitate, do the typical civilian thing and freeze up, but the woman had stones. Tears streaming down her face, crying baby in her arms, husband staying back to sacrifice himself, and she still did what was needed, just started moving. They went at a jog, Shannon scanning, the submachine gun ready. The air was cold and smelled like winter and algae.

Entering the tree line made her feel better, more cover, more room to do her thing. Plus, if Dr. Park was right, Soren might even ignore them. At the top of the hill she paused for a moment, looked back.

Just in time to see a slim figure enter the cabin by the back door.

Shannon snapped the weapon to her shoulder, sighted along it, but it was hopeless, and she knew it.

Amy saw the movement at the cabin. "We have to go back."

"Come on. Keep going."

"We could help."

Shannon grabbed the woman's arm and tugged her down the other side of the rise. "Move."

Half leading, half pulling Amy, she hurried toward the road. She could see her SUV parked on the shoulder. *Almost there. Come on, come on.*

A voice behind her said, "Shannon."

■

Natalie stood in the center of Epstein's cave and stared.

Most of the charts had vanished, replaced by video that hung in the air, live images from around the New Canaan Holdfast.

Each one a scene of unimaginable destruction. Fire and blood and smoke.

Her daughter clung to her, and Natalie knew she should tell her to look away, but couldn't find her voice. She just stared.

Stared, as a helicopter fell flaming from the sky, bodies leaping out of the open doors.

Stared, as the heavy turret of a tank rotated, the barrel lining up on a troop transport fifty yards away. A soundless recoil and a blast of flame, and the transport vanished in a cloud of upswept dust.

Stared as streaks of light crashed into the ground amidst fleeing soldiers, men and women in combat gear running in all directions as rockets rained down from drones hovering invisibly above. Each strike shook the ground, flung people like broken dolls, their bodies bent and torn.

There were thousands of soldiers just miles away, and by the thousands, they were dying.

"What have you done?" she said. "My God. What have you done?"

"I didn't want to. They made me," Erik Epstein said, his voice quivering. He wiped at his eyes with the back of his hands. "You heard. They made me."

■

Shannon whirled. The man had stepped from behind a tree, his assault rifle held with easy certainty. A man she had just seen this morning, fifteen hundred miles away, guarding John Smith.

"VanMeter," she said.

"What are you doing?"

He's not pointing that rifle at you. Not yet.

"Same as you. John sent me after Ethan Park." She tightened her grip on Amy's arm. "This is his wife and kid."

"John didn't tell me."

"He usually run his plans by you, make sure you approve?" Shannon shrugged. "Been a friend of his for ten years, one thing I've learned is that John always has surprises."

"You bitch!" Amy tried to yank her arm away. "You said you were protecting us."

Shannon let her go, then wound up and cracked the other woman across the face with a hard backhand. Amy gasped and staggered.

VanMeter's eyes were bright blue and quite pretty, but not quite convinced. "Where's the doc?"

"Soren is on him." She gestured over her shoulder with her thumb. "In the house."

Those pretty blue eyes flickered for just a second, and Shannon shifted. Slid sideways and dropped to one knee, knowing that VanMeter's eyes would come back scanning sideways, the change in visual plane buying her the fraction of a second she needed, and even as he brought his gun up she could see that he knew too, and then she killed him.

Well, John, you told me I was going to have to choose.

She stood up, grabbed Amy, said, "Come on."

The gunfire had the baby screaming again, and Amy's nose was bleeding, but she looked at the dead body, and Shannon could see her put it together. She didn't resist as they ran to the SUV. She beeped the locks and yanked open the driver's side. The other woman headed around the front, and Shannon said, "No."

"What?"

"This side." She passed over the keys. "You have somewhere you can go?"

"My mother. She lives in Chicago."

"There's enough gas for that. Don't stop for anything." Shannon turned and sprinted back up the hill toward the house.

■

In the movies, the cabin would have had a gun rack with a glass front, and Cooper would have smashed it and geared up. Unfortunately, it appeared the Hendersons hadn't read the script.

Cooper flipped open the revolver and dumped the empty brass. "You have more bullets?"

"We did. They were—"

"Stolen. Right." He glanced sideways, saw the TV playing footage of Wyoming, made himself look away. No time to get distracted.

Ethan said, "What now?"

"I'm working on it."

When it hit, it was so obvious he had the urge to slap his forehead. The two gunmen outside had both carried assault rifles.

He slid the revolver into his pocket and started for the door. Then froze. *You have to think. You can't count on your gift here.*

Cooper dropped to an army crawl. The position took core strength, and the moment he engaged those muscles, searing pain went through his chest, and that strange skipped heartbeat feeling. He gasped, then forced himself forward, elbow, knee, elbow, knee. Shivering splinters of broken glass tore shallow cuts. When he reached the base of the window, he put his back to it, then sorted through the window shards, selecting a daggered piece six inches long. Slowly he inched it up, angling it to see out the window.

The reflection was gauzy and translucent, but it framed the pickup well enough. He panned it sideways, trying to remember exactly where the guys had fallen. Trees and darkening sky, a blur, and . . .

And Soren, walking toward the house with that same absent calm, the long combat blade in his right hand.

Cooper yanked the fragment of glass down. His heart beat like a drunken drummer, heavy and out of whack. His palms were soaked, and blood dripped from a dozen small cuts.

No way to get to the rifles, not without facing Soren.

Options.

The back way might be clear. On the other hand, there could be a team of snipers back there who had been ordered to wait for their actual target. It made sense; Soren comes in the front and flushes them into fire.

Okay, a side window. They could climb out and haul ass, race into the woods. Only, same problem.

Plus, who are you kidding, Cooper? You can't outrun Soren, not now. Ethan might be able to, but then he's on his own, and that's as good as killing him.

His hands shook, and he gasped a deep breath like swallowing straight razors. There were no options. They had to make a stand, and the best place to do that was in the cabin.

But how? The last time he'd faced this guy, he'd lost spectacularly. Now things were far worse.

Think! Everything you have is on the table, and that roulette wheel is slowing, the ball about to drop.

He couldn't handle Soren, not in a fair fight. The man's gift just made him too powerful. A T-naught of 11.2, my God. An eye blink would last a second, a footstep five. It was a strange and terrible gift, one that—

Wait. For most abnorms, their gift is just a part of them.

But Soren's gift is different. In a very real way, he is his gift.

His perception of the world is entirely shaped by it.

He will depend on it utterly, and trust what it tells him.

—might be used against him.

Cooper scrambled across the floor, ignoring the pain. Unbelievable the risk. It wasn't just his life on the table, it was Ethan's, and the hope he offered the future. And it all depended on Cooper being right.

"Doc, I need you to trust me again." Still carrying the shard of glass he'd used as a mirror, he glanced over his shoulder. Out of sight of the window. He rose quickly, took in the room. Measured angles in his head. "You see that closet? When I say, crouch down, move to it, and get in. Whatever you do, don't look back."

Ethan laughed. "Are you serious?"

Cooper shared the urge to laugh, didn't. There was an archway out of the living room into what looked like a kitchen, the back way Shannon had taken. "Do it now."

■

Lionel Clay sat at the head of the table and stared around the Situation Room at a world gone mad. Men and women in uniform were yelling at each other, talking into phones, but all of them were looking at the same thing.

The wall of tri-d screens, where American troops were massacring each other.

A high-angle recon shot showed a line of vehicles burning. Those that could still move rolled into exposed positions and continued firing on one another.

A helicopter gunship hovered over a platoon of running soldiers, spitting bullets and bright tracers. Men staggered and fell as if shoved from behind.

A soldier missing an arm clawed his way across the broken ground.

The dead lay everywhere. Killed in groups and mowed down one by one.

Streaks of light hurtled down from tactical drones, each finger missile thumping into the ground with an explosion that tossed heavy trucks like toys, that tore bodies apart.

"What's happening?"

No one responded, and he realized his voice had been a croak. Clay pounded the table with his fist, said, "What's happening?"

General Yuval Raz, the chairman of the Joint Chiefs, was a forty-year veteran, a man whose uniform sagged with medals earned all over the world. He looked like he wanted to crawl under

the table. "It's a virus. A Trojan horse. They must have had it waiting in all our hardware."

"Can't we shut everything down?"

"Nothing is responding. The virus has subverted manual control."

"A computer program is massacring American soldiers by the
thousands, and there's nothing we can do but watch?"

"We're working the problem, but so far—"

"General!" The interrupting soldier wore a lieutenant's bar
and held a phone to his ear. He needed a shave, though the scruff
was patchy at best. *So young,* Clay thought. *So many of them, so
young.* "We have an unauthorized missile launch, a BGM-117."

"An Avenger?" Raz looked at Clay. "That will be out of Warren
Air Force Base in Cheyenne." To the lieutenant, he said, "What's
the ETA to the Holdfast?"

"Sir," the man said, eyes wide and face pale. "It wasn't from
Warren. Air command reports the missile was launched from the
USS *Fortitude,* a *Luna*-class attack submarine at latitude 38.47,
longitude -74.40."

"North 38 west 74? But that's . . ."

"Approximately one hundred miles east of Washington, DC."
The lieutenant swallowed hard.

General Raz laid his fingers on the table. "They've already
tried the self-destruct?"

"No response, sir."

"Activate all missile defense batteries." Raz spun. "Sir, we need
to get you out of here immediately."

"It's heading for the White House?"

Raz nodded.

"Can you destroy it?"

"We'll try. Meanwhile, sir, you have to go. Right now."

Lionel Clay stared. At the monitors, on which his soldiers
burned and bled. At the officers surrounding the table. At the
American flag hanging limp in the corner.

"Sir, the Avenger is our top-of-line technology. It's capable of more than four thousand miles per hour, five times the speed of sound. You have to go."

This was never what you wanted. Not the office, not division in America, not the war. You let others drive you here.

You knew better, and you let it happen anyway.

And now thousands are dying, and a missile is hurtling toward the seat of American democracy.

Where will you be when it lands?

"I ordered our troops to attack. I'm staying."

"Sir—"

"That's an order."

The general gave him an appraising look, then a sharp nod. "Yes, sir."

Clay stood up. Took his suit jacket from the back of his chair and slid it on. He'd been a history professor, not a mathematician, but the calculation wasn't complicated. If the missile could cover four thousand miles in an hour, it could do a hundred miles in a minute and a half.

Which meant they had thirty seconds left.

"Sir, antimissile batteries on the Chesapeake Bay are firing now." The lieutenant closed his eyes and bit his lip.

The White House was completed in 1800. It's been occupied by every president but George Washington. For 213 years it has stood as a symbol of all that America is.

Everyone in the room stared at the lieutenant, the phone held to his ear with fingers clenched bloodless. There was nothing but the sound of breathing.

And then something in the young officer gave. His shoulders slumped, and his head fell.

It was over. They all knew it even before the man said, "Negative. No contact."

Fifteen seconds.

Clay buttoned his jacket and straightened his posture. His eyes swept the room. Funny, only now did he realize who was missing.

You little shit-heel, Leahy. At the very least, you should be standing here too.

He wanted to say something. Wanted to find words that would make it all meaningful.

But what would they be?

Five seconds. He strained to hear a screaming, then remembered the missile traveled faster than its own sound waves. *We are never more clever than in the creation of ways to destroy ourselves.*

"I'm sorry," Lionel Clay said. And then, "God bless America."

White erased the world.

■

Soren walked.

Past the red Porsche, his fingers trailing along the hood, the metal cool. Past the shattered pickup truck, the windshield glass crunching beneath his feet.

As usual, John had been right to be prepared. The tactical team had failed, and it was up to him to finish it. The rook, but no longer on the back row. Now stalking the board, forcing checkmate.

His nothingness had been shattered, his stores of carefully hoarded oblivion squandered. *It's time to go away. But finish this for your friend.*

The presence of Nick Cooper had been a surprise. The man was resilient. But Soren had spotted the bandage on his hand, had seen him stumble and fall. All that resilience had accomplished was to delay the inevitable.

He walked toward the cabin, calm, alert, in the moment. Through the shattered bay window, he could see the living room, a television on, no sign of the people inside . . . until, low but not low enough, he saw Ethan Park hurry in a crouch to a door in the side wall. A closet, and in the leisure of his perception, Soren catalogued the items inside, the blankets and coats, fishing poles and board games. Park slid inside and shut the door behind him.

Soren paused, took thirty of his seconds to think. The doctor was intelligent, and hiding in a closet was the action of a child. Especially with Cooper inside the house. Which meant . . .

Of course. A trap. Soren was meant to see him go there. Cooper would be waiting somewhere he could cover the front door and the closet. He smiled, imagining John's amusement at such a simple gambit.

Ignoring the front door, he moved in a jog around the side of the house. As he rounded the corner, he took in the world, the pond, the trees, the woman Shannon moving into the forest with Amy Park and the baby. Good. No need to deal with her now.

The back door was ajar, no doubt left that way when she fled. Soren moved to it, light on his feet. Though he knew what he would see, he still moved carefully, easing around the edge of the doorframe.

Nick Cooper stood at the edge of the kitchen by an arch that led to the living room. His back was to Soren, the pistol up and aimed at the front door. Soren was almost sad; the man had proven resourceful, and while he would fail here again, he had fought to the end.

Soren slipped in the door. Four steps would take him there.

He took the first, then the second. Raised the dagger, the flat black blade so light it was an extension of his arm.

The third. Cooper held the pistol in his left hand, braced against the wall, his aim unwavering on the door. All his attention on the trap he had laid. His back exposed and unarmored.

The fourth.

Soren cocked the dagger back, lined it up between Cooper's vertebrae to the left of the spine, and lunged.

■

Cooper could feel the air moving in the room, could feel his blood pulsing in his veins. Could hear the tiny creaks of the cabin, smell the sweat and blood. His arm was tired, but he kept the revolver pointed at the door. Everything came down to this. He would have one shot, one, and if he failed, they were both dead. He had to be perfect. For his life, and Ethan's, and his children, and his country. One shot.

And when, in the glass shard he'd propped against the counter he saw Soren raise the dagger and lunge, he spun. Everything coming down to one instant, his left hand whipping the heavy pistol around, praying that he'd been right, that what Todd had shown him in the restaurant was true, and as he saw Soren hurling forward, the blade out and his weight shifted, Cooper's gift read his intention clear as neon, and he slid sideways and slammed the revolver into Soren's neck with all his strength.

The shock on the man's face was the second-most beautiful thing he'd seen all day.

The blow had been ferocious, crippling, and the knife fell from Soren's hand, but Cooper didn't pause to savor the moment, just wound up and swung again, across the man's face this time, and then the monster was falling. He hit the floor gasping, a gargling sound coming from his throat.

"Hi," Cooper said. Then he raised his foot and slammed it down, hearing the matchstick snap of fingers. Soren screamed, clutched at his ruined hand with his good one.

"Funny thing." He limped around the guy to the other side. "I realized the reason I couldn't beat you. You never attacked. You waited for me to move and then put the knife where I'd be. But once you commit to action, I can read you just fine."

Cooper raised his foot again. "You know how I realized that? The only time I could read you was when you were about to hit my son." He snapped the man's left shin like kindling. "So Todd says hello."

Soren screamed.

Outside, Cooper heard more gunfire, the same fast cluster as before. Shannon's SMG. There was no returning fire. Good. Cooper smiled. Then he tried to lean against the wall and fell down instead.

A moment later she was in the kitchen, moving fast, the gun up. "Nick!"

"I'm okay." He took the hand she offered and wobbled back to his feet. "You?"

"Fine."

"Hey, Doc," he yelled to the other room. "You can come out now. The good guys won."

On the floor, the man who had put his son in a coma writhed and moaned, his face a bloody mess, hand destroyed, a bone sticking out of his calf. Cooper watched. After a moment, he said, "Doc?"

"Cooper." Ethan's voice was faint from the other room. "I think you need to see this."

He glanced at Shannon, and she trained her weapon on Soren. Cooper limped through the arch, past the shattered pictures and the broken glass, to where Ethan stood staring at the television.

A line of tanks burned against the skyline of an apparently unscathed Tesla. Corpses lay everywhere, thousands of them carpeting the desert. The prefab buildings smoldered, black ropes rising into the sky. Helicopters buzzed through the haze, firing on the few soldiers still standing. Then the video cut to something new.

No, oh no.

Something that had once been the White House. The building had been replaced by a massive crater. The surrounding earth was bunched and rippled like carpet. A column of thick smoke obscured most of the strike itself, but the debris was everywhere.

The columns of the South Portico were scattered like children's blocks. Shattered glass glinted amidst piles of limestone and marble and bent steel. Paper blew in gusts, and small blazes flickered. Dust and dirt and flesh and blood mingled into an unholy gray. The trees on the north lawn were burning, a harvest of fire wavering like autumn leaves.

He stepped forward and found the volume.

"—a missile apparently launched from a submarine. The White House has been completely destroyed. We believe President Clay was inside at the time, along with . . . oh God." The announcer choked. "It was a computer virus, a Trojan horse triggered by the abnorms. The military force in New Canaan has torn itself to pieces. Casualties are in the tens of thousands. We—" A pause and a choke. "America is now at war. My God, we're at war with ourselves."

Cooper stared. Saw everything he had fought for burning.

They were no longer on the precipice. They'd gone headfirst into the abyss.

Without thinking, he kicked the television, the screen toppling over and smashing against the wall, sparks flying. Ethan jumped, said, "Jesus Christ!"

Cooper turned, staggered back to the kitchen. Soren had rolled to one side and lay shivering. Shannon looked up with wide eyes. "Did I hear—"

"Yes." He stared down.

Ethan joined them, saw Soren, said again, "Jesus Christ." Then, "Where's my family?"

"Safe," Shannon said. "Nobody's after them. She's going to her mom's."

Slowly, Ethan nodded. "Now what?"

Now what. Now what indeed.

Cooper had known that this plan was a long shot, known he was likely to die trying. And instead he'd survived, saved Ethan

Park, and it didn't matter. The White House was destroyed, the president dead, the nation in a civil war. John Smith had won.

No.

I won't allow it.

"Doc. Your boss, Couzen. You know him pretty well?"

"Sure. But he was kidnapped—"

"No. He faked it."

"He faked it?"

"Yes. He's out there somewhere, and he's got the recipe for the last best hope we have. You're going to help me find him." He turned to Shannon. "This isn't over."

"Nick . . ."

"It's not. It's not over unless we give up. Unless we let Smith win." He took a breath, tried to stop the shaking of his hands. "Everything is falling apart. But we can still fight. We just have to decide to do it. My children are still alive, and as long as that's true, I'm never going to quit."

She stared at him for a long moment, his fierce warrior woman, and then she nodded slowly. "What's the plan?"

"You're going to take this piece of shit"—he gestured at Soren—"back to Epstein."

"What? Why?"

"Epstein said that he's Smith's closest friend. That he understood Smith better than anyone." He read the confirmation in her eyes. "Good. We're going to need that."

"What about me?" Ethan said.

Soren groaned on the floor. Idly, Cooper wound up and kicked him in the temple. The man stopped moving.

Then he looked at the scientist. "You and me, Doc?" Cooper smiled. "We're going to go save the world."

END OF BOOK TWO

EPILOGUE

The diner had cracked Formica counters and photos of ugly children taped behind the register. The cook saw him standing there and said, "Two black coffees to go?"

The man nodded. *You've fallen into a pattern. This will have to be your last visit.*

He scanned the room. A fat man hunched over a plate with great concentration. Two guys in matching work clothes talked at the counter. The small tri-d showed a scene of devastation. Ah yes, the White House. He'd heard something about it being destroyed—a week ago, perhaps?—but he'd been too busy to investigate.

"Look," one of the laborers said, "that missile coulda been a nuke. They could have firebombed Manhattan. They didn't. So maybe we oughta—"

"Twists had their chance," the other replied. "There's ninety-nine of us to one of them. Let's see 'em use a computer virus against a bayonet."

The cook set the coffee on the counter. "Four bucks. My name's Zeke, by the way." He held out his hand to shake. It was plump and sweaty, and his nails needed a trim.

Dr. Abraham Couzen looked at it. "Sorry. I've got a cold." He laid four dollars down, picked up his coffee, and walked out.

Early December, the sky a chilly white. Abe peeled back the tab from one of the coffees and took a long sip, and then another, and then another. When he finished it, he tossed the blue and white cup in a trash can and started walking. The South Bronx was not a glamorous part of town, but he'd grown used to it. And it was the last place anyone would think to look for—

That man waiting for the bus. Didn't you see him yesterday?

The breeze smelled of gasoline and fish. Bits of trash in the chain-link fence hummed in the wind. Abe turned up his coat collar and walked another fifty feet, then spun on his heels. The man hadn't followed.

It didn't mean anything. There could be high-altitude drones tracking him right now. Government agencies, terrorist groups, Epstein's spies—so many dirty fingers picking through his past, scanning camera feeds for his profile, ransacking his home.

Pierre Curie did it.

The notion had occurred to him last night. A way to be certain his work could never be taken.

The building was a low, windowless brick rectangle. Abe unlocked the deadbolt and pressed a thumb against the biometric scanner. Bank after bank of fluorescent lights flickered on, illuminating two thousand square feet of previously abandoned warehouse space. It had been laughably easy to funnel aside enough of Epstein's money to buy the building and rebuild it to his exact specifications.

Barry Marshall did it.

A row of positive-airflow suits hung limp, respirator tubes trailing to the ceiling. Beyond that were lab counters broken out by function: wet bench, instrument bench, calculation space. Freezers and reagent refrigerators. A dry block incubator. A thermal cycler. A row of centrifuges. A micropipetter. Three DNA sequencers.

It was equal to the laboratory he'd abandoned in Cleveland. But no one knew about this one, not even Ethan. The bastards wanted his work, they'd have to find him first.

Jonas Salk did it.

There were things to work out, kinks, problems. Side effects. Tests that he should have been allowed to perform. Erik Epstein's hurry had prevented it. Along with the government's meddling.

But he was a scientist. His job was nothing less than wrestling the universe into a choke hold and making it cough out its secrets.

Abe took a long sip of coffee. Then he walked to the refrigerator, opened the door, and took out the syringe. The suspension fluid inside was milky.

This is foolish.

He tore open an isopropyl swab.

Reckless.

Rolled up his sleeve.

But Pierre Curie strapped radium salts to his arm to show that radiation caused burns.

Wiped his bicep with the alcohol.

Barry Marshall drank a batch of Helicobacter pylori *to prove that ulcers were bacterial.*

Picked up the syringe.

Jonas Salk inoculated his entire family with his polio vaccine.

Pushed the needle's tip through his skin and depressed the plunger.

And Dr. Abraham Couzen injected himself with non-coding RNA to radically alter his gene expression.

It was done. There was no going back. Abe set the syringe aside and rolled down his sleeve.

He'd always known he was a genius.

Now it was time to become brilliant.

ACKNOWLEDGMENTS

I am indebted to so many people it's embarrassing.

Scott Miller and Jon Cassir are the finest agents in the business, and it's an honor to have them watching my back.

The entire team at Thomas & Mercer is extraordinary. My FF Alison Dasho performed a masterful edit with a baby in her belly. Alan Turkus expertly took the reins when said baby insisted on coming out. Jacque Ben-Zekry will soon rule the world. Gracie Doyle is the Queen of PR. Danielle Marshall is a mysterious genius. Daphne Durham is unbeatable for bourbon-tinged book talk. Jeff Belle is the original class act. Thanks also to Andy Bartlett, Terry Goodman, Paul Morrissey, and Tiffany Pokorny.

I'm grateful to Alex Hedlund, Palak Patel, Joe Roth, and Julius Onah for their dedication to not simply making a movie, but making a great one. Thanks also to David Koepp for a rock-star script.

Robert Yalden, formerly of the Secret Service, helped me with the details of the White House and provided a frightening perspective on cyber-security.

Huge gratitude to my high school buddy Dr. Yuval Raz for figuring out how abnorms work on a genetic level, not to mention bringing Cooper back from the dead. Any errors, inaccuracies, or wild flights of fancy are mine.

Jeroen ten Berge knocked the cover out of the park, again. Thanks for never settling.

Joe Buice drew the flyer for Ringo's Army-Navy found early in the story, and Nick Robert designed the poster for *(Ab)Normal*.

Both did it for no other reason than they like the book, and that's just about the coolest thing ever.

Thanks to all the friends and family who read the draft and gave me notes, especially Darwyn Jones and Michael Cook, gentlemen and scholars.

Marjorie Braman's editorial pass offered exceptional insight into all the things I could do better. Jessica Fogleman caught all the things I'd screwed up.

My boys Sean Chercover and Blake Crouch were instrumental every step of the way. It's not just that without them this book would be worse—it's that it might well not be at all. Thanks also to Gillian Flynn for a ton of support.

Thank *you*, dear reader, for rolling the dice on my novel. I hope I didn't let you down.

My family means everything to me. Thank you Sakeys 1.0, also known as my mother, Sally; my father, Tony; and my brother, Matt.

Jossie, you're the best thing I've ever cocreated. I'm wildly proud of you, and I love you so much it makes me dizzy.

Finally, g.g.: my partner, my wife, my life. I love you.

ABOUT THE AUTHOR

Marcus Sakey's novels have been nominated for more than fifteen awards, including the Edgar and two ITW Thriller Awards. His book *Good People* was adapted into a feature film starring James Franco and Kate Hudson. Three of his other novels have been optioned for film, including *Brilliance.*

To research his work, Marcus has shadowed gang cops, trained with snipers, toured the morgue, flown planes, rappelled with SWAT teams, hung out with spies, and learned to pick a deadbolt. He was the host and writer of the acclaimed television show *Hidden City* on Travel Channel, for which he was routinely pepper-sprayed and attacked by dogs.

Marcus lives in Chicago with his wife and daughter.

His website is MarcusSakey.com, or follow him on Facebook (Facebook.com/MarcusSakey) or Twitter, where he posts under the clever handle @MarcusSakey.